TOO FAR

Copyright © 2023 by Abby Millsaps

All rights reserved.

paperback ISBN: 9798988800330

No portion of this book may be reproduced, distributed, or transmitted in any form without written permission from the author, except by a reviewer who may quote brief passages in a book review.

This book is a work of fiction. Any resemblance to any person, living or dead, or any events or occurrences, is purely coincidental. The characters and story lines are created by the author's imagination and are used fictitiously.

Developmental Consultation by Melanie Yu, Made Me Blush Books
Line Editing, Copyediting, and Proofreading by VB Edits
Cover Design © Silver at Bitter Sage Designs

Contents

Dedication	X
Content Warning	1
1. Locke	2
2. Josephine	7
3. Kendrick	12
4. Kendrick	16
5. Josephine	20
6. Josephine	30
7. Kendrick	33
8. Josephine	38
9. Kendrick	43
10. Josephine	47
Texts: The Boys	54
Texts: The Fab Five	56
11. Decker	60
12. Josephine	72

13.	Josephine	77
14.	Decker	81
15.	Josephine	92
16.	Josephine	95
17.	Kendrick	99
18.	Josephine	102
19.	Decker	106
20.	Josephine	113
21.	Josephine	116
22.	Josephine	120
23.	Decker	130
24.	Josephine	132
25.	Josephine	138
26.	Josephine	143
27.	Josephine	148
28.	Josephine	154
29.	Kylian	164
30.	Josephine	167
31.	Josephine	175
32.	Kylian	180
33.	Decker	183
34.	Kendrick	186
35.	Josephine	188

36.	Decker	192
37.	Josephine	194
38.	Josephine	197
39.	Josephine	199
40.	Decker	203
41.	Josephine	206
42.	Decker	209
Fullpage Image		212
Fullpage Image		213
43.	Josephine	214
44.	Josephine	218
45.	Josephine	222
46.	Kendrick	227
47.	Locke	230
48.	Kylian	234
49.	Josephine	240
50.	Josephine	244
51.	Josephine	250
52.	Decker	252
53.	Josephine	256
54.	Josephine	263
55.	Decker	270
56.	Josephine	275

57. Josephine	280
58. Josephine	284
59. Josephine	290
60. Decker	301
61. Josephine	309
62. Josephine	311
63. Josephine	315
64. Josephine	325
65. Josephine	329
66. Decker	335
Texts: The Fab Five	340
67. Josephine	345
68. Decker	351
69. Josephine	355
70. Josephine	359
71. Decker	361
72. Josephine	365
73. Decker	369
74. Josephine	373
75. Josephine	383
Josephine	387
Josephine	391
Josephine	395

Josephine	401
Kylian	407
Up Next	412
Afterword	415
Acknowledgments	416
By Abby Millsaps	418
About The Author	419

To the neurospicy readers, the chronic pain warriors, the spoonies, the fighters, the just-barely-getting-byers, the survivors, the caretakers, the struggle bus riders, and everyone who has to learn their lessons the hardest way possible: I see you. I love you. This book is for you.

I hope this story is a luxurious escape from reality when you need it most.

Content Warning

Too Far contains content some may find triggering, including mentions of past abuse and child neglect, brief references to past sexual assault of FMC (mentioned in chapters 29 and 45), discussion of death of a parent and grief, revenge by way of violence and blackmail, explicit language, recreational drug use, and chronic illness (rheumatoid arthritis and lupus in remission).

Chapter 1
Locke

Everything hurts. Everything always fucking hurts, but this time, the pain rattling through my bones isn't only physical.

My hand throbs. My head pounds.

But my heart—my heart is fucking shredded.

There's a gut-wrenching sense of dread percolating in my insides. The kind of fear I haven't felt in years.

"Nicky, look at me."

She's a vision. A fucking vision in a Crusader's T-shirt and my boxers. Though they might be Kylian's now that I'm looking closer. What I wouldn't give to sink into her softness. To let it engulf me like a plush cloud, providing all the comfort I need.

But I'm not the one who needs to be comforted right now.

Even though I lost control. Even though I'm the one who threw the punch.

I'm not the one who was arrested, handcuffed on the beach, forced onto the police boat, hauled to the station.

"Where is he?" Decker rages, tearing into the master bathroom, where we're holed up. The door leading from the patio to Decker's bedroom made this the easiest place to seek shelter.

"He's in shock." Kylian doesn't bother to look up from his phone.

"What the hell were you thinking?" Decker snarls at me.

He's right up in my face, spitting mad and dripping fury.

Bring it on, brother.

"He grabbed her arm," I grunt, clenching my throbbing fist and meeting his gaze.

I don't have to explain further. Yet what I did was too much, and what Kendrick did... *Fuck.*

Decker looks from me to Joey, then down to my bleeding knuckles.

Focusing on her again, he extends one arm and whispers "Siren" in an uncharacteristically docile manner for Decker Crusade.

I give her a nudge. At first, she moves closer to me, like she doesn't want to let go, but finally, she gives in and goes to him, receiving the comfort she deserves.

He tucks her under one arm, and she sinks into his side. That move alone gives me contentment. She belongs with him. She's safe with Decker. He can protect her from this in ways the rest of us can't.

Even if this whole debacle is happening *because* of him. I'd almost forgotten that detail.

Fuck.

Yes, he can protect her. Hire more security, set stricter limits for access to the house, use his name and money to keep her safe.

But none of that would be necessary if he hadn't allowed the camera crew on the isle in the first place.

They're here because of who he is. Because of the media's obsession with his family, his life, the entire Crusade dynasty. They're here because of who he's destined to be.

Fucking media. Fucking fame. None of it is worth it if she gets hurt—or if she leaves us all because of it.

"This isn't going to end well, Cap," I warn. "They were up in her face. They *touched* her. Filming hasn't even begun, and already, they're taking things too far."

Decker clenches his jaw, assessing me for a moment, then he takes in Joey, who's doing a poor job of holding back her trembles as she shrinks into his side. Finally, he turns to Kylian. "What's the damage?"

"Doesn't matter." His reply is instant and dismissive. "I blocked the signals and wiped the devices of everyone present. There's no remaining proof. It's their word against ours. And since they don't want to lose this job..."

"And since the man who confessed to assault is in custody..." Joey grouses.

What the hell was Kendrick thinking, taking my place like that? I wasn't in my right mind when I lashed out and hit the reporter, but I would have accepted the consequences of my actions. But then Kendrick stepped up.

Confessed to a crime he didn't commit.

Fuck. What I wouldn't do to hit rewind. If I'd known one of my brothers would take the fall for me, would I have lashed out like that? Hell no.

I lean against the vanity at my back, then sink down to the floor. "Why would he do that for me?" I groan into my hands.

K's got big dreams and a squeaky-clean reputation. He's a shoo-in for the pros. A mark like this on his record could destroy it all.

"He told you." Kylian's still focused on his device, his thumbs flying across the screen. "He said he did it for you and for her. For everything we're going to be."

"Kylian..." Josephine's tone is subdued, but it's a warning, nevertheless.

I don't bother lifting my head, even when Kylian squats in front of me.

"Nicky, look at me."

Despite the unfamiliar level of intimacy his proximity brings, I take a long breath in and obey.

Because a kind of blanket trust is forming between us, knitting together this new relationship we're forging. I might not have it in me to keep it together, and I might not know how to move forward right now, but I have no doubt they'll help me figure it out.

When one of us struggles, the others hold us up. Right now, I'm the weakest link. As much as I hate it, I need them to navigate whatever the hell comes next.

Meeting Kylian's light blue eyes, I open myself up, let him see my truth: the hurt, the heartache, the regret. Kendrick shouldn't have been the one hauled away. It should have been me. It should have been fucking me.

That realization hurts more than any physical ache.

"He's okay," Kylian assures me. "He's more than okay. He took his meds this morning. Worked out and stretched. We know where he is. He knew what he was doing, Nicky. He'll be okay."

"Come on." Decker offers an outstretched hand, and when I take it, he releases Joey and cups my elbow so he can ease me up off the floor. "We've got work to do. Kyl and I will find out who's going to set his bail. Then we'll figure out whose campaign we have to donate to so that this goes in our favor."

Joey scoffs. She should know better by now.

There's no price Decker won't pay when it comes to us.

"We'll have him home by dinner. Why don't you make something he likes? But maybe rest first?"

"I can't re—"

"Nicky." Joey steps in and wraps her arms around my waist. "Don't let Kendrick's sacrifice be for nothing. He'll be pissed if he gets home and you're sleep-deprived and still hurting."

She lowers her head and nuzzles into my neck. "I'll come up and lay with you. Just promise them you'll rest so they know you're okay."

Decker crosses his arms over his chest and lifts his chin, regarding me.

"Steer clear of anyone but us for now. They're setting up today and tomorrow. And they'll be back on Thursday to start the real coverage. Without evidence, I doubt anything will come of this. Kyl's right—they don't want to compromise this feature, but let's not give them any opportunity to retaliate."

"I'll meet you in your room," Joey offers. With one more quick squeeze, she drops her arms and turns to Decker.

"Come on," Kylian says, clapping me on the shoulder and leading me out of the bathroom.

Chapter 2

Josephine

"Decker," I whisper. The tears I refused to let surface while Nicky was in the room finally well in my eyes.

"Come here," he urges, opening his arms for me. "You did so well, Josephine. You did so well standing up to Misty, then keeping it together for Nicky."

I fall against him and hold him tight, but his embrace isn't enough to calm me. "Kendrick. What's going to happen now?" As good as it feels to sink into his hold, how I feel is the least of my concerns.

"We'll get him out. Soon. I meant what I said. I'd be shocked if he wasn't home by dinnertime."

"How do you know that?"

He smirks, but when he pulls back and really gets a look at me, his expression softens. Like he's just now realizing how intensely I'm distressing.

"K played his part knowing that Kyl and I would play ours, too. We'll get him back to you, Siren. I swear it. I won't stop until he's home. But first, I need to know... Who touched you?"

I exhale a swell of trepidation. Decker will go ballistic when he hears the details.

"It happened so fast," I hedge. "I was running down the stairs toward the beach, which was stupid, really—"

"Josephine."

I steel my spine and swallow my excuses.

"The guy with the red baseball hat. He sort of two-stepped so he was in my path, then ducked out of the way at the last second. I lost my balance when I tried to dodge him, but he shot his arm out and grabbed me here." I brush my fingertips along the underside of my upper arm and wince when I find the tender skin where the asshole manhandled me.

"It happened quickly, but I'm almost positive he intended to make me trip so he could grab me. Maybe I'm reading too much into—"

"No," he cuts me off, definitive and sure. "Don't make excuses for them. We need to know exactly who we're dealing with. If you say that's what happened, then I believe you."

I swallow past the emotion inspired by the way Decker accepts me at my word, trusts me so implicitly.

"Locke saw it happen, saw him cause me to stumble in the first place. That's why he hit him. He knew the guy wasn't helping me get my balance."

"Do you want him gone?"

My stomach knots as I search Decker's face. Is he offering to take care of the photographer the same way he and K and Greedy handled the South Chapel football players who took me captive during Shore Week?

"Josephine," he scolds mildly, like he can read my mind. "Not like that." Two fingers tip my chin up so I'm forced to meet his gaze. "I can't get us out of this feature, but I can control who's allowed in our home."

I bite down on my bottom lip, considering. "Would it be better to just let him stick around? I highly doubt he'll come after me again now that he knows the consequences."

If it were me, I wouldn't want to even breathe too loudly after being on the receiving end of that kind of reaction from the boys.

Decker blows out a breath and rolls his shoulders. "You're right. He stays. He'll be one less person to worry about now that he knows the lengths we'll go to protect you."

We'll is the problem, though.

I throw my arms around him and nuzzle into his chest, hoping like hell my affection is obvious before I speak my truth.

I don't know if I can do this.

It's not him. It's not them. It's me. It's everything I've survived.

"Decker... I don't want to be included in the feature. At all. I don't want to be photographed or have to worry about who's watching and when."

"I'm sorry. I wish it wasn't like this." His jaw ticks, and a bolt of pain flashes in his eyes, but he leaves it at that.

"That's it?" I push back. "You have no problem working around the law and paying off local judges, but Misty says jump, and you jump?"

He peers down at me, his cool, detached mask slipping back into place.

"There's a lot I can control, Siren. But this is out of my hands. It's a legally binding contract. It's a rider for the guys, too. It's in the NDA they signed when they moved in with me. Misty knows she crossed a dozen lines and that I'm fucking furious with her, but she's not going anywhere, and she knows it, since she represents my dad, too."

"Decker," I plead, not even sure what I want him to do. "You know what the cameras and the scrutiny trigger for me. Allowing this means they'll have the ability to take my picture and use it however they want."

"I have final editorial approval on the feature. But that's the extent of what I can control. We don't have a choice," he grumbles.

"*You* don't have a choice," I correct, my heart aching. "I don't have to be involved."

When he says nothing, I push harder.

"When were you going to share the magnitude of this feature with me? They're already here setting up, yet until now, you've only given me vague details. Did you think I wouldn't notice the cameras following you around all week?"

"They have access for ten days," he corrects.

"*Ten days?*"

Huffing, he pulls out of my hold and frowns down his nose at me.

"I planned to tell you. But I was still working out the specifics and putting fail safes in place to protect you, *Josephine*."

The frustration in his tone when he says my name sends me.

As if he's scolding me. As if *I'm* the one who's being unreasonable.

I plant my hands on my hips and prepare to square off. It's a position I've found myself in often when in Decker's presence, though not as often lately.

It's not that I *don't* believe him or trust him to take care of us the best he can. I believe he was working on a way to make this as painless as possible for all of us.

But people we both love have already gotten hurt because of it.

"Are there any off hours to the coverage? Timeouts from the monitoring? Safe places where they aren't allowed to follow us or photograph us?"

"Of course. They're not allowed to follow us into the bathrooms."

Now it makes sense why we're in here.

"And they're forbidden from photographing us, pursuing us, or using footage of us when we're out on the lake," he recites coolly. "My room is off limits unless I'm in here." He grits his teeth. "Kylian is working out a few other accommodations as well."

My stomach lurches as reality sets in. The lake exception makes sense, given the details of his mom's death, but besides that, this guarded man has agreed to give them unprecedented access to his life... to our *lives*. Why?

"I never thought about it before you," he offers, answering the question I didn't ask. "I cared how intrusive it can all be. I grew up living in the spotlight, and I've always been expected to go along with what Misty and my dad suggest. I resigned myself to being the rising star with the golden arm a long time ago. I didn't care if they wanted to follow me, photograph me, put pictures of me all over the Internet. I never cared before. Not like I care now."

"How are we supposed to—"

With a shake of his head, he silences me. "We just have to be careful." He takes a deep breath, his chest rising, then falling. "We're safe in here."

I scoff and fight back an eye roll. By "in here," he means his bathroom.

"It's only ten days, Siren. Ten days, then they're gone."

Silence shrouds us. There's nothing left to say. We're at an impasse—one where he's not in control, and for once, I wish he was.

Relenting, I rest my forehead against his sternum and will myself not to cry.

"I want more of you," I confess into the fabric of his shirt.

Humming, he bows down and kisses the top of my head. "You have me, Siren. Any minute we're not together—every hour they keep us apart—you're where I want to be."

For a long moment, we stay like that, my face buried in his chest and his arms holding me steady.

"We'll get through this," he says into the silence. "Any time you want to go out on the lake, say the word. I'll drop what I'm doing if it means giving you what you need."

I glance up into his onyx eyes, desperate to see something real. His gaze is a solemn vow. There's enough determination there to make me believe that this could all be okay.

"Promise?"

"With everything I am."

Chapter 3
Kendrick

I know it's him from the cadence of his stride. Each step is authoritative, purposeful. Formidable without wielding the kind of overzealous power stereotypical of law enforcement.

The cell door swings open, but I don't lift my head until he's seated beside me. It takes that long to garner the courage to face him.

His deep brown eyes flecked with gold are full of nothing but warmth and concern. The man sitting beside me isn't the Lake Chapel sheriff. This is my Pops.

He regards me, one eyebrow raised. "I raised you to be loyal, son. Not sacrificial."

He knows there isn't an impulsive, reckless bone in my body. There can't be. I'm a two-hundred-and-thirty-pound running back hoping to go pro. One indiscretion could ruin my career.

Damn if this wouldn't have been a hell of a lot easier if I was a nobody in this town. But I'm not, and I made a deliberate choice. One he doesn't agree with, if the disappointment on his face is any indication.

"You raised me to take care of my own, Pops. So that's what I did."

He frowns as he surveys me, the wrinkles in his forehead creasing deeply. "It wasn't for Decker," he declares after another moment's appraisal.

I roll my shoulders out in a shrug. "You don't know that."

I'm going for nonchalant, not disrespectful.

He's caught the lie before I even close my mouth.

"Maybe not. But here's what I do know." He drops his elbows to his knees. "We get a call from the Crusade isle. Reports of aggravated assault by a tattooed hulk of a man wearing a red Crusaders cutout."

Tilting his head, he makes a show of examining my long-sleeve fitted performance T.

I don't wear cutouts. Especially during the day. I can't risk exposing that much skin. He's been buying long-sleeve shirts like this for me since I was diagnosed with lupus more than ten years ago.

"The call is from a panicked out-of-towner who's making substantial claims and insisting he's got the whole thing on video. All this went down at the place where my son lives with his friends, where my baby girls go on the regular to visit their big brother."

He lifts one brow in a way that's always made my stomach sink. He's a fair man, but he's got high expectations of me. Especially when it comes to my sisters.

"I stay back at the station, conflict of interest and all that, and send Rodriguez as my eyes and ears. I sit in my office panicking, worried about one of my son's best friends, and down three cups of coffee in the process."

With his fingers steepled in front of him, he's the epitome of calm, even though he's raging on the inside.

"When Rodriguez returns, she doesn't have Nicholas Lockewood in custody. Nor has she obtained video footage or evidence. Because it's gone. Poof. Inaccessible. Corrupted. Wiped. Whatever it is Kylian does to make things disappear."

He watches me, waiting for me to argue or counter his assessment.

I don't. What's the point? He's not wrong.

Though I have no intention of admitting the truth or dragging my friends into this now that I've stepped up to take the heat.

"Aggravated assault. Potential evidence tampering. Obstruction of justice. You sure you know what you're doing, son?"

The question hits as intended.

Shuttering my eyes, I give myself two seconds to panic.

Two counts. One breath in. One breath out.

A blip in time to let the gravity of what I've done sink in and to acknowledge how it could send the whole castle crumbling down.

Do I know what I'm doing? Hell no. I'm so fucking out of my depth. I don't know what'll come of all this—the legal consequences or the disciplinary action from the school and the team. A smear on my record. A major hitch in my plans to go pro.

The scope of the potential fallout is unfathomable.

Yet I'd do it all over again.

Accepting my silence for what it is, my dad stands with a sigh and clasps my shoulder. "My hands are tied, Kenny. I love you, but I can't help you with this one."

I look up and lock eyes with him. This powerful, honorable man. A man I respect. A man I love.

He and my sisters aren't the only people I love these days, though. Is there any greater display of love than sacrificing for one's family?

"I know," I concede, placing my hand over his and squeezing.

I didn't take the fall thinking I could get off easier because of my last name.

I did it because I could take it. Come what may, I can handle the consequences.

"Your uncle is up for reelection this year. If he gets wind of this, or the media spins it and he feels compelled to make an example out of you..."

My uncle's a ruthless prick. Whereas my pops believes in justice, order, and civility, his brother is a county commissioner who revels in power and control and doing whatever it takes to come out on top.

"Understood."

He sighs again. "I see so much of her in you. Conviction. Honor. Love. You have my stubbornness, but you have your mother's spirit. I won't pretend to understand what the hell you were thinking, sacrificing all you've worked for so hastily, but I'm damn proud of the man you are, Kendrick."

His words slam into me so hard I have to restrain myself from hopping off the bench and pulling him into a hug.

He's never been stingy with his affection. Reserved and stoic, yes. But ever since my ma passed away, he's led our family with empathy and compassion. He's the kind of man who says what he needs to say when he needs to say it.

Swallowing past the gratitude and overwhelming sense of vulnerability coursing through me, I clear my throat, prepared to ask what happens now.

Turns out I don't need to.

He walks out of the cell and leaves the door wide open behind him.

"Decker posted your bail. I'll get one of the officers to take you home."

Chapter 4

Kendrick

They're lined up on the dock, every one of them so rigid the sight of them twists my gut into knots.

They're in size order, too. It would be hilarious if I wasn't so fucking keyed up and desperate to get back into the fold.

I don't bother waiting for the rookie tasked with accompanying me home to dock along the landing.

Two strides, a leap, and I'm home.

Among them.

Where I belong.

Decker holds out a hand, and I grasp it, allowing him to steady me on the wooden planks. Once I've got my footing, he pulls me in and hugs me fiercely.

"Fucking hell, K," he murmurs, cuffing my neck.

He doesn't need to say another word. I know the gravity of my actions. Maybe now he'll open his eyes and comprehend just how far gone we all are for this girl.

Releasing his grip on me, he pushes me toward Nicky. I lock eyes with my brother—one of very few people in my world who understand the physical aches and the mental anguish that come with chronic illness. A silent reckoning passes between us, but the moment is too heavy for me to fathom right now.

"Don't," I growl, cupping the back of his head and bringing it to mine. I wait for him to focus on me before I speak so I'm sure he understands. "I'd do it all again, just like that. For you. For her."

Tears well up in his eyes, and a pained groan escapes him.

It's difficult for him to accept this level of love; to feel worthy of any kind of sacrifice made on his behalf. That's a big part of why he and Kylian got on so well when they were kids. The emotions... the deep and heavy... neither one of them like to exist on that plane.

But that's what makes us human.

That's what makes us *family*.

"You're worth it, Nicky. This family is worth it."

He hangs his head, sniffs, nods. The guy is shutting down, so I won't push him any more. Despite not being locked up today, he's got to be in immense pain. He needs rest. Support. Meds. A chance to fully recover before our next game.

Pulling back, I tip my chin toward Kylian.

None of this would have been possible without him.

"They can't find any evidence," I confirm.

"Of course they can't."

I smirk at his smugness. "You did good, Boy Genius."

He glances at Locke, then over at Joey. With a nod, he gives me a pointed look. "So did you."

Finally—*fucking finally*—I reach the end of the line. When I do, I give her my full attention. Just being this close to her sends a wave of calm through me. Instantly, the tension in my shoulders ebbs and the vise clamped around my heart loosens.

She takes a tentative step forward, almost as if she doesn't know how to act or what to say. That hesitation grates on my nerves, snapping my resolve and all the level-headedness I've held tight to all day.

"Get the fuck over here."

Her pupils blow out at my demand.

She's barreling into my arms on the next breath.

The second she makes contact, I scoop her up and grip her tightly through the little shorts she changed into while I was away.

I pull her into my chest, desperate to be close.

She wraps her perfect legs around my waist, then cups my face and studies me.

The concern in her expression is like a punch to the gut, but I raise my chin and give her a half smile. "Miss me, Mama?"

She shoves my shoulder so hard I have to take a step back to keep from toppling off the dock into the water.

"Don't you ever do something like that again, Kendrick. I swear to god—"

With a palm on her ass, I squeeze, silencing her midsentence.

"I'm gonna stop you right there. It was the right thing to do, and I'd do it again in a heartbeat."

She huffs, then opens her mouth to no doubt sass me again.

I plunge forward, silencing her with a kiss. "Save your breath," I murmur against her lips. "You're gonna need it for what I have in mind when we get in the house."

Gasping, she wiggles out of my grasp. I'm reluctant to let her go until I notice the way Decker is scanning the shores across the way—his jaw is set, hands fisted at his sides.

Placing our girl gently on her feet, I shift so I'm standing between her and the open water.

"What's up, Cap?"

He turns to me and scowls. "The feature's still on. The reporter and photographers will be here soon to finish setting up the cameras and equipment. Let's get inside before they get back."

Nodding, I bend low and catch Jojo behind the knees, then hoist her over my shoulder. I grin at her laughter and half-hearted protests as I stride up the dock toward the beach.

"K," Decker warns as he follows.

I know his concern. I share his fucking concern.

The moment Misty got hold of photos and information about our girl's past, we put this woman at risk. That only compounded when Nicky threw that punch. The more the media knows about what she means to us individually and as a unit, the more scrutiny she'll be under.

This woman, who's been through more than enough.

This woman, who hates to be photographed, subjected, exposed.

Sighing, I place her gently on her feet, then turn her around and grip her shoulders so I can march her up the landing.

"My room, Jojo. I need you in my room right now."

Chapter 5
Josephine

It's been hours since I've felt truly safe, but that changes the moment we step into the sanctuary of Kendrick's bedroom.

Yet once I'm inside, I'm racked with indecision and confusion, because what happens now?

He doesn't give me time to overthink, though. I should have known he wouldn't.

He enters the room behind me and rolls out his shoulders, then closes and locks the door. Wordlessly, he saunters into the bathroom without looking back, no doubt expecting me to follow.

For a heartbeat, I take in my surroundings. I've never been in his room. The décor is dark and rich; a blend of black, maroon, and bright Crusaders red fills the space and gives it a depth. A set of framed jerseys is displayed on one wall: four sizes and teams, all number 24, with his name on the back. Framed pictures of the twins decorate the desk, along with a photo of him with his parents when he was much, much younger. His warm, masculine scent is everywhere: musk and vanilla, familiar and enticing.

The layout of the room is similar to mine, which makes sense, given that our rooms are down the hall from each other. A king-size bed dominates the space. It's centered on the far wall, with a desk and bookshelves on one side and a seating area on the other.

I'm still taking it all in when the sound of water hitting tiles snags my attention.

"Ohio."

The use of that nickname garners an immediate reaction. Irritated that he'd revert back to calling me that, I march into the bathroom, intent on putting him in his place.

Except I stop dead in my tracks the second my bare feet touch the cool tiles.

Before me stands Kendrick Taylor. Naked. Ripped and cut and polished like marble—and hard as fuck.

He strokes his cock with one hand, his lips parted, while he regards me through his thick eyelashes.

"Strip," he instructs.

"Don't call me Ohio," I counter as I wiggle out of my shorts.

He bites down on his bottom lip, tracking my every move as I grab the hem of my Crusader's T-shirt and lift it over my head.

His deep brown eyes go molten as I drop the shirt to the floor, because rather than standing in front of him wearing a bra and panties, I'm completely bare.

He strides across the bathroom, and he doesn't stop until he's got me backed up against the wall. With his head dipped low, he runs his nose along my throat, then licks a path up to my ear.

"I won't. But I knew that'd get you in here and out of your head," he teases, nipping at me. Grasping both wrists, he guides them up and pins them above my head. "Now be a good girl and let me lick your cunt. I want to taste you. I need a reminder of exactly why I did it."

He drops to his knees as his fingers trail over my shoulders, my breasts, my stomach, leaving hot tingles of arousal in their wake.

With both hands on my thighs to steady me, he encourages my legs apart and holds me open.

"Fucking perfect pussy," he whispers, his attention fixed on my core. Then he's diving in, sweeping his tongue over the entire length of my slit, and locking his lips around my clit and sucking. Hard.

"*Fuck*, K." I writhe against the wall, gripping his shoulders for balance.

He groans against me. "How does someone so sassy taste so fucking sweet?"

"More," I whimper, thrusting desperately against the hold he has on my hips.

In response, he sucks me into his mouth again, channeling all my focus to that one perfect pleasure point.

Arousal drips down my inner thigh.

"That's mine," he growls, licking me from mid-thigh all the way back up to my pussy. "Don't you dare waste a drop of this, Mama."

It's all I can do to keep my knees from buckling.

He pierces me with his tongue, then follows with relentless thrusts that are as ravenous and frantic as I feel. Each time he dips inside me, I only grow needier.

I want him deeper. I want to be fuller. I just want him.

More of him now. More of him always.

"Kendrick, please," I pant, digging my fingertips into the base of his skull.

"I know what you need, Mama. Come on my tongue, then I'll fill you up like you want."

He flicks my clit again, over and over, in rapid succession, then seals his mouth around the bundle of nerves and sucks.

I'm flying. I'm falling. I'm at the mercy of this man who's sacrificed so much for me.

My orgasm rips through me, forcing a scream from somewhere deep inside. Desperate, lost to the pleasure, I squirm against the wall as I release him and pinch my nipples. The intensity of his passion—the fire about to hit a boiling point between us—is everything.

It's everything, and it's consuming, and it's so fucking satisfying. But it's still not enough.

He's on his feet a second later, scooping me up, entering the shower, and pushing my back against the wet tiles as water streams from the dual showerheads.

One hand brushes down my body, between my breasts, to cup my sex. Squeezing, he kisses me, then pulls back slightly, his eyes still full of fire but his expression serious. "Can I come inside you, Mama?"

I swear my pussy clenches in response, and I practically swoon. He knows I have the implant, but he asked for consent anyway.

"You better," I reply, tipping my head back so he's forced to look at me. "Fucking claim me, K."

Without breaking eye contact, he grunts and lines himself up. In one single motion, he pushes in and fills me to the hilt.

"Fuck," I pant, gripping his neck tighter. "You feel so fucking good."

He thrusts up once, watching me.

Then he thrusts again, but at a slightly different angle.

He switches it up again, and this time, the hard, fat tip of his cock nudges the most perfect spot inside me. My cunt spasms in response, and my heart stutters at the way my body sings for him.

"There she is," he murmurs with a cocky smirk.

That single reaction was apparently all the confirmation he needs, because without a second of hesitation, he pistons into me with wild abandon, hitting that sweet spot over and over.

"So fucking perfect, Jojo. Perfect pussy full of sass and sweetness."

Fuck, his words alone could send me over the edge. "Don't stop, K. Please don't stop."

"Never," he grunts out, slamming his mouth into mine and sealing the promise with a bruising kiss.

Big hands cup my breasts and pinch my nipples. Every touch is electric. Every point of contact a stimulating connection that drives me higher.

He moves his tongue in time with his thrusts, and I swear I've died and gone to horny girl heaven.

Our kisses turn sloppy and desperate under the water, until we're a mess of tongues and groans, clashing teeth and desperate pants.

"Look at me," he demands.

Without hesitation, I obey.

"Now look down at how perfectly we fit together." He drops his chin. "Watch how you grip my dick like we were made to do this, Jojo."

I follow his line of sight, bowing my head to watch as his hard length disappears inside me.

He's right. My body greedily sucks him in with each thrust. Nothing has ever felt as good as the heat and pleasure emanating from us. Nothing has ever looked so utterly seamless. Every time he pulls out, the lips of my needy cunt stretch around him perfectly. Then, when he thrusts back in, my body clamps down like he's all I'll ever want or need.

"You take me so well, Mama." He pushes in again, pressing his body against mine and driving me into the slick tile wall, filling me to the hilt. Rather than pulling out again once he's seated, he thrusts deeper, the base of his cock driving into my clit as my arousal gushes around him.

The embers burning low in my belly ignite, sending waves of heat coursing through me. "Fuck, K. Fuck. I'm going to come again."

"Damn right you are." His thrusts grow rapid, desperate. He's got to be right there on the edge with me.

"Come for me, Mama. Show me how much you love what I'm giving you."

On command, I detonate, erupting with so much force I'm grateful he's got me pinned against the wall. My inner muscles convulse, tightening on the length of him as he grunts and pulses inside me, his release mixing with mine.

His thrusts don't slow as he comes, and by the time I'm done milking him, I'm desperate for a break from the exquisite, all-consuming fullness.

When I squirm in his hold, he lowers me so my feet hit the tile floor. But he doesn't let me go far.

Cupping my face with both hands, he peppers kisses along my mouth and my neck. Then he bends low to worship my breasts.

"Kendrick!" I giggle when the stubble along his jaw tickles my stomach. Still smiling, I close my eyes and revel in his proximity. In the security that envelops me now that he's home. Now that he's in my arms, inside me still, right where he belongs.

"Thank you," I whisper against his lips when he rights himself. Pulling back, and with a deep breath in, I push against his shoulders and drop to my knees.

His lip is caught between his teeth as he tracks my movement, instinctively gathering up my wet hair so he doesn't lose sight of me for even a second.

"What do you think you're doing down there?" he teases, grazing my bottom lip with the thumb of his free hand.

I quirk one eyebrow and peer up, admiring the way rivulets of water cascade down his body, into the divots of his chiseled abs, then over his strong, powerful thighs.

"Cleaning up our mess," I quip. With that, I lick down the length of his softening cock and make an exaggerated slurp as I suck him fully into my mouth.

Popping off, I sit back on my knees.

"And expressing my gratitude."

I kiss the tip.

"Showing you just how much I appreciate you."

With my tongue, I trace the ridge.

"How much it means to me. That you did that for Nicky... and for me."

I take him in my mouth again and swallow, eliciting a deep, appreciative groan before letting his dick slide out from between my lips.

"Proving to you just how well-mannered and coachable I can be."

I zigzag the tip of my tongue against his slit.

"Showing you just how much I love you." I sit back on my haunches and tip my head back so I can look him dead in the eye. "Because I do, Kendrick. I love you."

With another kiss to the tip of his dick, I rise up to my knees and take him fully into my mouth.

"Are you for real right now?" he demands, cupping my face and tilting my head back. "Did you just tell me you love me mid-blowie?"

"Mm-hmm," I confirm with a mouthful of him. Then I pull back with an exaggerated pop. "Would you prefer I stand up and say it again?"

Chuckling low, he thrusts his hips, driving his growing erection deeper into my throat. "Oh, you'll be saying it again. And again and again and again. I want to hear it every day for the rest of our lives, Mama. I love you, too. I'd do anything for you."

His declaration causes warmth to pool in my belly. The way his dick gets more rigid in my mouth by the second has liquid fire burning me from the inside out. I take him as deep as I can manage, and he hisses through clenched teeth, his fingers weaving into my hair and massaging the back of my head.

"You like the way we taste combined like that, don't you, Mama?"

I moan my confirmation around his length, relishing the way it pulses ever so slightly and the taste of the pearl of precum—or would it be postcum?—that leaks out the tip.

"Thank you," I murmur, holding his gaze as I lick his slit clean. "Can I have more, please?" With a deep inhale through my nose, I suck him all the way into my mouth and let him rest against my tongue.

"*Goddamn*, Jojo. You look so pretty on your knees for me. You can have it all."

I continue savoring him with slow, languid, reverent sucks. I can't help but groan as I explore, savoring the saltiness of our mixed releases as I lap at him. Every swipe heightens my arousal, prompting me to pour all my energy into making him feel good.

Swallowing around him again, I ghost my fingertips up his muscular inner thighs. I massage his balls, then travel higher and rub behind his sack until he's a mess of curses and praise.

"*Fuck, Mama. Goddamn.* Such a good girl. Such a polite, well-mannered girl for me. You like being on your knees with a mouthful of dick, don't you, JoJo?" he asks, combing one big hand through my hair.

"I love it," I purr. Then I go right back to sucking him.

He blows out a big exhale, clearly trying to hold it together. "You just gonna stay down there worshipping my cock while I clean up?"

I nod, careful not to let him fall out of my mouth as I tease my tongue along the ridge of the crown.

Reaching for his soap and loofah, he smirks down at me. He lathers up quickly, using one hand to wash his body while he places the other firmly on the top of my head. Before long, he's alternating between playing with my hair and stroking my face while he thrusts his hips gently.

He's hard and leaking in my mouth by the time he rinses his body, a feat I'm exceptionally proud of, considering he came less than five minutes ago.

"Fuck, Jojo. Your perfect mouth is almost as good as your pretty little pussy. I'm rock hard and ready to bust again," he groans, leaning against the shower wall.

"So do it," I taunt.

"Ask nicely." He shifts back far enough that his cock pops out from between my lips.

I whimper at the loss. "Please?"

Grinning, he smooths my hair back. Then he cups my face and tilts it up.

"You know just what I like to hear, don't you, Mama?"

"Please, Kendrick, will you let me suck on your big fat cock and swallow your cum?"

"*Goddamn*," he groans, his hand abandoning my head to circle his shaft. "Open that fucking mouth."

Eagerly, I rise up, lick the underside of his dick, and stick out my tongue as far as it will go.

"You want it?"

"Yes," I plead.

He grits his teeth, and his thighs tense under my palms. "Yes, what?"

"Yes, please. I want it. I need it. Come on my tongue, K."

On command, hot bursts erupt from him, and I catch as much as I can in my open, waiting mouth.

Groaning, I lick my lips and peer up through soaking wet lashes. When his eyes lock with mine, I swallow him in one gulp.

After one final caress of my cheek, he offers me a hand and gently pulls me to my feet. Before I can step out from under the spray, he tugs me against his slick, warm chest and cups my pussy as he kisses my neck.

I wrap my arms up and around him and lean back, letting him hold my weight.

"You did so good for me, Mama. I won't be able to step into this shower without thinking about you on your knees."

His praise makes my heart float in my chest.

"You want help washing your hair?"

As tempting as his offer sounds, he's had a hell of a day.

"I've got it."

"It's like that, huh? I know you can do it yourself, and I respect it. But I want to do it. How about *can* I wash your hair for you, please?"

My insides melt as I nod.

He makes quick work of squirting a glob of shampoo into his palm, lathering up, and massaging it into my scalp.

I sag against him, my back to his chest, and soak up his warmth as he takes his time working me over.

For as much pleasure as he's brought me tonight, Kendrick brings an equal amount of comfort. The way he cares is a sacred practice.

After I've rinsed and conditioned, he spins me in his arms and kisses me softly.

"You meant what you said?" He worries at his lip, his vulnerability on full display.

But he has nothing to be worried about. I meant it, and I'll say it to him every day, per his request, if that's what it takes for him to believe me.

"I love you," I whisper. "Not just because of what you did, K, but because of who you are. Because of how you nurture and love. I love you, and I'm in love with you, Kendrick."

His eyes flutter closed, and he sucks in a sharp breath through his nose. Eventually, he swallows, his Adam's apple bobbing, and he fixes his attention on me again.

"I love you, too."

With one last kiss to the top of my head, he moves to exit the shower. Naked and dripping onto the mat outside the enclosure, he turns and gives me a thorough once-over. "I'll leave you to finish up, but don't you dare wipe away what I gave you between those pretty little thighs. You hear me?"

"Yes, sir." I smile coquettishly and wink as he shuts the shower door between us.

Chapter 6

Josephine

"Come here."

When I exit the bathroom wrapped in a towel, he's sitting on the edge of his bed in nothing but white Calvins.

I take him in as I saunter over. He's so collected, steady, calm. He's an unfazeable force, not easily miffed or discouraged. Until now, I haven't fully appreciated Kendrick's cool demeanor. In fact, I've repeatedly categorized it incorrectly.

I interpreted it as grumpiness. Detachment. Aloofness. Except he's none of those things. He simply has an innate ability to read the room and remain stoically calm under pressure.

"Sit." He plants his hands on the terry cloth covering my hips and guides me to spin so my back is to him. Then he cups my shoulders and gently pushes me down to my knees.

Without a word, he rakes his fingers through my hair, combing out tangles and massaging my scalp.

The tension I've held on to all day ebbs as he works. I'm in such a deep, hazy, scalp-massage trance by the time he's done that I'm only pulled from it when he taps my arm.

I lift it in response, offering up the hair tie on my wrist.

His fingers trail over the red, black, and white Crusaders friendship bracelets first, then he slides the elastic off and uses it to secure what I've only now realized is a thick braid running down my back. His tone is light when he murmurs in my ear. "The girls haven't taken their bracelets off since you gave them to them."

"I miss them," I admit, tipping my head back so I can look into his deep brown eyes.

From above, he angles over me and places a gentle kiss on my lips. "We'll see them soon. They'll be at the game on Saturday."

The game. *Shit*.

Today has been a whirlwind, and when Kendrick came home, I was swamped with relief. Until now, I haven't even considered the consequences he'll have to face personally, academically, and where football is concerned.

My mind takes off, and one question after another pummels my brain, sending a wave of anxiety rising up in me until it's threatening to spill over. Will he be allowed to play this weekend? What about the rest of the season? Will there be disciplinary action? Legal proceedings? How does this affect his chances of being drafted?

"Not tonight, Jojo." He wraps my braid around his wrist and tugs, angling my head to the side and forcing me to focus. "I'm home. We're safe. We don't need to worry about anything else tonight."

I swallow past the emotion in my throat and try my best to steel my spine. If he wants to forget about the world tonight, to get lost in each other for a few quiet hours before we have to face the light of a new day, I can do that. I want to give him that.

He pulls on the braid again, making my scalp tingle, and drops his lips to the still-damp skin where my shoulder meets my neck. With a hum, he licks a path from my clavicle to just below my ear.

"Think you've got more in you, Mama?"

"Maybe," I hedge with a grin. "What did you have in mind, big guy?"

"No maybes," he growls with a corresponding tug of my hair. "It's yes or no, and it's *always* your choice."

Fuck. Yes.

K knows I don't need to be in control, but he understands that I *do* need to have the power of choice. The way he sees me... the way he just *gets* me... It makes me love him that much more.

"Yes, please," I amend, attempting to crane back so I can look at him but finding resistance.

He holds my hair tighter still, using it to move me until I'm right where he wants me. All the while, he grazes his teeth along my neck and suckles my skin. When I'm in position, he clamps down hard, and arousal shoots right down to my clit.

"Text your other boyfriends, Jojo. I want to watch them lick my cum out of your tight little hole and feed it to you."

Chapter 7
Kendrick

The knock is hesitant.

"Jo? Are you in here?"

She calls him in, and he doesn't even bat an eye when he finds her on her knees before me.

I knew he'd be good at sharing.

Kylian's practical. Logical. Strategic and quick.

He strides into the room and halts before us, his attention completely focused on our girl.

"You're okay?" It's more demand than question. With a tentative hand, he cups her jaw.

She hums in the affirmative and rises up on her knees to nuzzle against his thigh. "Kendrick wants to play." Pulling back a little, she takes him in, raking her teeth over her bottom lip. "I texted Nicky, too."

Behind his glasses, assessing blue eyes dart up to me. "First, define play. Second, it took a while for Decker and me to convince Locke to go to bed. He's asleep. I can wake him, if you want, but—"

"No." I lift my chin and hold his gaze. Nicky's not okay, and we both know it. He's far from it, in fact. The way he reacted when the photographer touched our girl was so out of character for him. He's not violent. He doesn't lash out. Between the physical pain he's dealing with after the incident and the mental anguish that comes with unnecessarily berating himself for losing his cool, he needs rest.

"Think you can handle her for me?" I ask. "She's already made me blow my load twice. I need someone else to tap in for the next round."

"Of course I can handle her." Scowling, he grips his shirt at the back of the neck and whips it off. "What kind of question is that?"

With a brow raised, I regard Jojo. I'll let her work her Kylian magic.

"He's not doubting you." She places her palms on Kylian's denim-clad thighs. "But if we do this, I want to do exactly what K says tonight," she explains. "For me?"

His eyes widen, like understanding has hit him.

Yeah, Kyl. You're not the boss in this room.

He holds out both hands and helps her to her feet, eyes ablaze as they scorch up and down her naked body. Shaking his head, he makes his declaration.

"Not just for you, Jo. For him, too." Then, turning to me, he asks, "How do you want us?"

I rise up and kiss Jojo on the back of her shoulder, smoothing my lips over her soft, supple skin. "You're still good, Mama?"

She nods, pressing into me and pulling me toward her until she's effectively sandwiched between the two of us.

With her consent, I regard Kylian.

"I already filled her up. Lick her clean and fill her up again."

He smirks, his focus flicking to Jojo for all of two seconds as he confirms that she's on the same page. "Yes sir," he finally replies, never taking his eyes off hers.

"Careful, Daddy," Jojo rhapsodizes, smoothing her hands up his bare chest. "He'll like it too much if we both call him sir."

Fuck yeah.

We're doing this.

"I bet he would," Kylian murmurs, kissing along her neck and ghosting his hands up the curve of her hips and over her ribs.

Leaving Jojo in his capable hold, I saunter over to the corner of the room and heave my reading chair forward. It scrapes against the floor, groaning as I drag it to the end of the bed. Once I've got it positioned where I want it, I make my way to my nightstand.

Over my shoulder, I watch Kylian press kisses into Jojo's jaw, all the while keeping his gaze fixed on me. Raising both brows, I pull open the nightstand drawer. "I assume you've seen the emails, Boy Genius?"

"Sent some and saw the responses, yes." He grasps Jojo's hips and guides her until the backs of her knees connect with the mattress. Then he deftly pushes her down until she's spread out on my bed for the taking.

She lets her head loll to the side and regards me lazily. Fuck, she's so beautiful—her lips swollen from sucking my cock, her neck and tits covered in little red reminders of all the places I've marked her.

So fucking beautiful. So fucking mine.

Brow furrowing, she reaches out a hand to me. "K... not tonight, remember?"

Ahh. So that's the rub. She thinks I'm asking about the emails because I'm worried. She doesn't want me upset.

I rummage through the drawer until I find what I'm after, then hold it up for her to see. "I know, Mama. I just want to know if I'm benched for sure. If there's no chance of me playing on Saturday, then I'm going to smoke a fat blunt as I watch you get fucked."

Her eyes light up in understanding. "You gonna share that with your girl?" she teases, running her hands down her body as Kylian pries her knees apart.

He stares hungrily at her swollen cunt for several seconds before tearing his eyes away to answer me.

"You're benched until the athletic advisory committee can meet and discuss the terms of suspension or probation. The next regular meeting wasn't supposed to be for three weeks, but Decker sent off a proposal for the SportsZone coverage that will require an emergency meeting to be held no later than next Tuesday. You won't play this Saturday," he states matter-of-factly. "You know I can take care of that anyway," he adds, nodding toward the blunt in my hand.

I pull out a smaller joint from my stash. "I know."

Kylian has to alter our test results regularly because of the antiquated rules around peptide use for college athletes.

Peptide hormones have been crucial to keeping my lupus in remission, and they help Locke with his RA. Yet even as a therapeutic measure, they're considered a banned substance.

Kylian could easily erase any traces of THC and tobacco in my system, but I was raised to be honest and forthright, so I'm more than okay playing by the rules when they don't interfere with my quality of life.

"Tonight's an exception." I place the blunt behind my ear, then offer the smaller joint to my girl.

She parts her lips, and I can't fucking help but lean over and swipe my tongue into that sweet mouth. Surprised, she opens wider and kisses me back, moaning with each sweep.

She's squirming on the mattress, and when I pull back, I see why. Kylian's already got his mouth on her tits. He works her over good, putting on a show, just like I asked, pulling and teasing one rosy bud into an erect peak before moving on to the other.

Grinning, I right myself. She's still writhing as she smiles dreamily at me, like I'm the one hanging all the stars in her universe.

"Keep doing that," I tell Kylian, placing the joint between her lips and lighting it for her. "Then check and tell me if she's wet."

She closes her lips, eyes on me, and inhales.

With a smirk, I bend low and kiss her senseless once again.

"She's fucking soaked. What the hell did you do to her?"

I suck on her mouth and massage along the slender column of her neck to encourage her to exhale. The musky cloud between us ratchets up my desire. Fuck. I'm already getting hard again.

"Fucked two of her holes and told her how much I love her." With one last kiss, I pull back and retreat to my chair. "Maybe if she's a good girl for you, I'll play with her ass when you're done."

Jojo arches off the bed, whimpering, her eyes begging me to come back and keep making her feel good.

"You want that, don't you, Mama? You want me in your ass tonight?"

"Yes," she mewls without hesitation. Her eyes are on me, but her hands are in Kylian's hair as he eats her cunt in earnest.

"Let Kylian take care of you first. We've got all night, and we're just getting started."

Chapter 8

Josephine

With every one of Kendrick's exhales, the room fills further with smoke, creating a soft haze. My nerves spark to life with each lick from Kylian as he absolutely devours my pussy.

I'm a loose, languid mess. Relaxed everywhere except for where it counts.

The promise of pleasure gathers low in my belly, then tingles up my spine. Bursts of sensation catch in my toes, my calves, up my thighs, and through my torso.

The anticipation is white hot. It's the kind of orgasm that promises blackout-level bliss.

I'm so close, and I can't fucking wait.

"Daddy, fuck. Please." I can't help it. I'm pleading for something I know he'll give me.

But then he pulls back and sits up, his face glistening with a mixture of my arousal and Kendrick's cum.

I yelp at the loss and scramble to sit up, ready to demand he finish what he started.

But Kylian isn't looking at me.

No, he's looking to Kendrick, who's wearing a wicked smirk as smoke billows around him. His legs are wide, his stance relaxed. Somehow, his Calvins have disappeared. He's lazily tugging on his straining erection, attention fixed on me, like he's ready for round three.

"I'm not the boss tonight," Kylian informs me. "Ask him if you can come."

Fuck. A shot of electricity zings through me.

Am I really being edged by these two?

I'm too lust-drunk and high to sass back and put up a fight.

So I do as I'm told.

"Please, K? I need it. Please let me come."

His wicked grin turns absolutely devilish. "You can come. Then when you're done, you can crawl over here and thank me."

Kylian dives back down, turning all his attention to my tender, needy clit. He laps at me, then presses the flat of his tongue against me, using his whole mouth to grind into me until I'm twisted even tighter than before.

My pussy pulses in anticipation, but the waves of pleasure keep gathering, each one more violent than the last, heating my body from the inside out.

Kylian sinks one finger inside me and expertly navigates to my G-spot, pressing with the perfect amount of pleasure and caressing me inside while never letting up on my clit.

That's just the trigger I need.

His name is ripped from my throat, followed by Kendrick's as I lock eyes with him. Kylian doesn't slow. He keeps lapping at me as I spiral.

K tugs on his cock, timing the pulls with the pulsing of my pussy. "Fuck, that looks like a good one."

Kylian grunts his agreement but still doesn't stop.

Finally, it's too much, and I slam my thighs closed, desperate to give my overstimulated nerves a break.

Kylian scoffs, pries my legs off his head, and spreads me open wider than before.

"Stay," he murmurs, shifting back to give Kendrick a clear view of my cunt.

"Goddamn," he murmurs at the sight of me. "She's so pink and swollen. You love his mouth on you, don't you, Mama?"

Chest heaving, I sigh. "Yes."

"You know we're not done with you, yeah?"

"I know." Already, heat pools deep in my belly again.

"Once you get feeling back in your legs, get on your hands and knees and crawl to me."

Fuck. My heart just about leaps out of my chest at his command.

Kylian wipes at his chin and grins at me. He offers a hand to help me up. Once I'm steady on my feet, I sink to my knees.

Then I do as I'm told and fucking crawl.

My breasts sway and my hips swing as I close the space between us.

"Ah, fuck," Kylian murmurs reverently from behind.

Kendrick chuckles. "Hang in there, Boy Genius. You're gonna get yours."

At the base of Kendrick's chair, I kneel before him, my legs spread wide and my head tipped back in submission.

"Goddamn, Jojo. You're so fucking pretty." He swipes at my bottom lip, then cradles my head in his hands. "She's a good fucking girl, isn't she, Kyl?"

"She is," Kylian murmurs in my ear.

His proximity startles me, but I relax again immediately and tip back, seeking his touch.

Kendrick's grip on my head tightens to keep me from arching away.

"Who's the boss?" he chides.

"You, K," I whisper as arousal drips down my thighs.

"Who gives you pleasure, Mama?"

My smile widens. "You, Kendrick." This time when I tip back, he releases my head. "And Daddy," I purr, finding Kylian's mouth for a hurried, sloppy kiss.

The combination of my flavor and Kendrick's on his tongue makes my pussy convulse.

"Hey now," K scolds playfully. Gripping my chin and turning my face, he regards me. "Don't you think your Daddy deserves to come?"

"Yes," I reply without hesitation.

"You're gonna suck him off right here in this chair while I eat your ass."

I practically black out as his words register, but I'm quickly pulled back to the moment when he rises, lifts me off the ground, and makes way.

"Sit," he tells Kylian.

The boys swap positions. Kylian lowers into the chair as Kendrick trails a finger over my shoulders and down the length of my spine before dipping between my ass cheeks.

"You don't stop for anything," K whispers, his voice husky and heated. He presses into my back, his hips encouraging me forward.

Kylian fists his cock in one hand.

"Suck him," K commands.

I've barely begun when big hands spread me open from behind. Kendrick dives in without preamble, pulling my puckered hole open and exploring with his tongue.

"Goddamn, Mama," he grunts, alternating long licks with greedy plunges.

Every time his tongue breaches the ring of muscle, I whimper.

Every time I whimper, Kylian fucks my mouth harder.

We're a chain of indulgence, perfectly in sync as we careen toward mutual pleasure.

"Close," Kylian announces after a few minutes of steady sucking.

Doubling down in earnest, I hollow my cheeks and swirl my tongue under his crown the way he likes. His hands massage into my hair and hold as he uses my mouth to find his release.

Kendrick doesn't quit as I suck down every drop of Kylian.

But then he pulls back and rises to his knees, and the loss of sensation has me gasping "no!"

"Stay down," he grunts as warmth hits my low back.

Sticky release trails down my spine like honey. I'm keyed up and trembling as I wait for what he's going to do next.

"You good?" Kendrick asks.

It's not until Kylian grunts a half-intelligible "uh-huh" that I realize he was talking to him.

"Sit up, brother. Rub her clit and suck on her perfect tits while I work on this last hole."

Fuck.

My pussy clenches at the very thought, then my whole body jolts and quickly tenses as Kendrick dips a finger through his cum on my back and rubs me.

"Relax for me, Mama. That's it. Ease back. Let us make you feel good."

His encouragement does the trick. That, and Kylian's mouth and hands expertly building me to orgasm number—fuck, I've lost count.

My breathing transforms to pants when Kendrick finally pushes in.

"You're mine," he growls in my ear as he crooks his finger inside my ass, claiming me in a way I've never been claimed before.

"Your mouth. Your cunt. This ass. All of you belongs to all of me. You feel me, Mama?"

I lean back, baring down as he works a second finger into my ass. Then I'm crying out as the finger fucking and Kylian's expert ministrations send me barreling over the edge.

Chapter 9

Kendrick

"Fuck. It's been a fucking day."

Grunting in agreement, I roll over and pull Jojo's pliant sleeping form into my chest.

I was shocked as shit when Kylian didn't take off the second she fell asleep between us.

He's welcome here—he's always welcome—but he doesn't usually jive with the constant group dynamics. Though since Joey, that's shifted.

I get it. The pull of her is enough to make a man reconsider his ways.

"You got another joint over there?"

I smirk into Jojo's messy braid. We rarely imbibe during the season, but today shook all of us to our core.

"Yeah, Boy Genius. Anything for you." Careful not to dislodge our girl, I reach over and blindly fumble through my nightstand, then fish out another joint and a lighter and pass them over.

I readjust, smoothing back the loose hairs along Joey's forehead and kissing her bare shoulder.

With a flick, a flame ignites, the only light in the dark room. Kylian's inhale is drawn out and languid, and his exhale is pure exhaustion.

The skunky scent infiltrates my senses, relaxing me further, so I close my eyes and will my brain to turn off for the night.

I'm beginning to fade when Kylian speaks.

"I didn't mention this earlier, because I didn't want to upset her. Or implicate her."

My eyes are wide open now, and I stiffen involuntarily. In a heartbeat, the calm I'd finally mustered is overtaken by a surge of adrenaline.

"What is it?" I reach over, signaling for him to pass the joint to me.

For a while there, I was hazy and sated, on cloud fucking nine. I appreciate his ability to read the room and not upset Jojo any more than she already is, but if there's more... if something else is coming for us—

"You're going to need to walk with a limp on campus this week. You might even consider employing the use of a crutch."

My stomach sinks. *The fuck?*

Before I can press, he continues.

"This morning, around 7:35 a.m., you were in the weight room with Cap. You tripped on a bench, snagging one foot in the process, and landed in an awkward lunge. It was a freak accident. The medical report indicates a suspected first- or second-degree groin tear."

In a way only Kylian can, he delivers this information all cool and collected, presenting only the facts.

Or, in this case, the lies masquerading as facts.

Passing the joint back to him, I mull over his explanation, searching for the deeper meaning behind his words.

"The email I sent from your account informing the coaches and training staff will bear a time stamp of 8:23 a.m."

And there it is.

The missing piece of the puzzle.

That means I was allegedly injured a few hours before shit went down at the house.

"The injury will take precedent over any fallout or disciplinary decisions," I muse, marveling at the simplicity and genius of the scheme.

"Precisely. The therapeutic protocol for a pulled groin is rest. The training team won't even attempt to evaluate, stretch, or massage it for several days. You'll be placed on the injured list for one or two weeks. There'll still be a review and potential disciplinary action based on who shows up to the meeting and how much sway Decker has with them, but it won't be the headline controlling the narrative. At least not right away."

An irrepressible chuckle rumbles through my chest.

I nuzzle deeper into Jojo's hair and inhale in an attempt to control my body's giddy reaction. Pride surges through me. Pride, and gratitude.

In this family, we take care of one another.

When I've finally reined in my natural physical response and I'm sure I won't wake her, I whistle low.

"That's clever. Cunning, honestly, even for you, Boy Genius."

"Anything for this family," he counters.

A-fucking-men.

His demeanor is far more serious than mine. It's probably more appropriate than the capricious relief rushing through me. There's a warmth and a resounding comfort to being part of a unit that functions so well and takes care of one another so completely.

I'm not out of the woods. There are still plenty of potential tripwires on the path back to the field and my future, but this is best-case scenario.

"Kylian," I croak, watching the cherry of his joint light up, suspended in the dark. "Thank you. I don't know how I'll even begin to repay you."

"You could start by upgrading my nickname. Daddy Genius has a nice ring to it."

I blink into the darkness, stunned and trying to make sense of the comment my most serious, literal friend just threw out there. A beat of silence thrums between us, and then he laughs.

He fucking *laughs*.

I've known this guy for over a decade, and yet as we lie in my bed, our girl between us, it hits me like a train careening down the tracks that I've never heard him laugh openly and genuinely. Not like this. Despite it being at my expense, I love it. I love him.

"I heard you had jokes now," I grumble, reaching over Jojo's still-sleeping form to shove his shoulder. "Finish that and go to sleep. You're welcome to stay in here if you think you'll be able to rest."

He puffs away, then puts the joint out and passes it back to me. I collected the others earlier, and I'll dispose of them accordingly tomorrow.

Based on the shit that's gone down over the last twenty-four hours, I'm not putting it past any of the SportsZone clowns to interpret *unbarred access* as permission to go through our garbage.

"You did good, Kyl," I whisper into the dark. "You did real good."

The mattress dips, and he moves closer. It's too dark to see him, but I hear him place a quiet kiss on Jojo's forehead.

"Anything for this family," he repeats with a yawn.

Chapter 10

Josephine

"Josephine."

Yawning, I peek one eye open and cuddle closer between Kylian and Kendrick. I swore I heard my name, but they're both still asleep.

Kylian doesn't usually sleep well outside the Nest, but from the way he's passed out beside me, it's obvious last night was just as satisfying and exhausting for him as it was for me.

"Josephine."

It's louder this time, and it's accompanied by a hand wrapping around my ankle under the covers.

I sit up like a shot, adrenaline coursing through my veins as I blink into the darkness.

"Shh," a shadow soothes from the end of the bed. "It's just me."

Coming to, I survey the trim waist and make my way to the set of broad shoulders before focusing on the tight-set jaw and onyx eyes locked on me.

"What do you want, Cap?" I groan, scrubbing a hand down my face.

"I want to take you somewhere." He tugs on both my ankles, pulling me down the bed toward him.

My heart leaps into my throat at the sudden movement. "Stop," I hiss, kicking out to force him to release me.

"Quiet," he scolds, looking at the guys on either side of me. "Get up and let me talk to you."

Wary about what he's up to, I slither down the middle of the mattress so I don't disturb Kylian or Kendrick. When I reach the end, I let my feet hang off the edge and pause as a yawn catches me by surprise.

"Josephine," Decker simpers.

I guess I'm not moving fast enough for him this morning.

With another yawn, I swing my legs, forcing myself to wake up. "I'm tired," I pout.

Kendrick kept us up way too late, and although I was more than happy to indulge in all the wicked, delicious fun, I assumed I'd get to sleep until a decent hour this morning. I don't even remember if I went to the bathroom before I finally passed out. All I know is that I was sore, sated, stoned, and so damn happy sandwiched between two of the men I love.

Decker bends low, and In the most tender move I've ever experienced from this man, he tucks my hair behind my ear, runs his nose along my jaw, and kisses my temple. "Josephine. I—I need you, okay?"

Chest constricting, I sit up straighter and wrap my arms around his neck. "What do you need?"

"I wanted to take you out on the boat before sunrise. I'll be tied up all day, so this is our only chance, but if you need more sleep, just say so. It's your choice, Siren."

His deference warms me. It's taken a few hard lessons, but I think he finally understands that giving me a choice is truly the way to my heart.

"I'd love to go out on the boat with you."

He smiles against the sensitive skin of my neck, then his massive, talented quarterback hands cup my ass and lift me up. I hold on tight as he wordlessly carries me from Kendrick's room.

Even once we're in the hall, he doesn't let me go.

I consider sassing him—I'm tired, but that doesn't mean my legs don't work.

But then he hoists me a little higher, holds me a little tighter, and hums, low and deep, into my neck, like I'm the most precious thing in the world.

Ugh. My heart.

I like to rile him up. Tease him. Make that damn jaw tic work overtime. But I love him like this. Sticky-sweet and soft, just for me.

His next words are heavy and set in a deep timbre that wasn't there a moment ago. "It's still dark outside. There shouldn't be any cause for concern... but just in case, I'll go down first and prep the boat, then you can follow a few minutes later."

Nodding, I brace myself as he carefully descends the stairs. When we get to the sliding glass door of the upper deck, he finally sets me on my feet. Reluctant to unwind my body from his, I loosen my hold but don't release him.

Grinning like he's eating up the way I'm clinging to him like he's my favorite pillow, he grasps my wrists and tugs until I'm forced to let go.

"You're underdressed," he states, his brow furrowed with worry.

"You pulled me out of bed, Cap. Not sure what you were expecting. You're lucky I love Kendrick's scent." I bring the collar of the shirt I slipped on last night to my nose. "Otherwise I'd still be naked."

His scowl deepens, so I decide against mentioning that I'm wearing Kylian's boxers.

"Here," he huffs, yanking his hoodie off. Before I have time to object, he works it over my head. "Count to one hundred, then meet me on the dock," he orders. Without waiting for a response, he slips out the door and into the cool morning air.

I push my arms into the sleeves, then wrap myself in a hug as I silently count in my head.

Shivering, I pull the cuffs of Decker's sweatshirt down past my wrists and let the too-long arms flop by my sides. If it's this cool inside, I can only imagine the chill that will hit me when I step outside.

I slip my feet into a pair of shoes as I watch Decker untie the ropes anchoring the boat to the dock and make his way aboard. Still shivering but warming more by the second, I bring my hands to my face and inhale deeply and shamelessly while I wait.

The hoodie is thick, butter soft and super warm, and suffused with not only notes of amber and sea salt but also the heat of Decker's body.

Is there anything better than an oversized, preheated hoodie?

The low hum of the pontoon's engine starting up is just audible through the glass.

I give it another ten seconds before I exit the house and follow after him.

The path that leads from the upper deck to the patio, then from the patio to the beach, is one I've taken so many times I can practically do it with my eyes closed.

Which is a good thing, considering it's pitch-black outside.

Decker has his phone light switched on, and I home in on it like a moth to the flame.

My feet find purchase on the pebbles that make up the shoreline around the lake, and I slow my steps, ready to hit the wooden planks of the landing.

By the time I'm at the end of the dock, he's offering out a hand to help me climb aboard.

With a grin, I scan the pontoon and tip my chin. "What? No love nest today?"

He closes his eyes, shakes his head, then hits me with a facsimile of his signature scowl.

"Just teasing." Popping up onto my toes, I peck his lips.

He catches my hip, steadying me but also holding me back.

"Wait until we pull away from the dock," he murmurs, eyes darting over my shoulder. "They've already set up the exterior cameras, but they're not allowed to capture or use any footage of us on the water."

Gulping past the worry that's collected in my throat, I peek over my shoulder.

"We're okay," he assures me as he grasps my hand. "I'd rather be too safe than slip up when it comes to you."

Weaving our fingers together, he guides me toward the captain's seat. Instead of sitting, he cages me in against the wheel, then reaches for the throttle and navigates the vessel out onto open water as he wraps his arms around me from behind.

"You sure you haven't changed your mind about boat sex, Cap?"

Decker nips at the juncture between my neck and shoulder as he continues to worship every inch of my skin he can access.

He's holding me in his lap, with one arm wrapped around my hips like a seat belt, while the other explores my body under his hoodie, playing with my nipples and making me writhe.

His unmistakable erection is pressing into my ass and has been for almost an hour, but he refuses to take things any further.

It's killing me. Fucking killing me.

Never mind that my pussy still feels like it has its own pulse after last night's very intense and thorough fucking. A thrill courses through me every time I think about how Kylian let Kendrick get so damn bossy with us both.

Another nip from Decker makes me jolt.

"Boat sex is still a hard no."

He follows up the bite with a soothing caress of his tongue over the tender flesh.

"But it wouldn't be right for me to get you all hot and bothered and leave you unsatisfied, now, would it?"

Sucking in a breath, I sit up straighter in his lap.

Is he kidding right now?

"Don't toy with me, Decker." I go for annoyed, but the effort is pointless when he's holding me tightly under the oversized hoodie and brushing his knuckles back and forth over one nipple.

All thoughts flee when his other hand dips low, lower, lower still, into the front of Kylian's boxers.

"You don't want me to toy with you?" he whispers in my ear, breath hot and minty, fueling the arousal simmering in my core.

I hold my breath, hoping, wishing, yearning, as his hand continues its journey.

"But what if I want to play?" he asks when his entire hand finally covers my hot, wet, needy cunt.

With a groan, I drop my head back against his shoulder. "Don't you dare tease me right now, Decker Crusade."

"Show me what you like," he replies, grasping my wrist with his other hand and guiding it to my waistband.

I slide my hand lower, until I meet his, and together, we rub my clit, our fingers slipping around each other as they stroke my swollen, slick pleasure point.

"Is this all for me?" he asks, pulling out his hand and inspecting the glistening arousal coating his fingertips.

I dive forward and capture his fingers in my mouth, sucking them clean.

"Fuck," he murmurs as he paints my tongue with my cum. He presses his fingers in and out of my mouth as my hips buck back and forth in his lap in time with his movements.

"I want you to come right here in my lap, Siren. Think you can do that for me?"

"I need—" I start, but he growls in my ear and dives right back into the boxers, like he knows exactly what I need and can't wait to give it to me.

I'm putty in his hands as he gently moves my fingers back to my tight bundle of nerves.

"Like this?" he confirms as he rubs me just the way I like.

Electricity zaps through me, lighting me up. "Fuck. Yes. Decker."

"Can I fuck you with my fingers?" he pants into my ear.

"Please," I practically beg.

The moment the word is out of my mouth, his thumb connects with my clit, and a steady pressure rises inside me as he slips two fingers into my pussy.

"Siren," he murmurs, the word husky and reverent. "You're so fucking tight, baby. So warm and wet and perfect."

He massages my tense inner walls, fucking up and hitting the perfect spot every time. With his thumb, he caresses up and over the hood of my clit, only occasionally pressing right where I want him.

He's doing it on purpose. It's the tension I crave: the back and forth I've come to expect from this man.

He plays me like an instrument, his fingers inspiring a sultry, slow, aching buildup as I writhe in his lap.

"That's it, baby. The fire between us burns so fucking hot. But I can make you feel good, too. I want to make you feel good forever."

I've never come at the hands of this man.

That thought is what sends me spiraling.

"Cap," I pant as I clench around his fingers.

"Say my name," he growls, pressing so hard against my clit I gush around his hand.

"Decker," I cry out, pulsing and writhing and reveling in our mutual flames.

"Decker. Decker. Decker." His name is a mantra, a prayer.

I melt into his body as he whispers reassurance and praise in my ear. Encouragement like *Thatta girl* and *I've never seen anything so beautiful* and *I love watching you come apart at my hand. So beautiful. So fucking beautiful... My Siren. My Josephine.*

Texts: The Boys

> Cap: Doing this via text because I'm afraid there's nowhere we can go that we won't be recorded. Kyl informed me last night that at least two of the mics in the kitchen are hot.

Kylian: Update. As of this morning, five mics are actively recording.

Locke: The fuck? How are they already recording?

> Cap: They're not supposed to be. But per the contract, they can use anything they collect.

Locke: Even if they're not supposed to do it yet? Bullshit

Kendrick: Get used to it. They own our asses until they're gone for good

> Cap: Sorry, man. There's nothing we can do now but get through it. I can't shut down what we've already agreed to. Official coverage starts Thursday.

Locke: She's not safe here

Cap: We can keep her safe. We can control how we function and what our priorities are. Our number one is to keep her safe.

Kylian: Obviously.

Locke: Agreed

Kendrick: Agreed. But she should be on this thread

Cap: She's asleep.

Kendrick: She should still be looped in

Cap: Fine.

Texts: The Fab Five

Cap: Josephine, we're discussing plans for the next two weeks. Filming isn't supposed to start until Thursday, but Kyl says some of the mics in the house are already recording.

Cap: I propose full coverage opposed to zone defense. We stick together, travel as a group as much as possible. When we can't, we should try to go two-on-one with Josephine.

Locke: Most of us are into two-on-one coverage when it comes to our girl

Kendrick: Hell fucking yeah we are

Cap: This isn't a joke. We need to shield her from this. Try to keep our private moments private. Protecting Josephine is our top priority.

Locke: Agreed

Kendrick: We're with you, Cap

Kylian: They're still going to record us.

Cap: I can't control that. But we can minimize scrutiny if one or more of us is always with her, and if we all make a concerted effort not to get too handsy or let on that she's more than just a roommate.

Kylian: Fine. I'll get behind this plan. The Nest and her room are dead zones, by the way. Cameras have been installed, but I've already tapped the feeds so I can scramble footage as it's captured. It looks like it's recording, but the playbacks will be gobbledygook.

Kendrick: You ran that past her?

Locke: You're okay with the cameras, Hot Girl?

Kendrick: And what kind of word is gobbledygook?

Kylian: Of course I ran it past her.

Kylian: Link: *gobbledygook*

Cap: She's not going to answer. I told you, she's asleep.

Josephine: It's cute you think I'm asleep just because I'm not arguing with you, Cap.

Kendrick: Hahahaha OWNED

Kylian: Why weren't you in bed this morning, Jo?

Cap: Can we focus here?

Josephine: Cap doesn't want you to know why I wasn't in bed this morning *winky face*

Cap: I have to be out the door in two minutes. I need to make sure we're all on the same page.

Cap: We stick together. Move as a unit. No PDA whatsoever when the cameras are rolling.

Locke: How about minimal PDA?

Kylian: Or equally distributed PDA? If the goal is to confuse them as to whom Jo is with, then, theoretically, if we all engage in equal amounts of physical contact, it should create the same illusion as none of us engaging in physical contact. I could make a spreadsheet.

Cap: The GOAL is to keep the cameras off her, period. To allow her to blend in. To make it seem like her presence is nothing special.

Locke: You are special, Hot Girl

Cap: I didn't say she wasn't special.

Locke: You literally said her presence is nothing special

Josephine: Let's not argue. I agree with Cap.

Cap: You do?

Josephine: *eye roll emoji* Don't act so surprised, Decker. We need to present a united front and keep PDA to a minimum. It's only ten days, right? If we make our lives look boring and routine, they won't have anything to harp on. I hate the idea of being included in any of this, but I refuse to be separated from any of you.

Kendrick: Whatever you want, Mama

Kylian: Always your choice, baby.

Chapter 11

Decker

A tinkling of laughter carries in from the deck, making the hairs on the back of my neck stand up.

I turn my head slightly, seeking, listening, an addict fiending for another hit of her happiness.

Fuck. What I wouldn't give to be responsible for that laughter.

Hell, I'd settle for just being in the vicinity of her brightness right now. To be granted the pleasure of her company, the gift of her proximity.

Anything but here. Anything but this.

It takes all the energy I've got to maintain my composure.

With a deep breath in, I tilt my neck to one side, then the other, relishing the way it cracks and the hit of relief that comes with it.

Misty hums beside me, regarding me with a coquettish smile. When she brushes her fingertips over my forearm in a not-so-subtle move to reach for the water pitcher, I flinch and yank my arm away.

She pours herself a glass, then suspends the crystal pitcher in the air in offering.

Shaking my head, I dismiss her.

"We're almost done," she whispers in what she thinks is a reassuring, placating tone.

We better be almost fucking done. We've been at this for nearly two hours.

My muscles are bunched and tense from sitting for so long. After a full day of class and practice, followed by two content shoots, my presence was required at what was titled *Strategy Meeting* on the calendar invite. Though it's nothing more than a ruse created by my dad and his lawyers so they can remind me who's boss.

And remind me, they have.

At my father's behest, we're reviewing the language of the SportsZone deal. Line by line. In his words, it's important that we analyze the fine print so that I "fully understand the significance of this opportunity."

The only saving grace is that in the two hours since this farce began, no one has brought up the incident on Sunday morning. Maybe the SportsZone photogs aren't talking. Or maybe my father has chosen not to rehash the events that led to Josephine being manhandled in a way that forced Nicky to come to her defense and K to then take the fall for it all.

Makes sense: why bring it up and risk angering me when they can hold me hostage and encourage specific behaviors through manipulation?

None of the information we've gone over is new. No, this meeting has been nothing but an excruciating exercise in revealing the full extent of the invasion of privacy that's about to occur in the name of marketing and promotion.

The SportsZone deal is all-consuming. They have unprecedented access to me, to the guys, to the house, to our lives.

Unprecedented.

And yet here we fucking are—establishing precedence.

"The right of first refusal clause outlined in 17.8.2 renews with each reprint," one of my dad's lawyers explains from the screen at the front of the room.

That's how I've started to think of them.

Dad's lawyers.

Not mine. Not ours.

His.

For the last few years, I've been resting on my laurels when I should have been taking a vested interest in the business dealings related to my career.

The goal has always been to hustle my ass off to secure NIL deals and to take the guys along with me for the ride. I've spent the last three and a half years actively pursuing every moneymaking opportunity available to me.

It has never been about money. Between my dad's legacy, my own deals, and my mom's estate, which I'm the sole beneficiary of, I'm set for life. I could walk away from football tomorrow and not have a single financial need if I made smart investments and lived conservatively.

But things are different for my boys.

Any time I could work Kendrick into a deal, I did.

When a local opportunity that wasn't too physically demanding of Nicky arose, I insisted he be included, too.

I welcomed the deals. Sought them out, even.

Nicky won't go pro. After this season, he's done. The toll is too high, his pain too great. He'll always be taken care of because he's family, but I wanted to ensure he has cash available while he figures out what comes after football.

K *will* go pro. We were supposed to enter the draft together.

That may change after the incident with the photographer. He's always kept his image squeaky clean, but aggravated assault will be a big blight on his reputation. Lots of athletes who find themselves facing similar charges still get picked up by professional teams, but then some don't. Only time will tell.

Regardless, he does a ton for his sisters, going so far as to pay their private school tuition. His father is well-known and highly admired in our community, but he's not making bank as the sheriff of Lake Chapel. Kendrick contributes more financially to his family than he lets on.

I yawn to force my jaw to relax.

I need to get up and move. Stretch. Take a hot shower.

Check on the guys.

Check on my girl.

"It's getting late," I interject when there's a lull in the conversation.

"Ah, that it is," my dad replies from his box on the screen, as if he wasn't fully aware of how long this session has been drawn out. "We've only got one more item on the agenda, so let's move on to that."

"Decker," one of the lawyers begins—I don't know his name, and I don't care to learn it. "It was brought to our attention that one resident in your home does not have a nondisclosure on file."

Crickets.

Silence.

Dazed, numb even, I'm lost in the ether of panic and protectiveness, paralyzed by fear, too scared to say the wrong thing or reveal too much.

The only sound is my own blood whooshing in my ears.

And then that tinkling of laughter again.

God fucking dammit.

This was a trap. A fucking setup.

This meeting.

My entire life.

"Son, you know the rules. I don't have an issue with your friends taking advantage of my goodwill and the accommodations I provide—"

My head snaps over to meet his eyes on the screen at those words. *Goodwill. Accommodations.* That was a veiled threat if I've ever heard one.

"But your roommates have signed NDAs, and they haven't caused problems during their time at the house."

"Josephine is not a roommate. She's my guest."

"Is she your girlfriend?"

Beside me, Misty scoffs.

Reining in my fury, I rise out of my chair. I give her my back, then cross my arms over my chest.

"It doesn't matter what she is to me. I trust her. That's enough."

A low chuckle echoes through the speakers.

My dad is sitting back in his chair, looking relaxed, bored even, wearing an amused smirk.

I grit my teeth and fist my hands at my sides, wishing he were here in person so I could punch his fucking face. This was a setup. And based on his cool, calm, collected demeanor, there's no way I'm getting out of this until he gets exactly what he wants.

"Trust is a fickle beast, though, isn't it? It can be given freely, or it can be hard-fought and earned. But at the end of the day, it's an illusion. A false sense of security. Blinders preventing us from seeing what's happening right in front of us."

He sits up straighter then, jerking his chin.

"Misty? You have the standard agreement on hand?"

"Right here!" Her response is far too chipper as she produces the requested documents.

"Is it safe to assume your *guest* is there now, Decker?"

I grip the edge of the dining room table to keep myself from throwing my fist into it.

"Get her in here," my dad demands. "Martin is a notary, and Misty can sign by proxy on my behalf."

Shit. Not only did I walk into a setup, but I'm already caught in the snare.

Fighting is futile. Arguing will likely reveal too much about the nature of our relationship and make matters worse.

I'm trapped. Fucked. My options are to do what he says or to chew my own leg off trying to fight this.

I slide my phone out of my back pocket and pull up the text thread between the two of us.

> **Decker:** Siren. Can you please come to the dining room ASAP?

Quickly, I pound out a second text, offering up details so she can prepare herself for what she's about to walk into.

> **Decker:** I'm on a call with my dad and his lawyers. Misty's here, too. They're insisting you sign an NDA. I had no idea they were going to force the issue. I'm sorry.

> **Josephine:** It's okay. Give me one second.

I close my eyes and focus on breathing. I'm unworthy of her compassion. It's *not* okay. None of this is. And nothing will be until she's safe.

They're not forcing the issue to protect me. No, they want power over her and over us, and this is the simplest way to get it. Yet the alternative—forcing her to leave, keeping our distance when we've seen firsthand how her association with us makes her a target—isn't an option either. Not one we'll survive, at least.

Heart lodged in my throat, I shoot off another text to remind her of our earlier discussion.

> **Decker:** Bring one of the guys with you. I don't want you walking into this room alone or giving away anything we don't want them to know.

I can't protect her from everything. But I can play my part. I can ensure that one of my boys stands by her side through this whole ordeal, since my hands are tied.

> **Josephine:** And what, exactly, do you not want them to know, Cap?

This girl.
She's flirting while knowingly being lured into a room of vipers. What I wouldn't give to tell her the truth:

That I'm in love with you.
That you matter more to me than anything in this world.
That I would give this all up if it meant I got to keep you forever.

> **Decker:** Just do as I say, Josephine.

"She's on her way," I announce. I slip my phone back into my pocket but remain standing.

Crossing my arms over my chest, I wait. I wait, and I steel my spine. I lock it in and put on my mask, knowing damn well that even the smallest blip of emotion could be used against me.

Misty keeps making little noises from her seat like she's hoping to garner my attention. I refuse to turn and acknowledge her. She's been colluding with my dad for years, but it's never felt so personal or vindictive.

Behind me, the dining room door groans on its hinges. I don't dare glance back. At least not yet.

Soft smacks on the hardwood floor confirm it's her. Barefoot. Probably without makeup. Her hair in a loose braid or gathered up in a massive bun on top of her head.

My jaw ticks with anticipation, anxiety. Fuck, I want to turn around and check on her myself.

But that's not my role. Not right now.

Heavier footsteps follow. Those are followed by a metronomic march, and finally, a slower, drawn-out gait.

I can't fight the smile that takes over my face.

She didn't bring one of the guys with her. She brought all three.

Clever girl.

"What's this about?" Josephine demands, coming to a halt across the table from where Misty and I are set up. Finally, she's in my field of vision, and I don't miss the terse side-eye she offers Misty.

Good. I don't trust her either.

One of the lawyers onscreen clears his throat.

"Hello, young lady. It's been brought to our attention that you haven't signed the standard nondisclosure agreement required of Decker's, uh, in-residence companions. We're here to dot the i's and cross the t's."

She waits for him to finish speaking, and when he does, she scoffs.

"Is that what you are, K? One of Decker's *in-residence companions*?"

I grit my teeth at her casual demeanor. This isn't a laughing matter. Fuck. So much is at stake here. They're asking too much, yet she immediately turns flippant.

With a breath in, I will my pulse to remain steady, then I finally home in on her. Rather than finding the calm I was searching for, the panic gripping my chest increases tenfold.

I don't want them to have her. She shouldn't be here or be vulnerable like this.

But she is. Because of me.

Light blue eyes meet mine, along with the most subtle nod of her head.

I breathe out an intense sigh of relief and drop into my chair once I see the trepidation in her eyes.

She gets it.

She's intentionally riling them up, joking around to lighten the mood, but she fucking gets it.

"Ah, well, uh, yes. Mr. Taylor signed his nondisclosure as soon as he turned eighteen." My dad's lawyer stumbles through his response. "Misty?" he inquires, brows raised.

Every eye in the room turns to her, and the smarmiest smile stretches over her pink lips. She doesn't even look up or regard me before she dives right in, giddy with power.

"You're required to sign a standard NDA. It'll be retroactively enforceable from the day you first took up residence at the Crusade mansion. Based on my recollection, that was sometime in early September. There's a place to list the date if you can provide it." She finally looks up, the ugly smile still plastered on her face. "Or, if you don't know, we can check the camera footage to ensure accuracy."

"It was September third." Kylian's response is delivered with such intensity and vitriol I swear Misty does a double take.

Inhaling, Josephine stands straighter. She assesses Misty with a look full of disdain, her lip practically curling. Then she plasters a passive expression on her face and turns to the men on the screen.

"My permanent residence is actually Sam's Salvage and Parts. That's what's listed in the Lake Chapel University database. My uncle can vouch for me. I can give you my word that I'll stay out of the way and won't cause any trouble, but I'd prefer not to sign anything."

My father barks out a laugh. "Your word?" he mocks, his tone dripping with derision. "Your word means nothing. You're playing a game of semantics, girl. Don't bother trying to bullshit me about a permanent residence. Where did you sleep last night? And the night before that?"

The atmosphere in the room shifts swiftly and acutely, right along with the hackles that raise along my back. Judging from the murderous expression each of my boys is wearing, they're right here with me.

He doesn't get to talk to her like that. *No one* talks to her like that.

Kendrick catches my eye, shifting forward so he's standing by her side. Locke crowds her back, and Kylian sidesteps in front, positioning himself between Josephine and the screen.

I yearn to move. To rise. To break out of the shackles that bind me to this chair—to this life—and protect them all.

But keeping them all safe requires I do nothing. Show nothing. Give nothing away.

If there was a doubt in my mind that our girl couldn't fend for herself, even against the likes of Thomas Crusade and his slimy lawyers, those are laid to rest the moment she opens her mouth to respond.

"Do you make a habit of asking women half your age where they've spent the night?" She wrinkles her nose, then grimaces. "That seems kind of inappropriate, don'tcha think?"

It's the casual *"don'tcha"* that sends me.

I have to bite down hard on the inside of my cheek to stifle a laugh.

My father is unaffected, though, and clearly uninterested in being put in his place. "You'll sign or you'll leave. It's as simple as that." His obsidian eyes don't stray from her through the screen.

But Josephine doesn't miss a beat.

"And if I'm not comfortable signing something I haven't even had time to read?"

A glimmer of cruelty flickers through his bland expression.

"You're welcome to read it. In fact, you can take it with you and have your lawyer review it. Take all the time you need. You can return to the isle, and to my house, when you're ready to sign."

My rage is simmering so hot it's moments from boiling over. Apparently, I'm not alone in that regard.

"Jo."

All eyes are on Kylian with that single word.

"You don't have to do anything you don't want to do. They're making it seem like you only have two options. You've shown me time and again that things aren't always black and white."

Locke hums his agreement, and Kendrick slings an arm over her shoulders, letting his hand brush casually along her bicep. He plays the gesture off as nothing more than friendly, but as I observe them, it's obvious the contact soothes her. Instantly, her shoulders lower a fraction.

When he bows his head low and murmurs, "We'll back you up, Mama," her tight expression softens imperceptibly. "All of us," he says. "If you don't sign, we'll figure it out."

Misty huffs beside me. K's statement was quiet but clear from where I sit. Though I doubt our virtual friends caught the sentiment, she obviously did.

I'm still frozen where I stand. And I really fucking hate it.

This is happening because of me, yet I'm helpless in this moment—useless.

My brothers get to support her. They get to say the words I desperately wish I could say. I fucking hate it, but I have to believe that by holding back now, I'm protecting her in the future.

It's all I have to cling to.

The hope that when this is all over—the feature, the extreme access, our lives on display for public consumption—the life waiting on the other side will be filled with peace. Privacy. Long nights of passion and pleasure. Slow mornings waking up with her in my arms.

The hope of what could be is enough to sustain us all through the sacrifice of now.

Josephine catches my gaze as she wordlessly walks around the table. She holds her head high as she passes in front of the projector, momentarily cutting out the feed.

When she reaches me, her fists are clenched and she's quietly cracking her knuckles.

"Let me use your pen," she says, bumping my chair with her hip.

I gulp past the trepidation burning a hole in my esophagus and obey, willing my hand not to shake. Misty shuffles a stack of papers beside me like she's preparing to present them to Joey. Before she can, I snatch them out of her hands and cut her out of the exchange.

My girl may be required to sign away her privacy and dignity to stay here with us, but I refuse to let her give away another piece of herself. I won't let Misty get the satisfaction of making her any more uncomfortable, especially after the stunt she pulled with the photo slideshow the other day.

With her lower lip pulled between her teeth, Josephine takes the pen from me.

I cling to the papers like they're my last will and testament.

With one brow cocked in a way that almost makes her look unaffected, she rests a palm on the polished surface of the dining table.

"Siren," I whisper, overwhelmed by both reverence and sorrow, wishing I could say more.

Her brow line softens, and she gives me a subtle nod. "It's okay, Cap," she whispers back, taking the papers out of my hands and placing them on the table in front of her.

While she takes her time reading over the first page, every person in the room—physically or virtually—is focused on her. Seconds turn into minutes, and all the while, no one dares to speak. The only sounds come from the occasional shuffle of paper as Josephine reads through each word.

After close to ten minutes, she clicks her pen, tilts her head enough to catch my gaze, and nods once more.

"It's okay," she mouths. Then she scrawls her initials on the bottom of the first page.

Chapter 12

Josephine

As the green numbers illuminated above the stove creep higher, I grimace. It's almost midnight. I had no intention of staying up this late, but I won't let myself sleep before I talk to Decker.

Finally, I hear footsteps down the hall.

Hopping off the barstool, I hustle in the direction of his wing of the house, intent on intercepting him between here and the weight room.

We need privacy for this, and with the plethora of cameras that have been installed, my options are limited.

He's looking down at his phone, panting, but as I round the corner, he tenses. It isn't until he lifts his head and spots me that he blows out a breath and lets his shoulders sag.

"Siren—" he starts, his brows jumping to his hairline like he's surprised to see me.

I don't stop walking. As I pass him, I catch his elbow, altering his path and forcing him to follow me into the pantry.

As soon as we're safely inside, I kick the door closed and melt into his frame. I lace my fingers behind his neck and press my front into his broad, hard chest.

His hands find my hips and hold me steady for one breath, and on the next inhale, they pull me closer.

I'm hyperaware of every place our bodies connect, me leaning into him, him gently cocooning me in his arms.

He's just finished his nightly workout, so heat radiates off his skin, and his breathing is still heavy.

Maybe he wouldn't have to end each night sprinting on the treadmill and lifting to exhaustion if he'd stop cockblocking himself and allow things to naturally progress between us.

I bite back a smirk at the thought.

As much as I like pushing and testing him, there are universal truths I've accepted when it comes to Decker Crusade.

He believes his plans are for the best. They're not always, but because he means well, because his true intention is always to protect me, I'm okay letting him think that sometimes.

A semblance of control brings him peace, and if anyone is in need of a little extra peace, it's this man. Plus, I've learned from experience that he's much more willing to compromise when he understands that I won't fight him for control. Not when there are bigger issues at hand.

And what I need from him right now is bigger than my libido. By just a smidge.

"Hi." I lean into him and rest my cheek on his drenched tech shirt.

"What's wrong? Are you okay?" He tips my chin up, searching my face with a frown, looking for some sort of problem to address.

He's always on high alert.

He has to be.

I don't want him to feel that sense of alarm with me.

Nodding, I close my eyes and breathe him in. Warm amber and sea salt caress my senses. His usual scent is amplified by the saltiness of fresh sweat dripping down his body.

"Josephine," he scolds, grasping my arms like he's going to peel my body off his so he can assess me more thoroughly.

"I'm fine," I insist, gripping him tighter around the waist and tipping my head back so he can see for himself. I rest my chin on his sternum and raise both brows. "I just wanted a minute alone with you."

Understanding registers in the inky black pools of his irises, and the harsh lines of his face soften. Though he doesn't stop studying me like he's looking for a buried truth.

"Hi," I repeat. With a smile, I press up to tiptoes and kiss him on the lips.

He doesn't kiss me back, but he does run his hands along my back until his palms rest against my low back and he's pulling me closer. "You didn't have to sign," he whispers against my lips.

My response is a swift punch to his side.

He lets out a satisfying *umph*, although I know he barely felt my hit.

"That's not what this is about, Cap. Can you just let us have a moment here? Just one minute?"

He sighs again, clearly exasperated. "I just want to make sure you understand that I didn't know they were going to pull that bullshit. If I had, I wouldn't have even—"

"Decker. Stop." I pull back and run my palms up his chest. Pressing into his shoulders, I force him still. "One minute. Sixty seconds. One minute where it's just you and me. No contracts. No lawyers. No outside world."

"One minute," he repeats warily, as if he can't fathom letting his guard down for even the briefest of moments.

"One minute," I whisper back.

And then I make the most of my sixty seconds in heaven with Decker Crusade.

On my toes again, I pepper his jaw with kisses, then trail my mouth along the muscles of his neck. His skin is warm and salty on my tongue. With a hum, I nip at his ear, then continue to savor every inch of skin I can get my mouth on before stopping at his lips.

I hover. I wait.

He exhales, attention roving over me. Then his tongue darts out to wet his bottom lip.

It's the consent I need. I dive in, kissing him with an intensity that he quickly matches. I moan into his mouth, captivated by the way he grips my face, positions me right where he wants me, and strokes his tongue against mine.

Most of the time, I'm well-matched against this man. Our stubbornness pairs well, and our tempers both run hot. It's rare I don't rise to any challenge he presents me.

But when Decker kisses me, I melt. All combativeness drains out of me as I inadvertently welcome his dominance and invite it to stay. The moment our lips touch, I'm done. Mindless. Needy. So fucking desperate for him.

I want nothing more than to be ravished and savored as his tongue explores my mouth, his hand grips my face, and he pours himself into the kiss like his entire sense of purpose in life hinges on stealing my breath and making me moan his name.

Too soon, Decker's pulling away, rubbing his forehead against mine, shifting back into his broody, surly go-to persona.

"You didn't have to sign," he repeats, panting.

I press my cheek against his chest, listening to the beat of his heart as it hammers against his breastbone. With a kiss to his sternum, I look up and raise both eyebrows. "Why can't you trust that I know what I'm doing? That I want to be here? That I want to be with *you*?"

He says nothing.

Annoyed by his silence, I huff. "Decker, I'm in too deep. I couldn't leave now if I tried. There isn't an alternative for me. I'm here. This is now. You need to accept that I'm part of this family, too."

"I do." It's a growl, low and fierce.

Lifting my chin, I ready for battle. "I don't see you trying to push the guys away."

"They know the deal. They've been putting up with this for years."

"And now it's my turn. I signed the papers, Decker."

He tips his head back and stares at the ceiling, anguish rolling off him in waves.

"You shouldn't have had to."

I press a hand flat to one cheek and wait until he's looking at me again before I speak. "But I did. Willingly. Knowing all that it entailed."

When he tries to look away again, I frame his face with both hands. "I'd do it again. I'd do it every day from now until eternity if it meant I got to be with you, Kylian, Kendrick, and Locke. Now is not forever. We'll get through this. Just promise me we'll ride this out together. This isn't the time for you to play the hero or push us away to protect us. You aren't in this alone. We're in this together."

My declaration is met with silence.

"Don't let me down. I need you to be strong enough to let me in and let me stay."

He bows his head low, running his nose along my jawline, but still, he doesn't speak.

"Decker..." I hedge.

"I heard you."

Heart sinking in my chest, I accept that's all I'm going to get out of him tonight.

Chapter 13

Josephine

A familiar sense of unease greets me the moment I open my eyes. It's not panic, exactly, but something's not right.

I'm in my own bed, alone. It feels too big, and the room feels too empty without at least one of my guys here with me.

I reach out and search my nightstand for my phone. Squinting at the too-bright screen, I blink away the sleep and register the time.

4:31 am.

It's too damn early. With a yawn, I climb out of bed, but every move makes my body ache. A few days have passed, but it's possible that I'm still sore from all the escapades of Kendrick's homecoming. Thankfully, I don't have to leave for class until midmorning, so after I empty my bladder, I'll crawl back into bed and get a few more hours of sleep. Maybe I'll feel better once I'm rested.

Wincing, I shuffle into the bathroom and turn on just one light.

The second I sit down to pee, I know.

The burn grows in intensity the longer I urinate. Dammit. I groan, recognizing the telltale signs.

I've got a fucking UTI. Ouch. And ugh.

I sit on the toilet longer than necessary, desperate for any measure of relief from the burning urges. Eventually, though, I force myself up, wash my hands, and splash cold water on my face.

Once I've dragged myself back to bed, I pick up my phone, considering my options.

I don't want to panic Kylian. Because he *will* panic.

I refuse to wake up Nicky. He's still recharging, and in an effort to encourage him to rest, we're each in our own room tonight. He's really struggling—with the pain, with the aftermath of the run-in with the photographer, and with the guilt and trauma of Kendrick taking the fall for him. The last thing I want is to keep him up late or leave him feeling isolated while I'm snuggled up with the other guys. So separate beds for a night or two is our best option.

Decker's a nonstarter. Despite all the progress we've made, I would rather ride a bike in a wet bathing suit with a UTI all the way to the drugstore than ask Decker for help. Probably more of a me problem, but still.

That leaves one person.

> **Jojo:** Are you up? It's not an emergency, but I need help.

The knock on my door comes less than sixty seconds later.

"Jojo? You in here?"

The door opens silently, and Kendrick peeks in. When he finds me buried beneath the covers, he quickly enters the room and shuts the door behind him. The second he turns and really looks at me, he falters.

"What's wrong?" he demands, striding to the bed like he's running the ball down the field.

He's shirtless, which is a sight to fucking behold. His silky athletic shorts rest low on his hips, putting his expanse of hard, defined muscles on full display. Even in my current state, I can appreciate the beauty.

Weakly, I hold out one hand. "I think I have a UTI."

"Shit," he murmurs, coming to stand beside the bed. "Does it hurt? What do you need?"

My heart flips in my chest at the care and adoration in his voice. This man. This beautiful, kind, sweet grump of a man.

"I love you," I whisper when he takes my hand and sits on the edge of the bed.

"I love you, too. Now tell me what you need." He tucks a strand of hair behind my ear. "Would pain meds help?"

I nod, dropping an elbow to the mattress so I can sit up.

"Stay down," he murmurs, gently pressing on my shoulder while simultaneously whipping out his phone. He combs his fingers through my hair as he scrolls.

"The Internet says you'll need an antibiotic. Do you have any allergies?"

I try to sit up again—the keyword being *try*.

"Woman, I swear to God," he snaps. "Lay down and let me take care of you."

Ugh. My heart.

And ouch. My urethra.

Curling up on my side, I close my eyes and blow out a slow breath. "No allergies. A week of antibiotics and a few days of pain meds usually does the trick. Lots of water and a heating pad will help, too."

"Kyl's probably got some antibiotics on hand. He keeps us well stocked. Do you want me to see what I can find, or do you want to talk to a doctor?"

I sigh. "Of course Kylian would have drugs on hand. But I should probably talk to a doctor just to make sure I get the dosage right."

Kendrick rises to his feet, keeping his attention fixed on me. For a long moment, he hovers, one brow raised like he knows I'm tempted to sit up again or challenge him. Finally satisfied that I'll stay down, he nods. "Good girl. Do not move from that bed. I'll sort out an appointment, and I'll round up a heating pad and pain meds. You need food, too. You can't take them on an empty stomach."

He kisses the top of my head and strides to the door as urgently as he strode in.

"Wait. K?" I call after him.

He pauses with his hand on the knob, his eyes still fixed on his phone.

"Don't wake the others. Locke needs sleep…" I trail off with a yawn.

"I got you, Mama." He nods and peers up at me. "Hang tight while I get what you need."

Chapter 14

Decker

It's officially nine thirty and I haven't seen another soul but Mrs. Lansbury.

The silence of the kitchen is eerie. For years, the house has been filled with noise. Especially when we're all headed out the door at the same time.

Their quiet makes me anxious.

Gripping the edges of the smooth quartz, I pull in a deep breath, then another, listening for any sign that the others are approaching or even awake.

We leave at nine thirty. They all know we leave at nine thirty a.m. If there was ever a day to deviate from our routine, this isn't it. Filming starts tomorrow. We're supposed to be sticking together.

Sighing, I push off the counter and stalk toward the stairs.

I'm halfway up the staircase when the first murmur floats its way to me. Then another. It's obvious by the time I hit the landing that they're coming from Josephine's room.

I approach with caution, bracing myself for what I may find when I open the door. I'm aware that she's with the others. Individually. Together. I don't know all the details, but the guys, and more often Josephine, tease me enough that I get the fucking gist.

If we're late this morning because one or more of my boys decided he needed to get his dick wet and couldn't wait—

"Oh."

Everyone freezes when the door opens and I step inside.

I scan the scene before me, then pull out my phone again.

It's Wednesday. Wednesday morning. The display on my phone confirms it. Nothing about what's happening in this room fits with the plan.

Something has to be wrong.

Locke and Josephine are in her bed. He's sitting up against the headboard with one arm around her shoulders and the other stroking her hair. She's curled up against him, her head nestled against his chest.

Kendrick is perched on the end of the bed, surveying me over the top of his phone.

The only person missing is—

"Coming through."

Kylian breezes past me without a glance my way.

He approaches the bed with total confidence. He's undeterred by the sight before him, confirming the inkling in my gut.

Something's wrong. And I'm the last to know.

"What's going on?"

Kendrick's still watching me, but his blank stoicism gives me nothing to go on.

Josephine's eyes are closed, but she hums to acknowledge she heard me.

Kylian and Locke disregard me as if I haven't spoken at all. Neither takes their attention off Josephine, even as I stomp toward the bed.

As I approach, I home in on the paper bag Kylian is holding up.

"These side effects are hellacious. When did she eat last?" he asks without looking up from the document stapled to the bag.

"She had toast around five this morning," Kendrick replies.

Kylian scoffs and drops the hand holding the bag to his side. "That's the last time she ate? How about her water intake? How much has she had to drink?"

Shifting from one foot to the other, I ask, "What's wrong?"

Not only am I ignored once again, but Josephine isn't inserting herself into the conversation. Something must be *really* wrong if she isn't getting after them for talking about her like she isn't here.

"She's had plenty to drink. She knows the drill. Just give her the meds, Kyl."

"Absolutely not. The instructions say to take them with food. Toast that was consumed more than four hours ago does not meet the qualifications. I'll go make her real food—"

"I'll do it," Locke insists. He shifts toward the side of the bed, making Josephine groan in protest.

"Josephine," I snap with more force than I should. I snake around Kylian and take Locke's position by her side before anyone can beat me to it.

"Hey," I say, softer. I shift until I'm close enough to stroke her shoulder. "Talk to me. What's going on?"

Locke bends over me to kiss her head, then takes off.

I brush the hair out of her face and tuck a section behind her ear. Finally, she peeks up at me with one eye.

"Why are you still in bed?"

The corner of her mouth turns up in a smirk, though it's weak.

"Because I knew it would piss you off."

Kendrick snorts and mutters a "behave, Mama" under his breath as he grabs her half-full water bottle.

"I'll go fill this up. You want me to pop your heating pad back in the microwave? Should I bring the Tylenol up? We could start alternating pain meds."

"Yes. Both." With another groan, she shifts and pulls a rice pack from under the covers, then holds it out for him.

My chest is so tight I can barely breathe, and no one will fucking answer me, but I affect calm and keep my voice soft. "Are you hurt?"

She rolls to her back and blows out a slow, clearly pained breath.

"Are you sick?" I press, peering at the orange prescription bottle in Kylian's hand as he continues to glare at the instructions and warnings as if they're personally offending him.

"Sort of," she mutters.

I sigh, checking the time again. It's 9:36 a.m. We're running out of time. I'm running out of patience. "How can you be *sort of* sick?"

Instead of answering me with words, she reaches for my hand and pulls, guiding me closer to where she's curled under the covers.

"Will you rub my low back?" she whispers. "Nicky's hands are hurting, so I didn't ask him."

My knuckles instantly find her spine and knead into the muscle so intensely she lets out a whimper.

"Sorry, sorry," I mutter, using my fingertips instead. "Better?"

"Mm-hmm," she murmurs, eyes fluttering closed in what I hope is contentment.

Pride surges through me, but it's quickly replaced by dread when I catch sight of the clock on Josephine's bedside table.

9:38 a.m.

"We should have left eight minutes ago." I tip my chin toward Kylian but maintain pace as I massage Josephine's low back.

She arches her back and sighs softly when I hit a particularly tender spot. Damn if it doesn't make me feel like I'm the king of the world when I get that kind of reaction from her.

"I know," Kylian confirms. "Today we will be late."

Josephine goes rigid and pushes up with one arm so she can turn to look at me. "I'm making you late?"

"Yes," I reply as Kylian adamantly declares, "No."

"I'm sorry. I didn't realize what time it was." She stifles a yawn with the back of her hand.

Scrutinizing me through his glasses, his expression cool, Kylian continues. "Time is irrelevant in moments like this. You needed us. We want to be here for you, Jo. Once they confirmed the diagnosis—"

"Which is what, exactly?" I press through gritted teeth. It takes all I have to maintain my pace, smoothing one hand over Josephine's low back in methodical strokes, as I glare at Kylian.

He scoffs. "I'm not committing a HIPPA violation right in front of the patient herself."

Josephine barks out a laugh but is surprised by another yawn. She's never this lethargic.

"Siren, if you're sick or contagious—"

Her shoulders tremble as another laugh works its way out of her. "I promise you can't catch what I have, Decker." She reaches behind her back and snags my hand again, pulling me closer and guiding my limbs around her body until I'm basically spooning her.

"What is that supposed to mean? What do you have?"

Groaning, she rolls to her back and regards me.

Her hair is loose and wavy, the ends tickling my forearm. Her freckles have started to fade now that the weather is changing. I resist the urge to kiss the bridge of her nose, dismiss Kylian, and just hold her for the rest of the damn day.

But then she purses her lips and side-eyes me.

"You're a mother hen, you know that, Crusade? Has anyone ever told you—"

"Josephine," I contend, clenching my jaw so hard it aches. It's not just that she's withholding information or that she's making us late. It's that everyone but me, it seems, knows what's going on. "If something is wrong with you—"

"I have a UTI, Decker!"

My chest constricts, even if I don't have a fucking clue what she's talking about. "A U-T-what? What does that stand for?" I rack my brain, flipping through the diseases and ailments I know of.

She blinks at me, deadpan. "Urinary tract infection. It's something girls get sometimes. I'm a girl—remember?"

Kylian snickers.

"How do you know that's what's going on?" If she has an infection, she needs proper medical attention. She needs to see a doctor, or at the very least—

"Because I had a telehealth appointment this morning. And because I've had them before. Most women are familiar with the symptoms, Cap. Plus, I got dairy dicked a week ago"—she tilts her head toward Kyl—"then I fell asleep before I had a chance to pee after Kendrick and Kylian tag-teamed me on Saturday night."

My heart pounds in my chest, and a wave of concern washes over me. Concern. That's what I'm feeling. Concern about her health. Concern for her well-being. That's it. The heat creeping up my chest has nothing to do with jealousy.

I'm ready to lay in to Kylian and drag Kendrick up here and demand he explain himself, but Kylian cuts me off.

"Wait. Sprinkles caused this?" The abject horror in his voice is almost enough to pull me out of my frustration.

"Meh." Josephine lifts a shoulder but winces and drops it quickly.

I knead the muscles of her lower back with a little more force and cocoon her frame with my body.

"That feels good," she whispers over her shoulder, just for me. "Don't stop?"

"I won't," I vow. Fuck making it to campus on time or even going to class at all. If she needs me, then I'll be here.

She reaches for Kylian, and like a magnet, he scoots closer. "Multiple factors contributed. Thankfully, I recognized the symptoms early. I'll feel better tomorrow, and by the weekend, I'll be good as new. If I start taking my meds now, that is."

Kylian gives the orange bottle one last glare and hands it over just as Kendrick walks back into the room.

He saunters over and joins us on the bed.

Josephine sits up, accepts the water bottle from K, then dutifully takes the antibiotic.

"Nicky will bring breakfast up in a few. What else do you need?"

"Nothing. I'll be fine after I eat and take some more pain meds," she insists. "I'll just go heavy on the water today and rest as much as I can. You'll take care of my classes?" she asks Kylian.

"Already done."

"Mrs. Lansbury's off this afternoon," I remember out loud. Biting down on the inside of my cheek, I consider the options.

"I'll be fine," Josephine says through another yawn.

"You'll have to walk down to the kitchen to eat… and every time you need to refill your water."

"I have legs, Decker," Josephine snipes, side-eyeing me.

"But the cameras are already rolling in the main living spaces," Kylian surmises, connecting the dots.

I pull in a steadying breath. Then scoot closer to Josephine on the bed.

"Siren," I start. I've got to choose my words carefully. Her first instinct will be to say no to my suggestion, but I need her safe. I need her to understand. "We can't be here with you today. Mrs. Lansbury is off until Friday. You're going to be home alone."

She waggles her brows weakly and smirks. "Afraid I'm going to go Kevin McCallister on your room, Cap?"

Kendrick snorts.

This girl.

"I can't prevent them from filming you or from using footage they capture of you. I think—" I lick my lips as I formulate the words in my head.

This has got to sound more like a suggestion and less like a demand.

"I would feel better if you'd stay in my room while you're home alone."

Her brows shoot into her hairline, and her nose scrunches up. With a huff, she opens her mouth, surely ready to argue, but Kylian rests a hand on her hip, garnering her attention and effectively interrupting her.

"I would feel better knowing you're in Cap's room, too, baby. It would be less work for me later when I pull footage."

"They can't use anything from the master bedroom that doesn't feature me," I explain. "Don't ask me how the hell that of all things is a contractually binding point. I have a suspicion it has to do with my dad and the company he keeps."

"Oh. Okay."

Uneasy silence ensues as I look to Kylian, then over to K.

"What?" Josephine asks with a soft laugh. "That makes sense. I'll camp out in your room. I don't argue with you just to argue, ya know."

"Sure, Mama." Kendrick scoffs lightly. "I'm gonna help Nicky get things set up downstairs. Take it easy today, okay?"

She turns to him silently, expectantly. As if he knows exactly what she wants, he catches her chin with two fingers, tilts her head back, and kisses her on the forehead.

"Love you," he murmurs when he pulls back. "Be good and text me later."

"Only if you text me before practice," she teases, peering up at him with sleepy eyes.

"This seems like an ideal opportunity to remind you all that I have access to everyone's data and can see when you send alleged 'thirst trap' pictures from the locker room."

"Lucky you," Kendrick quips as he rises from the bed. "Let's go, Daddy Genius."

Josephine laughs in response, though it's subdued.

Me? I'm frozen in place, unsure of what to make of their exchange.

Deeper connections are developing on the fringes of our group. Friendships are evolving, growing stronger.

As if Josephine fortifies us.

Of the four of us, Kylian and Kendrick have the least in common. They care about each other, even consider one another family, but they've never been all that close.

Apparently, that's changing.

Kylian leans over and whispers in Josephine's ear. She bites down on her bottom lip as he murmurs words I can't make out.

When he's done, he pulls back slightly and wraps one hand around the side of her neck. She cranes up to whisper her response. He groans, then kisses her quickly on the lips before pulling away and leaving the room.

My nerves are already frayed. With a long breath out, I sit up. I've got to get my head on straight so I can face this day. I can't shake the feeling that something's missing, that I'm missing out. I can't pinpoint the cause or identify a solution when my mind is swimming with frustration like this. I need a workout. A few hours in the weight room. Maybe even a stiff drink.

It's obvious that my boys are gone for this girl. I knew it, but until now, I didn't understand to what magnitude. The kicker? I am, too. Only we're not competing on the same level.

They've gone pro, while I'm still playing JV. I'm being left behind. I have no one to blame but myself, and yet—

"Hey, Cap?"

"Yes, Siren?"

She rises to her knees so we're face to face.

"I know you have to get going, too... but do you have one more minute to spare?"

I search her face, taking in the concern behind her blue eyes and her soft smile.

"Are you in pain?"

"Yes" is her response.

I run a hand through my hair and tug on the strands. "Josephine, just lie down. You need—"

"I *need* a minute with you."

She doesn't need a damn thing from me. She needs rest. To keep hydrating. To give the antibiotics time to work and the pain meds a chance to kick in.

"One minute," she repeats, running her hands over my shoulders, then linking her arms around my neck.

When she presses her lips to mine, it's like a needle meeting a helium balloon.

There's a jolt, then an instant, supremely satisfying release of tension. Every worry, every ounce of anxiety and stress I was holding on to, it all releases.

I fight back a groan as I smooth my hands over her hair. I kiss her back, matching her intensity when she starts soft and sweet, then turns more urgent.

The energy between us doesn't fizzle out as much as we tamp it down, both aware of each passing second, both desperate for just one more moment together.

I let her pull away first. I'll be damned if, after all this time, I leave her wanting.

More than anything, I want to make her happy. Protect her. Love her. Keep her safe.

How can such base desires feel so convoluted?

I accepted years ago that who I am, what I do, who I'm destined to be, is all too much. It's overwhelming even for me most days. How could I expect a partner to navigate the pressure, the criticism, and the constant scrutiny I've invited into my life?

The guys and I have made it this far despite it all. We've figured it out, made it work. Their loyalty has given me hope, possibly false, misguided hope, but hope, nonetheless.

Hope that there's a future for me that is more than public appearances and highlight reels.

Hope that it could be me and her.

And them.

That we could forge our own path.

That we could make this work, together.

Josephine hooks her chin around my shoulder, locking me in place as she strokes through the hair at my nape.

"I—"

"I know," she insists. "I just wanted to hold on to you for as long as I could."

She unwinds her body from mine, but I don't let her pull away completely.

Hoisting her up in my arms, I hug her tightly: soft, supple breasts push into my pecs; strong, toned legs wrap around my torso.

"Want me to carry you downstairs?" I ask, snagging one more kiss as I readjust her in my arms.

She laughs against my mouth, her spark warming me from the inside.

"I already told you my legs work, Cap. Put me down and get to class."

Chapter 15

Josephine

"Josephine. Could you please pass the peas?"

I press my lips together to stop myself from outwardly reacting to the ridiculousness of this whole charade.

At least he didn't ask for nuts.

Beside me, Locke snorts, clearly not as in control of himself.

I offer the bowl to Locke, but don't release it when he's got it in his grasp. He gives me an over-the-top assessment as he playfully fights me for the dish. Then, just as quickly as the game began, he schools his expression.

During our little exchange, the camera operator—Nate—circled the table and now has his obnoxiously large lens focused on the two of us.

Decker clears his throat, and both cameras whip around to focus on him.

"Let's take the pontoon out after dinner."

Kendrick raises his brows and locks eyes with Cap. In the span of a blink, they hold an entire silent conversation.

K relaxes—an imperceptible tip of his chin that I only catch because I've become so familiar with his mannerisms.

I let out a breath I didn't know I was holding. If K's okay with this plan, then we'll all be safe.

The other person hiding behind a camera—Tina? Tonya, maybe?—lowers her equipment and moves around the table. She can't be more than a few years older than us, with bright blue eyes and a watchful, knowing gaze.

She wears heavy makeup—dark eyeliner whipped into a cat eye, bold lipstick perfectly painted on her cupid's bow lips. She's a tiny thing. Next to Locke and Kendrick, her frame is comically small. She's quiet but clearly perceptive as hell.

She's the one to watch out for.

Heat creeps up my neck as she stops at Misty's side.

Misty, who hasn't left us alone during waking hours since the cameras arrived.

Misty, with her clipboard in hand, as if she's part of the production team.

Maybe she's looking for film credit.

I snort quietly at the thought.

At the sound, she directs her venomous gaze at me. Unblinking, she listens to the cameraperson chirping in her ear.

Her brows furrow, then she nods once. Stepping forward, she puts a hand on Decker's shoulder from behind and caresses.

Startled, he sits up straight and goes eerily still.

I bristle and hold back the indignant huff threatening to escape as she claws at my man.

Mine. She's touching what's mine.

"Decker," Misty purrs.

With a subtle shrug, he dislodges her hand, then he turns his head to give her his ear. His onyx eyes settle on me, his gaze sweeping over me with so much vigilance it makes my heart rate accelerate.

Not deterred by his lack of attention, Misty crouches until she matches his height.

"Per your contract, the camera crew can't follow you out onto the water. They need you to stay—"

"They don't need me to do anything," he snaps, his tone so harsh she shuts her mouth with an audible snap.

She straightens, smoothing nonexistent wrinkles from her skirt.

"I'll go with you, then," she declares. "To take note of any conversations we may need to recreate for the feature."

Kylian, sights set on Misty, sets down his fork. Then his knife.

"If you even consider stepping onto that vessel, I will wait until we're in the middle of the lake and throw you overboard."

Locke slaps the table, and Kendrick has to bring a hand to his mouth to stifle his laughter. Kylian just stares at Misty, deadpan.

For her part, she doesn't react. Must be all that PR training. Instead, she crouches lower, bringing her face level with Decker's.

Before her lips even part, he dismisses her with a wave of his hand.

"We're taking the pontoon out after dinner. Just the five of us."

Chapter 16

Josephine

"Why does it feel like we're in trouble?" I cup my hand to my mouth and fake whisper, wiggling on the smooth leather bench between Kendrick and Locke.

"Seriously. He's giving 'I'm not mad, just disappointed,'" Locke quips. He catches one of my belt loops and pulls me closer.

"It feels like we've been naughty, and now dad's mad," Kendrick adds in a low simper.

Across from us, Kylian's head snaps up. "Don't call him that."

I snort.

Kendrick chuckles, his deep timbre vibrating through the seat we're sharing as he slides one hand along my low back. Once he's got a handful of me, he pulls me toward him, reversing the direction Nicky was just moving me in.

"Hey," Locke grumbles, reaching around me to shove Kendrick in the shoulder.

Kendrick cocks a brow. "Bro. Chill. I haven't seen her all day."

Not interested in their ridiculous need to piss on me, I rise to my feet, find my footing, and shuffle to Kylian's bench.

"Josephine," Decker grumbles from the helm, no doubt chastising me of standing when the boat is moving.

With a huff, I roll my eyes at the overprotective ass and settle beside Kylian. "I'm good now."

"Hi, baby," Kylian murmurs. His attention is still glued to his phone, but he loops one arm under my knees and pulls my legs across his lap, arranging me the way he wants me. "Okay?" he asks, finally peering up to make sure I'm comfortable.

Humming, I rest my head on his shoulder. "What's this about?" I whisper after a few breaths.

He looks up from his phone and regards Decker before he turns back to look at me. "No idea. He didn't mention anything to me."

Decker doesn't keep us in suspense long.

He eases off the throttle, and in moments, the pontoon is stopped in the middle of the lake. From here, the lights from the isle and the dock lights from the marina on the other side seem to be equal distances from us. Out here, we should be far enough from land to avoid scrutiny, even if a rogue cameraperson with a telescopic lens got any bright ideas.

When the anchor's been set, he turns. "Typically, I would have brought this up at dinner." He regards us all, holding court at the helm instead of joining us on the benches. "But given the audience and the timeliness of the issue, I thought it best to bring you all out here and address it, man to man."

It takes every ounce of willpower I possess to not hop to my feet and remind Decker that I am, in fact, a girl.

Kylian, probably sensing my frenetic energy, slides one hand up my thigh and squeezes in warning. I press my lips together, schooling my expression, and keep my focus from wandering to Nicky or K, because I know without looking that they're fighting back smirks.

"You all hurt Josephine last week."

Kendrick pulls his focus from Decker and assesses me, while Kylian's hand freezes on my thigh.

"We hurt her?" Nicky challenges, crossing his arms over his chest and lifting his chin. "When? How?"

"Josephine explained to me how she, well, what caused her to be sick."

This time, I can't hold back. I slap my palms on my knees and sit up straight.

"Good grief, Decker Crusade. You've got a lot of gall for a guy who didn't even know what a UTI was until two days ago."

He grunts in response. By his scowl, I'd say he's just as annoyed as I am. "We're all grown ass adults, so I knew you'd bristle at this. But you all can't just run a train on her like that."

While that simmering under my skin ratches up to a low boil, Locke slaps his hands to his face, attempting and failing to hide his reaction.

Kendrick shakes his head at Decker, then shoots me a knowing smirk.

"Easy," Kylian warns under his breath, one hand still clamped down on my thigh. Probably to keep me from lunging.

These three? They know me. My quirks, my go-to responses. They get me. Each one of them can so accurately predict my reactions.

Why does the self-appointed leader among us insist on learning lessons the hardest way possible?

I cross my arms over my chest and hit him with a deadpan stare. "You're forgetting one important part of the equation, Cap."

"What's that?"

"*Me.*"

Across the vessel, his eyes narrow to slits. "I specifically brought this up because of you, Josephine."

"But you didn't ask. Did it ever cross your mind that I wanted them to, how did you so eloquently put it? 'Run a train' on me?"

"Josephine—"

"Don't *Josephine* me, Decker Crusade." I hop to my feet and plant my hands on my hips. I can't sit still while fury and annoyance rage inside me. "You think you're being chivalrous—feminist even—by insisting your friends aren't allowed to rail me when I want to be railed?"

Kendrick whistles low.

Kylian leans forward, wrapping one arm around my hips to steady me, even though the boat is barely rocking.

"Like you said, we're all adults here." I throw out an arm and glance at each of my guys. "There's never been an instance where I didn't have a say in what we were doing or how things went down. The four of us have been navigating this for a while now. You, though? You're awfully concerned about our game plan for a man who hasn't fully committed to this team."

With a low growl, Decker turns and looks out toward the isle, his jaw ticking as it always does when he's angry.

"You don't get to tell me what to do. Not about this, Decker. *No play, no say.*"

Around me, my guys sit up straight. They're prepared to back me up, but they're giving me the space to handle this.

With a deep breath in through my nose, I rise to my feet and take a tentative step forward. Kylian brushes a hand over my ass, then secures it at my hip, anchoring me and ensuring I'm steady, but never holding me back.

"Although," I start, taking another step. With the next, Kylian's hand falls away.

I swear Decker's holding his breath as I approach. He's raging with Big Decker Energy and a broody attitude after being scolded.

"There is a way you *could* have a say."

As soon as I'm within his reach, his hands are on my hips. He's not holding me the way Kylian did. No, this overprotective brute is worried about my balance despite my steady footsteps.

I look over my shoulder at each of my guys, then turn back to Decker. Lifting my chin, I give him the sauciest look I can manage.

"You could join us, Cap."

"Careful, Mama," K warns under his breath in a low rumble.

I ignore him. I'm tired of being careful. Treading lightly. Tiptoeing around the reality of the dynamics forming between us—at least between most of us—and what I'm dreaming of for our future.

"What do you say, Crusade? Want to hop on board at the next stop and be the conductor of the train?"

Chapter 17
Kendrick

The energy on this boat is charged and eager. We're all watching the unexpected show Josephine is putting on as she bates Cap.

Our girl is playing with fire, and we all know it.

But Kylian, Locke, and I sit back and let her do her thing. She's already proven to be flame resistant. And I, for one, am curious about how this will go down.

Nicky and I have been with our girl together. The night she called Kylian to my room last weekend was, hands-down, the single hottest experience of my life.

Though I've only played on a team twice so far, those events won't be the last. We're all committed to this. All the way in, in every fucking way.

Except Decker.

It's obvious he wants her, and the man isn't so traditional or narrow-minded that he's opposed to an unconventional relationship.

If I had to guess, it has more to do with some sort of martyr mentality. He's under constant scrutiny, and that's only going to increase in the future. He wants to shield Jojo from the world. But he wants her, too.

Maybe he'll never come around.

Or maybe he just needs a little push.

He can't have her all to himself and he knows it. It's time to make his intentions known.

Decker's position on the fence doesn't serve anyone, least of all her. It's not fair for him to be one foot in and one foot out with her or with us.

We've always been a team. It's about time he was reminded of that.

She's propped up on tiptoes, murmuring words I can't make out. His eyes are darting around, searching. He scans the water, looks to the shore. Eventually, he glances at Kylian, then over to Locke and me.

"Brother," I call out, chin lifted.

His eyes widen in the dark. It's a gut-punch reaction, as if he's a child who's been caught doing something he knows he shouldn't be doing.

A small scoff escapes me. "There's no need to be on high alert. Not with us. We're all fine. She's good, too. Aren't you, Mama?"

Jojo nods, looping her arms around Cap's neck.

When she buries her face in his neck, he closes his eyes in pleasure, accepting her affection.

I hold back a groan, knowing exactly how supple and warm her mouth feels on his skin right now. Despite the lavish attention she's giving, his fists are still clenched at his sides and he's still focused on me, his expression rigid.

"Come on, Cap," I tsk. "You have to know none of us would ever intentionally hurt her. In any way. We trust her. We *love* her." I pause on the confession, letting it carry on the cool breeze making the pontoon sway. "If she says she's good, she's good."

Kylian clears his throat. "Cap needs proof. Show him just how good you are, baby. Show him how much we want this."

Jojo peers over her shoulder in Kylian's direction. "Cap has a rule about boat sex."

Nicky chortles. "Cap has a rule about everything."

That gets him.

Decker shoots Locke a cutting glance, then gingerly peels Jojo's hands off his body, holding her at arm's length.

Shaking his head, he blows out a long, defeated breath. "Don't push me tonight, Siren."

I look across the boat to gauge Kylian's take. The man's an emotionless fortress most of the time, but he's been different lately. More open. More forthright with his opinions. It has everything to do with taking on more of a leadership role within the group.

He asserts himself more. Cares more. In the past, he's always gone along with Decker, but now, he has a reason to speak up and defy him.

When he meets my gaze, I get all the confirmation I need.

The slight quirk of his lips tells me we're on the same page. We know our girl. And we both know exactly how this is about to go.

Jojo isn't going to back down. Cap's got two choices. He's either gotta get on this train once and for all or clear the tracks, full stop.

Stepping back into his space, she takes his face in her hands, forcing him to look at her.

"What do you say, Cap?" she murmurs. "We're out here alone. You very clearly need to blow off some steam. Let me take care of you for once."

I hold my breath, waiting for his response. Anticipation courses through me, lighting me up.

Eventually, I have to exhale, because he's an obstinate motherfucker. He won't give anything away unless he chooses to. Even in the name of pleasure. Even in the name of pleasing *her*.

Nicky sighs beside me. "Don't underestimate his stubbornness, Hot Girl." He slumps, like Decker's resistance is a personal defeat.

"Don't underestimate my commitment to keeping her safe," Decker growls in reply.

"Decker." Jojo wraps her arms around his waist this time, pressing her cheek into his chest and holding him close. "I know I'm safe with you. With all of you."

She tips her head and rests her chin on his chest. "You're so good at protecting me, Decker. At taking care of us. But I want to take care of you right now. Will you let me?"

With her eyes locked on his, she releases him and slowly drops to her knees.

Chapter 18

Josephine

"I want you," I whisper up at the man standing at the helm.

My beautiful, stubborn, obstinate man with the onyx eyes.

A man who's made it his mission in life to maintain composure and exude control.

His jaw ticks as he glares down at me. The trepidation rolling through him is so thick it's palpable.

He wants to say no. The word is on the tip of his tongue. Hasn't he learned yet that denying me is the most surefire way to make me push him harder?

I want to unravel him in the most primal way. I want to break his resolve because I can, right here and right now.

"Josephine," he hisses when I tuck my fingers into the waistband of his pants. "Someone could see." His argument is weak and contradictory to the way his body tenses at my touch.

Licking my lips and keeping my attention fixed on him, I graze my fingertips against the definition of his lower abs.

That's not true, and he knows it. He knows it, because he was the one getting me off on this very boat at the start of the week. Plus, it's late. Pitch-black. Even if prying eyes could see through the distance and the dark, they're not allowed to photograph us.

I lower his shorts just an inch, ignoring the very clear erection demanding attention and instead focusing on the warm patch of stomach I've revealed.

"It's your choice, Cap," I assure him, placing a soft kiss below his belly button.

His midsection is a defined slab of granite, peppered with dark hair that gathers into a thick, inviting happy trail.

Running my nose through it, I inhale warm amber and sea salt and smile when he sucks in a sharp breath.

He grasps the back of my head, but he pulls away just as quickly, as if battling with himself, clinging to any shred of control, grasping for any excuse he can find.

"You're okay with them watching?" he growls under his breath, his head bowed and cast in shadow, making it impossible to read his expression in the dark.

Now I really can't fight back my grin.

For once, he's not arguing. Or calling me off. He's not demanding I stand up or telling me this can't happen.

No, he's confirming how this works and ensuring that we're all consenting to this situation.

I lick my bottom lip, and my core heats further as his eyes track the movement. Nodding, I peer up and wait for him to acknowledge my attention. Then I make him a promise. "I want them to watch. I like it when they watch me."

Hands fisted, Decker turns to the boys.

The boys, I might add, who are all observing silently, their focus locked on us. They're rapt, waiting to see how this is going to play out.

"You're okay with your girl doing this right in front of you?" His brows are pulled low and his words are clipped.

If the words had come from anyone else, I would be insulted.

But this is Decker, and he's trying so, so hard.

"They're good boys," I declare before anyone else can respond. "They can wait their turn."

I peek over my shoulder, first to a smirking Kylian, then across from him to Kendrick and Locke. I grin and raise my brows, offering an unspoken promise that they'll each, in fact, get their turn.

When my focus shifts back to Decker, the vein in his forehead is pulsing and sharp breaths saw in and out of his lungs. He's so on edge, strung out and stressed, pent up and frustrated. If anyone needs a release, it's him.

We're all on the same page. We all want the same thing.

Yet I worry that Decker's need for control will prevent him from going for what he wants.

So without another moment's hesitation, I boldly help him out.

I peel down his pants, pushing down his boxers as I go.

His thick, rigid cock springs free, and instantly, a pearl of precum seeps from the tip.

Licking my lips in anticipation, I say, "Ready when you are, Cap."

He glares down, his eyes impossibly dark. He's still fighting to maintain his composure, breathing hard through his nose and gritting his teeth as his gaze shifts from me to the guys, then back again.

I wait with bated breath, willing him to make the first move.

But he's determined to win this standoff.

So I concede and take what I want.

When I grip the base of his cock, he flinches. He doesn't pull away, and he doesn't stop me. His eyes flash with heat and desire, despite his glower.

I fist him slowly, stroking from root to tip, then lean forward and kiss the crown of his penis. That's all I give him—for now. This has to be consensual. I know he wants it, but he has to allow himself to have it.

Nuzzling into his muscular thigh, I focus on his face and whisper, "You can take what you want and still be in control, Decker. If you change your mind and need me to stop, just tap three times. They won't see you. They won't know. But I'll stop immediately."

He scrubs his hands down his face. "I want you so bad it hurts."

"So have me."

Another beat passes. It's silent except for the water lapping at the side of the pontoon and the harsh rhythm of Decker's breathing.

Finally—fucking finally—he groans and bats my hand away. Gripping the base of his cock, he weaves his other hand into my hair. "Fuck it."

Behind me, one of the guys murmurs an encouragement as Decker finally lets go, thrusts forward, and drives his cock between my open lips.

Chapter 19

Decker

Her mouth. Her mouth. Her motherfucking mouth.

She's kissed me and sassed me and whispered reassurances with those lips.

But never has her mouth felt this good.

Each slide in and back out sends sparks dancing up my spine. I bite the inside of my cheek until I taste blood, distracting myself enough to hold back the orgasm threatening to blast off and paint her warm, wet, supple, wonderful lips.

"This fucking mouth," I groan, stroking her head as she worships me on her knees.

Never has anything felt this good.

Never has anything felt so right.

"Fuck, Siren." I tug on the ends of her hair to steady myself.

With a mewl, she pops off my dick. "Harder," she whispers.

Growling, I fuck her face hard and fast: a pent-up, feral beast who's been fiending for this exact moment for what feels like a lifetime.

The moment I give in.

The moment everything changes.

She does some sort of swirling motion with her tongue, then she pulls on my balls and hollows her cheeks.

"Fucking hell, woman," I grit out. The tingling sensation escalates to pinpricks of pleasure and pain.

My attention is solely focused on her.

Although I know three others have their eyes locked on us.

I don't dare look. Wouldn't dream of pulling myself out of this moment or breaking the spell.

I'm done fighting her.

I'm done fighting this.

Want and need and the carnal urge to claim her braid together into an unstoppable force as pleasure surges through me. Warmth spreads up my thighs, traveling to my balls and pulsating through my cock.

"Coming," I grunt in warning.

Josephine doubles down, sucks me deeper, and moans when the first spurts of my release hit her tongue.

Euphoria like I've never experienced washes over me. The deluge is unending. I fill her so full she has to swallow twice before I'm done. It just keeps fucking coming.

I groan, lost in the way she laps at me as my dick softens in her mouth.

Finally, she pulls off and kisses the tip, finishing the way she started.

"Now that wasn't so bad, was it?" she croons.

Smirking, I tip forward, intent on helping her up and pulling her into my arms.

But she leans back and shakes her head, her brows lifted as mirth dances in her eyes.

"I'm not done," she whispers with a wink.

Then she turns and crawls on her hands and knees straight for Kylian.

I swallow past the concern bubbling up inside me. She's fine, she's safe, and Josephine only ever does what she wants to do. I take a breath and force myself to settle. If she wants more, it's hers for the taking.

Kylian scoots forward on the bench and spreads his legs wide. He watches her approach, his eyes full of primal lust behind his glasses. "You did so good for him, baby," he praises, pulling his cock out of his pants.

She murmurs something I can't make out, and his face lights up in response. Without hesitation, he reaches out to line up her pouty, swollen mouth with the head of his cock.

"Suck," he demands, filling her mouth entirely in one smooth thrust.

Fuck. It's been moments since I experienced the most intense orgasm of my life, and already, my dick twitches and grows to a semi.

I'm tempted to look away, to pull back, sit down and turn around in the captain's chair to give them privacy.

Until her words from earlier echo in my mind.

She likes them watching. She likes being watched.

"Fuck yeah. You look so perfect sucking his cock, Mama."

The words smack into me, jolting me from the carnal spell I've fallen under. Across from them, Kendrick blatantly grips his length through his shorts.

Beside him, Locke is even less discreet. He has his dick out, and he's leaned back, squeezing the tip like he's forcing himself to hold out.

Kylian unloads with a grunt a minute later, both of his hands tangled in Josephine's hair as she sucks him down.

At this rate, she's going to make a meal of us.

The thought of all of us filling her with cum and mixing together inside her sends another spark of arousal through my gut.

With one hand, Kylian puts his dick away, but he doesn't release her head.

Instead, he bends low and kisses her, sweeping his tongue into her mouth like he's ravenous to taste himself on her lips.

He groans and dives in for another taste.

I gulp past the urge to remind him that he's likely tasting my cum on her tongue, too.

Maybe this is how it works? Maybe this is what they like.

Admittedly, I don't *not* like it.

My completely hard length is evidence of just how much I like the scene taking place right now.

Kylian finally pulls back. "Who's next?"

I expect one of the boys to answer, but instead, it's Josephine who speaks.

It's Josephine they always defer to.

It's Josephine, ultimately, who always has control.

"I want them both at once," she declares, glancing over her shoulder to where Kendrick and Locke are sitting side by side on the bench.

"Will you hold my hair for me, Daddy?" she asks Kylian.

Fuck. I swear her words alone have cum leaking from my tip.

Kylian's sly smile is the only answer he provides before he stands, gathers the loose strands around Josephine's face, and wraps it around his fist.

"Come," he grunts. Then, like he's walking a dog, he guides her across the pontoon boat.

Crawling on hands and knees, she obeys without argument, allowing Kylian to lead her.

They stop in front of the others.

"You heard our girl. She wants you both."

He tilts Josephine's head back, exposing her throat. With her face uplifted like this, her swollen lips glisten. She's wearing the most serene smile as she gazes up at them all.

"And our girl always gets what she wants." Kylian straddles Josephine's body from behind, grasps her throat with his free hand, and gives her a sloppy, upside-down kiss.

When he straightens, he keeps his hold on her hair.

"Cocks out. Face each other. Put one knee on the bench if you have to, but get as close together as you can. Give our girl what she wants."

Both men eagerly comply. Locke groans and gives his already freed cock a stroke. K's murmuring low as he pulls himself out of his pants. They make quick work of rearranging until their tips are nearly touching.

"You want them both, baby?" Kylian asks, pulling Josephine's head back again. "Look how hard they are for you. Look how ready they are to feel your perfect mouth stuffed full."

Puffing out my cheeks, I grip my own length, half-afraid I'm going to blow my load from watching them.

Josephine looks to Locke first, then to Kendrick. Checking in with each of them, I think, to make sure they're good.

They both grin in response, eager and willing, ready to comply with her every desire.

"Suck their cocks, baby. Make them feel good."

Positioning herself as close to the bench as she can get, she reaches out to caress each man's balls as she makes a slow, languid pass over their cocks with her tongue.

"Fuck," Locke draws out, readjusting immediately to offer more of himself to her.

His back is to me, partially blocking Josephine's movements, but the hunger on Kendrick's face is clear in the barely there light of the moon.

I shift slightly, peering over the helm, no longer trying to control the cum that leaks out of me each time one of them moans or groans her name.

"You can get closer," Kylian says.

His crisp words startle me, and I pull back.

He snickers, but then he doubles down on the encouragement. "Come on, Cap. Get up here. Come watch her work. She loves being watched, don't you, baby?"

Josephine whimpers in what I assume is assent.

Her mouth is working overtime to stretch over two dicks at the same time, so that whimper is probably the clearest response he'll get.

"That's it," Kylian encourages.

As I inch closer, Josephine's head bobs faster.

"Fucking hell, Siren." From this new angle, the sight in front of me is the most erotic thing I've ever seen.

She has them both by the balls, and Kendrick and Locke are stroking their cocks, jacking themselves hard in unison. Josephine pops from one mushroom head to the other, and every few seconds, she takes them both into her mouth at the same time.

She's a mess of spit and moans as Locke grunts out a warning. "Get ready, Hot Girl."

"Right there with you, brother," Kendrick confirms.

"Come on her tongue," Kylian demands, tilting her head back, encouraging Josephine to open wide.

In almost perfect unison, my brothers explode, ropes of cum streaming from their cocks and painting her mouth. They keep jacking until they're spent, and Josephine keeps her lips parted, greedily capturing every last drop.

When they're done, Kylian tugs on her hair again. "Don't swallow."

His eyes glint with authority as he turns to me.

"Get the fuck over here and give her yours."

My lungs seize. I already came. She already swallowed for me. He can't possibly think—

"Cap."

I take Josephine in. Still on her knees, her mouth full of spit and cum as Kylian strokes her cheek affectionately.

"She wants it. Don't you, baby?"

Pleading blue eyes connect with mine as she whimpers her desire.

I can't deny her.

Not anymore.

Not ever again.

I work my cock out of my pants so fast I almost come on the spot. Sensing my struggle—I'm so fucking out of my depth here—Kylian takes the lead, helping Josephine turn as I stumble closer and slide myself right back into her warm, willing mouth.

The veins running along my length disappear as they're painted with the cum of my brothers. The warmth and slickness of their releases is an otherworldly sensation as she swirls around my cock and coats me in their fluids.

"Fuck, Siren. This mouth... this fucking perfect mouth."

I piston my hips in shallow thrusts, chasing another orgasm I didn't think was possible.

"What are you doing to me?" I groan, cupping her cheeks affectionately as my balls tingle in warning.

I last less than a minute, shooting off again as she opens wide, welcoming my load.

When I'm finally, Kylian releases her hair, crouches down to her level, murmurs, "good girl," and kisses her right on the mouth.

"Now you can swallow," he concedes.

He stands up and shifts back to the bench, giving me a clear view of our girl still on her knees for me. Her eyes lock with mine as she grins, chokes down the mouthful we gave her, and licks her lips clean.

As soon as she swallows, her gaze turns soft. Her arms snake around my thighs, hugging my lower half as she nuzzles her face into my quads and hums contentedly.

Stunned by the sudden affection, I smooth one hand over her hair and cradle her head against my body, awkwardly holding her as she clings to me like I just gave her a gift she'll cherish forever.

I look down in awe, fascinated and wholly captivated by this woman.

What the fuck is she doing to me?

Chapter 20

Josephine

The gentle rocking of the boat lulls me into a state of sated exhaustion. I feel like I'm floating, suspended on the surface of bliss.

Based on the guys' lackadaisical postures, the feeling is mutual, four times over.

We're still on the pontoon, savoring the privacy the lake affords us. If I could stay out here all night, make the magic last just a little longer, I would.

Kylian runs his hands through my hair, massaging my scalp to ease the tenderness. With a hum, I nuzzle into his lap, wishing I could get even closer. His fingers are magic.

Decker jackknifes up into a sitting position like he just realized he's late for practice or forgot about an important homework assignment. "Wait. You didn't get off."

"I'm still getting over my UTI, Cap," I remind him.

The burning is gone, and I feel tons better, but I still have a few more days of antibiotics.

"Besides, it doesn't always have to be tit for tat," I add. "This one's gotten me off dozens of times without reciprocation."

Kylian scoffs above me. "You know my thoughts on the matter, baby. Your pleasure is my pleasure."

"I know," I murmur.

Though I also recognize that this is all new for Cap.

"It won't always be fair," I hedge. "If we're doing this—*all of us*." I focus on Decker so he knows he's included in the *us* I'm referring to. "Then we have to commit to not keeping score. I know you're all competitive in nature, but I don't ever want you competing or trying to one-up each other in our relationship.

"It's not about numbers." I sit up and rest my head on Kylian's shoulder.

"Not about numbers?" he questions under his breath. Naturally, my stats guy would begrudge such a concept.

"What's it about, then?" Locke asks, sporting a teasing grin. He's playing my game. I appreciate the assist. Heavens knows Cap wouldn't ask himself.

I look to each of my guys, hoping the smile I give them communicates my sincerity. "It's about love," I offer softly. "It's about giving without expectation."

Kendrick murmurs his agreement, another reassurance that we're on the same page. Every time they show me just how devoted they are, my heart squeezes.

"It's about showing up for each other," I continue, "not because we have to, but because we want to."

"Love, huh?" Decker asks, his shoulders suddenly tense again. As if the concept is foreign. As if he doesn't know what to make of this new information.

"Love." I yawn, stretching my arms overhead before settling back against Kylian. "At its core, love is honoring a person where they're at and committing to cherishing the future versions of them, too. There's uncertainty to it." I have to acknowledge that point, because I know how Decker's mind works, and I know what I'm asking is pushing him outside his limits. "But it's worth it."

With a smirk, Locke strides across the vessel and hauls me to my feet. Then, with his hands on my hips, he drops onto the bench I was just occupying and pulls me into his lap. "Sure you don't want to be a philosophy major, Hot Girl?"

"I love you, but no," I murmur against his lips, kissing him to drive home the point.

When another yawn catches me by surprise, Kylian squints at me, then turns to Decker.

"I know we'd all rather stay out here than be under the microscope at the mansion, but she needs sleep, and so do all of you if you want to win a football game tomorrow."

Rather than raise the anchor and start back toward the isle immediately like I expect of the ever-prudent, always-sensible Decker, he stays put and nods to Kendrick.

"What's up, Cap?"

He presses his lips together, hesitating. "Would you mind getting us home?"

Stepping away from the helm, he approaches me and offers a hand. After one more kiss for Locke, I slip my palm against Decker's and let him gingerly help me to my feet.

He leads me to the now-empty bench and pulls me into his lap. And that's where I stay for the ride back to the isle—wrapped up in the arms of Decker Crusade.

Chapter 21

Josephine

Sitting on a cold, backless metal bleacher instead of beside Kylian leaves me feeling vulnerable and exposed. The crowd around me is too loud and the field is too far away.

I've never watched the boys play from anywhere but the sideline. I've never experienced a Crusaders football game without Kylian.

I miss his presence: the certainty of him at my side, the way he'd reach over and idly squeeze my thigh or tuck my hair behind one ear without ever losing focus.

But now is not forever. For the moment, I'll cling to the temporary nature of this arrangement. It's game day and day three of the feature coverage. Next week at this time, we'll be counting down the hours until the camera crew clears out and we're free to live our lives.

Today's game is only an hour from Lake Chapel. I don't typically attend away games—it's rare I'm at home alone, so I savor those quiet moments—but I had no interest in hanging back at the house with cameras rolling twenty-four seven.

Decker was visibility relieved that I didn't push back when he suggested I tag along today.

We all agreed it was safest for me to sit in the stands where I could blend into the crowd. Here, I'm strategically positioned between Emilia and Jade Taylor.

It was Hunter's idea, actually. SportsZone didn't obtain releases for the girls; they're minors who can't consent to being photographed for commercial use. It's so simple, but also genius. My best friend is going to make a badass lawyer someday.

It's the top of the second quarter, and we're already leading fourteen to three. This morning, the guys had a long discussion about what has to change since Kendrick is out. There's less focus on the run game and way more calls for Decker to throw the ball.

My favorite running back is on the bench today. He's wearing generic Crusaders gear rather than his own jersey. He's on the injured list, just as Kylian expected.

There's nothing I can do to fix the situation, but I can support him. Which is exactly what I'm doing tonight.

He may not be wearing number 24, but I am.

Along with Emilia and Jade.

The girls were thrilled when K invited them today. Just like me, they typically only attend home games with their aunt—Kendrick's Pops rarely has the time off to accompany them—but again, the proximity to Lake Chapel made it feasible.

Satisfaction percolates through me when I look at them. Kendrick trusts me with his sisters. Not only that, but they seem to like spending time with me, too.

The warm contentment chills a little, though, when the game of twenty questions sets in.

"Is K your boyfriend?" Emilia blurts before she shovels a fistful of popcorn into her mouth. She side-eyes me as she chews, clearly expecting a response.

I smooth one hand over my hair. One of the Crusaders bead bracelets on my wrist catches, so I give it a tug to free it.

"Yes," I finally answer, picking at the loose strand attached to the beads.

As if he knows we're talking about him, K chooses that moment to turn around and seek us out in the stands.

When his eyes find mine, he breaks out into a grin and tips his chin in that cool guy way.

I grin right back with absolutely no cool at all.

I woke up beside him this morning. We made a big breakfast together. He sent me his customary locker room thirst trap pic before the game, despite not dressing. Yet I'm still so thoroughly affected by his charm and swagger. Even fifty yards away.

"So K's your boyfriend," Emilia repeats, "but Jade saw you kissing Kylian when he dropped you off."

"Millie!" Jade hisses.

I roll my lips. *Shit*. How the hell do I explain to preteens that yeah, well, he's my boyfriend, too?

"And Nicky calls you Hot Girl," Emilia continues before I've formulated a response. "Which makes it sound like he like-likes you, too."

She's still side-eyeing me, looking both skeptical and unimpressed. She's throwing major shade for such a little thing.

"Kendrick is my boyfriend. I also have special relationships with Kylian and Nicky."

"What about Uncle Ducky?" Jade presses, finally letting her curiosity show.

I stifle a laugh. "Uncle Ducky, too. I care about all of them." I shift against the cold metal of the bleacher, looking from one sister to the other. Solemnly, I vow, "Your brother knows how I feel. I wouldn't do anything to hurt him or to break his trust."

"We know, Jojo," Jade rushes to reassure me. She links her arm through mine and rests her head on my shoulder. She's so sweet and unassuming. I could gobble her up. I fight back the urge to kiss the top of her head—something her brother does to me often to show affection.

Cautiously, I look to Emilia.

She's the more cynical of the two. She's so much like Kendrick in that way. After holding eye contact for several seconds, she shrugs and turns away, dismissing the conversation.

Jade comes to my rescue once again. "Millie, don't be rude. Kendrick hasn't been nearly as grumpy as usual lately and you know it."

She keeps her gaze on the field, muttering under her breath as the Crusaders set up at the line of scrimmage. Finally, she turns back to me and gives me a once-over. "That's true."

"If you have more questions, you could ask your brother," I offer.

Her eyes go wide with something that looks like horror as Jade bursts out laughing.

The laughs quickly become cackles that force the bleacher seat beneath us to vibrate.

Wiping tears out of her eyes, she finally calms enough to speak. "Yeah. No." She sucks in a breath. "We'll take you at your word, Jojo. You might be K's girlfriend, but you haven't experienced him at his grumpiest until you're his little sister pestering him about girls."

Chapter 22

Josephine

The Crusaders won. The celebration at the end of the game was far more subdued in the stands than it is in the thick of things on the sidelines.

That anticlimactic vibe has shrouded us all night.

Nothing is wrong, but nothing feels right, either.

We're all quiet as we trail up the dock. Kylian leads the way to the house, and I follow. Nicky and Kendrick are behind me, with Decker bringing up the rear, a physical barricade separating us from the cameraperson trailing him.

A familiar cameraperson, I realized the moment we stepped off the boat.

Red Hat Grabby Hands is on duty tonight. With each step I take across the beach and up the stairs with him on our heels, my stomach twists into tighter knots.

We made the right call, allowing him to stay. He hasn't made a comment or so much as glanced my direction the few times I've noticed him with the crew.

He's terrified of my guys, and rightfully so.

The normal postgame party is on tonight, according to Kylian, even though the game was away. Part of me dreads the chaos, but at least the commotion of a victory party at the Crusade mansion will ensure there are plenty of other targets for the cameras and likely far more interesting scenarios.

But the atmosphere around the five of us grows warier the closer we draw to the house.

It's like the hum of humidity in the sky before a storm. Or the smell before rain.

It's unsettling and unnerving.

I shudder from the unease. I'm not cold. I'm just... confused.

The lights are on, but there's barely a sound coming from the house. From here, the water lapping against the dock and the boats is audible. On party nights, those subtle noises are drowned out by music and chatter.

I turn back and scan the lake, only just realizing that the ferries aren't running.

One is docked down on the beach, but the guys manning it are sitting wide-legged on the vessel and fiddling with their phones like they're on break.

I stub my toe on the step and hiss as I find my footing.

"Careful, Mama," Kendrick murmurs from behind. One hand finds my back, supporting me as I climb the last few stairs.

His fingers graze the waistband along the back of my leggings. The touch is featherlight but full of so much meaning. I *know* we have to be careful. We're all just trying to get through this week. But feeling K's fingertips on my skin, knowing that he wants nothing more than to wrap me in his arms, it's enough for now. It has to be.

"K, why—"

"Let Decker explain."

Pressing my lips together, I resign myself to waiting for answers.

Kylian holds the door, but Kendrick weaves around me so he can enter first. They're keeping me positioned between them, I realize, always making sure someone's at my back and at my front.

Not that I mind. Kylian and Kendrick sandwiches rank pretty high on the list of my favorite combos.

I sidestep into the main living room and lean against a floor-to-ceiling window as I scan the space.

The DJ is set up in their usual spot, though the music is much lower than normal. The couches are all occupied, and the kitchen is full of people, too.

For all intents and purposes, it looks like a party. But the energy is nothing like the usual vibe.

Even when Decker strolls through the door, the mood remains muted. A few people call out congratulations. One guy approaches, arm extended, to commend them for the win.

The cameras are rolling, aimed on Decker's every move, intent on capturing every second of the postgame celebration.

Yet everything about the scene surrounding us is fake.

"Joze! My girl!"

At the sound of those words echoing through the house, I shoot up straight and turn toward the kitchen to see Greedy striding toward me, wearing—I have to do a double take to confirm—Crusader's red.

"His girl?" Kylian deadpans in the way only Kylian can, shifting just enough so he's in front of me now.

I grasp his shoulder. "You know how he is," I murmur, going for soothing. "Although now I'm even more curious about why he's here."

Kylian hums, never taking his eyes off Greedy. "The Sharks owed us a favor."

His words don't have time to register before Greedy is sidestepping him and scooping me up until my feet skim the floor.

"Damn. I haven't seen you for ages. Where have you been, girl?" He spins me, turning us in a half circle so he's standing between Kylian and me.

I have to look away immediately to keep from laughing.

Kylian's livid, shooting daggers at the back of Greedy's head.

Before I can quietly assure him that I'm okay, big hands catch my hips, gently but firmly dislodging me from Greedy's grip.

"Careful, Mama," K repeats in my ear, his low timbre husky and melodic. Goose bumps crop up along the length of my spine.

"Watch yourself, Greedy," he adds, his voice a little louder.

I wiggle back, ready to sink into his hold. My back barely grazes his chest before he catches my arms to stop me. A second later, his heat disappears.

I glare over my shoulder, ready to put him in his place.

Only to be met with a look of frustration and agitation.

"Cameras, Jojo. Anything and everything we do..."

Shit on a crumbly cracker.

It's the reminder I need. But damn if it doesn't sting like rejection.

As if he can read my mind, Kendrick whips out his phone and nods, silently signaling that I should do the same.

> **Kendrick:** You're perfect. You feel so fucking good in my arms. I wish I could take you out on that dance floor right now and show everyone what's mine

> **Jojo:** This sucks

He chuckles, and Greedy catches on.

"Yeah. Okay. I'm not going to stand here while you two sext. Find me later, Joze, and we can catch up. I'm Hunter's ride home, so I'm sure I'll see you in a bit."

Oh. Hunter.

We had plans to meet up at the party like usual. I got distracted by the very un-party-like atmosphere when we walked in.

> **Joey:** Hey girl. I'm back

Kylian leans forward, brushing against my body not so subtly, but in a way that wouldn't be noticeable on camera. Probably.

"I'm heading upstairs," he tells me. "If you need a break from Big Brother, head to your room. Cap's room is safe as long as he's not in there, too. Come to the Nest if you need me."

He kisses the back of my neck, a barely there peck that inspires a full body shudder.

I need more. Want more. I swear I didn't realize how much PDA we engage in until it was off the table. It's only been a few days, and I've turned into a needy, touch-deprived bitch.

"I'll see you in the morning," I whisper. My world may be topsy-turvy because of the feature, but I know damn well Kylian's not going to allow a break in our Sunday morning routine.

Nothing beats starting the day with multiple orgasms as Kylian eats me for breakfast.

"You'll be down here for a while?" I ask Kendrick as Kylian walks away.

"Until midnight. That's the official end time."

Huh. That's also new.

"I'll find Hunter in a bit and let her know I saw you," I tell Greedy.

His face falls. "I'm sure she'll be thrilled to hear it."

I smirk. At least Greedy's self-aware enough to realize how Hunter truly feels about him.

"I'm going to go find Cap," I announce.

Crossing his arms over his chest, Kendrick turns so he's the one with his back to the window and scans the crowd.

"Check the gym," he suggests, propping one knee up behind him and settling in to stand guard.

Weaving through the people scattered about is easier than usual. It's noticeably less crowded tonight; the typical chaos and excitement are a barely discernible buzz.

I take advantage of the quiet kitchen and empty hall by pulling out my phone.

> Joey: Where are you?

> Hunter: I'm in your room. They were making everyone sign NDAs downstairs. Corbin let me up before they got to me.

> Joey: Clever. I want to find Cap, then I'll come up and join you. Any idea why Greedy's here?

> Hunter: *eye roll emoji*

> Joey: It's like that, huh?

> Hunter: Sharks had a bye week. Decker called in a favor.

My heart trips in my chest. All this was Decker's doing?

I find him in the gym, like Kendrick thought I would. Why the man thinks he needs to run on the treadmill after winning a football game is beyond me.

Not wanting to startle him—he's legit sprinting on an incline—I wait until he sees me in the mirror. He quickly slams the emergency stop and whips his head around, scanning me from head to toe.

"Are you okay?" he wheezes.

I fight back a smirk. "All good." I prop myself up against the doorjamb rather than enter the room. Kylian discovered that hovering in a doorway makes it harder for the cameras to capture our conversation.

"I just wanted to check on you. Congratulate you. Ask about the party..."

I raise one brow and scrunch my nose.

His gaze shifts to the camera clearly mounted in the corner of the gym, then he focuses on me again.

"It's just our regular party, Josephine. It'll wrap up around midnight. You don't need to hang out downstairs if you're not in the mood to celebrate."

Nodding, I turn my head just a little, looking into the hallway, then back again, silently willing him to recognize the invitation.

He stands, stretches his arms overhead, and cracks his neck, like he's in no rush at all.

When he starts toward the door, I turn and stride away.

I don't falter or look back to confirm he's following.

Holding my breath, I turn the handle on the pantry door, check that it's empty, and duck inside.

The door latches closed behind me.

I spin on my heel and fight back a smile. "Are we alone in here?" I whisper, not bothering to flick on the light.

There isn't a B-roll camera here, but there are mics throughout the house. That leaves us with few places we can find true privacy this week. Regardless, I'm itching for a moment of solace with this man.

Leaning against the closed door, Decker nods and beckons with one finger. "We are. Get over here."

I rush into his arms. The warmth and strength of his hold instantly settles all the stirred-up emotions that have run rampant inside me since I spent the game in the stands instead of on the sideline.

He cups the back of my head and ducks low, mouth at my ear. "Kylian knows what you like to get up to in this pantry, Siren. He thought it best to scramble the feeds and mics in this part of the house, too."

I play punch his side, and he lets out a *hmph*. Lightning quick, he catches my wrist and raises my hand to his mouth. With his free hand, he unwinds my fist, then he places a kiss on the center of my palm.

He keeps his eyes on me the whole time, onyx orbs filled with desire.

The air around us hums. It's rare for the two of us to have a true semblance of privacy.

Day in and day out, I feel his gaze in the very marrow of my bones as he watches me.

But I live for these moments.

Sweet moments. Singular minutes. Secret seconds where it's me and him, and he's not worrying about anything else.

"What's really happening out there?" I whisper against his lips.

"We had to give them something tonight. I called in a favor. It's South Chapel's bye week. Greedy had no trouble convincing his boys to come drink my liquor and possibly be filmed for SportsZone."

My fists tighten around the fabric of his sweat-dampened T-shirt. "Who all—"

"I vetted everyone, Siren. No one here saw you that night. Greedy wouldn't do that, and you know I wouldn't allow it."

As the air presses out of my lungs, I rest my cheek on Decker's chest, then inhale, breathing him in. Instantly, my heart rate begins to regulate.

A kerfuffle in the hallway reminds me that we aren't alone.

Sighing, Decker drops his head back against the door. "We have to get back."

I fist his shirt tighter. "Decker."

He rests his lips against my forehead. "I know."

"One minute?" I quietly request.

"One minute."

And then he kisses me.

It's soft at first, a subtle greeting. A reacquaintance. It's like arriving at a beloved destination I haven't visited for a long time.

Never mind that I had his cock nudging the back of my throat on the boat last night.

His kiss right now is full of promise, brimming with unspoken potential.

It's a kiss to assure.

It's a kiss of surrender.

It's a kiss meant to encapsulate everything we're going to be.

As seconds tick by, our movements become frantic, and the kiss evolves into more.

We're desperate.

Not just for each other.

We're both desperate for more.

We're desperate for time to stand still or, at the very least, slow. To give us pause. To give us a fighting chance at more.

I trail my fingers down his torso and burrow beneath the fabric of his T-shirt until I graze warm skin. His abs are impossibly defined: taut valleys of strain and discipline from the exertion of the game.

We don't break the kiss as he slides his palms under my shirt, finding my low back.

He rests there. Holding me. Linking us.

Giving all he has to give in this moment.

We whisper silent but unified prayers against each other's lips.

Let this be enough.

When it's all over, when the feature wraps and the cameras are gone, when we're free to examine our reality and consider how we'll make this work with the guys.

Please. Let this be enough.

At what could be a full minute or maybe only a beat of my heart—because all semblance of time and logic evaporates from my mind where Decker Crusade is concerned—he pulls back.

It's subtle. But it's there.

A necessary retreat. Commitment, determination, and discipline that I don't possess.

He places one last achingly soft kiss on my lips. "Be good tonight, Siren. Next week at this time, we'll be home free. Everything will be different soon."

I nod, dazed and more than a little love drunk as Decker extends his arms, shifts away from the door, and ensures I have my balance before turning away from me.

When the door opens and light from the hall spills in, I watch him leave, focusing on the strain in his shoulders and the way he holds his head high. He's all confidence and swagger as he exits the pantry without a glance back.

Fuck. Watching him walk away guts me.

Emotion clogs my throat, and my eyes well with tears.

It's ridiculous, an overdramatic reaction to the responsible choice he's making. The choice he and I both know is right.

We just have to get through this week.

Tread lightly for a little while longer.

I blink away the moisture in my eyes and take a long, cleansing breath.

We're so close to having what feels like a beautiful version of something real.

But as I slip out of the pantry and gently latch the door behind me, I can't help but feel like it's not enough.

What I want, what he's able to give.

What will we do if, in the end, it's simply not enough?

Chapter 23

Decker

I would have stayed in the pantry with her forever.

I could drag in a mattress. Build a pillow fort. Hole up in our little hideaway, just me and her, soft lips and lingering touches.

Hell, I'd even let the guys join us.

They make her happy. So damn happy.

And after last night?

I want to make her that happy for the rest of my life.

If she wants to be with all of us, I want to give her that. I want to make the life we're daring to dream for ourselves possible.

But my current position comes with responsibilities I can't avoid. Boxes that must be checked before I'm afforded a life where privacy is a given, not a highly sought-after privilege.

I blow out a long breath, forcing myself to forge on.

I don't dare look back.

Because I'm a coward.

I can't stand the thought of seeing the expression on her face as I walk away from her.

Seven more days. I just have to get us through them.

Almost there is the mantra playing on repeat in my mind as I stride into the kitchen.

People call out to me.

One of the camera people—Tonya, I think her name is—rushes forward to focus the shot.

I offer her a terse smile, never looking directly into the camera, per the instructions Misty has drilled into me over the years.

Smile more. Look natural.

Hold your head high, but not too high. Don't clench your jaw.

I crack my neck to alleviate the tension.

Seven more days.

Everything will be different in seven more days.

Chapter 24

Josephine

I give Corbin a fist bump and wave at the other security guard stationed at the base of the stairs. With what could almost be considered a smile, Corbin lifts the rope hooked through one side of the stanchion, allowing me to pass.

A sense of ease settles around me when the metal lobster claw clinks back in place.

Halfway up, I pull out my phone and check the time. It's not even nine, and yet a yawn escapes me.

Pausing where I am, I check in with the group text and tap out a message.

> Josephine: I'm heading to bed. Great game tonight, guys.

I quickly scroll through my pictures as I climb the last few stairs and send a few selfies of the twins and me celebrating after they won.

Kendrick replies instantly.

> K: They adore you

That simple response makes my heart float in my chest.

> Josephine: Good. The feeling's mutual. In fact, I'm pretty fond of all the Taylor siblings

> K: Yeah you are

> Kylian: Enough. This exchange is an unnecessary use of the group chat.

My smile transforms into a snort.

> K: Don't be jealous, Daddy Genius. You know I got love for you too

> Nicky: DADDY Genius??

> Nicky: WTF?

> K: See? If we weren't using the group text, the others wouldn't know about your promotion and new nickname

> Kylian: Irrelevant to the initial complaint. We each have individual texts with Jo for these types of conversations.

> K: Believe me. Jojo and I make good use of our individual text thread. Don't we Mama?

> Decker: There are cameras on both of you right now.

> Kylian: I'm upstairs, Jo. Come up if you need me.

> Josephine: Yes Daddy

> **Nicky:** OH GOD MAKE IT STOP

> **Kylian:** See you in the morning, baby.

Yes he will. My Sunday morning tradition with Kylian is my favorite. While it's still dark, I sneak up to the Nest, where he spreads me out on his bed and eats my pussy while I watch the sun come up through the stained-glass panels of the cupola.

I'm grinning so wide my cheeks hurt by the time I open my bedroom door.

Once the door is closed securely behind me, I turn on my phone flashlight rather than flick on the lights.

"You're good. I'm awake."

I'm startled by the sound of Hunter's voice. It took longer to make my way upstairs than I anticipated, so I didn't expect to find her awake and sitting in the dark.

Although in my defense, I may have been lost in thought, thinking about Kylian's head between my thighs.

"How long have you been up here?" I make my way to the bathroom, shedding my clothes as I go, careful to fold my Taylor jersey so I can return it to Kendrick in the morning.

"Since just after I arrived," Hunter replies through a yawn.

I flip on the dim light over the shower and pull a makeup wipe from its packaging. "Did you come with Greedy?"

There's a long pause before she answers. "No. I had no idea he was going to be here. I've already sent Decker a scathing text about it. A heads-up would have been nice."

Once I'm finished in the bathroom, I grab a T-shirt from my drawer and pull it on.

"I'm sorry." I climb into bed and turn to face her, propping my head on my hand. "I didn't know he'd be here, either."

From this close, I can make her out, even in the dark. Her face is red and blotchy, and her eyes are puffy.

"Hunter," I soothe, squeezing her leg. "What's wrong?"

She shakes her head and turns away so she's facing the French doors to my balcony.

"Hey," I try again, softer. I scoot a little closer and take her hand in mine. "You know you can talk to me. About anything. I would never judge you."

She stays focused on the doors, breathing with audible effort and the occasional sniffle.

Then, with a shuddering breath, she turns back to me. She's got a fake smile plastered to her face, and she's doing everything she can to not make eye contact.

"How was the party?" she asks brightly.

Too brightly.

My heart sinks and I deflate. Hunter is my closest friend, and yet some days, I swear I don't know her at all. I understand more than most that not every issue consuming a person is one they can talk about, but I'm desperate to support her or, at the very least, console her. I feel like a shitty friend. She's done so much for me in the short amount of time we've known each other, yet here I am, unable to do the same when she's obviously struggling.

I'd be an even shittier friend, though, if I pushed her to talk when she's not ready to share or forced her to reveal secrets she's not comfortable telling me. So I let it go for now.

"The party was uncharacteristically Shark-ish," I quip.

"You know what Jimmy says. Beware of Sharks that can party on land."

For a minute, my head swims in confusion, but when I get it, I snort. She's talking about Jimmy Buffett. Only Hunter…

"What if I told you I was down there dancing with your not-brother?" I tease. I flip my pillow, savoring the feel of the cool fabric on my cheek as I settle in.

Hunter holds my gaze for all of three seconds, her face neutral. "I'd call bullshit. Your boyfriend wouldn't stand for that."

"Which one?" I challenge.

"Exactly!" she squeals, shoving me playfully until we're both laughing.

It feels good to laugh. It feels even better to lie down.

God, I'm thankful Kylian has blockers on the camera feeds in this room. Despite the glow of the little red light in the corner, I trust in his expertise and have absolute faith in his assurance that there will be no usable footage of what happens between these four walls.

With a soft groan, I relax my muscles and settle in for sleep.

But then Hunter speaks.

"I'm going to sleep here tonight, if that's okay with you."

I hum, gripping her hand. "Of course it is." Then, pushing my luck, I add, "Are you sure you're okay?"

"Yes." A sigh. "No. I don't know."

"Hunter..."

"It's my mom."

My eyes pop open and a surge of surprise courses through me. So much for relaxed muscles. I assumed Greedy's presence at the party tonight was the issue. Her mom, though? Since the first day she and I hung out, she's been tight-lipped about the woman.

"Your mom?"

That's all it takes to convince her to continue.

"It's been almost a year since I heard from her last. Now, all of a sudden, she's been calling. Leaving voicemails. She keeps saying she's coming home... that she can't wait to see me."

Her tone is filled with trepidation and her voice quavers, making the words sound more like a threat than a promise.

"You don't want her here?" I guess.

Hunter flops to her back, sighing. "She's my mom. I feel awful saying I don't want her here, but..."

"But?"

"She's not a good person, Joey," she whispers. "She's manipulative. Mean. Greedy hates her. Those two together..." She trails off, sounding utterly defeated.

I press my lips together, forcing myself to hold back the litany of questions I want to ask.

Silence ensues.

I'm okay with silence. I understand its importance.

But I need her to know that if there's ever a time when silence doesn't serve her anymore, I'll be here for that, too.

Still gripping her hand, I mirror her position and lie flat on my back.

"Nothing you could say would ever change how I feel about you."

She squeezes my hand in reply and lets out a small, sad hum. "Thank you. Love you. Good night, Joey."

I take that as the cue that we're done. At least for tonight.

Chapter 25

Josephine

"And what, exactly, are you making there?"

This cameraman is acting like he's auditioning for the role of documentary filmmaker this morning.

He's standing unnecessarily close to Mrs. Lansbury as she peels fresh ginger root. His bulky frame towers over her, and the camera is so close it almost grazes her shoulder as he swoops in for a different angle.

When she shoots me yet another wary glance, I can't help but jump in and save her.

"I'll take it from here," I announce, prying the paring knife from her grip.

With a sigh and a grateful smile, she takes off toward the pantry.

I turn on the cameraman, offer a saccharine smile, and point the knife in his direction. "Nate, was it?"

"Yep," he confirms as he adjusts the lens. He's been here since before we woke up. I know, because he was roaming the upstairs hallway when I crept down from the Nest.

"Right. You're standing too close to me, Nate. The contract states that your presence cannot interfere with anyone's ability to perform daily tasks and functions. Currently, you're interfering."

It really does pay to have a best friend majoring in prelaw.

He chortles, but takes two steps back, giving me enough room to at least finish peeling slivers of ginger.

I make quick work of getting everything into the pot on the stove and give it a good stir. Already, the aroma of the anti-inflammatory tea Mrs. Lansbury started for Nicky permeates the air.

"It appears there are too many cooks in the kitchen," Kylian announces, bypassing his usual seat at the island to come stand behind me.

He peers over my shoulder, then quietly kisses the side of my neck the camera can't see.

"We should have stayed in the Nest," he murmurs, a hand trailing against the cotton covering my stomach.

Each caress is strategically placed so as not to be documented by the insufferable lens of the camera. Little touchpoints, just for me.

I lean back so our bodies barely brush, and he hums low. It's a recognition of how badly he wants to hold me, but it's also a warning.

In my periphery, Nate shifts, trying to not so subtly capture our embrace.

My mood sours further... *fucking Nate*. Fucking feature.

"I promised Nicky I'd go with him to his appointment." Murmuring low seems to make it difficult for the mics to capture our conversation, so we've been doing a lot of that over the last couple of days. "I want to get this tea brewing quickly so it's ready when he comes down."

"There's an outing planned for today?" Nate's inched closer again, camera still in one hand. Now he's holding a rolled-up piece of paper in the other and squinting at the page.

"Not for you, there isn't."

The cameraman shoots a glare at Kylian, but Kylian's completely unaffected.

He has the least at stake with SportsZone. He doesn't have NIL contracts to be concerned about. Although he's required to be on camera as part of his roommate agreement, he's rarely the primary focus of the footage.

"If there's an opportunity—"

"Nicholas has an appointment with a medical professional," Kylian says, cutting Nate off. "Per the contract, he's not required to disclose any medical information. If you have questions or don't understand HIPPA, I suggest you contact Misty."

Shut. down.

Grumbling something unintelligible, Nate lowers his camera. He sets it on the island countertop so it's pointing in our direction, then stalks off toward the living room.

Kylian snags a dish towel from the handle of the oven and drapes it over the lens.

"Whoops."

I meet his gaze and finally allow myself to laugh. To really laugh. God, this whole situation is absurd.

He catches me around the waist and spins until I'm backed up against the side of the fridge.

"Cameras can't see us here," he confirms, tilting my head to the side to expose my neck.

Groaning, he captures me in a deep, passionate kiss.

My clit throbs with need—like he didn't already get me off three times this morning.

He sweeps his tongue against mine. "I can still taste my cum in your mouth, dirty girl."

With a hand at my throat, he pins me to the fridge. "As soon as the cameras are gone, I'm going to fuck you on every surface of this kitchen."

I kiss him back, my breath coming in heavy pulls as I lose myself in the caresses of his tongue and the strain of his fingers wrapped around my throat.

"Are you wet for me, baby?"

"Yes, Daddy," I pant.

"Still, or again?"

Boldly, I dip two fingers into the front of my shorts and swirl my fingertips around my opening.

"Again," I confess, lifting my hand to show Kylian the proof.

He squeezes my neck with a growl, then clamps his mouth around my fingers and sucks them clean.

"You like it when I've got my hand on your throat, don't you? You like it almost as much as when I've got my tongue up your cunt. And when Kendrick's got a finger in your ass."

I squirm, which he reads as a cue to loosen his grip.

"Don't let go," I counter, grasping his wrist and guiding his hand back to my neck. "Harder," I practically beg.

He does as I ask, and my pulse picks up, along with the throbbing of my clit.

"Fuck. You look so hot with my hand gripping you, baby. I wonder if I could talk you to orgasm just like this."

Blood whooshes in my ears, and my vision goes fuzzy on the edges in the most delicious, promising way.

"Would you like that? If I told you all about how I want to fuck you while one of the boys chokes you with their cock?"

He kisses me again, stealing what little oxygen I have access to.

"Who do you want it to be? Who's fucking your face while I pound you into the mattress?"

"Decker," I answer instantly.

With a chuckle, he squeezes my throat again, then moves his free hand to my lips. I open without instruction, whimpering when he murmurs, "Good girl."

"You loved having Decker's fat cock in your mouth Friday night, didn't you, baby?" He presses two fingers into my mouth and drags them back and forth against my tongue. "You're desperate to get him off again and to make us all watch, aren't you, dirty girl?"

"Yes," I rasp. Saliva dribbles down my chin, and carnal passion heats me from the inside out.

"Yes what?" Kylian demands, sticking his fingers so far down my throat I nearly gag.

"Yes, Daddy," I purr, trying so damn hard not to cough.

"Good girl."

Suddenly, he pulls back. He removes his hand from my mouth and the other from around my throat. Then he shifts away and puts a bit of space between us; enough that I stumble forward, horny and practically delirious.

"You better get going," he deadpans, swatting my bum when I gape at him.

"Are you kidding me right now?" I hiss, just as Nate returns.

Kylian reaches for my coffee mug and brings it to his lips to hide his grin.

I've been cockblocked by cameras. Edged to the point of delirium, then left wanting because of Nate.

Fucking Nate.

I ought to knee him in the—

"Jo."

My head snaps up, heart still pounding, as I meet Kylian's gaze.

"Locke's waiting for you," he reminds me with a wink and the smuggest smile.

Chapter 26

Josephine

Logistically, I understood what was involved when I agreed to accompany Locke to his infusion today.

I just didn't give myself time to think about how it would feel to walk in the back door of Lake Chapel Radiance beside a man who played a part in flipping my world upside down the last time I was here.

I didn't leave my place of employment on good terms.

I didn't have a choice, thanks to Decker and his insistence that I stick by one of the guys at all times.

So I quit my job via email, giving no notice. I didn't even return the uniform.

My feet stop of their own volition as we reach the door.

Nicky's got one hand in mine, the other outstretched to turn the handle.

At my resistance, he glances over his shoulder, his brow furrowed in confusion.

Willing the nerves that have suddenly flared up inside me to abate, I meet his gaze.

He scans my face, and his expression softens. I don't have to say a word for him to register my trepidation. "You're okay. Only a couple of staff members are here on Sundays, and we won't see anyone besides Dr. Kline anyway. That's part of the arrangement."

He removes his hand from my hold and slides his arm around my shoulders. Pulling me close, he drops a kiss to my hair. "That's why Kendrick reacted the way he did when you followed us out that day," he explains.

I blow out a breath and stand a little straighter. "And here I thought he reacted that way because he's a big grump who doesn't know how to process his feelings."

Nicky snorts. "That, too. Come on, Hot Girl. Let's get this over with so I can take you home."

Nicky's words proved to be true. We didn't see or interact with another human until Dr. Kline greeted us, ushered us into the biggest treatment room, and shut the door.

Locke introduced me as his girlfriend. It would have been cute if Dr. Kline hadn't shaken my hand enthusiastically and acted like we'd never met before. Although I can't really blame him for not remembering the girl who worked all of three shifts before disappearing.

Now I'm sitting by Nicky's side in the wide lounge chair, tracing the ink on his knuckles as he lies beside me with his eyes closed.

"Is the treatment the same every time?" I ask, eyeing the bags hanging on the drip above him.

Eyes still closed, he clasps my hand. He's been doing that more lately—wrapping my hand up with his instead of interlacing our fingers.

He's been in near-constant pain for these last few weeks, and it only escalated after the altercation. I feel so helpless, not being able to soothe the aches.

"I've got a whole laundry list of treatments on rotation. Today's cocktail is specifically designed to help with the swelling in my joints. The hope is that it'll help me feel better faster in the mornings. We'll see." He sighs, as if he's already prepared to be disappointed by the results.

"Is it always this bad during the season?"

He opens his eyes and focuses on me for a long moment. Finally, he clears his throat and squeezes my hand. "No. It's never been like this before."

As gently as I can, I wrap one arm around his midsection, desperate to comfort him. He doesn't flinch or readjust, so once I'm sure I'm not hurting him, I nestle into the crook of his arm.

"That sucks," I acknowledge. No amount of saying I'm sorry or encouraging him to look on the bright side will change the physical pain and the reality of his situation.

He pulls in a deep breath, his chest rising and falling beneath my arm before he swallows audibly and speaks again. "Can I tell you something?"

"Anything."

He sighs, readjusting his arm under my head. "I keep thinking it might be time to call it quits. I've always justified the pain that comes along with football. Relished it, even. But lately, I can't help but question if it's all worth it."

Holding my breath, I listen without judgment.

"Cap and Kendrick will enter the draft. They're destined for the pros. For a long time, I've known that football isn't my future. Lately, I've been caught up in wondering if powering through the way I have been will do more harm to my body long term. To what end? Just to say I finished out the season?"

"What do you want after college?" I ask, tracing my fingertips along the veins of his forearm.

Head lolling to the side, he bites his lip and gives me a thorough once-over.

"What else?" I laugh, because he's made that particular *want* clear.

"A life with you. With the guys. A home we can all share. A job I don't hate."

It's such a simple list. Unremarkable to some, but more than enough for my Emo Boy.

"Anything else?" I push.

He closes his eyes and smiles.

"I want to have good days. I know they won't all be pain free, but I want them to be easier than this." He sighs, peering up at the IV drip. "I want to play on the floor with my kids. To coach their sports teams. Rake leaf piles for them to jump in. Take them swimming."

"You want kids?" I squeak out, my heart lodged in my throat. He's already made it clear his vision for the future involves me. And yet I still have to ask. "With me?"

"I mean... you're my first choice," he teases. He rests his arm over mine along his torso and hits me with a serious expression. "Of course I want kids with you."

Surely, any second now, my brain will go haywire. How could it not?

I'm twenty-one. I haven't even finished my first semester of college. We've only been dating for a few months, and our relationship is less than conventional.

Instead of being hit with the urge to bolt from this man's arms at that declaration, I'm flooded with visions of mini Nickys. Babies with warm hazel eyes, or maybe blue eyes, like mine. They'd have dark hair and sweet smiles, toothy grins that light up their little faces, and sweet, tinkling laughs.

"Nicky," I sniff, my bottom lip quivering.

"Too much?" he guesses, squeezing my arm.

"Not at all," I whisper. "I just hadn't thought about any of that before. About you and me, the guys... *babies*. All that our future could entail." I bow my head and kiss his shoulder. "I want kids with you, too. In like, ten or twenty years."

He snorts. "The timeline's negotiable. I want us all to get what we want out of this life. I can be patient."

He brings his free arm over so he can pull me closer. His hold is a comfort and a promise of everything we're going to be. Now isn't easy, but our future is so damn bright.

We lie together, lost in thought, cuddling and connecting without speaking. We readjust every few minutes so Nicky can stay comfortable, but I'm happy to do it. Even if we're here because of not so great circumstances, I savor the time alone with him.

"What do you think about the football thing?" he eventually asks.

I shake my head. "That has to be your call, Emo Boy. I don't want to persuade you one way or the other, but I'll support you through whatever you choose."

His serene smile fills me with so much joy—a calm peacefulness that feels like hope.

"I love you," he says.

Three simple words that wrap me up in a warm embrace. Words that serve as a promise that now is not forever, that better days are ahead.

Chapter 27

Josephine

Misty's heels click obnoxiously as she dutifully marches the guys down the too-bright hallway to the next location, carrying on about—god, I don't even know anymore.

It's been a feat holding back the eye rolls today. At her comments, at the looks she keeps shooting my way, at her insistence that she accompany us to begin with.

As if we couldn't possibly navigate a children's hospital without her guidance.

On my right, Kendrick keeps brushing his hand against mine, catching my pinkie with his and giving me secret little smiles.

On my left, Decker is a stoic, emotionless wall. He's sent a few wary glances my way, his gaze always filled with worry. I don't know how many ways I have to say "I'm fine" before he'll actually believe me, but here we are.

"Knock, knock!" Misty singsongs, pushing open a door marked Family Lounge.

Behind her, we file inside, smiles plastered on our faces as we prepare to greet the next round of patients.

We've done this twice already today. First in the burn unit, then on the oncology and hematology floor. Now we're in a wing marked Palliative Care.

The expectations are simple: the boys greet the kids, take pictures, and sign all sorts of things. I have a dozen permanent markers stashed in my bag for this very reason. The visit was heavily promoted in advance, so siblings and other relatives of the patients have gathered to meet the guys, too.

The best part? Because they're meeting with minors, the camera crew is nowhere to be found.

According to Decker, Misty tried to move this engagement once she was aware of the scheduling conflict. Both he and Kendrick refused, full stop.

As I follow the guys farther into the room, I take in the scene. It's far less crowded here than what we've experienced so far.

In fact, there are just four kids in the room, along with a nurse who doesn't look to be much older than us.

The nurse looks up and greets us with a smile. "Hey. You're the football guys?"

"We are." Decker's jaw twitches as he fights back a smile. It's not often people don't recognize him. Or, in this case, seem completely unfazed by his presence. The flash of amusement in his eyes makes my heart lift. He's enjoying the obscurity.

"Well, you can leave," one girl declares from her seat at a craft table. "There aren't any boys here." She doesn't even bother looking up from the fuse bead she's placing on the template as she dismisses us.

"Pretty sure her name's Emilia," Kendrick says under his breath so only I can hear.

"Girls can like football, too." I step out from behind the guys.

That garners a little interest. All the girls peek up at me.

Except the designated spokeswoman speaks up again before any of the other girls can get a word in. "They can. But we don't. You can leave."

"Well, okay then!" Misty clasps her hands and draws in a breath like she's eager to agree.

Beside me, Decker holds up a hand. He shakes his head once, effectively silencing her. I have to hold back a laugh as the air deflates from her lungs. Resigned to her fate, she click-clacks to the corner of the room, pulls out her phone, and focuses on the screen.

So much for helping the guys relate to the public.

"I've got this," I murmur, brushing past both boys. "So if you don't like football," I start, moving closer to the apparent leader of the group. "What do you like?"

I'm close enough now to make out the butterfly template the little girl is hyper-focused on. She's working on an intricate, perfectly symmetrical pattern for the wings. I wouldn't want to be bothered in the middle of that project, either.

She pauses and looks up at me like she's noticing me for the first time. Our eyes lock, and the authoritative look she gives me makes me stand a little straighter. I don't think I've ever met someone so young yet so commanding.

She scans the room, looking at each of the other three girls in turn, having some sort of silent conversation. Finally, she speaks.

"We like crafts. But good crafts, like loom bracelets and fuse beads. Not baby crafts like coloring."

Noted. No baby crafts.

She can't be more than seven or eight, but I have to assume, given where they are and the reality of their lives, the last thing they want is to be babied.

"And we like games," the smallest girl in the corner pipes up. She's dressed in a hospital gown, but she's got a bright pink boa draped over her shoulders and heart-shaped sunglasses perched on her head.

"Do you have any games here we could play?"

"Of course we do!" she cheers, hopping to her feet and ambling over to a big storage locker. She wraps her tiny, pale fingers around the silver handle and opens the door to reveal a cabinet practically overflowing with board games and puzzles.

Wow. It's like being in the toy aisle of a big box store. They've got everything.

I scan the selection, racking my brain for memories of rules and objectives for the games I recognize.

My hunt doesn't last long. As soon as I see the box, I know.

"Anyone who wants to play a game, come over here!" I announce.

The smallest girl is still by my side, and another rushes over. A third stands slowly, then, with the help of the nurse, wheels her IV stand and oxygen cart over to join us.

Their leader is the lone holdout.

"You can join in at any time if you change your mind," I tell her. Shifting slightly, I survey Decker. As I expected, he hasn't taken his eyes off me since we arrived.

I give him a small smile, then turn back to the girls surrounding me.

"Come closer," I mock whisper. I eye the guys and cock a brow, making it clear they are not supposed to hear. Kendrick bites back a smirk. He has little sisters. He can probably guess how this is going to go.

"Make room." At the command, the circle widens a bit, and the leader joins us.

Everyone loves a secret.

I smile at her so she understands that she's welcome and wanted and that it's okay to be standoffish or even skeptical. Those are facts of life I know all too well.

Crouching low, I take each of the girls in, then smile up at the nurse who's also joined us.

"Here's my idea." I keep my voice low as I explain what we're going to play and who is going to play with us.

"The boys won't do that!" one of the little girls exclaims.

I can't help but grin.

"Oh yes they will," I singsong, turning to reach for the game box.

Princess Decker and Princess Kendrick are glaring at each other over the game board. Each man is locked in and determined to win. They're seated on opposite sides of the craft table, their massive frames comical in the kid-size chairs.

"Come on, Crusade," Ciara bemoans. "You *have* to get an earring."

"I know, I know," Decker mutters, glowering at the game board as he flicks the spinner.

Collectively, the girls hold their breath.

The air whooshes out audibly when the all-star quarterback comes up short.

"*Yes*!" Kendrick shouts, high-fiving Morgan and Sawyer with such enthusiasm the green clip-on earrings dangling from his ears sway.

The green team wins, and after another moment of celebration, I encourage the girls to get together and pose for a picture with their princess.

"Oh, good thinking!" Misty chirps, popping up from her perch in the corner.

I shoot her my surliest scowl I can muster. "These pictures aren't for the public. They're just for us."

She scoffs, indignant, but I turn back to the team and ignore her.

Ciara—the leader of the bunch—is explaining to Decker what he should have done differently when he landed on *Put One Back* a few turns ago.

He harrumphs, his attention fixed on K as Ciara chirps in his ear. Kendrick doesn't notice. He's too busy teaching the girls the victory dance he typically reserves for the endzone. I fight back a grin as he eagerly poses with them, still fully decked out in his green costume jewelry.

"That was an unexpected turn of events," the nurse comments, stepping up to adjust the settings of the one child's IV drip.

I smile as my chest inflates with a sense of pride.

"Do people come in like this often?" I ask.

She shakes her head. "Most of our visitors on this floor are the regular hospital volunteers. It's rare to have anyone under fifty interested in volunteering, though. It's a shame. All it takes is a background check and a commitment to a minimum of one shift a month."

Her words tumble around in my mind as Kendrick comes to stand beside me.

"Yo, Cap. Your crown's crooked," he teases.

Decker brings a hand to his head, then rolls his eyes.

Kendrick snickers. "Oh, that's right. You didn't win a crown," he chirps, twirling the piece of bejeweled plastic around his finger.

"Be nice," I warn, though I can't fight the smile splitting my face.

"You're a genius, you know that?" he asks, wrapping his arms around me from behind and dropping his chin to my shoulder. "Look how happy they all are."

They are happy. Every one of them is smiling and chattering. The scene makes my heart squeeze in my chest.

"You're so good with them, Mama." His praise is a whisper, the words meant only for me.

Beaming, I run my fingers over his hands and sink into his hold.

"I used to think I wanted to work with older populations, like I did with hospice," I tell him. "But maybe I want to do something with kids."

"You'd be great at that. You could go into social work. Or hospital administration?"

I nod, still spinning ideas around in my head.

With a featherlight kiss below my ear, Kendrick releases me. "You'll figure it out, Jojo. And we'll be here to support you every step of the way."

Chapter 28

Josephine

Tucking my hair behind my ears, I follow Kylian up the garden-stone path illuminated by solar powered lights. "Are you sure we shouldn't have brought something? Dessert? Or a bottle of wine?"

Kylian side-eyes me but doesn't slow. "How would we bring wine without knowing what's being served for dinner?"

Fair point.

"I just feel weird showing up empty-handed."

He reaches for my hand and interlaces our fingers.

"Now your hand's not empty," he declares.

I laugh, but his literal view of the world soothes the holes in my confidence.

"You've already met my parents, baby. They invited you here tonight, so I assume they like you just fine."

It's not the most reassuring sentiment, but I get where he's coming from. He's right. I've already met Mr. and Mrs. Walsh, and I say hi to them at football games when I see them.

Sometimes it's just a smile and a wave.

Other times we exchange pleasantries, or his mom catches me in a quick hug on the sideline.

But never has it been them welcoming me into their home for dinner.

I tug on my hand, the urge to free it and crack my knuckles taking over, but Kylian just grips it tighter.

"Why are you acting nervous?"

We stop on the stoop, and he immediately goes for the handle.

My stomach drops to my feet at the thought of crossing that threshold. "Wait."

"Jo."

I take a deep breath, willing my pulse to remain steady. "I just... I don't know how to do this. I mean, I've never done this before."

"Done *this*?" he questions, tilting his head to one side.

I shift my weight from one hip to the other and inspect the maroon door with the pretty fall wreath affixed to the front. Mrs. Walsh probably changes them with the seasons. I bet she does lots of little things like that to make her house feel like a home.

"I've never met my boyfriend's parents."

Kylian adjusts his glances and assesses me. "The last time I checked, you have more than one boyfriend."

"Exactly!" I throw my hands up. "What am I supposed to say about that to your parents?" A bead of sweat gathers at my nape and rolls down my spine in slow motion.

"Jo." Kylian's voice is stern, triggering my body to snap to attention. "I highly doubt my parents are going to ask about monogamy or the emotional and sexual components of our relationship."

He's right, but regardless, I feel thoroughly under-prepared for what tonight entails.

"And if they do?" I pull my shoulders back and stand a little straighter, tapping into a defiance I usually reserve for Decker. That alone is evidence of my anxiety level.

Dropping my hand, Kylian skims his knuckles up my back, tracing the path of that bead of sweat in reverse. He threads his fingers into the hair and tugs, then cuffs my neck and brings his lips to my ear.

"If my parents inquire about our relationship—which is extremely unlikely, based on the conversational topics they statistically stick to during meals, and because I already informed them that you are, in fact, my girlfriend—I will tell them the truth."

"Which is?" I whisper.

"That I love you. That I'm in love with you. That I share you with my best friends, and that we're all happier than we've ever been. Ever." With that, he releases my neck and brings that one hand to the base of my spine again.

I blow out a breath and will my heart rate to even out. His words are the reminder I need.

His hold, his touch, his love? It's always been a cocoon of safety against the torrential storm of intrusive thoughts and overwhelm.

Clearing the lump of emotion from my throat, I step in closer, prepared to tell him that I love him, too.

But before I can reply, the front door swings open.

"There you are!" Mrs. Walsh's smile is bright. "I thought I saw the car pull up. Come in, come in!" She ushers us inside, giving Kylian space as he removes his jacket and takes mine as well.

"I'm so happy you're here!" She clasps her hands at her chest and grins. She's practically bouncing on the balls of her feet, looking from Kylian to me, then back again.

She's holding back, I realize, as I watch her wring her hands and shift from hip to hip.

She's keeping her distance, honoring the space she knows her son requires, but it looks like she just might burst with excitement if someone doesn't hug her.

I take it upon myself to lean forward, arms wide.

"Oh, Jo," she murmurs, wrapping me up in the tightest, most sincere embrace. "I'm so happy you're here," she whispers, smoothing over my hair with one hand.

The tender, affectionate gesture incites a swell of emotion inside me. It's so unexpected and so genuine. I have to take a deep breath to keep the tears at bay.

"Mom."

Mrs. Walsh pulls back, keeping her hands on my shoulders as she holds me at arm's length. Her bright blue eyes are so similar to Kylian's. Except right now they're filled with unshed tears.

"Mom," Kylian repeats, clearly annoyed with her gushing.

"Oh, leave me alone," she counters with a lighthearted laugh. "It's not often someone actually wants to hug me," she quips.

Kylian takes the comment in stride. "Nicky hugs you every time he sees you."

"True," she admits. "How is he?" she asks, softer. "I invited him, but he said he hasn't been feeling well."

I nod, choosing my words carefully to avoid walking into the line of questioning Kylian assured me wouldn't come up tonight.

"He's had more bad days than good lately."

She studies me, her lips pressed together, and I hold my breath, trying in earnest to hide the truth of just how much it hurts me when Nicky's in pain.

Understanding washes over her features, and her smile softens slowly.

It's then I realize maybe I don't have anything to hide at all. At least not from her. She cares about Nicky, too. Loves him like a son. That love, though, doesn't mean she cares for her biological child any less.

Maybe the concept of loving them both isn't that outlandish after all.

"I'll send you home with food for him." She nods her head once, resolute. "Oh, where are my manners? Come in! Come in!" The smile is back. "Dinner will be ready in about half an hour."

She turns and heads toward the kitchen, and I follow, but Kylian catches me by the belt loop before I make it more than three steps.

"I love you," he murmurs into my ear, wrapping his arms around me from behind.

When we arrived, he didn't hug his mom. Based on their exchange, it seemed like she didn't expect him to.

Yet Kylian lavishes physical affection on me generously and frequently. He knows I love it, and he knows that the reassurance and reminders help keep my anxiety at bay.

I sink into his arms and smile, extra grateful for his embrace.

"How long has this been happening?" Kylian questions, examining the two devices in front of him as his dad peers over his shoulder.

"Well, uh, a couple of weeks? Right, honey?"

Mrs. Walsh looks up from the sink. "At least," she offers. Then, to me, she murmurs, "He doesn't like bothering Kylian to ask for help with these things."

"Fixed."

"What? How—"

"If it happens again, let me know immediately," Kylian states, standing from the table and handing the devices back to his dad.

"How long until dinner?" he asks his mom.

The table is set, and she keeps insisting she doesn't need help. The house smells amazing—savory and homey, like she's been cooking all day. I've already decided Kylian and I will do the dishes. It's the least we can do.

"Another fifteen or twenty minutes. Why?"

"I want to show Jo something upstairs. We'll be down in twenty."

He grabs my hand and marches out of the kitchen, around the corner, and up the stairs.

He doesn't look back and he doesn't slow until we reach the end of the hallway. Even then, he only pauses to turn the handle, push through a door, pull me into the room. Then he closes and locks that door behind us.

"What's gotten into you?" I laugh, breathless from scurrying up the stairs.

In answer, he pins me against the door and kisses me.

Hard. Fast. Deep.

It's an urgent kiss—one meant to banish doubt and soothe anxiety. One I so deeply appreciate. One I'm happy to return in earnest.

Gripping my waist, he pulls me closer, teasing my mouth with his tongue and nipping at my bottom lip.

He shuffles backward, and I follow him willingly.

I'll follow him anywhere. I'll follow him always.

When he stops, he bends at the knees and crashes into a seated position, taking me with him, his hands on my ass, grinding my hips against his.

"Is this what you wanted to show me?" I tease, shifting in his lap as he grazes both hands up my back under my sweater.

Without answering, he unfastens my bra, then leans back on his elbows.

"Did I say I wanted to show you something?" he asks. His gaze is hot, intense, and predatory, but there's a hint of mischief in his tone. More and more, that humor appears, and every time, I want to stop and savor it. "I meant I needed you to show me something."

My heart rate spikes, but now is not the time or the place.

"Kylian," I hedge.

"Jo."

He flips me until I'm flat on my back on a buoyant surface, practically floating.

"What is this?" I crane my neck and take in our surroundings.

"This is my childhood bedroom."

My stomach tumbles at the notion of being in this space. Predictably, every item in the room is classic Kylian. The walls are painted a navy so deep it's almost black. One is covered in schematics and diagrams of electronics. A small computer is set up at a clean desk. The double bed is pushed against the opposite wall.

The entire space smells like him: citrus and eucalyptus, with maybe a hint of spice that makes me think of the body spray teenage boys are so fond of.

The ceiling is painted a soothing Caribbean blue: The color of the sky. The color of his eyes.

But the most remarkable feature is whatever the hell is below me that makes me feel weightless, like I'm floating, or maybe flying.

"I can see we're in your room. But what am I laying on?" Kylian is looming above me, his thumb tracing his lower lip as he surveys me.

"It's a zero-gravity beanbag that I modified to my liking."

The hunger in his expression is so visceral I can't help but play along.

"This is to your liking?" I give him a coy smile as I slip my bra off one arm, then the other, without taking off my shirt.

"Or is this the modification you had in mind?" I peel my shirt off and gently set it on the floor so it won't wrinkle before dinner.

"Fuck, baby," he groans, bringing a fist to his mouth. "My sixteen-year-old self would have busted a nut if he knew the girl of his dreams would one day be spread out on the beanbag chair in his bedroom."

I squirm, giggling each time I reposition and it molds to me. It's the strangest sensation—or lack of sensation, I guess.

"Girl of your dreams, huh?" I run my knuckles over my breasts, mewling when my nipples pebble on contact.

Kylian sinks to his knees, which causes the beanbag to ripple like an ocean wave. He grips the hem of my leggings, fucking smoldering as he fixates on me. If the man knew he could smolder, he'd scoff, I'm sure, but damn, is it hot. "Girl of my dreams. Woman of my every desire. Beat of my fucking heart."

He pulls off my pants with a flourish, giving me no time at all to protest. Making out on the beanbag chair sans shirt is one thing, but lying completely naked in the middle of his bedroom with his parents one floor below us is another.

"*Kylian*," I hiss. "We're here for dinner."

"We are. I'll take my appetizer now."

I stifle a laugh as he kisses one of my bare hips. A shudder rolls through me when he runs his tongue along my stomach and kisses the other.

I tweak my nipples again and welcome the arousal warming my core, no longer fighting him.

Kylian caresses my inner thighs. "That's a good girl." His praise encourages me to relax into his touch.

Stretching out, I savor the weightless support of the chair and the feel of his hands and his mouth on my body.

He kisses lower, lower, and lower still, but just as he makes it to the place I want him most, he freezes.

A rush of air leaves me, and I sag against the soft surface below me.

"I want to try something new. Trust me?"

A smile spreads across my face unbidden. "Always."

"Roll to your side."

He supports my hip as I follow his instruction, his palm warm and comforting.

"Now, scissor out your legs—just like that, perfect." He guides my body until I'm positioned the way he wants me.

I shiver with anticipation, which he notices, of course.

"Cold?" he asks. Before I can answer, he adds, "You won't be for long." With a lift of both brows, he removes his glasses and lines his mouth up with my pussy.

The first lick is exquisite: warm and hard with the flat of his tongue, exploratory and curious when he teases my hole with the tip.

This activity is by no means unfamiliar. Kylian swears he could eat me out every day, and at this point, he does.

But this angle is new entirely.

"Oh." I preen, arching my back as he licks. My body is perpendicular to the position I'm usually in when he goes down on me, so he's licking me from one side to the other.

He presses his tongue against my clit again, and it's not just my clit that sparks with arousal. Warmth spreads through my insides, and pleasure blossoms deep in my belly as my entire lower half tingles.

He rubs up and down, which, in this position, is more of a side-to-side motion, alternating between that and sucking my lips into his mouth.

When he spears me with his tongue, he goes deeper than he's ever gone during oral before.

I moan. "Fuck. How are you doing that?" With a gasp, I slap a hand to my mouth, remembering his parents are close by.

"You like it?" He fucks me again, this time holding his tongue deep inside and swirling it so it tickles against my inner walls.

"I love it," I pant. I'm so turned on my arousal is dripping down my thighs. My pussy flutters and tingles, the surest signs of an orgasm already developing.

"I've been researching new ways to get you off. This is the Kivin method."

Of course it's a method he researched and studied. Only Kylian.

"Fuck. Kylian. I'm already close."

I shift my hips, desperate and needy. I don't want him to stop lapping at my clit, but I want his tongue inside me, too.

He doesn't make me choose. Like he can read my mind, he fucks me with his tongue while teasing around my pulsing bundle of nerves. He's rubbing everywhere but my actual clit, building me higher and higher.

As if he's detonating a bomb, he presses his thumb to the spot. My orgasm crescendos, and I lose myself to a silent scream.

Hungrily, he laps at me as I gush with each wave of pleasure. My insides are on fire, my chest and cheeks burning with heat.

I squeeze my eyes shut as I ride out the cresting ecstasy. Little bursts of light flash behind my lids as my body unravels. The orgasm consumes me, from my neck to my toes. I continue to soar. The weightlessness of the antigravity chair makes it feel like I'm suspended in air.

With nothing to brace against, my body gushes again, and I moan softly before finding my voice. "Fuck. Okay, okay!" Sawing sharp breaths in and out, I search for Kylian. When I find him, I tug on the ends of his hair, silently begging for a reprieve.

Sitting back on his haunches, he eyes me salaciously, his mouth and chin glistening with my release. Even his shirt is damp around the collar.

"Oh shit," I murmur as I try to sit up.

Try being the operative word.

All the blood must have rushed to my pussy, because I'm lightheaded and dizzy. I search for purchase so I can attempt to rise up again, but as I slap the surface below me, my hand lands in something wet.

"*Kylian! I soaked your beanbag.*" Fuck. The shock of the sensation, though, is quickly replaced by satisfaction. Maybe it's strange, but I'm impressed by the little puddle pooling between my thighs.

I fight against gravity—antigravity?—to sit up into a straddle and blot at the wet spot.

"I'm sorry." My face flames, this time from embarrassment. Holy hell, I made a mess. And quickly, too. Ten out of ten stars for the Kivin method.

"Stop." Kylian grasps my hands, then he dips his head between my thighs and inhales deeply.

"Fuck. This is going to smell like you from now on, baby."

He hauls himself to his feet and looks down at me with a smile full of love and affection.

Never taking his eyes off me, he picks up his glasses and settles them on the bridge of his nose. "You're perfect." His words are a whisper clouded with an unusual level of emotion. "So fucking perfect, baby."

He runs a thumb along my jawline in the softest caress. "I always want to remember what you look like right now, laid out and fully satisfied. Naked. Still dripping on my beanbag chair. What I wouldn't give to have a picture of this."

My heart stutters in my chest in a wholly unexpected way at the suggestion. "So take one."

His spine straightens and his eyes go wide. Above me, he's frozen. Stunned.

Lowering onto the buoyant cushion once more, I peer up through hooded lashes, confident and eager for what I'm about to request.

"Take my picture, Kylian."

Chapter 29

Kylian

My mind kicks into overdrive, the urge to protect her igniting every nerve in my body.

"Take my picture, Kylian." Her voice is so calm. As if that isn't the most vulnerable thing she could ever ask me to do.

My answer is swift and solemn.

"Jo. No."

"Kylian. *Yes.*" She pushes up on her elbows, making her breasts press together.

She's a fucking dream, laid out in front of me. Her hair's a mess, her body relaxed and soft. Her creamy pale skin is still pink in all the erogenous zones because of her orgasm. It's a vision I want to remember forever. But not so badly I'll risk hurting her.

"Take my picture," she repeats, as if saying it multiple times will persuade me. "Please."

I inhale, then let the breath out slowly, knowing it won't do much to steady the hammering of my heart, but trying anyway.

I can't take her picture. I would never forgive myself.

This is what I've been working to eradicate from her life. I've vowed to myself that I would remove every invasion of privacy of her stripped-down, naked body from the Internet. Taking a new picture of her like this would transgress those efforts.

As if she can read my spiraling thoughts, she reaches out. "Hey." Her expression is soft. Her words are soothing.

I don't deserve the solace she provides. Not after such a careless suggestion.

With a shudder, I sink to my knees. Remorse and regret war for dominance. "I'm sorry I said that. I shouldn't have even brought it up."

I don't often think without speaking anymore. It took years of practice, but I've mastered the ability to slow down and think through the implications of my words before I voice them, especially if they have the potential to hurt someone.

She pulls me closer and kisses my knuckles. "This doesn't scare me, Kylian." She tilts her head and dons a small smile. How can she smile about this? "There's a big difference between having pictures taken of my unconscious body as it's being violated and posing for a nude to share with a person I love.

"I wouldn't have offered if I didn't want it. And I do, Kylian. I want it." She squeezes my hand. "Take my picture, please. Let me give this to you freely and willingly, from a place of love. I know you'll keep it safe. Just like I know you'll always keep me safe."

"Always." I smash my mouth against hers in an urgent kiss.

Fuck. We're doing this.

"You're sure?" I whisper against her lips.

By the time I've heaved myself to standing again, she's already posed her body for me, tits pressed together, legs spread wide.

"Take my picture, Daddy."

Taking her at her word, I pull out my phone and assess my girl on the screen. Once I have the shot lined up, I look over the edge of the device and lock eyes with her.

She gives me the coyest smile and the slightest nod.

I press the shutter button with my thumb.

It's done.

"You're so fucking pretty," I muse, pulling up the image and handing it to her for approval.

She sits up and surveys the screen. Her cheeks flush, but the small smile remains.

"Still okay?" I hedge. "I can delete it. Or you can delete it, if—"

"More than okay," she insists as she stands. "And now we've both taken a step to rewrite our pasts and make our sixteen-year-old selves proud."

She kisses me, hands me my phone, and collects her clothing.

Not a minute too soon, either.

"Kylian! Jo! Dinner is ready!"

I help her into her shirt and untangle her leggings. All the while, she giggles and peppers me with kisses.

"You're perfect," I tell her again as she brushes her hands over her pants. "Let's go."

Chapter 30

Josephine

"Why are we so old?" I bemoan, latching my laptop closed and resting my head in my hands.

"Who are you calling old, sister?"

I peek up at Hunter. She's sucking down what has to be her third or fourth matcha tea latte of the afternoon, pencil stuck in her hair to keep the messy bun in place, surrounded by open books and a wheezing laptop.

She works harder than anyone I know.

"I hate feeling behind. The guys all registered two weeks ago. I don't think Kylian or Decker even have in-person classes in the spring."

Hunter snorts. "Of course they don't."

I blow out a breath. "I feel sort of lost looking at all these options. I like college, but I still have no freaking idea what I want to be when I grow up."

Hunter gnaws on the end of a pen and scrutinizes me over her glasses. They're only blue-light blockers, but she swears the secret to combatting fine lines and wrinkles is prevention.

Another tick in the *why are we so old?* department.

"If money wasn't an object, what would your dream job entail?"

With a sigh, I drop my elbows onto the table and take a moment to truly think about the question.

I liked working in hospice. Loved it, actually. It was heavy work, and losing clients I'd developed relationships with was difficult, but the work itself—taking care of people, making them feel seen and respected when the world offers so little care to the elderly—was fulfilling.

Then there are the little girls from the hospital. Thoughts of them have been dancing around my mind for days. I'm not sure I'm cut out for the medical side of patient care, but I could see myself working in a hospital setting, developing programs and activities that allow kids to be kids.

And then there's my quietest fantasy. One I didn't even know existed until Nicky breathed life into it.

I want to be a mom. I want to raise a family.

Years from now, when Kendrick and Decker are playing professional football—when Kylian, Locke and I feel content with our education and careers—I could see myself taking care of my people. My boys. Our kids.

Hunter's cackle pulls me out of my daydream.

"What?" I ask, shaking my head slightly to clear it.

"It looked like you were having an out-of-body experience there for a minute, babe."

With a light huff, I shrug.

I wouldn't admit this to anyone—not even Hunter—but dreaming is new for me. For most of my life, I operated in survival mode, just trying to get by as a kid, then trying to get out as a teenager.

Considering my future and all that's now possible is novel and overwhelming, but in the most wonderful way. It's easy to get lost in my head when I allow myself to dream. But it's a good kind of lost. It's limitless. Hopeful. Powerful.

"I want to take care of people." I declare. It's true. Every version of my dreams for the future involves helping others in some capacity.

"How about social work? Or teaching?"

"Maybe," I hedge. Both are admirable, but I'm not sure either is quite right for me.

With a waggle of her brows, Hunter upturns her palms and sweeps them across the mess in front of her. "You could always follow in my footsteps and go into law."

I snicker. "I said I want to take care of people, Hunter. Not ruin their lives."

"Hey! I fully intend to take care of people." She lifts a hand to her chest, feigning outrage.

"For a billable rate of three hundred dollars an hour."

"Bible."

A gasp slips from my mouth and my eyes go wide. "Isn't that Greedy's thing?"

"Oh God." She drops her head into her hands. "I can't escape him. He's everywhere. He's even infiltrating my speech patterns."

"Hey, as long as that's all he's infiltrating..."

She's still got her face buried in her hands, but I swear her cheeks flush at that comment.

Giving her the space she so obviously needs from that scrutiny, I hold back another jab and check the time.

"We should get going," I murmur. Stacking my books, I push my chair back and stand. "The guys want to be home by dinnertime so Decker doesn't have to face the camera crew alone for too long."

With a nod, Hunter goes about organizing and packing up her copious notes and books.

She offered to hang out with me in the library tonight since Kylian had a meeting and the guys had practice. Decker is the only one required to spend a certain amount of time at the house and on camera each day. The rest of us have made a concerted effort to stay away from the isle as much as possible, so this worked out well.

Hunter heaves her backpack over her shoulders, then loops her arm through mine. "Let's get you home, Josephine Meyer."

We spot the guys the moment we pull into the marina parking lot. Kendrick and Locke are leaning against the front of K's Suburban, heads bowed low in conversation. Kylian stands tall between Decker's G Wagon and my Civic, his attention fixed on Hunter's headlights as we approach.

Always watching. Always waiting.

He's safety and security, passion and care, packaged up in a brilliant, beautiful man.

I exit Hunter's car, call a quick bye over my shoulder, and head straight for my target.

"Hi, baby." He catches me by the belt loops and pulls me flush against his body. Sliding one hand up my spine to grip the back of my neck, he kisses me. Then, instead of backing away after a moment like I expect, he deepens the connection, sucking on my bottom lip and groaning into my mouth like he can't get enough. "How was your day?" he asks when he finally pulls back.

I inhale deeply, lightheaded from the intensity of his greeting.

"It was good," I finally answer, snuggling into his chest. "Missed you."

He tightens his hold on me, the move settling the loose threads of worry that have pulled me in different directions all week.

Savoring his touch, I inhale his citrus and eucalyptus scent. I could stand in his arms for hours. I love that he leans into the contact nowadays—more often than not, I have to pull away first.

Neither of us breaks the hold for a while. Tonight, we're in no rush.

Our routine has been more or less the same all week. We take our time getting back to the isle, treasuring the quiet, the privacy, the sanctity of darkness and lack of cameras in the marina parking lot.

My heart rate picks up when one of my other guys approaches from behind. I don't have to see him to sense his presence, and I don't bother to even unwind my arms from around Kylian's waist until big hands grip my hips from behind.

"My turn," Kendrick purrs, pulling me against him so my ass lines up with his crotch.

"Hi, Mama." He sweeps my hair to one side, exposing my neck so he can kiss and suck and greet me the way only he can.

I'm squirming within seconds.

"K," I whine. Everything this man does turns me on.

Though we all know now is not the time.

He sighs, acknowledging my concern, but then he kisses me a dozen more times along the neck. The man doesn't let up until I'm lost to a fit of giggles.

Goose bumps erupt along the right side of my body, leaving me tingling.

"Not fair," I cry, wrenching around so I can counterattack.

He anticipates the move, though, and scoops me up, hitching me over his shoulder.

"Hey now." With a chuckle, he spins until I'm laughing so hard I can barely breathe.

"Kendrick!"

I pound on his back, but it's pointless. I'm like a toddler beating her fists into a solid brick wall.

I wiggle and squirm, but it only makes him clamp down harder on the back of my thighs. That is, until I peek up and see Locke watching me.

He's still settled against the front bumper of K's Suburban. It takes a moment of closer inspection to realize he's not just leaned against the hood but slumped.

"Put me down," I quietly command.

Without argument, Kendrick places me on my feet, then follows my gaze.

"He had a rough day."

I tilt my head and focus on K again, imploring him to go on.

"Let him tell you," he encourages. "He needs you tonight." Cupping my jaw with one hand, he leans in close and murmurs "love you" below my ear, inspiring one last round of shivers.

I make my way over to Nicky, my heart sinking at his defeated posture.

"Can I hug you?"

A sad smile blossoms on his face. "Always."

Taking care to be gentle, I loop my arms around his waist. He flinches from the slight touch, pulling in a sharp breath as his abs contract.

"I'm fine," he mutters, hauling me in closer and squeezing me tight.

I relax against him, savoring the rise and fall of his chest and timing my breathing to match his.

We're in no rush, I remind myself. If this moment is what he needs, then I want to give it to him.

We hold each other as seconds tick into minutes. His posture gives him away—he's bone-tired and more than ready for bed. Yet he doesn't let go. He doesn't rush us back to the house so he can rest.

We should go. We all know it. Yet we hang back. A sense of foreboding washes over me each time we get on the boat and head to the isle. Based on the way the boys hesitate at the marina, I think they feel it, too.

Right here. Right now. This is the only sanctuary we're guaranteed. Anything we want to do or say has to happen in this parking lot.

"How was practice?" I hedge.

Thick lashes fan against his cheeks as he closes his eyes and shakes his head.

"Nicky..."

"I'm out this week."

It takes a few seconds for his words to register.

"You talked to your coaches about sitting out?"

He barks a sad, defeated laugh and releases his hold on me to bury his face in his hands. "Fuck. I wish."

The frustration rolling off him is palpable. When I pull him back in, his hands clench into fists at my back. An instant later, though, he hisses in pain and drops them to his sides.

"I'm here," I remind him, nuzzling into his chest. "Talk to me."

His responding sniff snags my attention. I glance up in time to see a tear start its lonely trek down his face.

Pushing up on tiptoes, I kiss it away.

It takes several more heartbeats, but finally, he speaks. "Couldn't make it through practice." He sniffs again. "Couldn't even set up on the line of scrimmage. Coach is worried I'll trigger too many false starts. Both knees... the knuckles on my right hand... Fuck. Everything hurts, Joey."

He hunches forward, resting his forehead on my shoulder, and shudders.

Gingerly, I run my hands up and down his back. "I'm so sorry you're in pain," I murmur, hoping to give him a modicum of respite from his misery. "But I'm glad you don't have to stress about the game this weekend."

With a huff, he snaps up. "I wanted the choice, though. I know it's the right call... but I wanted it to be my fucking choice."

My heart crumples for him. That's a sentiment I understand completely.

Glancing over my shoulder, I find Kylian and Kendrick focused on us. They've maintained their distance, though, respecting that this is the only moment of authenticity we'll be granted all night.

To that end, I hold Nicky tighter, mourning the lack of control that comes with his RA right along with him. There's nothing to say. There's nothing I can do. So I hold him, and I hope that, in my arms, he knows he's not alone in this.

After another minute, a shiver ripples through me. I try to stop it, to hide it so the moment doesn't have to end, but I'm unsuccessful.

"You're cold," Locke says, rubbing his hands up and down my arms. "We're all tired. Let's go home."

I plant my feet and shake my head against his chest. "I'll stand out here with you all night if you want."

He takes me in and holds my gaze, then kisses me on the forehead. "I know you would. And knowing you love me that much is enough. Let's go."

Chapter 31

Josephine

Kendrick stands at the helm, charting a direct course over the lake as we head toward the isle.

It's a cooler evening. The sky is filled with clouds that cast full coverage over the half moon as they move. Each time they block out its light, the darkness that veils us is potent, eerie. Surely we've been out on similar nights, but tonight, my thoughts linger on the black sky and lack of stars.

Once we boarded, I sat on one of the speedboat's cushioned benches and convinced Nicky to lie down with his head in my lap.

Kylian is seated across from us, the bright blue and white light from his phone reflected in his square lenses.

As I mindlessly play with Nicky's hair, my stomach gurgles. Loud enough, apparently, for Kylian to hear from his side of the boat, by the way his head snaps up at the sound.

"You hungry, Hot Girl?" Locke asks, grinning up at me with the first genuine smile he's offered all night. His eyes hold a warmth and affection that not even debilitating pain can mask. The glow of the moon peeking out from the clouds once more shines on his eyebrow piercing.

I can't resist stroking my fingers over it and massaging his temple. "Always," I finally answer, looking up to gauge how far we are from home.

We're halfway across the lake when my stomach growls again.

Nicky chuckles, his head bouncing against my thighs with his laughter. "I'm sure Cap has plenty of food waiting for us."

We've kept Mrs. Lansbury away from the house as much as possible this week. The camera crew is in her way more often than not, flustering her with their presence.

Decker offered to cook tonight since he would be home first, but he didn't mention what he was making.

"I hope it's pasta. I could really go for pasta and meatballs tonight."

Nicky squints, holding back a snicker. "There's a ball joke in there somewhere, but I'm honestly too tired to make it."

"Ha. Ha." I would play punch him if he wasn't in so much pain. Instead, I press my lips into a straight line and hit him with my most unamused stare.

"Who the hell is that?" Kylian demands, standing.

He's fixated on something off in the distance, in the direction of the marina.

"Camera crew, maybe?" Kendrick suggests, glancing over his shoulder.

I crane my neck to look for myself. I don't want to jostle Nicky, so I stay seated. From here, all I can make out is a small yellow light glowing on the water. It's quite a way off, but it appears to be increasing in size.

Shrugging, I drop my attention back to Nicky and stroke his hair again. "Looks like another boat or PWC."

Kylian widens his stance and studies his phone. "No one new is scheduled to arrive until seven tomorrow morning."

The feature coverage is meticulously scheduled, so as not to overcrowd the dock or interfere when we are coming and going for class and other commitments.

"Those fuckers are past the buoys now."

Nicky sits up at that.

"The fuck?"

Kendrick alternates between watching the water ahead and peeking over his shoulder while the rest of us are focused on the singular source of light. Which, now that I'm paying attention, does seem to be traveling toward us at a fast clip.

A hushed silence blankets the group as we watch the light get closer at an alarming rate.

It's not until my chest starts to burn that I realize I'm holding my breath.

As I exhale, two things happen: the other vessel's engine revs, as if it's accelerating, and Kendrick lets out a string of curses.

"Get a life jacket on her. Now."

Kylian is by my side before I can blink, shoving one arm into a bright orange vest that he procured from under the seats. On my other side, Nicky does the same.

"What's wrong?" I whisper, popping to stand between the guys.

No one answers.

"What's happening?" I demand. The words come out in a shrill panic. I look to the light, then to Kendrick, then to the light again.

"Sit down," K barks when I meet his gaze.

I'm tugged backward, and when my calves hit the seat, I stumble onto my ass.

"Hold on!" he calls again.

We accelerate. The weightless sensation the movement causes makes my stomach turn as we fly over the choppy water and go momentarily airborne.

"What's—Who—What..."

"Joey. Hey. Hey. Look at me. You're okay."

Locke's words are soft, soothing, but his body language betrays the calm he's trying to affect. He's sitting up on the edge of our shared seat, wearing an expression of sheer torment as he looks from me to the pursuer. The longer I look, the more acute the panic swirling inside me becomes.

"God dammit, motherfuckers," Kendrick curses, his voice barely audible over the engine. He's focused on the lake, on the isle that seems too far away.

Kylian's still standing in the middle of the boat, his stance wide to maintain his balance, rapidly typing on his phone.

"Hey," Locke calls out to the others. "Should I strap her?"

Kendrick glances our way, but only for a heartbeat. We're going too fast, and his attention needs to remain on the water ahead of us. When he looks at us again, I see the question nagging at him—the tightness of his jaw, the grit of his teeth.

Kylian lifts his head and drops his phone to his side, looking from me, to Locke, to Kendrick, then behind the boat toward our pursuer once again.

He has an entire conversation with K in the span of three seconds.

And yet neither says a damn word.

"Yes or no? Should we buckle up?"

My gaze volleys between the boys.

The vessel coming after us is close enough that the constant hum of the engine is audible.

Finally, it's Kylian who shakes his head.

Just once. Decidedly.

"She can swim."

My heart plummets. "Wait—*what*?"

He drops to his knees in front of me. "Jo," he says, planting a warm hand on my knee. "Look at me."

Though my breaths are coming faster and my chest feels tight, I do as he says.

"If I tell you to jump, you jump."

"No. No, no, no, no, no." The taste of tears I didn't know I was shedding surprises me when I open my mouth to argue. They're salty and familiar, merciless and hopeless.

"Baby," Kylian soothes. "We're okay. You'll be okay. There's only one boat following us. I checked the radar to be sure. If they don't let up, and I tell you to jump—"

"*No.*"

Kylian lurches forward, catching himself on my knees.

A bolt of panic stabs at my chest. Certain we must have hit something, I turn to Kendrick—

"Brace yourselves," he yells, gripping the steering wheel as he looks over his shoulder, his face etched in a mix of fury and fear.

Kylian falls right on his ass this time.

I slide off the seat after him.

Beside me, Nicky grunts in pain.

Tipping my head back, I blink up at the moon, stunned by its brightness as the cloud that has covered it for the last few minutes reveals its gleam.

Stunned and horrified.

Because our boat has been hit.

Chapter 32

Kylian

The floor of the boat vibrates as Kendrick cuts across the water.

Though the twin inboard one-thousand-horsepower engines can reach one hundred forty miles per hour, K won't push it that hard. He won't take a risk that great.

Not with her on board.

Especially since she refuses to jump off the damn boat.

My phone vibrates in my pocket.

As if he can sense our distress. As if he can feel the wrongness of our situation.

"Switch with me," I scream at Locke over the wind.

He nods, and we move as a unit. I take his place beside Jo, wrapping my arm around her shoulders. He slinks to my previous position on the floor and crouches low, holding her legs to brace her for impact as Kendrick punches it harder.

I turn off the fear and run the numbers, only pulled out of the calculations when my phone buzzes in my hand again.

This time, I accept the call. "Give me ten seconds." He'll have to wait.

I take eight seconds to compute the calculations—the direction of the wind, the estimated distance to the dock, and the exact speed required to get the nose of the boat on land without smashing it to smithereens.

One and a half seconds to double-check the math.

Half a second to yell instructions to Kendrick.

"Seventy-eight miles per hour until the last buoy, then shut it down and coast. Bring it in between the sandy alcove and the rocks to the right of the dock."

When my ten seconds are up, I greet him properly.

"Hey, Cap."

"I see you. I fucking heard you. What the fuck is going on, Kyl?"

"We're being pursued across the lake at high speeds. They've rammed us twice, but K was able to put some space between us. We should be home in fifty seconds or so."

There's no "or so" about it if Kendrick follows my directions.

My calculations are precise. Thank fuck, too, because there's no margin for error.

"Fuck. *Fuck.*"

On the other end of the line, there's a loud crash. The call remains connected, so he didn't throw his phone.

Breathing heavily, he curses again. "You're all together?" he grits out.

"Yes." Before he can inquire, I elaborate. "Jo's got a life jacket on. She's sitting beside me. Locke is bracing her and keeping her steady."

"Seat belt?"

"No."

"Good. She can swim."

My thoughts exactly.

"Put her on." His voice is more hollow than I've ever heard it. Desperate.

I pause, considering.

We're in the midst of a crisis. This could all end disastrously if the pursuer feels extra bold or Kendrick misses the soft, marshy target we're aiming for.

Chatting on the phone helps no one.

In fact, it could make things worse.

There's no comfort she can offer him or that he could lend to her. I don't grasp why he thinks—

"Kylian."

Right.

Sighing, I lean over and yell into her ear. "It's Decker. He wants to talk to you."

Chapter 33

Decker

"Cap?"

Thank fuck.

My heart is pounding so hard there's a good chance it'll beat right out of my chest, but I push the terror away and tamp it down. For her. I have to keep a level head for her.

"Siren. You're okay. You're okay."

It's a question and a statement and a mantra I'm determined to manifest into reality.

"I'm scared," she whimpers.

I'm fucking scared, too.

"You're safe," I assure her.

It's a hollow offering, but it's all I have to give right now.

"Decker, if something happens, and—"

"Stop," I snarl. "I can fucking see you, Josephine. I'm standing outside. I can see the boat. I can see you on the phone. You're heading right to me. You're coming home." I swallow over the lump in my throat, willing my voice not to waver. "You'll be in my arms in a few minutes. Don't you dare think a single thought to the contrary."

I take the stairs from the upper deck two at a time and pause halfway down so I can survey the status of the speedboat carrying my family and the motherfucker on the modified WaveRunner chasing after them.

At least there's only one of them.

But the parallels are astounding and abhorrent. The nightmare of what my mom endured, the visions of what it must have looked like, how she must have felt.

I'm standing on the isle, helpless, witnessing it firsthand.

This time, it's not just one person I love. It's all of them. The friends who've stood by my side no matter what. The family we were forming as we fought for a future.

I close my eyes and inhale four counts.

"Decker?"

I hold the breath in until it burns through every bronchiole and my body screams at me to exhale.

"Yes, Siren?"

"I love you."

My eyes fly open.

"I just want you to know, in case—"

The line goes silent at the same second I hear the boat accelerate.

Straining to see in the dark, I survey the water. They're close now. Close enough they could swim if they had to. If we were sure the maniac chasing them wouldn't pursue them in open water…

I launch down the steps two at a time and take off at a sprint for the dock.

I'm halfway there before I realize that Kendrick's not aiming for the dock. He's coming in for a hard landing.

Halting to a stop in the middle of the yard, I keep my eyes on them. I watch it happen in slow motion.

I watch it happen thirty yards from where I stand.

Powerless. Useless.

I can't help them. No amount of control or effort I assert will make an iota of difference.

The bottom of the boat crunches and scrapes against rock, the sound like nails on a chalkboard, but the landing is good. The speed and angle are just right.

Kylian.

The sound of the personal watercraft catches my attention. It whips around, and the driver throws himself to one side, causing the vessel to spray a violent stream of water that makes it impossible to see the make or model.

I laugh, cold and emotionless, because it doesn't fucking matter.

Nothing does.

If I can't protect them... if I can't keep her safe...

I take off toward the boat, desperate for confirmation that my people are as okay as they can be, given the situation.

Kylian's got his back to me. I can't see Nicky or Josephine. Kendrick, though, is at the helm. He meets my gaze and nods.

"Thank fuck," I choke out on a sob.

Chapter 34

Kendrick

I don't realize I'm still gripping the steering wheel with both hands until she's at my side, peeling my fingers from it.

Wordlessly, she places my hands on her hips, then smooths over my jaw with her fingertips. Her pale blue eyes study me, inspect me, relieved but flooded with an overwhelming sense of dread.

There's so much I want to say: Truths I want to share. Parts of my soul I'll readily bare. Words I want her to hear every day.

Only moments ago, we were inches away from losing our shot at forever.

She brushes her hands over my neck, then holds me tight.

We're both still too stunned to speak.

But I make sure she knows. I make sure she fucking feels it.

Gripping the back of her neck, I tilt her mouth to mine and kiss her hard. Claiming her. Forcing my tongue between her lips and caressing until she sighs.

She opens for me—my beautiful, responsive Jojo—and then she matches my intensity, as if sensing this is what we both need.

To feel alive. To restore our connection.

To take the hurt and the pain, the fear and terror of the last few minutes, and transform it into something good.

Something real fucking good.

I don't back off, don't even give her a chance to catch her breath as I kiss her harder, devouring her. I'll swap out the fear for lust. Until every nerve in her body is on fire. She'll feel me everywhere, and I'll make this nightmare feel like nothing more than a bad dream.

A throat clears behind me. I ignore it. The sound comes again. Then again. Persistent motherfucker. Finally, I pull back.

But not before I tell her my truth.

"I love you. I'll do whatever it takes to make sure you feel that. Always."

It may not always be easy. I can't promise her that.

I don't even feel confident enough to swear I'll always be able to keep her safe.

But showing up, staying true, loving hard?

That I can do.

And it's exactly what I intend to do for the rest of our lives.

Chapter 35

Josephine

A strange calm has settled over me. I'm barely shaking as Kendrick helps me off the boat.

The ground is soggy beneath my feet, making it hard to get traction. Eventually, we find more solid ground, though we have to dodge sharp rocks and stay mindful of the uneven earth.

Finally, we reach the more familiar pebbled beach.

Decker closes the distance. In a heartbeat, he's in front of me.

I'm silent as I collapse into his arms.

With one hand at the back of my head and the other at my waist, he maneuvers me this way and that. First to look me over, then to hold me tight against his chest.

Like he never wants to let me go.

His heart hammers against his ribcage, his breathing erratic. I smooth my fingertips over his pec.

"Decker, I—"

"One minute, Josephine. Give me one fucking minute. Let me hold you and try to convince myself you're safe."

I nod and swallow past the lump in my throat.

Resting my cheek against his shirt, I open my eyes. When I do, all I see is the mangled boat.

We were on that. We were chased. We almost—

"The fuck, Cap? At least get her inside. What is fucking wrong with you?"

Nicky's words are frantic, shouted from twenty feet away, but a direct shot at Decker that I feel into the depth of my soul.

Kylian and Kendrick give him a wide berth, the three of them standing on the soggy earth still.

"How many times are we going to go through this? Hold her through the panic? Panic *we* caused."

Nicky's hands are in his hair, tugging on the ends.

Decker grunts like he's been physically hit.

"This life... this so-called family... it's not fair to her. It's never *fucking fair*."

My heart aches at the pain so blatant in his every move and every word. I yearn to get closer, to comfort my spiraling, broken boy.

I pull away from Decker, desperate to get to him. To assure him I'm okay.

Instead of releasing me, Decker tightens his grip and tucks me under his arm.

"He's in shock," he growls under his breath. He surveys me, looking down his nose in the way he does. His onyx eyes are darker than normal, if that's possible. So dark they match the cloud-covered sky. "So are you."

His words don't register. I can't focus on anything but Nicky. He's unraveling. He needs me to hold him up.

I want to go to him, but...

I don't want to leave Decker's side, either.

A shiver racks through my body.

Then it doesn't give up.

"Siren."

Again, I hear him, but I don't know what he needs or what he wants me to do.

"She's shaking. Let's get inside. Then we can regroup."

My shoes and socks are soaked. The cold registers, and like a shock of electricity, it travels through me, up my legs, then down my arms, inspiring goose bumps all over my body.

Decker leads the charge over the uneven terrain toward the house, keeping me locked to his side. At the bottom stairs, we stop and wait for the other guys. Once we're gathered, we move as a unit.

"Motherfuckers," Kendrick mutters behind me.

I lift my head on the next step.

On the deck above us, waiting, watching, leaning against the railing like this is their home, not ours, are three crew members with two cameras pointed at us.

"Block her," Decker barks out.

Sticking close, we increase our pace.

"Switch with him," Decker orders.

Who he's speaking to and why are lost on me.

But then the boys move with military precision, and Kendrick replaces Nicky on my right, putting himself between the cameras and me while also ensuring Nicky is as far away from the prying lens as possible.

The crew says nothing as we pass, and I don't bother trying to meet their gaze.

Our directive is clear.

Get inside.

Get to Decker's room.

Get away from them and this day and all the shit that's weighing on us now as a seemingly new threat has emerged.

As we file into the living room, the toe of my soggy sneaker catches on the threshold of the sliding glass door.

With a *humph* I stumble, then startle when several sets of hands reach out to steady me.

"I'm fine." I right myself as a fresh shot of adrenaline sends my heart rate skyrocketing. "I'm fine," I repeat, though heat licks through my body, lighting my nerves on fire, even as I shiver from the cold.

"I'm—I'm—"

I crumple.

The wet heels of my shoes soak through my pants as they connect with the backs of my thighs, and then I'm on my knees, limp and shaking, struggling to keep myself from tipping to one side.

Chapter 36

Decker

Crouching, I scoop her off the floor. Then I stride out of the living room as fast as I trust my feet to carry me.

Behind us, the camera crew enters the room. I can hear the murmuring and the shuffling of feet.

I can feel them pursuing us, trying to keep up and get the shot they're so desperate for. To make content of what they're witnessing.

But they can't have her. They can't have any of us like this.

I don't slow until I reach my bedroom door, though I keep my body angled to protect Josephine's head. She's still conscious, thank god, but silent, nonstop tears cascade down her cheeks.

She's in shock.

They all are.

I might be, too.

How this could happen—how history could nearly repeat itself...

But no. They're safe. They're home.

I can't allow myself to dwell in any version of what-if.

Despite my efforts to push them out, Nicky's words play on repeat in my head. Fuck. He's right. This isn't fair. This life. The positions she's put in over and over because of me.

She's not safe. I'll never be able to keep her safe.

As the guys file in behind me, I set Josephine on the bed. Kylian kneels at her feet, taking her hands in his, while Kendrick sinks onto the bed beside her.

A throat clears near the door.

It might as well be the starting shot of a race for the way I jump to my feet and charge.

"This is a private moment. Get the fuck away from us."

I slam the door in the faces of our audience, then lock it for good measure.

Not that closing the door on the crew gives us a modicum of true privacy.

With an inferno raging inside me, I haul the trunk at the end of my bed to the far wall.

"What are you doing?" Locke demands.

I don't bother answering. I won't let anyone stop me.

Standing on the trunk, I'm just tall enough to snag the camera mounted in the corner of the room. I pull, and it falls away easily. Then I tug so hard the cords rip right through the drywall.

I throw it onto the ground, jump off the trunk, and smash it with my heel.

When I finally look up, all eyes are on me.

Kylian cocks one eyebrow so it raises over the black frames of his glasses. "We're still not—"

"I know," I relent, hanging my head and planting my hands on my hips.

"Bathroom," Kylian reminds me.

Wordlessly, I nod, and we all make our way to my en suite.

Chapter 37

Josephine

There's nothing we can do.

There's nothing to say.

We're all so ravaged and hollow. Not one of us is in a position to comfort or support the others.

Kylian has asked me half a dozen times what I need.

I can't give him an answer because I honestly don't know.

"I want you to go to sleep," I implore, my attention fixed on Nicky. The pain of sitting on the cold tile floor has to be excruciating. Yet he hasn't moved since we shuffled into Decker's bathroom half an hour ago. The second the door was closed behind us, we all sank to the floor.

Kendrick climbs to his feet, then offers Locke a hand. "Come on, brother. I'll help you shower and get settled in."

"I'll come lay with you in the morning," I promise. "After you've rested."

Without argument, he nods once, then he lets his head hang as if he's too depleted to hold it up any longer.

Kendrick murmurs in his ear. Then, as Nicky exits the bathroom, he squats in front of me.

He taps my jaw twice with his knuckles, then kisses me on the lips. "Chin up, Mama. I love you."

The same defeat that's ensnared Nicky washes over me. All I can do is nod.

"Where are you sleeping tonight?" K asks.

"She's staying in here with me."

No one bothers arguing with Decker. None of us have any fight left in us right now.

Kylian's on his feet again, standing tall in the middle of the bathroom, arms crossed over his chest. Once the others clear out, he peers down at Decker and me. "I'm not going to take my meds tonight," he declares.

"Yes you are," I counter.

Kylian takes medication to sleep. The last time he chose to not take it—the days immediately after the disastrous Charter Cruise—he was up for three days straight.

"I need to stay up and watch over you. I need to know you're okay."

"You *need* sleep," I argue. "You were on that boat, too, Kyl. We all deserve a chance to recover."

He sits beside me and cups my face with one hand. "You want me to leave?"

No. Yes?

My mind is scrambled and blank at the same time.

"No, Kyl. I just... I—I..."

Shit. I blow out a breath while I search for the right words. I don't want to hurt him. I don't want him to think I'm pushing him away. But I also can't turn off the urge to take care of him—of all of them—despite being in no position to do so.

I'm so close to slipping into a panic attack I can't tell up from down.

I don't want to break down in front of Kylian, Kendrick, or Locke. They lived through the situation right along with me. They don't need a reminder of what we survived tonight. Just like none of us should be saddled with the responsibility of looking after each other. Not now.

We need to recover. We need a chance to process what the fuck is going on, and to figure out how we can ensure a situation like that never, ever happens again.

Decker hauls himself up and looms over us. "I'll take care of her, Kylian. I swear."

Frowning, Kylian looks up, his eyes narrowing. "If she needs me—"

"I want to stay with Decker," I finally articulate. "If I need you, I'll text you. I promise."

Kylian's shoulders sink, and he averts his attention, but it only takes a moment for him to press a kiss to my lips and rise to his feet.

"I love you," he tells me as he makes his way out of the bathroom.

"I love you, too," I mumble, closing my eyes.

The exhaustion running through me is bone deep and widespread. Maybe sending them away is the wrong call. Maybe it's exactly what I need. If I was clearheaded, maybe I'd have the right answer. I just know I can breathe a little easier when I'm not so worried about keeping it together in front of the guys.

What just happened—how and why, the terror in the moment, and the reckoning of the consequences had we not gotten back to the isle safely—it's all too much to process.

Fear and dread wash over me in waves. Just as one ebbs, another crashes down. The anxiety continues on like this, cresting higher and higher.

This isn't the first time an incident like this has occurred on Lake Chapel. That isn't lost on me.

Neither are the ramifications or the realization that despite his absence on that boat, Decker will likely be the one most affected by tonight's tribulation.

Chapter 38

Josephine

"Let me help you."

The offer sounds more like a strained, desperate plea.

Nodding, I lift both hands and let Decker pull me to my feet.

He wraps his arms around me, but his hold isn't tight enough.

"Decker." I nuzzle against his chest, wishing I could meld my body and his, and inhale the scent of amber and sea salt I've come to associate with my stoic, complex man.

"I've got you," he promises, holding me tightly in his arms.

It's still not enough.

"What do you need?" he whispers. His breath is warm against my ear as he breathes me in, revealing just how intensely he needs this, too.

Gulping past the fear of rejection, I tip my chin and meet his somber gaze.

"I need to get out of my head," I confess, my heart hammering so hard against my chest it aches. The trepidation lingers, but now it's for a completely different reason. This time, it's mixed with a heavy dose of anticipation. "I need to stop thinking. I just want to feel."

He inhales, his broad, defined chest rising and falling beneath my chin. His grip on me is tight, full of hesitation, as he studies me with a dark expression.

I brace for rejection, but I double down anyway, before he can come up with an excuse.

"I need to feel alive, Decker," I whisper. I push onto tiptoes and kiss the corner of his mouth. "I need you to help me feel alive."

He's rigid against me, his jaw locked and his eyes hard. Then, as if a switch has been flipped, the air whooshes out of his lungs and his hands are on my face and he's kissing me like I've never been kissed before.

My body lights up like a firework: a chaotic explosion that's as beautiful as it is powerful.

He grips my face harder, his hold borderline painful.

But I relish the sensation.

I want to flourish. I want to thrive.

This is what living feels like.

It's almost impossible to keep up with him as he ravishes my mouth with his own. He's brutal and fervent and merciless in the way he consumes me. But I give everything I have, nipping at his bottom lip, teasing the tip of my tongue into his mouth. It's as if, now that he's made his decision, he can't tamp it down or hold it back.

He tilts my face, putting me where he wants me, feeding me his tongue and groaning with every sweep.

His hands smooth over my torso, along my hips, down my ass. When he lifts me off my feet, I wrap my legs around his waist, and when his belt buckle presses right where I want him, a whimper escapes me.

He doesn't break our kiss as he carries me out of the bathroom. He takes the long way, double-checking the lock on the bedroom door with one hand while holding me to him with the other, then stalks toward his bed.

"You're sure?" he asks, breathless, as he stops at the foot of the mattress.

Oh no he doesn't. I've suffered too much tonight to be cockblocked by Decker Crusade.

"I need to feel connected to you, and I need to come on your cock. I've never been more sure of anything in my life."

Chapter 39

Josephine

He lowers me onto his bed and takes a step back. Without taking his focus off me, he rips off his shirt over his head and whips the belt off his pants.

Hating the distance between us, I tip forward and stretch a hand toward him. He steps within my reach, and when I wrap my arms around his torso, he tenses. His heart is pounding so loudly it thunders through me as I rest my cheek against his abs. I hold him tighter as he takes in long, steady breaths.

"I can't lose you, Josephine. Not to this life."

Silent tears stream down my face, catching in the strip of dark hair that disappears below his waistline as I squeeze him tighter.

He cups my face in both hands and regards me. His eyes are filled with so much devotion. Taking a knee in front of me, he kisses away the moisture, then closes his eyes and rests his forehead against mine. "I love you, too," he whispers into the inch of space between us.

I'm so damn tired of the ever-present space that separates us.

"Show me."

Decker pushes me back and climbs onto the mattress, straddling me as he captures my mouth with his.

With shaky hands, he rips at my shirt, my bra, my pants and underwear. I'm naked in no time.

Shivers rack up my spine as he takes in every inch of me. His examination is like a physical touch, heating me, winding me up tighter, triggering the need for him that's been hounding me for weeks.

He hauls himself up onto his knees and shoves down his boxer briefs. When he's naked before me, he buries his face in my hair and kisses me like it's his last day on earth and I'm his final meal.

Pressing his forehead to mine, he searches my eyes for a long moment. Then, with his lips parted, he lowers us onto the bed, lines himself up, and pushes in.

I gasp, and he groans. Finally, our bodies come together in a union I've anticipated for so, so long.

"Decker." I grip his shoulders, pulling him closer, desperate for him to bury himself as deep as he can and never let me go.

"I'm right here, baby. I've got you. I won't let anyone get to you ever again." His words are a solemn vow.

Slowly, he thrusts, pulling all the way out, then sliding in to the hilt, over and over, making sure we both feel every inch of this connection.

Tears well in my eyes. Intrusive thoughts try to burrow their way in, threatening to steal away my grasp on reality, but I push them away.

I can't let them win, because I can't lose him.

Not now that I love him. Not now that I know he loves me, too.

But he's holding back. Why does it always feel like he's holding back?

"Decker," I whimper, tears flowing freely as I lose the battle with my emotions.

"What's wrong?" He freezes, holding himself in a plank above my body.

It's too much.

It's not enough.

It never has been with him.

"Please." I grasp at his shoulders, begging him to lower himself again. Pleading for the closeness I crave. "Please, Decker. Hold me. Fuck me. Make love to me. Make me forget."

His eyes widen and his lips part, but he gives me what I want. He lowers himself and covers my body with his own. That's all I need in this moment. He's all I need.

"You're okay, Siren. You're okay."

He repeats the words, over and over, grinding his hips against me. Now, his cock barely moves as he fucks me into the mattress, keeping us wholly connected.

"Right here, baby. Look at me."

Obediently, I meet his gaze, and in that moment, every worry and every fear are sapped from my soul. I lose myself in Decker's eyes, in his solemness, in his assurances.

"No one's getting to you. Not today. Not ever again."

His words soothe me as his body takes me higher. Every thrust grinds his pelvic bone against my clit. I wrap my legs around his lower half, desperate to be even closer now that he's finally letting me in.

"Don't let me go." I claw at his scalp, pulling his face down to meet mine, begging him to keep me.

"I won't let them take you," he promises with a kiss.

Slow and steady, my orgasm builds. It's deep, bottomless. Every emotion I've been hit with tonight gathers in the pit of my stomach and swirls, mixing with the pleasure he's providing.

"Decker," I whimper again. This time it isn't with want.

I have no more requests, only the desire for him to meet me where I am. To join me as we tip over the edge together.

"Come with me," I whisper as the first wave erupts in my core and my walls clench around his length.

He kisses me, groaning into my mouth, and with a few hard thrusts, he joins me.

We're silent as we come down, wrung out from the horrors and the ecstasy of this night.

He rests his forehead against mine once more, then kisses me tenderly.

"Never again." His words are soft and low, but the meaning is overpowering.

With a final kiss, he wraps his arm around my midsection and rolls to his side, cuddling me close.

Chapter 40

Decker

Her chest rises and falls. The hair fanned out around her tickles against my chest with each inhalation.

I hold her. I kiss her. I watch for and relish each breath she takes.

The visual of her in my bed, the knowledge that tonight, she's in my arms and she's safe, are gifts I don't take for granted.

She looks gorgeous; peaceful; sated. She looks like mine.

I allow myself to commit this moment to memory. To revel in the fantasy that this is real, and that Josephine and I are just getting started.

I allow myself to indulge in the way she feels curled up beside me, the press of her ass against my bare thighs, the tickle of her cold feet between my calves.

I allow myself to feel it all.

Because this is the one and only time I'll ever allow this to happen.

Tonight wasn't just eye-opening, it was course-correcting.

It was the reality check I sorely needed.

As devastating as it was, I'm grateful it came when it did.

Tonight was a stark reminder of who I am and what's required of me.

I won't allow her to give what the world wants from me. They don't get her—they can't have her.

Protecting her means letting her go. It took far too long, but I'm finally ready to accept that fate.

My heart beats out an erratic rhythm every time my mind wanders to what the morning will bring. I shake off the thought again, burying it down for now. It's for the best.

For her.

For them.

We can't go on like this.

If one of us has to break, it will be me. From where I'm standing, it's the only way I can ever truly love her. I'd rather break both our hearts than break my girl's spirit.

The heart can mend.

But the spirit—the soul of this woman, the very essence she fought so damn hard to resurrect by coming to Lake Chapel—won't survive the life I'm going to lead.

Sighing, I home in on her eyelids, watching her lashes flutter as she dreams. I fight back the urge to touch her, to wake her. To make love to her again and again, until she's burrowed so deep into the core of who I am that nothing can tear us apart.

She's so beautiful: inside and out, body and soul.

What I wouldn't give to walk through life admiring her, learning from her, loving her with everything I am.

For the rest of my life, I'll keep this memory close. This moment will have to be enough.

Maybe this is how it was always supposed to be.

Maybe this is why it had to be her, and them.

Maybe this is why I never inserted myself into their group dynamic. Not fully. Why I never fit, no matter how much we all wanted it to work.

I served my purpose. I'd like to think I played a small part in reigniting her flames. I witnessed firsthand how her spirit sparked to life, then just kept glowing. I got the very best parts of her, if only for the briefest time.

No one has ever seen me the way she does. Challenged me. Made me feel so alive and so out of control.

She was worth it.

She's so fucking worth it.

I swallow past the dread threatening to take over again. I've made my choice. It's one I'd make a thousand times over to ensure she leads a long, beautiful, private life.

A life so different from the fate I'm resigned to.

I'll trudge along without her, without them, even. After tonight, I don't see how I can keep any of them. Because they love her. She loves them. And I love them all.

I'll break my own heart if it means she gets some version of happily ever after.

I don't care about the state of my heart anyway. Fractured or fragmented. Broken or tattered. None of it matters if my sacrifice fortifies her path and brings her a fraction of peace.

If my heartbreak is her salvation, then let me shatter.

Come tomorrow, she's going to hate me, but it's for the best. Her hatred will make it easier on all of us. It will give the fire that burns in her the outlet it needs.

That fire, painful as it may be, will feel brighter than any love I've ever known or will ever experience again.

I welcome her flames. Relish them.

I swore I was done calling the shots and pulling the power card. She's my equal. She's the best of me. She's the best of all of it.

Come tomorrow, she's going to hate me.

But she'll survive.

And not just survive—she's going to live.

I want her to live. I want her to thrive.

Tonight, she loves me.

Tomorrow, I'll destroy us to save her.

Chapter 41

Josephine

It's still early when I roll over, sated and sleepy, still tired but safe.

Safe.

With Decker—in his arms, with his love—I'm safe.

I crack one eye open to find his focus already fixed on me. He's wearing the softest, most tender expression.

"Josephine."

I press a kiss to his lips to silence him.

"One minute," I murmur. Snuggling into his chest, I revel in the warmth of his arms.

Last night went from devastating and horrifying to so unimaginably beautiful I can't believe it was real. For the first time in my life, I feel complete. Fulfilled. So in love I can hardly stand it.

"Hey, Decker?"

He exhales, a wary sigh.

God, I love riling up this man. I want to spend a lifetime making him sigh like that—teasing him and pushing his buttons, forcing him to not take himself so seriously. Encouraging him to let others take care of him the way he takes care of us.

A lifetime together. A lifetime of love.

"Do you remember what I said on the phone last night?"

In my hold, he goes rigid. His physical response triggers alarm bells in my mind, but I have to get this out. I have to make sure he knows it wasn't just a trauma response—that it's real, and true. So I take a deep breath to garner my courage, then speak my truth.

"Those words? They weren't said out of fear or panic. I didn't just say them because we were in danger. I said them because they're true. I love you, Decker. I love you so much."

A tremor rolls through him—from overwhelm or happiness, I hope. Without a word, he pulls me closer, wraps both arms around me, and inhales deeply.

I melt in his arms, soaking in every reciprocated emotion as he silently pours into our embrace.

It's okay if he's not ready to say it again. By his actions and care, he shows me. Ours is the forever kind of love that will blossom and shine over time.

"Minute's up," he murmurs, clearing his throat and jettisoning me out of the moment.

His mouth moves from my neck to my lips, then to my forehead, where he places the gentlest of kisses.

"I need to get downstairs and take care of some things," he explains. "Kylian's probably already got you out of classes for today, so take as long as you need before you come downstairs. I want my sheets to smell like you for days, Siren. I want to remember for as long as I live every detail of what it was like to have you in my bed last night."

I bite down on my bottom lip, prepared to hit him with a sassy remark about how I'll gladly refresh the sheets with him tonight. Or tomorrow. Or next week, once the cameras are gone for good.

But he's sitting up and climbing out of bed before I can even open my mouth.

Heart aching with so much love for him, I watch him walk away. This perfect specimen of a man—*a man who's finally mine*—strides into the bathroom with purpose and power.

When he turns on the shower, I consider joining him.

But that would defeat the purpose of his request. So I stretch my arms overhead, yawn, and roll to the center of the bed to drift back to sleep.

The next time I open my eyes, Decker is dressed. He's hovering over me, his brow furrowed and his expression unreadable.

Onyx eyes meet mine, and then he nods once.

"Come down to the dining room when you're ready."

He turns on his heel, and then he's gone, leaving me alone in his bed.

Chapter 42

Decker

It's more than an hour later when I hear Josephine in the kitchen.

I've been in the dining room waiting all this time, too sick to my stomach to eat.

The boys are seated on either side of the table. They know very little, but I asked them to stay. As always, they've got my back. They're supporting me, despite the lack of information I've given them.

"As soon as Josephine joins us, we can wrap this up."

They're here because I need them to witness my resolve. When they do, they'll know this is the real deal.

I also need them to be here for her, to clean up the mess I'm about to make.

Josephine pushes through the dining room door with a coffee mug in hand. "Oh." She stumbles to a stop when she takes in the four of us seated around the table.

I clear my throat, garnering the attention of everyone in the room. "I want to talk about what happened last night."

Silently, our girl nods and makes her way over to Locke.

Their girl.

Their girl.

"I've sent away the camera crew, and I've notified SportsZone that we're done."

"Thank fuck," Kylian mutters.

Kendrick hums in appreciation.

"How—" Locke starts.

I raise a hand to silence him. If I don't get the words out quickly, I won't see it through.

"They have enough footage, and we have final approval over everything shared or published. I made it clear that I wouldn't approve anything captured after five o'clock yesterday, so collecting additional footage was a waste of resources. I also implied I'd be hard-pressed to approve much of anything if they insisted on coming back to the house."

"I've also hired outside counsel to review my NIL commitments for the rest of the year so we aren't surprised by something like this again. I'm happy to have them look over yours, too," I add, regarding Kendrick, then Locke.

"That's probably a good idea," Locke mutters as Josephine leans her head on his shoulder.

Their girl.

Their girl.

"Yeah," Kendrick adds. "Thanks, Cap."

With my heart in my throat, I rise to my feet. Looking at each of my boys, I will them to feel the sincerity of my next words. I will them to forgive me for what I'm about to do.

"What you all did last night... what you went through and how you handled it, thank you. And I'm sorry." I fist my hands at my sides to keep them from shaking, to keep my composure. "We always knew there'd be ups and downs. Knowing you've got my back even through the lowest points... that makes this worth it. I appreciate it more than you could ever know."

The guys murmur their support, but their individual responses don't reach me. I can't focus on them or I risk falling apart. With a deep breath in, I fortify my heart and lock down my resolve.

There's a high-pitched whining in my ears, a pit of despair nestled in my gut. It's now or never. And never isn't an option.

"One more thing."

Fuck.

She was everything. She is everything.

This is for her.

For them.

For all of us, and for the future they're destined to share.

Kendrick. Kylian. Locke.

And Josephine.

My Siren.

Their girl.

Jaw clenched so tight it sends a bolt of pain through my temple, I force myself to look her in the eye. Force myself to make my resolve unmistakably clear.

I swear she can sense what's coming. Before I've spoken, her face screws up in disbelief. An instant later, her expression morphs into anger. She's ready to push back and fight me, all before I've even opened my mouth to speak.

"There's no easy way to do this, so I'll just say it. You and I..." I nod to her, swallow down the vomit threatening to spew from my mouth, then steel my spine. "We're done."

The room is silent.

Silent and still.

Still, yet forever changed.

Closing my eyes, I allow myself to remember how she felt in my arms last night. How she clung to my body. How she pulsed around me.

It was enough.

It has to be enough.

Because she's not mine anymore.

From this moment forward, she's not anything to me.

Now, she's just their girl.

Like the coward I am, I keep my head bowed as I stalk for the door. "Either you can move out, Josephine, or I'll leave. It's your choice. But we're through."

Chapter 43

Josephine

It's been raining for two days.

Not storming, *thank god*, but a persistent, miserable drizzle.

In those two days, I haven't slept.

I've mulled over every excuse as to why. I've tried so damn hard to drum up reasons that aren't so pathetic.

Because I refuse to accept the truth: That it hurts. That it's not getting better. That I'm incomplete. That he's not going to change his mind.

The erratic rhythm of droplets pelting the roof makes it impossible for me to drift off. That's my most valid excuse. It's the rain. Or the sounds of Scout scampering in the junk yard. It's the unfamiliarity of this too-small bed. The scratchiness of the sheets, which were perfectly fine until I lay in a bed of thousand thread count Egyptian cotton at the Crusade mansion.

Fucking fancy sheets on that annoyingly comfortable bed.

I considered going to Hunter's. Her offer is open-ended, but she warned me that she expects her mom to waltz back into town any day, and that when she does, things may go sideways.

Being back at Sam's will have to do for now.

My uncle's typically gone during the week anyway, and here, I'm close to campus. Here, I can bypass the lake. Avoid the marina. It's easier here.

No. That's a lie.

It's been nearly three weeks, and nothing is easier. Nothing hurts less.

Beside me, Nicky groans and blows out a breath as he tries to stretch out his arms overhead in a way that won't jostle me.

"You're okay. I'm awake."

He goes rigid for an instant at the sound of my voice, but then he rolls to his side, kisses my hair, and spoons me from behind.

It was his turn to stay with me tonight.

Even though he's not comfortable here.

Even though cramming onto this too-soft twin-size mattress in my makeshift bedroom at Sam's place leaves him sorer and achier than usual the next day.

None of them are comfortable here, but they all refuse to stay away.

Secretly, I'm grateful.

On the rare occasion I do manage to sleep, I wake up in fits. My heart races, and flashes of boat rides I wish I'd never taken and words I wish I'd never whispered haunt me.

I thought we could press past it.

I thought if I gave him time, he'd cool off.

Foolishly, I thought he would change his mind.

"What time is it? Why aren't you sleeping, Hot Girl?"

Keeping my back to him, I shrug. I don't have a clue what time it is. As for his second question, I don't have an answer.

Silent tears drip down my cheeks and fall to the sheet beneath me. I blink, and more join them.

Somehow knowing, he sits up and tugs on my shoulder until I'm flat on my back.

His lips find my cheeks in the dark.

The tender way he kisses away the tears only inspires fresh ones to fall.

I love and appreciate what he's doing, what they're all doing to support me through this.

I should cherish the one-on-one time with each of them, but I can't shake the longing that consumes me. To experience the unique intensity of the five of us together again.

That's the rub. Because it's no longer an option.

Decker destroyed us.

He broke my heart, and he shattered all of us in the process.

A muffled sob escapes me, and in response, Nicky holds me tighter.

As yet another deluge of tears escapes, I resign myself to giving up on that dream. There's no use in crying over it. There's no sense in yearning for something that's not meant to be. The five of us will never be together again. Decker will make sure of it.

"Nicky?" I sniffle.

He remains silent, but he squeezes my hip, so I know he's listening.

"What's it like to always hurt?"

For a moment, I'm not sure he'll answer the question, but finally, he clears his throat. "Hopeless. It feels fucking hopeless."

Another sob racks through me.

I knew he wouldn't sugarcoat it, but to hear the reality spoken out loud like that makes me so queasy I might actually vomit.

"But it doesn't always hurt the same. Some days the pain is less intense. Some days the sun shines a little brighter."

"I just don't know how to go on," I confess into the dark.

It's a truth I can't reveal to Kendrick. If I do, he'll want to comfort and console me until I'm better.

It's a candidness I won't share with Kylian. He's been just as deeply affected by Decker's rejection as I have.

I can talk about it with Nicky. No one understands pain quite like he does.

"Adjust your expectations, Hot Girl. Keep chasing the light. Savor the good days. Accept the new standard for what decent, good, and great all mean."

It's good advice.

It doesn't temper the all-consuming, ever-present ache in my chest.

Determined to focus on the rain pattering on the rooftop, hoping it will clear my mind, I let out a sigh and wrap his arm around me.

I doubt I'll sleep at all, but I owe it to myself and to my guys to try.

As his breathing slows, I caress his forearm, ghosting my fingertips over his warm, smooth skin. Keeping my voice low, I ask, "Do you ever forget just how good it felt before the pain set in?"

He inhales, then releases a shuddering breath. "No... Never."

Chapter 44

Josephine

"What are you working on?" I can't help but smile at the way Kylian aggressively types on his tablet. He's sitting on the other side of the table in my uncle's home, and he's got his phone out, too. Every few seconds, he refers to it, then the typing starts up again.

He startles, as if I've caught him off guard, but he doesn't take his eyes off the screen. "A personal project. It's something I've been working on for a while."

"Oh, I assumed it was something for the team," I muse, turning back to the business writing assignment I'm slogging through.

A clattering sound in the office breaks my concentration. When it continues, loud and chaotic, Kylian peers up over the rims of his glasses and raises one eyebrow.

It's Jeannie, my uncle's assistant.

She's here a few days a week, and in her defense, she's typically alone.

Loud doesn't even begin to describe her standard volume, even when she's alone, I've discovered. Apparently, she's quite clumsy, too.

Her mess of tightly permed curls appears around the corner of the kitchen-slash-living room for a second as she peeks out.

"Oh. Oh!"

"Hi, Jeannie," I call out.

With a sigh, Kylian hits the lock button on his iPad. There's no sense continuing to work. We both know what comes next.

"Oh, Sugar. I'm sorry. I'm being loud again, aren't I? And you're in here trying to work. I'm not used to people being here, s'all. I'm all nerves and jitterbugs today anyway. I may have had a few too many cups of coffee last night while I was tracking the storm coverage."

Across the table, Kylian goes rigid as I ask, "What storm?"

Jeannie props herself up on the doorframe and hitches a thumb over her shoulder. "Haven't you seen the news? Tropical Storm Theo is heading right for us. Rumor has it the governor's going to issue the evac warning during her broadcast tonight." She waves us to follow, then scurries back to the front office, more frenzied than usual.

A tropical storm? My stomach sinks, and instantly, my thoughts get jumbled.

We're a couple of hours from the nearest beach, but I guess that doesn't matter. I know nothing about tropical storms and hurricanes. I'm from the Midwest. Snowstorms? Sure. The occasional tornado? I've spent a little time hanging out in the closet of my mom's trailer, waiting for the all-clear.

Kylian scrutinizes me as he rises from his seat at the table.

Offering me a hand, he pulls me to my feet. When I'm standing, he slides one hand down my back, and then he guides me to the front office, where Jeannie's got the news blaring on the TV mounted on the wall.

It isn't until I step into the space that serves as the office and main entrance for Sam's Salvage and Parts that I realize Jeannie isn't alone.

On the other side of the room, below the TV, two men stand with their arms crossed, watching the storm coverage.

They turn when Jeannie walks back in waving a file and telling them she found it.

They focus on her for a moment.

Then, almost in unison, their eyes flit to me.

"I'll be damned," one of the men says, a brow raised and a smarmy smile on his face.

Kylian takes a step closer and moves his hand from my back to my side, holding me at my hip.

With an elbow, the first guy nudges his buddy, who's still staring at the TV as the meteorologist standing in front of a radar image projected onto a green screen goes on about the storm's predicted path.

"That's the girl, isn't it?" he asks his friend, not bothering to lower his voice. Then, to me, he lifts his chin. "Aren't you that girl? The one who was with Decker Crusade but hasn't been to any of the games lately?"

Stomach twisting, I close my eyes and shrink into Kylian's side.

"No." Kylian's tone brooks no argument. "You need to leave," he tells the two men. Then he turns to Jeannie. "You need to close for the day."

Then, with the kind of energy he usually reserves for the bedroom, he takes my shoulders, turns me on the spot, and marches back down the hall to the living area.

"Those men know nothing. Those men mean nothing. Don't let them get to you, baby."

But it's too late.

My heart sinks, knowing so many people blame me for ruining the Crusaders' perfect season. They didn't say anything that the rest of the town isn't already saying.

The Lake Chapel Crusaders have lost their last two games.

One game is a fluke.

But two? When the whole town—hell, the entire state—expects at least two of the star players to go pro? That's unheard of. Unacceptable.

It was only a matter of time before people started asking questions and looking for clues.

I've been photographed with Decker on numerous occasions. We were together on campus all the time and seen together at his NIL events.

Now? We're nothing.

Since I've been out of the picture, the Crusaders have lost their shot at a perfect season. Now they run the risk of missing the playoffs.

Never mind that their star running back has been out for the last three games with an alleged groin injury. Or that their right guard has been benched for the last two games because of his arthritis. Not to mention there are at least three guys on defense who are grappling with injuries or illness.

But yeah. Sure. It's my fault that the Crusaders aren't Crusading.

It's ironic. Pathetic. Just plain sad.

Because at the end of the day, it doesn't matter that Decker Crusade cut me out of his life.

I can't seem to cut him out of mine.

Chapter 45

Josephine

I wake up to a vibrating phone dancing on the nightstand and all sorts of banging in the kitchen down the hall.

I'm alone.

The lack of companionship was expected, but it doesn't dull the pain that hits me square in the chest when I remember. I'm alone, and I'm lonely. It's nothing new. I've been lonely for most of my life. Yet now it hurts more than it ever has before, because I've spent the last few months basking in the attention of four passionate, devoted, borderline-obsessed men.

How can a twin-size bed feel so empty?

Last night was Kendrick's night, but he was needed elsewhere.

As the sheriff, Mr. Taylor's working around the clock to prepare the town for a smooth evacuation in light of Tropical Storm Theo, so it was up to K to look after his sisters.

I refused to let Nicky suffer through two nights in a row on this tragically small mattress. He's doing better, but he's still not well. Sleeping in his own bed helps, so it wasn't difficult to convince him.

Kylian, on the other hand, was exhaustingly adamant that I not be alone.

If not for the storm, he would be here. When he checked coverage sometime during the night, he decided it was time to secure a safe place to shelter once we leave Lake Chapel.

His commitment to keeping me safe is the only reason I don't stress when I read the messages Hunter sent early this morning.

> **Hunter:** Hey girl. Greedy's pestering me about you and the evacuation. Do you have plans to go with the guys?

> **Hunter:** We're heading to Dr. Ferguson's cabin near Beech Mountain. Do you want to come with?

> **Kylian:** I'll be by to pick you up at ten. Kendrick wants to get on the road before lunch.

Yawning, I type out a reply to Hunter.

> **Joey:** I'm fine. Kylian has a plan. We're leaving in a few hours. Stay safe!

> **Hunter:** Where are you guys going? Decker's place in the mountains?

Shit on a crumbly cracker.

I didn't even bother to ask. I just trusted Kylian to handle it. Surely he doesn't expect me to cohabitate with the man who broke my heart. The guys can barely stand to be around him on the nights they're not here. There's no way they'd willingly push us all back together.

Sam raps his knuckles on the door. "Hey, kiddo," he says from the other side. "You up?"

"I'm up," I reply, sitting up in bed.

"Are you alone?"

The words slice through me with such intensity I startle.

I'm alone.

I have three men who love me. Yet we're all broken and battered. Is there a difference between being alone and being incomplete? Will the crater of loneliness created by the decision Decker forced on our group fill in over time, or will we learn to live with the emptiness?

Gulping past the overwhelming sadness, I shoot for upbeat when I respond. "Yep, just me. Come on in."

Sam pushes the door open, but he doesn't step into the room.

The forced smile he wears is far too bright for the circumstances.

"I made breakfast. Hungry? I also wanted to check in about the evacuation orders. I was planning to head to Louisiana this afternoon anyway. You're welcome to join me."

My heart warms at his offer. This man has done nothing but support me since the day I arrived in Lake Chapel.

"I have plans," I assure him. "But thank you." I gulp past the emotion burning up my esophagus. "It's nice to know I have this place—and you—to fall back on."

"Of course, Jojo," Sam chides, his brow furrowed. "Always. That's what family is for."

The ride to the marina is mostly silent. The whole way, Kylian keeps his hand on my thigh, squeezing now and then to assure me.

When we arrive, he angles close and places his hand over the seat belt latch. "Before we get going…" Then his lips are on mine. At first, the kiss is desperate, but as we melt into each other, a peaceful calm washes over us both.

"I love you," he whispers against my lips. "But last night was bullshit. I didn't sleep, and I'm not doing that again."

Frowning, I pull back and get a good look at him.

His eyes are watery and a little bloodshot, and the lines in his forehead are more defined, as if he's been deep in thought for hours.

"When this storm is over and we get back to Lake Chapel, things have to change. Either Decker leaves the isle, or we get our own place, or—"

Pressing my lips to his, I nod frantically.

There's so much to figure out. Logistics. Finances. So many of the resources we're all accustomed to are either provided by Decker or are made possible because of him, but I have no doubt that Kylian will find a solution. Just as I'm certain all three guys will do whatever it takes to move on and get us back on track.

High-pitched squeals catch my attention then. Before us, Jade and Emilia are running circles around Kendrick and Nicky.

A rush of love washes over me, and a smile so big it hurts stretches across my face.

"The girls are going with us?" Quickly, I unbuckle my seat belt and collect my things. I packed enough for three days; Kylian assured me we'd be gone a few nights at most.

"I told you, everyone will be there. Sherriff Taylor has to work. They always come with us when we evacuate."

Nervous to ask my next question, I worry my lip and scan the marina parking lot. "And by *everyone*, you mean..."

"He's not riding with us." Kylian's tone is firm, sure.

Dropping my shoulders, I let my head fall forward and close my eyes. That answer is more telling than Kylian realizes.

"He'll be there, though?"

For a breath, he doesn't respond. When I pull myself together again and turn to him, he's inspecting me from behind his glasses.

"Yes. He'll be there."

My heart pounds out an anxious rhythm in my chest. "And *there* is where, exactly?"

These are questions I should have asked earlier. Details I should have considered, even if the outcome would ultimately be the same.

"Decker's cabin. It's just beyond Beech Mountain."

And there it is.

My stomach sinks. Because we're heading off the grid, running from one storm, straight into the eye of another.

Two clashing, warring tempests, each raging for their own reasons. Neither can be dissuaded by the other, and in the wake of their battle, they'll leave nothing but a path of destruction.

A reunion between Decker Crusade and me won't go any other way. I fear I'm not strong enough to survive it.

"How far is the drive?" I whisper. It's all I can manage.

Kylian's still taking in my every move, like he's cataloging them all so he can figure me out. "He knows to stay out of your way. You won't have to see him at all if you don't want. This was the best option for everyone, though, Jo. There's enough room for all of us. The girls are used to the cabin—"

"It's fine," I insist. It has to be. "How long is the drive?" I repeat.

"Usually, it's two hours and thirty-four minutes. But with the whole town evacuating, and given the evacuation reroutes, I expect it to take us three or three and a half hours."

Three hours.

I developed a raw form of resilience when I had to return to high school after I was raped and filmed without my consent. It's an armor of sorts, but it adapts on a dime, molding me into the version of myself most fitting for survival in each situation.

There's no conscious effort involved. The resiliency clicks into place on instinct.

In years past, it often meant donning my bad-bitch, no-shits-given armor. Other times, it served me best to blend in and move through the shadows, remaining unseen.

It took years of therapy to recognize the coping strategy. Even if it's not a healthy one, it's undoubtedly useful, especially when confronted with my own personal version of hell. Like now. I've got three hours to get my shit together before I have to dwell in the presence of Decker Crusade.

Chapter 46

Kendrick

I've made this drive a few dozen times.

My surroundings are familiar as I merge onto the designated evacuation route.

Nicky's riding shotgun, looking more lively than he has in a while.

Thank fuck.

I won't go as far as to say his flare is over, but his pain has significantly decreased. The new drug regimen Dr. Kline's got him on was a bitch to cross taper, but my boy stuck with it, and now he's finally beginning to reap the benefits.

Turning my way, he raises his pierced eyebrow.

"You good?" I ask, just to make conversation.

He grins that signature Nicky grin. The one that can't be met with anything but a smile. The one we've sorely missed for the last few weeks.

"Yeah, man. I've got a drawer full of spoons and an unexpected vacation with my friends and my girl." He hitches a thumb over his shoulder. "Never better."

Gripping the wheel and focusing on the road, I dip my chin once and blow out a long breath. "This isn't going to feel like a vacation for her."

He scoffs and rubs his hands over his thighs. "Yes it will. I'll make sure of it."

With my eyes trained on the road and the accumulating traffic, I mull over his words.

We're all on the outs with Cap. Have been since the morning he gathered us together to break up with Jojo.

The unexpected blow hit every one of us hard. None of us would have allowed it to go down like that had we known. But once Decker sets his mind to something...

Shaking my head, I tip my chin to Nicky. "We're aligned in our feelings, but tread lightly for the next few days, brother. We're playing with fire putting everyone under one roof. I know you want to protect her and avenge her, but despite the whole 'lone wolf' bullshit he's got going on right now, I'd reckon you can't burn him without hurting her, too."

Locke crosses his arms over his chest and watches the scenery out the window.

"Oh shit," a small voice mutters behind me. A voice that shockingly sounds like one of my sisters.

"What did you just say?" I whip around just as Emilia is reaching for the floor.

"She dropped sixteen beads in the seat and on the floor," Kylian announces from the back.

How he knows the exact number, I don't bother asking. I have no doubt he's right.

Turning forward again and easing off the accelerator as we get closer to the car in front of us, I shoot a quick glare at my sister through the rearview mirror. "What did I tell you about making friendship bracelets in the car?"

With her chin held high, she meets my gaze. "Not to do it."

"And yet you deliberately disobeyed me?"

"*Ohhh*," Jade whispers.

Sitting up straighter, I eye her in the mirror. "Hush."

Emilia scowls at me, indignant and self-righteous. "I was making a bracelet for Jojo. She's sad, Kenny. I wanted to cheer her up."

We come to a full stop. The traffic is getting heavier as we approach the metro area outside of Charlotte. Shifting in my seat, I look at my girl—my beautiful, gorgeous, sad girl.

Jojo's tipped forward, searching between the captain seats, talking low to Emilia as she hunts for fallen beads. She must feel my stare, because she lifts her head, still murmuring reassuringly to my sister, and offers a meek smile. Fuck. It's so incongruent when compared with the enigmatic smile or playful smirk I'm used to seeing plastered on her face.

My sister's right: she's sad.

Unlike Emilia, I know the reason behind her sorrow.

"Why are you sad, Jojo?" Jade twists in her seat, but she's trapped by her safety belt.

"Stay buckled," I warn.

She dismisses me with a wave of her hand. Little sass pot.

Jojo smiles at me in the rearview mirror, the smallest reassurance that she's got this one.

"I haven't seen your brother in a while. I missed him."

"*Aw*. That's so sweet," Jade gushes.

Emilia groans. "Gross. I better not have to watch you kiss at the cabin."

My girl laughs, a hollow reply that contains only a fraction of her usual joy. But at least she's laughing. At least she's trying to smile.

Running a hand down Emilia's arm, Jojo pulls back and sits up straight again. "I promise you won't have to watch anyone kiss at the cabin."

Beside her, Kylian lets out an indignant *hmph*.

"It'll be fun to all hang out over the next few days," she adds.

"So maybe this storm isn't such a bad thing, since we all get to be together," Emilia announces.

I don't need to look at Jojo to know she's fighting back tears. As it stands, "all of us" will never be together ever again, even if we are sheltering under the same roof for the next few days.

Chapter 47

Locke

Outside the Suburban, I stretch my arms overhead and inhale the crisp mountain air, savoring the chill on the breeze.

I love the mountains. I love getting away from real life, losing myself in nature, away from the buzz of school and the media.

I haven't felt this good in a long-ass time.

Each time I come off a bad flare, I'm wary. It's hard to trust my body, or even my mind. I'll feel incrementally better one day, but I don't let myself hope. Not until I've made it through multiple days of reduced pain. Only then do I accept that maybe the worst is over.

Then, when the agony is diminished, I question whether it was really as bad as I remember. Sometimes I swear it was all in my head.

It's ridiculous. Pain is pain, and mine is debilitating. It affects all aspects of my existence, and there's no way to quantify what it feels like or how it'll compare to the discomfort of the following day.

Today is the first day I woke up confident that I'm on the upswing.

The absence of pain is sweet.

The presence of her is even sweeter.

Being back in the mix with my girl—holding her without aching, kissing her, playing with her, and worshipping her the way she deserves—is the sweetest reward.

Once Jade has climbed out with her backpack and is dashing toward the cabin after Emilia—while Kendrick yells at her to put on the coat she has tied around her waist—I offer Joey my hand. When she emerges from the back seat, she looks suspiciously rosy-cheeked and satisfied.

"You fucked in the back seat," I deadpan as she hits the running board on her way out.

"Finger fucked, yes," Kylian declares as he climbs out behind her and moves past us toward the house.

With a gasp, Joey smacks him in the chest.

"Emilia said you were sad," he counters, clutching her hand. "An orgasm always cheers you up."

Joey rolls her eyes, then sets her sights on me.

She gives me a once-over, and when she finally meets my gaze, she breaks into a playful grin. My girl likes what she sees, and I'll be damned if Kylian's the only one who gets to cheer her up with orgasms over the next few days.

Taking a step closer, I lower my head just a little. "Hey, Hot Girl."

Her eyes twinkle with delight. "You're back." Looping her arms around my midsection, she squeezes hard. Just how I like it.

With a groan, I pull her impossibly close, and because I can—and because she needs the lighthearted moment—I lift her off the ground and spin in circles.

When I settle her on her feet again, I bring my lips to the shell of her ear. "I'm back." My voice is gravelly, even to my own ears. "I'm sorry it was so rough for so long."

Slipping from my hold, she plants her hands on her hips and scowls. "Can I punch you?"

I can't help the snicker that slips out at her odd request. "I mean, I guess?"

Her little play punch lands right in my abs.

With an exaggerated *hmph*, I stumble. "You know I like it when you get violent with me, Hot Girl."

She crosses her arms and holds her head high. "Don't apologize for things you can't control or for doing what you need to do to be okay. I don't want you to ever say sorry for that again."

I love it when she's feisty. I love it even more that she's so unconditionally supportive.

"Come here." I grin and wave both hands until she's biting back her own smile and waltzing back into my arms. "I love you," I murmur into her hair. "I promise not to apologize for my arthritis again, but can I at least say thank you?"

With a drawn-out sigh, she snakes her arms around my waist and melts into me. "Yes. That, I can accept."

"Thank you. Thank you so much, Joey. For loving me. For sticking it out on the bad days. For making me tea and forcing me to sleep." My chest gets tight, and I have to clear my throat before I can continue. "For just being present and doing everything in your power to support me."

She sniffles against my chest. "Always, Nicky. I'll always be here for you. On the good days. But especially on the hard days."

I smooth my hand over her hair, savoring just how incredible it is to have her back in my arms.

"There'll be more hard days in the future," I warn. "Weeks. Hell, maybe even months or years." I pull in a breath and let it out slowly. Fuck, I hate the inevitable truth of chronic illness. "I'll have flare-ups for the rest of my life."

My girl tips her head back and rests her chin on my sternum. Her smile is soft and sincere when she says, "We'll face every hard day together."

I'm damn near teary eyed as I bow low to kiss her. It's one thing to stick with a person through the good days. It's hard for me to accept that this woman loves me enough to slog through my lowest lows, especially knowing there's no limit to how low I'll go or how long that low will last.

"I love you, Hot Girl. I know it's been awful for you these last few weeks. Maybe the fresh mountain air is what you need, too. I love this place. I think you will, too." Pulling back, I take her hand. "Come on. I want to show you around."

"Wait." She doesn't budge when I tug on her hand. "You've been here before?"

"Been here?" I tease. Just the thought of this place makes me feel lighter. "This is one of my top five favorite places in the world." She grins and turns to retrieve her bag from the car. I take it from her, grasp her hand once more, and start up the incline toward the house, following the stone path that leads to the wraparound porch.

"What are your other top favorite places?" she asks, squeezing my hand.

"Beach. Pantry. My bed."

I side-eye her and waggle my brows.

"And buried inside you."

Chapter 48

Kylian

Forget the god-forsaken beach and the sand that's impossible to leave behind when it's time to leave; give me a cabin built into the side of a snow-crested mountain any day.

The visible puffs of our exhalations create a cloud of hazy carbon dioxide that drifts over the ledge of the porch as it evaporates into the atmosphere.

Jo sits up and reaches toward the planks of the heated deck. I wrap one arm around her legs to hold her steady as the hammock sways gently.

She takes a sip of her hot toddy—courtesy of Mrs. Lansbury, who's been at the cabin since yesterday when we finalized our evacuation plans—then sets it on the ground, lies back against my arm, and sighs.

"You good, Mama?" Kendrick asks from the other end of the deck.

He's helping Jade and Emilia do their school assignments for the week. Standing between them, he looks on and offers corrections as needed. Except he's messed up two equations so far. Maybe he's trying to make it appear as if a fourth-grader really did complete the assignment.

"Better than good," our girl replies. She stretches. Leans over the edge again. Makes the fabric of her thin black leggings pull tight around her ass as she bends to take another sip of her drink.

I can't see her face, but based on the hungry look Kendrick's sporting, I would guess she's eye-fucking him right back.

One of the twins asks a question, and Kendrick turns away, breaking their spell.

Jo relaxes back into the hammock between us.

"I can see why you love it here," she murmurs to Nicky as she snuggles closer.

With a relaxed hum, he smooths one hand down her body so his tattooed knuckles rest between her thighs.

Theoretically, the colder air should worsen his arthritic pain. But this cabin is built low enough into the side of the Blue Ridge Mountain Range that the barometric pressure is reduced. Decker has it outfitted with a state-of-the-art dehumidification system, and all the decks and porches feature propane heaters to ward off the cold.

I asked him for a spoon check when we arrived; Decker usually does it, but Decker's not part of us anymore, so I've stepped up in regard to his health and Kendrick's. I've also been keeping watch over Jo's since the urinary tract infection incident.

Nicky insisted he was on cloud nine, which I surmise to mean he's in good shape, mentally and physically. No telling what the barometric pressure is on cloud nine, but he's better than he was, and that makes Jo happy. If Jo is happy, then I'm satisfied.

I sit up and sip my own drink. When I settle, this time on my side, I brush a kiss to the soft skin of Jo's neck and tease one hand along the elastic of her waistband.

"It feels really good to all be together again," she whispers.

As if that's some sort of secret.

She's right.

We've all been hurting. Reeling. Coping in our own ways. All without the support of one another. It's obvious each of us is carrying a heavy weight, yet I don't want to burden Jo or either of the guys with my concerns. If that's the case, then it's safe to assume they each have a similar mindset. The complexity of our situation and how deeply our day-to-day lives are intertwined with Decker's only make the emotional pain more acute.

A simple solution to getting off the isle with our girl—all three of us—doesn't exist. So we stayed. We took turns. We avoided Decker. Now we've started making plans for what's next.

"I know, baby. We're working on an arrangement that will allow us to be together permanently," I promise, kissing the warmth below her ear. "I'm sorry it's taking so long."

"Kyl." She grasps my hand. On the other side, she's already holding Nicky's. "It's okay. None of us has had time to formulate a plan. We were *all* blindsided."

That we were.

"Hey. I have an idea. Worst-case scenario, you and I can move back in with our parents," Nicky says. "K and Joey can take turns going between our houses. I've slept on that zero-gravity moon chair you used to have in your room. It's pretty comfortable, honestly."

Jo snorts. Damn, is she awful at keeping secrets and maintaining her composure.

"What's so funny?" Nicky asks, propping himself up with an elbow and eyeing her, then me.

She peers over at me, eyebrows raised. I shrug in response. If she wants to share, then I won't stop her.

With another snort, she turns her head to Nicky. "Sleep isn't the only thing that beanbag chair is good for."

Frowning, Nicky sits up a little higher. "Wait. What am I missing?"

Jo laughs again. She can't stop laughing. She's losing it, and now we have Kendrick's attention, too.

"Don't worry about it, Emo Boy." She tries to brush it off, but at the same time, she sits up and clutches her stomach, garnering even more scrutiny from our audience.

"Wait a minute." Nicky curls up fully and points an accusing finger at us. He keeps his voice low, but it's cutting, nonetheless. "Did I miss out on beanbag sex? Seriously?" He tugs on Jo's hand. "When? Was it when your parents had you over for dinner a few weeks ago? Your mom invited me, but I was in too much pain!"

Jo's doubled over now. I rest a hand on her shoulder to keep her from rolling forward off the hammock.

"Sorry, pal," I offer with a shrug.

Nicky flops back, groaning. "I fucking hate RA."

He didn't keep his voice down that time.

"Nicky said a bad word!" one of the twins shouts from the table.

"That he did," Kendrick grits out, his jaw locked tight. "Maybe Nicky wants to come over here and help with this long division to make up for it."

Huffing, Locke lifts up on his elbows so he can see K and the girls. "Dude. I'm a philosophy major. I didn't understand old math, let alone *new* math." With that, he reaches over a still-cackling Jo and shoves my shoulder. "I bet Daddy Genius here could help you."

When Jo dissolves into a fresh round of giggles, he smirks. The twins are both turned our way and wearing perplexed frowns that make them look just like their older brother.

"Kylian is not anyone's dad!" Emilia sasses.

Jo, now laughing so hard she's crying, slinks off the hammock and onto her knees. The lightness and playfulness emanating from her is contagious. Her laugh is a soothing melody, a perfectly curated balm.

When she's finally caught her breath, I stand and offer her a hand. Her shoulders are still shaking as she accepts my help, and there's a mischievous glint in her eye.

But as soon as she's fully upright, the laughing stops.

As if the joy has been sapped from her body.

As if the world has been shrouded in darkness.

She's so silent and still it's eerie. Telling.

Though I suspect what I'll find, I glance over my shoulder to confirm.

There he fucking is. The man of the hour. The man of all the hours, until he destroyed the most perfect, beautiful human I've ever known and left the rest of us to make sense of the pieces he scattered as he broke her.

At the door, Decker hovers. He knows he's not supposed to be here. He's got one foot on the deck, one foot still in the house.

He knows better. Yet there he fucking is.

I agreed to come to the cabin because the storm evac plan we have in place is solid and there was no time to create another I could guarantee was as safe. I agreed so long as he vowed to stay out of sight and out of our way.

It's evident that plan is shot to hell.

He clears his throat. The sound grates against the silence that's fallen over the group.

"Sorry," he offers evenly.

As if being in her presence for the first time in weeks doesn't affect him. He's a liar. A liar and a thief.

"I didn't realize…" He runs a hand through his hair and looks over his shoulder, into the house. When he turns back, he regards me. "I'm just heading out for a hike."

The sound of a chair scraping against the deck breaks the silence that's enveloped us once again. At the table, one of Kendrick's sisters shifts in her seat. "Don't forget your bear spray, Uncle Ducky."

Innocent Jade.

She's unaware that most of us here wouldn't mind if he forgot his bear spray. Not to cause fatality, of course. A mauling resulting in severe injury would suffice.

I give him a second.

Then two.

At the three count, I'm releasing Jo, glaring daggers, and striding toward the door.

"Whoa." Kendrick steps in front of me, cutting me off a few feet from where Decker stands.

I try to push past him, but the man's massive, and he anticipates my sidestep.

"Whoa. Whoa. Whoa. Chill, brother. We're going to have to start calling you Kyller if you go guard dog on his ass every time he makes an appearance."

Heart pounding and fury running through me, I cross my arms over my chest. "We had an agreement," I remind Decker. "We would all come here like usual. You could see for yourself that we're safe. In exchange, you agreed to make yourself scarce."

He raises both hands in surrender.

But then his eyes flit over my shoulder—considering, searching.

"Don't look at her," I snap.

Because this is the exact moment I was determined to avoid. The one where she's forced to face the man who broke her heart.

The fucker encroached on our first lighthearted moment in weeks, and he's audacious enough to look at her and remind himself of what he pushed away.

No one is getting out of this unscathed.

Though I hoped we could get through this weekend without creating fresh wounds.

Apparently, it was too much to wish for.

I struggle against Kendrick's hold, fully prepared to get up in Decker's face if he needs the proximity of my fury to communicate the severity of his transgressions.

"I'm going," he relents, shifting back into the house and out of sight.

Kendrick doesn't back away from me as I crane my neck and watch him go, fighting down the urge to charge after him and lock the front door once he's gone.

Chapter 49

Josephine

Decker didn't resurface for the rest of the night.

Thank fuck. Once was enough.

It's impossible to avoid his presence altogether, of course. Not with the number of promotional posters that feature his likeness all over campus or the footage of him on the local news Jeannie insists on blaring while she works.

Though I hadn't considered it a possibility before today, seeing his image everywhere made facing him for the first time hurt less than I anticipated.

Oh, the irony. Maybe there's merit in his whole exposure therapy concept after all.

I'm loading the last of the dinner plates into the dishwasher when Mrs. Lansbury catches me.

"Child," she murmurs in her melodic accent. "I told you, dear. I'll take care of the dishes. The cooking. Everything. It's the least I can do…" She trails off. By the sympathetic looks she's been giving me since we arrived, it's safe to assume she's privy to the heartbreak and damage caused by her beloved employer.

Tightening the bow of the apron around her waist, she steps up to the sink. Softer, she says, "It helps me feel useful. Gives me purpose. The boys are always trying to pitch in, too, but I need to keep busy during times like these."

Times like these.

I'm tempted to ask her if she means the storm heading up the coast or the tempest that's torn our group apart.

But I don't find the courage before Kylian sweeps through the kitchen.

"Jo. Let's go."

He's all business as he marches deeper into the house. Ahead of me, his stride doesn't falter as he calls back, "Good night, Mrs. Lansbury."

I have no idea what we're doing, but I'm more than intrigued to find out what's got Kylian so hyper-focused.

Catching up to him, I link my arm through his. "Where are we going?" I whisper as he weaves down a hallway to a set of stairs.

"The Den," he replies.

That's his only explanation.

When I pause on the landing, still holding tight to his arm, he stops on the second step. Turning, he peers at me through his glasses. Standing like this, he has to look up at me.

"What's the Den?"

Despite Kylian's assurance that there would be no more run-ins with Decker, trepidation washes over me. This is his house, so I have no desire to hang out in public spaces.

Kylian tips his head to the side. "I forgot you've never been here." A playful smile paints his face. "The Den is the cabin's version of the Nest. Except it's in the basement, so it's pitch-black when I want it to be. Nice and cool, too. Ideal for sleeping."

"We're going to bed?" I glance over my shoulder, then back at him. I don't know what time it is, but it can't be that late.

"We're going to the Den," Kylian corrects, squeezing my hand. "The private, fully soundproof Den."

Oh.

"Soundproof, huh?" I tease, lacing my arms around his neck and raking my fingers through the short hairs at his nape.

"Fully soundproofed. Well-appointed bathroom. Mini fridge. I already moved your bags down there."

That gives me pause.

I pull back a fraction. "Kyl, you don't sleep well—"

"I'll be fine," he insists. "The Den is bigger than the Nest, and so is the bed. I'd feel more at ease if you were with me tonight. I—" He clears his throat and blinks at me, his lips turned down. "I need to know you're okay more than I need good sleep tonight, baby. Come down and let me take care of you."

My heart patters out of my chest at his confession. Kylian is my rock, my safety, my harbor, and my anchor. He rarely communicates his own needs to me. It doesn't come naturally to him.

"Okay," I agree. My heart is still pounding, and as an idea knits itself in my mind, a low, liquid heat develops in my core. "We *are* going to do more than just sleep, yes?" I angle my lips over his, running my tongue along the seam.

He lets me kiss him for two seconds before nipping at my bottom lip. "It's a soundproof room with a king-size bed, Jo. While your safety is my top concern, I'm excellent at multitasking, so yes, I plan to be buried deep in your perfect pussy for a large portion of the night."

Hit with a bolt of lust, I ask, "Can Nicky come, too?" Before he can respond, though, I elaborate. "He's finally feeling better, and I miss him, but I miss you, too, and—"

He cuts me off with a bruising kiss. Grasping my shoulders, he guides me back as he walks up the two stairs he had descended. Once he's positioned on the landing, hovering above me, his lips are on mine again and he's feeding me his tongue.

Sparks dance up my spine as he grips my throat.

I know what that tongue feels like lapping at my cunt. I know exactly how intense tonight will be if he's already squeezing my neck.

"You want to play with two of your boyfriends tonight, baby?"

Moaning into his mouth, I smooth a hand down his torso. When I reach the crotch of his joggers, he's already hard and straining. He thrusts into my hand once. Then again.

Suddenly, I wish I hadn't stopped and asked for an explanation. Now I'm frustrated that we're not already downstairs.

"Hmm?" he doubles down, pressing his cock into my hand as he awaits my words.

"Yes, Daddy," I answer on a shaky breath.

He pulls back and smacks my ass. "Text him. Tell him he has three minutes to get down there or I'm starting without him." He's halfway down the stairs when he calls over his shoulder. "And you better be spread out on the bed and dripping on my sheets in two."

Chapter 50

Josephine

"Lie on the bed."

Kylian's instructions begin the second Nicky steps into the room.

"All right, all right. What have we got going on here?"

"Jo requested your presence for sexual relations. We're going to have a three-way."

Behind me, Nicky snorts. "You her spokesperson now? Didn't know you were considering a career in PR."

"You asked a question. I gave the answer. Jo's mouth is full, so she can't answer for herself anyway."

Nicky steps into my line of sight as I take Kylian's cock deep. He's planted firmly at the end of the bed, and I'm already naked, on hands and knees, my thighs spread wide so I can sink low enough to take his full length into my mouth.

Kylian grips my hair, thrusting and holding until I gag. He groans as my throat constricts around his cock. With a shift of his hips, he pulls back a fraction to give me a break.

I grunt my refusal and dig my nails into his thighs until he gets the idea and fucks the back of my throat again.

"Jo," he groans, drawing out the single syllable like it's a prayer. "Fuck, baby." He thrusts again.

I peek up, enamored by the sight of his head thrown back in ecstasy, and pull back just a little so I can lock eyes with Nicky. Holding his gaze, I swirl my tongue around the ridge of Kylian's penis.

"That's hot." Locke's got his bottom lip pulled between his teeth and he's fisting his erection through his pants.

"I told you to get on the bed." Kylian grits his teeth, as if he's doing everything in his power to keep it together.

"Bro. I love you. But I only take orders from her." He shoots me a wink.

Kylian scoffs, but he cradles my jaw with a touch far too tender for the commanding tone he's taken. "How do you expect her to give you orders when she's being such a good girl and letting me fuck her mouth?"

My stomach erupts with butterflies. Praise like that from Kylian does it for me every time.

"We don't need words. Our connection is so deep I can read her mind."

"Oh yeah? Oh—*fuck*, hold up."

The warning is for me. Kylian's cock pulses in my mouth. He's close, but he doesn't want to come yet.

Easing off, I focus on the tip, tonguing the end of his leaking slit.

"Yep. For instance..." Locke approaches, shucking off his shirt, and sinks to his knees. "Right now, our girl wants me to suck on her perfect tits and play with her clit while she deep-throats you until you explode."

The heat between my thighs intensifies at the prospect.

"Is that what you want, baby?" Kylian shifts his stance to make room for Locke.

I pop off his dick and grin. "Yes, Daddy."

"Don't smack me too hard with your nuts." Locke's wearing a devious smirk.

I stifle a laugh. It's a fair request. He'll have to sit on the floor right in front of Kylian to make this work.

Before Kylian can respond, I take his full length into my mouth and hum. I love the feel of him. The fullness. The trust he bestows on me when he lets me play with his cock.

I moan as arousal drips between my legs, both from pleasuring Kylian and from the proximity of his best friend. Nicky angles in and kisses my neck, my chest, and finally scrapes his teeth against the peak of my breast while his big hands caress and massage every inch of skin he can find.

He lavishes me, going from one side to the other, biting my breasts and sucking my nipples into hard, pointed peaks.

"You're so fucking sweet. You love when I suck on these perfect tits while Kylian fucks your pretty mouth, don't you, Hot Girl?" He dips low again, capturing one breast in his mouth while he pinches the aching nipple of the other. "What's that? You want me to rub your clit too?"

I grin around Kylian's cock, delighted by the return of Locke's playful nature.

Peering up, I check on Kylian.

He's very clearly in his own world. With his head thrown back, he's muttering under his breath. When he grips my hair and holds my head in place, I know he's ready.

I hollow my cheeks and suck hard. At the same time, Nicky pinches one nipple, sucks on the other, and grinds the heel of his hand against my clit in quick, urgent thrusts.

As an orgasm crashes into me, Kylian groans, and the first spurt of his release hits my tongue.

Nicky works me through my orgasm as I suck Kylian through his.

We're a mess of moans and cum as our indulgence peaks and our joint releases crash through us.

Pleasure. Pleasure everywhere. Giving and receiving. Feeling and loving.

For as long as I live, I'll never get enough of these boys.

When we're done, we're all breathless. With a groan, Kylian scrubs his hands down his face and looms over us so he can see Nicky, who's still splayed out on the floor.

"Now are you ready to get on the fucking bed?"

Locke rolls his lips and turns his head in slow motion, clearly deferring to me.

"On the bed, Emo Boy. Don't make him say it again."

Without a word, he scrambles to his feet, salutes Kylian, and flops back on the mattress, legs and arms splayed wide.

Kylian grasps my waist and helps me to my feet. Once I'm steady, he spins me around and presses into me from behind. He rests his chin on my shoulder and brings his lips to my ear, sending shivers racing through me, as the two of us take in the sight of Nicky spread out before us.

"You're going to ride him while I finger your ass."

It's not a question. It's not even a request.

It's a command I can't wait to obey.

Locke yanks his pants and underwear down in one quick movement and tosses them off the bed.

My heart pounds against my chest as I climb onto the bed and crawl closer to him.

Kylian follows right behind me. "Plant your feet, Nicky. Ease her down, then get her nice and stretched out on your cock."

Locke grins up at me as I straddle him and lower myself onto his length.

I'm dripping from my orgasm, but I still take my time. Savoring the stretch. Savoring the sensation of being filled so impossibly full by Nicky's massive size.

Locke squeezes his eyes shut and clears his throat, then opens them and focuses on our lower halves, hazel eyes blazing. His focus is set on the apex of my thighs, at the place our bodies connect and two become one. "I'll never get over the sight of us together."

"It is one of your top five favorite places," I tease, bending forward so I can pepper his neck with kisses.

"I'm serious, Hot Girl. I love this. I love *you*. You're my ultimate favorite place." The kiss he plants on my lips is tender. The thrust that follows is hard enough to force his pubic piercing into my clit. Our lips are still touching when he whispers, "Right here. Right now. Inside you. There's no place else I'd rather be."

Kylian trails his fingers down my spine, pulling me back to the moment.

The warmth of his lips against the back of my neck is so erotic my pussy clenches around Locke's length.

"I've got plenty of lube. It's going to burn a little at first. Tell me to stop, and I will."

It's sweet that Kylian's done his research, but Kendrick's been fingering my ass almost every time he fucks me lately. We're all in with the ass play and prep these days. We all have the same end goal in mind.

Behind me, Kylian pops the cap off the bottle, and a moment later, his finger is probing.

"Relax for me, baby. Kiss Nicky. Let him make you feel good."

"Yes, Daddy." Obediently, I dip my tongue into Nicky's mouth and grind my hips back and forth in his lap.

When Kylian breaches my hole, I freeze. Not because it hurts, but because it feels so deliciously carnal and forbidden.

"Holy shit," Nicky breathes out. He grips my hips and holds me down. "I can feel his finger inside you. Holy shit. *Ah*, fuck. That's so fucking good. Too good. I'm not going to last at this rate."

"Oh yes you will," Kylian murmurs.

Locke jolts and lets out a yelp. "Dude. What the fuck? Did you really just yank on my balls?"

"Yes I did. You need to hold off. Make our girl detonate. She comes first. Always."

"*Fucking hell*, Kyl. That was never up for debate. No more spontaneous ball grabs, understood?"

"Yes."

Their banter would probably have me rolling with laughter if I wasn't so focused on the stretch and the pull and the hot and fiery sensation flooding me as Nicky fucks my pussy and Kylian fingers my ass.

I rise up slightly, then lower again, and we all groan in unison.

"You love this, don't you, baby?" Kylian murmurs in my ear. "You love rubbing your clit on Nicky's piercing while you're full of his cock. And you love my fingers plugging your ass."

"Fuck. Yes," I pant, unable to control my breathing. I'm desperate to move, desperate to chase what's promising to be an utterly satisfying orgasm.

"You're so perfect, baby. Letting us fill you up. Showing us how well you can take it."

I grind harder on Nicky's piercing, the edges of orgasm within reach.

Kylian moves my hair to one side. "As good as this feels, imagine what it will be like when Kendrick's fucking your ass while I'm buried deep in your cunt for the first time."

I was already on the precipice. The sensations are all too much. Adding his dirty words and carnal promises is all it takes to send me spiraling.

"That's it," Nicky grunts. "Right fucking there."

His cock pulsates inside me as his orgasm takes hold.

"That's our girl," Kylian praises. "Ride his cock and fuck my fingers, baby. Show us how pretty you look when you come for two of your boyfriends."

We come, the two of us, under Kylian's direction and praise.

Our joint release is so much more than pleasure: it's a promise and a vow, a manifestation for our future.

I want it to always be like this.

Together. Figuring it out. Making it work.

We come together, and my body trembles with a vulnerable sense of need I've never felt before. I've always been fiercely independent, and I've never needed anyone like I need my boys, but as the final spasms of my orgasm roll through me, I admit the truth to myself: I never want to be apart from them again.

Chapter 51

Josephine

Kylian wasn't kidding about the size of the bed in the Den. The three of us fit easily. In fact, it's so large that I wake sometime in the night, shivering, because neither of my boys are cuddled close.

Kylian's flat on his back, off to one side, well and truly asleep. Nicky's got an arm draped loosely around my hips, but he's not holding me close enough to share his body heat. I'm tempted to snuggle up against him, but even though he swears he's past his flare, I won't risk causing him pain.

Quietly, I peel myself out of bed. As I do, my shivers intensify.

I packed for the evacuation quickly and carelessly. Without much thought, I threw a few changes of clothes and my regular toiletries into a bag. Even if I'd had more time, I wouldn't have many options. My wardrobe consists mainly of clothing ideal for the typical temps of North Carolina, not for sleeping through cold nights in a basement in a cabin built into a snowcapped mountain. I'd have to put on everything I own to be warm enough down here.

There are a few items of clothing on the floor, but the selection isn't much better than what I arrived with. Locke runs hot, so he came down wearing nothing but sweatpants, and Kylian redressed before falling asleep.

I snag Nicky's oversized black joggers off the floor and step into them. I have to roll the waistband three times to make them stay up. Then I find and slip on the tank top I was wearing earlier.

Accepting that this is the best I can come up with in the dark, I venture upstairs in search of more layers. Or even an extra blanket.

The house is quiet, the sound of my bare feet against the hardwood steps echoing off the exposed timber of the cabin.

It's a beautiful place. Cozier than the mansion and not nearly as sleek or showy. It feels more like a home.

Yawning, I step into the living room and immediately spot a stack of blankets near the fireplace.

"Yahtzee," I mumble, beelining for the pile.

I grab one and wrap it around my body like a robe, moaning at the feel of the ultrasoft fabric and its plush thickness. I take two more blankets from the stack, then turn to head back to the Den.

But when I spin, a hand catches my shoulder. Another gently presses against my lips.

"Don't scream," he rumbles.

Gasping, I stumble back and look up into the onyx eyes of Decker Crusade.

Chapter 52

Decker

Her breath caresses my palm.

Her clear blue eyes go round with shock and shoot up to mine.

Panic. Trepidation. Unease.

Her eyes go even wider, then she inhales a sharp breath.

Removing my hand, I pacify her. "It's okay. It's just me."

I was afraid I'd scared her, emerging from the dark the way I did.

As her fear transforms into resolve, her brows hitch higher and realization trickles in.

She's not scared. Startled, maybe. But it's not the unknown presence looming in the dark that's throwing her.

It's me.

I watched her walk into the living room. Looking for what, I didn't know.

I watched her, satisfaction settling in my gut as my longing manifested into reality.

I thought I was hallucinating.

After I'd wished for her to appear before me all night, she waltzed right back into my orbit.

Close enough that when she passed, I could feel the shift in the air.

Close enough that the sweet scent of her shampoo assaulted me.

I've been up for hours.

Nursing three fingers of bourbon. Desperate to find a way to escape the ever-widening pit in my stomach. Willing myself to ignore the discontent overshadowing my existence.

It's all in vain. I can't ignore anything about how she affects me or how much I fucking miss her. Being in the same house only compounds the yearning.

I'm so attuned to her, so desperate for a glimpse of her face or the hint of a smile. I swear I sensed her before she'd made it to the top of the stairs.

My pulse hammered so loudly I was certain it would give me away.

But she didn't see me where I sat, shrouded in darkness, slouched in a wingback chair.

She didn't even sense me, not the way I always sense her.

It hurts. It hurts to know she's moving on.

In search of a blanket, she wandered through the dark house, wearing a tiny tank top and sweatpants that clearly belong to one of the guys. She just wanted a blanket.

And I can't leave well enough alone.

Her hair is wild and loose. She's fresh-faced, her cheeks rosy and lips swollen. I want to ask if she's cold. If she's hungry. If she's even remotely okay. Because I'm fucking not. I haven't been since the second I told her we were through and obliterated the most cherished relationship I've ever had. That I'll ever have.

All I want to do is hold her.

"Siren."

She blinks out of the spell we were both under.

She pulls the blanket around her shoulders tighter.

I know before she opens her mouth that the moment is gone.

Vanished. Dissipated. Over before it even truly began, just like us.

She averts her gaze. "I wasn't expecting anyone to be up." She won't even look at me. Her focus is fixed on a spot over my shoulder.

"Josephine," I try again. Surely she can feel my desperation—the despondence and pain that lurches through me at just the sight of her. If only she'd let me hold her. If only we could slow this all down so I could explain.

I reach out. Only enough to test her resolve.

She shifts back before I've moved an inch.

"Kylian said we wouldn't see you again this weekend." Her words are clipped, her tone as tense as her posture. She barely sounds like herself as she speaks, and she still won't meet my eye.

She wasn't supposed to see me.

That's what I promised when I persuaded them to come to the cabin.

How the hell did I convince myself I could stay away from her when every breath I take burns with regret?

She wasn't supposed to see me, but the instant I laid eyes on her, I couldn't hold back.

"I'm sorry. I'm only out here because I didn't think anyone would be up at this hour."

She nods, pulling the blanket draped around her shoulders even tighter.

"I just needed…" She trails off, still looking everywhere but at me.

A blanket. She needed a blanket.

Which confirms my suspicions. She's sleeping downstairs with Kylian.

I didn't dare inquire about sleeping arrangements. I was just so damn grateful that they'd all be here. That I can see with my own eyes that they're safe. That they're sheltered, under my roof, together. Despite how begrudgingly they came.

But now she's here. Standing two feet in front of me.

"Wait. Josephine," I croak. Desperate to get through. Desperate for her to look at me, to open up, to stop pushing me out.

Her eyes find mine, and for a second, just a second, I swear there's a flicker in those blue irises.

A flicker of curiosity.

A flash of pain.

A second suspended in time where we exist in an alternate universe. One where I didn't break us and our story wasn't over before it had a chance to begin.

She blinks, and it's gone.

But it was there. I saw it. I fucking felt it.

I refuse to accept defeat. The moment may have passed, but I have to try.

"One minute," I request, planting my feet wide and squaring my hips.

I'm warm and unsteady from the bourbon I've been nursing all night. I maintain my posture and hold the position while I await her answer.

"One minute, Josephine," I plead. This time, I hold my breath.

Her eyes narrow, searching. If she's considering whether I'm worthy of that minute, she should know I'm not. But I am relentless.

I'm not above begging. She's here. Right fucking here. Within arm's reach. Even if she's further from being mine than she's ever been.

I'm still holding my breath when she tips her chin and shakes her head.

"I can't."

The pain of her rejection doesn't even register. I stow it away, keep it for later.

She takes a step forward: a long stride, sidestepping me in an effort to give herself a wide berth.

I fall back into the pocket, willing to stand directly in her path and take the sack.

"Josephine," I try one more time. "One minute. You can't even give me that?"

She hesitates. It's a micro-movement, a barely there drag of her momentum. But it's enough.

She peers over her shoulder, this time with tears in her eyes, and assesses me. The scowl she so often reserves for me is firmly in place.

"No, Decker. You can't have a minute. Not now. Not ever again."

Chapter 53

Josephine

Heat rushes through me as I flee.

By the time I make it back into bed, I'm so hot and agitated that I have to kick the extra blankets off.

Despite the way my pulse pounds in my ears, I'm as quiet as I can be. I don't want to wake either of my guys or let on to my encounter with Decker. Not until I've processed it.

What the fuck happened up there?

Because that was real. The emotions and whatever just passed between us—whether it was a moment of weakness or a peek at the truth I've been so desperate to uncover—Decker was there. Waiting for me? Hoping I'd show up?

I lie awake, huffing as adrenaline courses through me for what feels like hours.

I can't sleep.

Can't breathe.

I can't do anything but envision his face: The initial hope followed by the horror in his eyes when I rejected him. The shock that slid over his features when I denied his request.

My fight-or-flight instinct kicked in once the implications of his plea hit me. Because what the fuck did he expect to happen? Did he really believe we'd hold each other for a minute? Allow ourselves sixty seconds to surrender to what we both want, but what he so unceremoniously and single-handedly destroyed?

And then what? Did he think that one minute would be enough to galvanize us until the next run-in? That it would pacify him for a while? That he could come back looking to steal another minute of my time when its effects wore off?

What about my wants? My needs?

What about the fresh wounds, just beginning to heal, that he'd reopen if I said yes to him?

Heat creeps up my neck as I silently seethe.

How dare he?

After I've lain in bed for what feels like an eternity, I sit up, more heated and aggravated than when I left Decker standing in the living room.

I quietly scoot to the foot of the bed for the second time tonight, grateful when both Locke and Kylian stay sound asleep.

When the door is latched behind me, I hoof it up the stairs, on a mission.

I don't bother going slow or being quiet this time.

I don't care if he knows I'm coming. He deserves everything coming his way.

The living room is quiet, but it was quiet before.

I scan the space, and when I find nothing but an empty room, I check the kitchen and the dining area. Unoccupied.

Hands fisted at my sides, I venture deeper into the house and down the hallway that leads to a set of bedrooms. I helped Kendrick get the girls settled into their room earlier, so I know which one is theirs, just like I know that K's is right next door.

There's another door at the end of the hall, which I discover is a linen closet. Then there's a small half bath and an empty bedroom on the other side.

I turn the handle on the last door in this part of the house, and I'm met with another empty room.

Sighing, I take a step back, ready to pull the door closed, but the sound of water striking tiles stops me.

Then a tattered, broken cry echoes through the dark.

A bolt of concern shoots through me. I scurry toward the haze billowing out of the doorway, panicked.

But when I cross the threshold, I'm met with nothing but steam from the shower and the fogged-up mirror above the vanity.

That's when my brain catches up. That's when the identity of the person in the shower dawns on me.

"Decker?" I ask tentatively.

Because it could only be him.

I step farther into the room, shivering when my bare feet hit the cold floor.

Another step.

Another strangled sob rings out, reverberating off the tiles.

My heart bursts into a billion pieces.

Fragments. Fractures and slivers so thin, there's no way to piece them back together. The edges don't line up. It's senseless to try to salvage something so utterly destroyed.

Because that's what Decker did. Before we even had a shot at solidifying our connection. Before I could show him how deeply I loved him, he pushed me away and shattered my heart.

I freeze where I stand, my self-preservation warring with my desire to comfort him.

I should leave. Every iota of logic and reason I possess is urging me away from this place, from this man.

Vindication thrums through me as I listen to him cry. He wasn't completely unaffected by what he did, despite the cool, heartless mask he wears. He's hurting. He's hurting so badly he's sobbing.

Yet he's the root cause of our mutual pain.

God dammit, Decker Crusade.

I should have known better.

I should have pushed back harder, refused to come here in the first place.

This is why I can never go back to the mansion.

It's not about dancing around one another and what almost was.

It's not about avoiding each other the best we can.

It's constantly battling against the invisible strings and palpable pull that link us together.

"Decker?" I call out, louder.

There's a startled grunt, then silence ensues.

The shower turns off.

But he makes no move to emerge from behind the steamy glass enclosure.

He knows it's me. He has to.

I take another step further into the room.

Anxiety thrums through my veins as I wait for him to speak. To acknowledge me.

A massive palm slaps against the fogged-up glass. It remains there. Inviting me. Resting. His open palm calls me forward like he knows I'd give anything to touch him for real. To feel the warmth of him again, even for a minute. Even though he was the one who brought about the bitter, cold darkness I've existed in for the last few weeks.

"Decker. Talk to me. Let me in." I'm practically pressed up against the glass now, with no recollection of how I got all the way across the room.

His answer is nothing more than a choked-out, hollow sob.

Even so, he makes no moves to slide open the glass shower door. To reach out. To put us both out of our goddamn misery.

I swallow past the nauseating emotion lodged in my throat, not even bothering to fight the tears that fall freely down both cheeks.

"Decker, please," I beg, placing my palm against the glass, lining it up with his massive hand.

The shower door shudders, startling me, as he presses his forehead into the panel between us.

"I'm sorry." His words are muffled, and his face, all but his forehead and brow line, is hidden by the steam.

"Josephine. I'm so fucking sorry."

A guttural sob shakes the glass, triggering an onslaught of my own tears. They well and crest over my lashes, falling fast and splattering against my chest like raindrops.

"Decker. Open the door."

He shakes his head, and the glass shakes with him.

This stubborn, obstinate, bullheaded man.

"*Decker Crusade*," I plead, grinding my own forehead into the smooth, warm glass.

We're so close. So fucking close. Why can't he let me in?

"I'm so sorry, baby. I thought I could save you," he sobs. "I thought I could push you away and stay away. But all I did—all I've ever done—is hurt you."

He's spiraling. He's unraveling in front of me, and yet I can't reach him.

"It doesn't have to be like this," I urge. "We can go back, Decker. We can figure this out."

He didn't give me a chance the morning he broke us. He didn't give me even a minute to collect my thoughts or catch my breath.

I would have fought for us. I would have committed to finding a way forward, even if it hurt. Even if it was hard. Even if it required sacrifice.

He never gave me a chance.

He never gave *us* a chance.

"Decker." I pull on the handle, determined to get through to him, but the door doesn't budge. His weight holds the glass in place. "Decker. Let me in."

"I can't," he cries.

"You can!" My heart hammers against my ribs as heat creeps up my chest and neck. "Decker, open the door. We can figure this out. Just give us a chance."

"*No*," he barks. The word echoes off the tiles. "We fucking can't, and now I'm hurting you more. It's killing me. It's killing me to put you through this, and yet I can't stop. I'm a fucking masochist when it comes to you, Josephine." He shudders. "I'm not strong enough to do what I know has to be done. You were right to deny me. Don't give me any more of your minutes, Siren. Promise me you'll stay away. You *have* to stay away."

The glass rattles as he pulls back, removing his hand and his head and all hope in one fell swoop.

A second passes. Then another.

Tears fall in rapid succession as I sense the emotionless mask he wears for the world slipping back into place.

His tone is sharp when he speaks again.

"There's nothing left between us. There can't be. There won't be, ever again."

His words land like a physical blow. My stomach bottoms out, and all the air escapes my lungs. He's so determined to push me away.

I press my forehead harder against the glass as the tears fall faster, dripping straight to the floor now.

They aren't tears of sadness, though. I'm sad, of course, but my heartache will keep.

These are tears of frustration. Anger. Tears of outrage and devastation.

Because it doesn't have to be like this. There's *always* another way. Yet he's so fixated on protecting me that he can't see past his own bullheadedness to consider alternatives.

The world we live in isn't black and white. There's always another option, a new idea, an alternative. If only he'd let us try.

I'm willing to try. I'd put in the work. I could learn to deal with the media, agree to more security, spend a lifetime learning to accept that he's a public figure.

If only he'd let us fucking try.

This realization hits so hard it's almost enough to knock me off my feet.

He's already given up on us. He's not even willing to try.

"You're a coward," I whisper, the words raw as they scrape out of me. "You're a coward, and I wish I could hate you. But I can't. I can't hate you, Decker. I'll *never* hate you the way you want me to. I can't even stay mad at you the way you deserve. I know you too well. I know you're doing this to protect me. And I know you're destroying yourself to do it."

I wait, letting my words fill the space between us, holding on to one final glimmer of hope that my words, who I am, what I have to offer, will be enough to break through.

It's not.

It never has been. And clearly, it never will be.

"I loved you. Even after everything. Even now, I love you still."

Silence ensues.

Just like it always fucking does when Decker digs his heels in.

"I loved you," I whisper one last time, the words barely audible to my own ears above my ragged breaths and the erratic beating of my broken heart.

His continued silence is the only reply I receive, and it's all the answer I need. I pull myself away and walk out of the bathroom without looking back.

Chapter 54
Josephine

Not even Kylian's breathing or Locke's light snores are perceptible through the dark.

With a groan, I spread my arms out, reaching for the guys. All I find are cold bed sheets.

I'm alone.

The realization carves a groove into the pit in my stomach that still festers from my confrontation with Decker.

Seeing him, seeking him out, finding him and begging him to let me in and give us what we both crave.

It was infuriating, seeing the crack in his armor when I bumped into him in the living room. I saw the tears, and my stupid heart felt the pining and sensed his longing. That's all it took for renewed hope to take root.

Hope for what, I don't know.

I'm a fool to hold out hope that Decker will ever come around. That he'll allow himself to be vulnerable enough to let me back in permanently.

I roll out of bed, wincing at the pain behind my temples.

I'm hungry, and I need coffee.

I feel hungover, despite not drinking a single drop of alcohol. Emotional hangovers can be just as horrid as the real thing, but without the fun.

Padding up the stairs, I clasp the edges of the blanket at my chest. The Den is absolutely frigid. Next time we come here—if there's a next time, seeing as how this is Decker's place—I'll bring my warmest, fuzziest pajamas. Maybe even a robe.

As I ascend the staircase, the arguing becomes audible. Dread percolates in my belly.

Voices are raised.

Talking over one another.

Ignoring the pounding in my head, I take the stairs two at a time. As I turn the corner to the eat-in kitchen, Decker's voice booms above the rest.

"I thought I *did* have a lawyer review the contracts." He's standing at one end of the table, gripping the back of a chair.

Kylian is facing off directly across from him, arms crossed and looking utterly annoyed.

Kendrick is seated between them, his forehead resting on his steepled fingers.

Locke is propped up against the island, cradling a coffee mug. "I'm lost. Why does it matter what he signed or what it says? Decker's out. He's made that clear."

As if he can sense my presence, Decker looks up. He locks eyes with me, and I'm instantly transported back to last night. To the moment in the living room. The breakdown in the bathroom. The palpable desperation and yearning.

They're just as pronounced this morning, churning just below the surface. I can feel it in the way he looks at me. I can feel it in my soul, despite his silence and hurtful actions.

He's not out.

He's *never* been out.

I'm so fucking mad at him for playing the martyr, for trying to fix everything on his own, for abandoning what we share because of some twisted ideal of sacrifice and love.

He stares long enough that the others turn and follow his line of sight. The energy shifts as I step into the room.

Locke holds one arm out, and I go to him. He holds me close and brings his mug to my lips so I can take a sip.

"Hey, Hot Girl. Did you sleep okay?"

Nodding, I pull the blanket around myself tighter. "It's cold down there."

I nuzzle into his chest and wrap my arms around his waist. Leaning against him fully, I let him take my weight, something I haven't done for a long time because he's been in so much pain.

"Okay?" I ask, peeking up at him to look for signs of discomfort.

"All good," he promises with a soft smile and a kiss on the head.

"Why is Decker here?" I ask through a yawn. "And why are we fighting before breakfast?"

"We've already had breakfast. We saved you some." Kylian's eyes are set on me, but I can't make sense of his agitation.

I need more coffee.

As I gingerly take Locke's mug out of his hands and bring it to my lips, Kylian continues.

"Decker was just sharing some interesting revelations about his NIL deals and upcoming commitments."

He stops there. His tone is short. Accusatory. Kylian isn't usually sarcastic or purposely obtuse. "Meaning?" I press.

"That's what I want to know," Locke mutters. "What does all of that mean for us?"

Kylian raises his brows at Decker. Decker glares back in response.

Kendrick flattens his hands on the table and clears his throat. "Cap has a multiyear contract with HiDef Enterprises, which owns several big apparel and merchandise brands. They also own SportsZone, NewsAction Now, and a national sports bar chain."

"Is something wrong with the contract?" Locke presses.

Decker pulls the chair he was just leaning on away from the table and sinks into the seat, digging his elbows into the wooden tabletop. "The whole thing's fucked."

He roughs a hand down his face and scans us, wearing a hard, tortured scowl.

"Once I realized just how intrusive the SportsZone feature deal was, I hired outside counsel to review my other contracts. They're looped. All of them. Everything I've committed to over the last few years is interconnected in a way I didn't truly understand when I signed the contracts at eighteen. Our monthly appearances. Long-standing brand partnerships. It's all interlinked. If I cancel or attempt to renegotiate anything, we could lose it all."

Kylian speaks up this time and paces to one end of the table. "He's trapped. We're trapped. Each deal is stacked in a way that affects the others. Ending the feature coverage early was a breach of contract. SportsZone issued a warning, like we expected they would. But what's at stake is so much more than we realized."

When he's made it to the other end of the table, he spins on his heel and plants his feet.

"It's not just his deals. It's K's. Yours." Kylian nods at Locke. "All current revenue streams for the three of you will dry up if Decker is in breach of contract again."

Kendrick looks to Decker, his dark eyes swimming with unease. "The girls' tuition for next semester is due at the end of this month."

Decker sits up, nodding solemnly. "I know."

I'm not the most financially savvy person. The most money I've ever had to my name was the forty-two hundred dollars Alice left me when she died. But the guys have been doing these NIL deals and appearances for years.

"Don't you have savings?" I ask. "Earnings from past deals you can use, or—"

Decker grunts. "We were advised—"

"By his father's financial planner," Kylian adds.

Decker grits his teeth, causing his temples to pulse. "We were advised," he repeats, "to structure our contracts so we didn't make more than we needed for spending money while we're still in college. Most of our deals won't pay out in full until we graduate."

"It made sense when we signed," Kendrick says, blowing out a breath. "We both expect to be drafted to professional teams, so we'll hit a higher tax bracket next year regardless. At the time, the logic was sound. We just didn't know we were being played."

"Who owns your cars?" I ask, my focus on Decker again.

"K and I have loaners from the dealership. They're part of a promotional deal."

My stomach sinks. "And the house?" I ask, though I'm starting to understand the gravity of the situation.

"My dad holds the deed. I always intended to buy it, but it didn't make sense to move on it while we were still in school."

Beside me, Locke has gone rigid. "So you're telling me that we're shit out of luck and broke as hell because of Decker?"

"Not yet, we aren't," Kylian says.

"My plan was to cancel several NIL deals and restructure those worth salvaging. That's why I hired my own legal team. I was trying to ensure we never have to go through something like this again."

He swallows, his Adam's apple working, and scans the four of us.

"The reality is that, as it stands, I won't be free. Not anytime soon. Probably not for years. It's best for all of us if I just accept—"

"No."

I don't know what he was going to say. What I do know is that his plan will be to cut himself out completely. That's Decker's way. To take the brunt of the attack, to shield us and sacrifice himself.

With my stomach twisted in knots, I wiggle out of Nicky's hold and stride toward Decker.

"No," I repeat, more resolute this time, as I stop beside him. "There has to be another way."

That damn jaw tick of his is at it again as he surveys Kylian across the table.

He doesn't glance my way. Like he's scared. Like he physically can't. He doesn't even look at me when I touch his shoulder.

"Time-out," I whisper.

That word finally snags his attention. Those onyx eyes find mine and hold. He doesn't blink. Doesn't agree. But he doesn't outright argue, either.

Bolder, I look to each of the other guys, one at a time, pausing until they meet my gaze. "I call a time-out. We're here for at least one more night, right?" I look at Kylian for confirmation.

He glances up from his phone, shoots daggers at Decker, then turns his attention to me. His expression softens a fraction. "At least one, maybe two. All campus activities are canceled this weekend, including the game. The storm has passed Lake Chapel, but there's still a good amount of cleanup. No sense rushing back since we don't have a home to go to."

"It's decided, then." I seek out Decker again.

He doesn't argue or glare or huff. His expression is almost blank, his mouth set in a straight line. Either he agrees with me for once, or, more likely, he's out of fight.

"Today is a time-out. We can all think about the best course of action, then come back together to discuss it tomorrow."

Three of my guys nod.

I know better than to take Decker's silence as assent.

Shucking the blanket still wrapped around my body, I unceremoniously plop into his lap. The move startles him, causing him to sit up and catch me around the hips.

"Time-out," I whisper. I keep my chin tipped up and my eyes locked on his so he knows it's not a request. "No one is making any decisions today, Decker. Tell me you understand. Tell me, after everything you've put me through, that you can give me this."

Instead of agreeing, he closes his eyes and leans against the seat back, as if he's trying to distance himself physically.

Finally, he swallows and nods.

Over his shoulder, I catch sight of Locke. With a frown, he shrugs.

If that's all he can give right now, then I can accept that.

"Time-out," I repeat once more. Then I rise to my feet and go in search of my own cup of coffee.

Chapter 55

Decker

I was wrong. So damn wrong.

About so much.

There's no comfort in that realization.

I rub at the tension gathered at the base of my skull and turn my head from side to side to ease the pain. The fabric of the hammock bunches as I shift. With a shrug of my shoulders, I rearrange myself again in a seemingly futile struggle to get comfortable.

"Oh. Sorry, brother."

Kendrick.

I jackknife up to sitting so quickly I almost spin the entire hammock.

"Easy," he chuckles, holding out a hand. "I didn't realize you were out here. I'll give you space." Pivoting, he heads back to the door.

The urge to talk about what the fuck I'm supposed to do now is too strong to let him go. "Wait. K. Stay."

He stops in his tracks and regards me over his shoulder, his brow furrowed.

Clearing my throat, I double down. "Please stay. I could use the company."

Nodding, he approaches my end of the deck. "What are you doing out here anyway?"

Shifting in the hammock, still sitting upright with my legs dangling over one side, I sigh. "Feeling sorry for myself."

He scoffs, then laughs. Like I'm a joke.

Anger burns hot in my veins, mixing with the self-loathing I've let consume me. "Is something about this situation funny to you?"

Towering over me, he rolls his lips and assesses me. "Yeah," he admits. "Kind of."

I grit my teeth, waiting for him to elaborate on how my misery and the situation I put us in could be humorous.

With a huff, he drags a chair across the deck. The way it scrapes against the composite surface sends a shudder through me. He spins it around, then straddles it, so close that I can see the golden flecks of warmth in his irises. He's close enough that the disapproval coming off him is palpable.

"You're Decker Crusade."

As if I could fucking forget.

What I wouldn't give to forget...

"What excuse could you possibly have to feel sorry for yourself? Bro, you're laying on a hammock at your private cabin in the mountains. You're the golden boy of Lake Chapel—the future prince of professional football. You'd be hard pressed to find anyone to take pity on you."

I grind my molars at the scolding and will my indignation to remain at a low simmer. He's not wrong. Yet so much of my life is out of my control these days. The reality of it isn't even remotely aligned with what I want for my future.

At least not anymore.

"And if I don't want to be the golden boy of anywhere or the future prince of anything?" I cross my arms and lift my chin. I look like a petulant child, I'm sure.

Kendrick, naturally, takes it in stride. With a nod, he considers me.

Few people in my life have known me as long as K. He's seen it all, and he's stood by my side for years. Our paths have always run mostly parallel, our lives routed on the same course. We've been dreaming of going pro, with the hopes of eventually playing together again, since our days with the Little Dukes U-12 team.

"Want to know what I thought about during the nine hours I was locked up last month?" he hedges.

We share matching smirks. He didn't even sit in a cell for a full day.

"I thought about how I stepped in for Locke and how, no matter the consequences, it was worth it. All of it. I had faith that you and Daddy Genius would figure it out and I wouldn't be in there long—"

I cough out a shocked laugh, but Kendrick scowls, shutting me down before I can hound him for calling Kylian "Daddy" anything.

"Don't ask," he mutters. "Anyway, I came to terms with what was, and I decided I could accept whatever happened next, as long as it ended with her."

Sighing, I scrub my hand down my face. "So you're allowed to make sacrifices, but I'm not?"

He tsks. "A sacrifice is a choice you make for the greater good, Cap. It's not stubborn, bullheaded, arbitrary action that benefits no one in the end."

Balling my hands into fists in my lap, I glare, collecting my words, ready to argue my reasons yet again.

He doesn't give me the chance. "Who are you helping by pushing her away? What sort of life do you envision for yourself these days, without her, without us? One where it's your dad and Misty congratulating you after games? One where there's an occasional warm body and nameless face in your bed, but you fall asleep alone each night?"

"Of course not."

"Then what? I, for one, can't imagine my life without that woman. But obviously, you can. So what does your version of the future look like? It must be good if you're working so damn hard to preserve it."

His words hang between us while I put myself through mental gymnastics trying to visualize what my future *does* entail if I stay on the current path.

I used to relish the idea of following in my father's footsteps: fully stepping into the spotlight, carrying on the Crusade name in the world of professional football.

Now, when I consider the next six months, the next year, the next *anything* without her, all I taste is bitterness.

The draft. Training season. My first professional game. My first pro win.

None of it holds any appeal if I have to go it alone.

"If this isn't what you want anymore, then figure it out. There's always an alternative. An answer. An option that allows you to push reset and start over. People you know—people you love—have done it with a lot less certainty on their side."

Josephine's accusation from last night ricochets through me.

She called me a coward. She was right.

"What if it's too late?" I groan, my heart sinking in my chest. So much is already in motion. My career is a freight train barreling toward the future. A future, I'm realizing, I don't even want. Not without my boys by my side. Not without *her*.

Kendrick doesn't give me an answer, and he doesn't let me wallow in self-pity. Instead, he lobs another question my way.

Gripping the back of his chair, he leans forward and locks eyes with me. "What are you willing to give up to prove it?" He pauses, raising both eyebrows. "If it all went away tomorrow—football, the deals, the money—would we be enough? Would she be enough?"

"Yes," I reply without a millisecond of hesitation.

"Then there's your answer."

I scoff. "That doesn't *solve* anything." I'm so fucking frustrated I could scream.

K holds up both hands. "You're right. It doesn't. But you don't need to know the solution to have your answer. The solution is what we figure out together, Cap."

Together.

She asked for together.

The gaping hole in my chest, the one I created when I ripped my own goddamn heart out and walked away from Josephine, suddenly doesn't hurt quite so acutely.

I can give her that.

I can give her so much more.

If only I get my head out of my ass.

They're right. I can't handle everything on my own. I have to let them in, commit to the version of my life I want. Even if it looks nothing like the dreams I created long ago.

Kendrick rises to his feet. Looming over me once more, he stretches his arms overhead and jerks his head to the side until his neck cracks. "You want to run later?"

I nod absently, lost in thought.

He returns the chair to its place at the table and tips his chin once more. "How much money did your mom leave you?"

My lungs seize at the question.

My mom was wealthy in her own right. Long before my dad came into the picture. Honestly, I think he resented her for it. She didn't need his money, and that meant he couldn't use it against her. He got especially nasty when he found out she'd left me a trust he knew nothing about.

"Five million when she died. I'm sure it's grown since then. You know I can't touch that money, though. The trust is ironclad."

Taking a step back to me, he crosses his arms over his chest. "What were the terms again?"

I let out a huff and roll my shoulders. He knows the terms. We used to talk about how we'd spend our twenty-fifth birthdays on a private island together. That dream didn't keep as we got older, but it was our favorite fantasy to lean on during grueling workouts and two-a-days in the heat of summer.

The terms of the will are simple. Beautifully simple, in a way that's symbolic of my mom's love. Her will mentions nothing about football or my education. She designed the trust so I didn't have to meet any sort of metrics to access it.

"I get the money when I turn twenty-five," I remind him—more than three years from now—"or when I get married. Whichever comes first."

He nods again and raises a hand. Then he walks into the house.

Chapter 56

Josephine

"So. Jojo."

Kendrick chuckles softly. He squeezes my hand once, but he doesn't let go as we pick up our pace to catch up.

In my periphery, he smirks. "She wants something."

Blinking at him, I try to make sense of the lighthearted warning. How can he interpret her intentions from those two small words? I'm endlessly fascinated by their tightknit connection.

We're hiking around the property on a footpath that K swears is safe. Even though we had to bring bear spray.

The girls are walking ten yards or so ahead of us, and every so often, they peek over their shoulders. We can't hear their conversation, but I catch the sound of their laughter every few steps. Kendrick calls out to them when they get too far away for his liking—which earns him matching unamused glares each time.

The way he cares for them makes my heart flip-flop in my chest.

Emilia stops and turns to face us, donning an angelic expression. "Did you bring your nail stuff with you?"

"Millie," Kendrick scolds, keeping his voice low.

"What? It's a fair question!" She plants one hand on her hip. "If we're stuck here for another day or two, how else are we supposed to pass the time?"

"You got somewhere to be?" Kendrick deflects.

Jade steps up beside her sister and offers a saccharine smile. "Oh, she does. She wants to go to Kayla's party tonight."

Kendrick frowns. "Why in the world would she be having a party tonight? We've barely made it out of the timeframe for the storm warning."

Emilia places her other hand on her hip, doubling down. "Kayla's family has a condo near Charlotte. She said the roads are open and there isn't any damage in their neighborhood."

"Damn private school," Kendrick mutters. "Their friends have houses all over the state."

I hold back a laugh, because I so acutely remember what it was like to be a preteen and care about nothing else besides who's hosting the next party and whether I'd be able to go.

Hand in hand, we make our way closer to the girls.

"You know the rules," Kendrick says.

Emilia shoots him a surly glare that makes her look so much like him. "I know. I'll have her mom call you later. Okay? Please, Kenny? Please, can we go?"

Kendrick holds her gaze for so long and with such intensity that I start to squirm. "I'm not making any promises until I talk to this girl's mom and confirm a few things. I'm also not committing to leaving here at a specific time."

"Mrs. Lansbury could take us!" Jade pipes up.

With a scowl, Emilia elbows her in the side.

"What?" she demands, whipping her head around so quickly her beaded braids swing with the force. "She already said she would."

Oh, sweet Jade.

Emilia hisses a warning under her breath, catches her sister by the elbow, and marches her away from us.

Good thing, too. K's outrage simmers just below the surface as details of their scheme hit him.

I squeeze his hand once and shuffle closer so my arm brushes his. They're just kids. Clever kids, yes. But their plotting is harmless.

"You're strict," I tease, pulling him forward so we can follow the girls. "We might have to talk to Kylian about joint custody of his nickname."

Kendrick chuckles, low and melodic. The sound inspires a kaleidoscope of butterflies to riot in my belly.

"You're a comedienne now, huh?"

I hit him with a cheeky smile. "Something like that."

He returns my flirtatious grin, but his face quickly falls. He stops, and his hand still encompassing mine forces me to stop, too.

He grasps my other hand and tugs until we're standing toe to toe. "I take care of the people I love, Jojo. Them. The boys. *You*. It's my duty and a privilege to take care of you."

Big hands skim up my arms until he's pulling me into an embrace. His nose nudges against mine, his lips ghosting along my jaw.

"When we leave here, I go where you go."

They're words I didn't know I needed to hear. His promise fills me with warmth, the reassurance quelling the anxiety that's been kicked up from sharing a roof with Decker.

Emotion catches in my throat, and I have to blink back the tears threatening to escape me. The sentiment behind his declaration is identical to Kylian's. We won't go back to the way things were. Living separately, stealing moments every few nights. Deep, appreciative understanding rolls through me, a wave so strong I let the tears well and crest over my lashes.

We don't know the details. How or where we'll go.

But we'll be together.

It's so close to being all I've wanted for weeks—all of us, together.

If this is as close as I can get, then I accept.

"I love you," I whisper, tipping my head back and circling my arms around his waist. He's so sturdy. Solid. Hard on the outside, but ooey-gooey where it counts. "I love you so much, K."

He bites down on his plush bottom lip like he's holding back his grin, but his eyes dance, giving him away. Two fingers catch under my chin and tilt my head further as he lowers to kiss me.

Our lips haven't even touched before the sound of fake retching hits our ears.

"Gross," Jade draws out.

"Get a room," Emilia jabs.

"Hey!" Kendrick shouts, pulling up straight and pointing at his sisters. "Inappropriate. And most definitely *not* the way to convince me to let you go to a party tonight."

Jade's eyes go wide as she slaps her hand over her mouth.

Emilia skips over to us, squaring up with her brother like she isn't intimidated by his six-two frame whatsoever.

"If we go to Kayla's, you could kiss Jojo all night without us making a single peep." She presses her lips together and smirks.

Kendrick glares at her for a beat, then another.

His deadpan expression cracks into an exasperated sigh as he scrubs a hand down his face.

"What am I going to do when you're actually teenagers?" he bemoans.

"Jojo will have to step up," Emilia declares, pulling her shoulders back.

The confirmation that my presence is a given in K's future, that we'll all be present for one another, warms my insides.

"Speaking of..."

Jade tentatively joins us now.

"Was that a no for nails?" Emilia asks me.

"Get going," Kendrick snaps, pointing down the trail.

With a laugh, I shake my head. "I'm sorry. I was in a hurry to pack and didn't think to bring any of my supplies. I'll do your nails next week, once we're back home."

The girls take off again without complaint, instantly moving on, but a sense of dread trickles in as the promise I just made hangs in the air around me.

Home.

Where is home?

My boys are my home, yes, and we all share the same goal of sticking together from here on out. The where and how, though, are still in question.

My breath hitches on the inhale as panic ignites inside me, sending my heart rate skyrocketing.

K notices instantly.

"Not today," he reminds me.

He smooths a hand down my spine in a move that's both reverent and mollifying and rests his palm on my low back. He doesn't let me stop. With that hand, he gently guides me down the path after the girls.

"Nothing to worry about today, Mama. You called a time-out. Honor that."

I swallow past the worry and push down the panic.

Time-out.

I am here. This is now.

Everything else will keep.

Chapter 57
Josephine

"You just let them go to a stranger's house to spend the night?" Kylian asks.

Locke and I share a knowing look. K is *not* going to appreciate this line of questioning.

The girls have been gone for an hour, but we're still hanging out around the table after dinner. Locke and Kylian insisted that since Mrs. Lansbury was charged with dropping off the twins, they'd take over dinner duty. They grilled steaks and vegetables, then made enormous baked potatoes with all the fixings, plus a dish of rice pilaf for Nicky.

The girls gobbled up their food in a hurry, but Kendrick made them sit with us until it was time to clear the table. He may or may not have cut into his steak at a painfully slow pace just to mess with them. Once we devoured our dessert—peach cobbler with huge scoops of ice cream—he sent them on their way.

It feels good to sit around the table with my guys without worrying about cameras or busy schedules. Wrapping my arm around Nicky's bicep, I nuzzle into his shoulder and breathe in the familiar scents of sugarcane and mint. He shoves back his chair and hauls me into his lap before I can exhale.

This is what we needed. This is what's been missing for weeks.

Time together. Time to just be.

The time-out was the right call. I've never been more grateful for a storm.

Kendrick scowls and raps his knuckles twice on the table. "Hold up. What makes you think I didn't do my due diligence?"

Kylian scoffs. "You didn't ask for my help."

"They're eight-and nine-year-old girls, Kyller. Not sure you'd be able to dig up much about them on the dark web."

I smile into Nicky's chest as Kylian opens his mouth to bicker.

And they like to say *I'm* sassy.

Leaning back in his chair, Kendrick crosses his massive arms over his chest. "You underestimate me. I called the parents this afternoon. Asked my usual questions—who would be at the house and their ages, including siblings. What the sleeping arrangements are. Who's staying up with the girls. All that. Their answers checked out. There are only five girls in total. All from the girls' school. Plus," he adds, "Jade's an awful liar and has no poker face. If anything questionable goes down, I'll know."

Kylian squints, unconvinced. Or maybe he's just insulted that K didn't ask for his help. Either way, he eventually nods. That's all the approval he's going to give, apparently. Not that Kendrick's asking for it.

"Hey, wait." Locke shifts me in his lap and sits up, brightening. "*We* should play poker. Do you know Texas hold 'em, Hot Girl?" He runs his hands over my hips and around to my stomach.

Dropping my head back on his shoulder, I cock a brow at him. "Do I know how to play poker? Yes. Will I sweep the floor with you before the night's over? Also yes."

A cacophony of disgruntled disagreement fills the kitchen.

"If you're all so confident, then let's do it. We could even up the ante and play strip poker," I suggest, looking at each of my guys with a wicked grin.

"I'm a mathematical genius on the brink of earning an honors degree in statistics. You'll all be naked before I've removed my sweatshirt," Kylian pronounces, sitting up straight in his chair.

Oh, it's on.

Kendrick rises from the table, rubbing his hands together. "Easy, Daddy Genius. If our girl claims she's got skills, then we owe her the benefit of the doubt."

"You can't just 'have skills' in poker," Kylian counters. "You can have discipline. You can develop a strategy and rely on standard deviation to determine—"

Locke reaches over and hits Kylian with a playful punch. "Bro. Flip the switch. We don't need a lecture on probability right now. Joey wants to play *strip poker*. As in, clothes are coming off, no matter what. If you want to run your mouth, stop the nerd talk and dish up some of your signature dirty talk."

Kylian raises both brows, giving Nicky a pointed look. Then he sets his sights on me.

Arousal swirls low in my gut as he stares me down. The switch has officially been flipped.

Game. On.

Crooking two fingers, he juts his chin and beckons. "On the table, Jo. Crawl to me."

Liquid heat pools in my belly, and instantly, I'm a moth to the flame. Under his spell, I rise from Locke's lap and place both hands on the table.

"Oh, hell yeah." Kendrick pushes back and rises from his seat. "I'll find cards and grab drinks. What are you having, Mama?"

Before I can answer, Kylian clears his throat.

I whip my head around to tell him to wait his turn and practice a little patience, only to find his eyes no longer on me. Instead, they're hard, ice blue and piercing, and fixed on the opposite side of the room.

Heart lurching in my chest, I lift my hands off the tabletop and spin.

"Decker."

The sight of him instantly sends my heart plummeting to the floor. His shoulders are slumped, his eyes sunken, and his skin stretched taut. He looks exhausted, tormented. So unlike himself.

"I'm just grabbing food." He glances at me, then turns to Kylian. "I planned to wait until you were done in here, but it's getting late..."

"Of course," I insist softly, sliding off the table. "There are leftover steaks and potatoes in the fridge. You can eat at the table and join us if you want."

"Jo," Kylian scolds. "You don't have to give him the time of day."

Spinning on my heel to face him, I plant my hands on my hips. I take a deep breath in, tempering the annoyance bubbling up inside me. "I called a Time-out this morning." Then I turn back to Decker. "Grab some food. We'll sit with you while you eat. We were planning to stay up a while anyway."

Kylian makes a noise of protest, so I shoot him a warning look.

Kendrick sidles up beside me, grazing along the curve of my waist and gripping my hip. "You're good?" he double checks, his low tone soothing and supportive.

Nodding, I peer up into his deep brown eyes. "I'm good," I promise. "We'll play later."

"Yeah, we will." He strolls deeper into the kitchen to fetch our drinks.

Behind him, a despondent Decker follows.

Chapter 58

Josephine

I was wrong. So damn wrong.

Despite calling a time-out, despite desperately craving normalcy and civility, sitting at the table with Decker is agonizing.

Kylian looks unbothered. Smug, even, like he knew it would be this awful.

Locke and Kendrick both seem to be tolerating Decker just fine.

It makes sense. They've spent more time with him over the last few weeks. Between games, practices, and going back and forth to the mansion when they weren't with me, Decker has been in the fold more than I have.

Decker and I are the ones struggling.

And fuck, are we struggling.

"Did you, uh, did you have a chance to get outside today?" His question isn't pointed at anyone in particular, but with the cold shoulder he's receiving from the guys, I feel compelled to answer.

"We did." I nod, sipping the hard seltzer K placed in front of me twenty minutes ago. I've palmed the can so much it's already warm. "Kendrick and I took a hike with the girls."

His gaze drifts to Kendrick, and unspoken words pass between them. K shakes his head once, and Decker turns back to his food.

The interaction is another reminder of how close they are, how long they've known each other, how awful the current state of things between them is.

Decker shoves another forkful into his mouth, chews, swallows, and clears his throat.

"It's nice now, but the woods are especially beautiful in winter. You can come back here then if you want."

He's reaching.

"You could all come for the holidays."

He's trying too hard.

"I mean, just you. I wouldn't have to be here. I just mean, if it would make you happy…" He trails off, ducking his head and focusing on his plate.

It's all too much. And yet not nearly enough.

Awkward silence lingers, so I take the reins this time to fill in the void.

"I haven't celebrated Christmas in years." The confession is directed to no one in particular. I keep my focus trained on my hands and pick at the corner of my thumbnail.

Kylian's responding growl has me shooting up straight and watching him.

I offered that up without thinking, and the blue flames burning in his eyes make it clear that was the wrong line of discussion for this already too-tense scene.

Decker just stares at me, unblinking.

I don't have the courage to look at K.

Locke reaches out, offering a hand that I gladly accept. After I interlock our fingers, I sneak a glance at him and offer a soft smile.

He gets it. Christmas is just another day for kids who are living in survival mode. It's also a very long day. When school's been out for a week, and they don't know when their next meal is coming, it can be brutal.

"We'll make this year extra special," he promises, giving my hand a squeeze.

The promise lingers, heavy and tense.

After several seconds where the only sounds are our breathing and the scrape of Decker's fork against his plate, the table quakes.

"This can't stand." Kendrick scans the room, his face set in a glower, his fist pressing into the tabletop.

"K," I warn. "Let it be. We're still on a time-out." As painful as this is, it's almost over. Decker's almost done eating. He'll most likely excuse himself, and head to bed.

Then tomorrow.

Tomorrow...

My heart cracks and my eyes well with traitorous tears just thinking about tomorrow.

I slump back against my seat when realization hits. All we have left is the rest of this meal. The forced civility and tolerance around the table are only promised for a few more minutes.

Ignoring me, Kendrick clears his throat and lifts his chin. "This can't stand," he repeats. "This is bullshit, and you all know it. He's just too stubborn to make the next move." He points an accusatory finger at Decker.

I let out a sigh, willing my emotions to stay in check. They threaten to escape anyhow. The longer this goes on, the harder it is to hold back the tears. I don't want them to fight.

Not now. Not over this. Not when we only have a short amount of time left.

"I'm calling you out, Cap."

All eyes fly to Kendrick.

"Cards on the table. Full stop. What do you want?"

The silence that ensues is suffocating.

"Kendrick," I whisper in warning, pushing back in my chair to go to him. To assuage his anger. To make him see reason.

I didn't ask Decker to join us to force him into a confrontation. I don't want him to think—

"No." Kendrick raises a hand. "He needs to man up."

Fuck, I love him. Leave it to Kendrick to imply that processing emotions and talking about feelings is the definition of manning up. "He needs to step up and own this. What do you want, Cap?"

Around the table, we're all holding our breath.

K is sharp and emotionally intelligent in a way that's uncanny for a twenty-one-year-old student athlete. Maybe it's because he lost his mom so young and was raised by a single father. Maybe it's his role as caregiver to two young girls. Or maybe it's the lupus and the acute understanding that goes along with chronic illness.

Life is short.

Say the words.

Embrace the grief.

Lean into the good.

Lean on others through the bad.

Though my stomach is in knots, I watch him and wait.

K is smart. He's *so* smart. He wouldn't put Decker on the spot like this if he didn't know, if he wasn't sure—

"I swear to God, Cap. I don't want to hit you, but I'm not above beating your ass to force this conversation. *What. Do. You. Want?*" he grits out through clenched teeth.

Decker shoves up from his seat and storms away from the table.

I close my eyes. The sight of him turning away only pulverizes the shards of my heart into smaller, sharper pieces. How much longer, how many more rejections can it take, until all that's left of it is dust?

But before he reaches the doorway, he pivots.

With a murderous look on his face, brows low and jaw locked tight, he storms back to the table.

He grips the top of his chair with such force it falls to the floor when he pushes it out of the way.

Stepping up, he glares at Kendrick. Looks at Locke. Eyes Kylian. Then finally, settles his gaze on me.

"Her."

It's a whisper. A despondent murmur. A pained and hopeless plea.

"I want her. I want you all." He scans the boys. "I want this life. Together."

The confession hangs in the air before it thuds onto the table like an iron cloud.

I refuse to hope. I refuse to go down this path again.

We've been here. We've done this. I can't keep enduring this cycle. The one where Decker admits his feelings, then refuses to act on them before finally pushing me away.

"Please don't," I whisper, hollow, broken. Each time we battle it out, I lose another piece of myself.

K thinks he's helping. He thinks Decker can be reasoned with. Only, he doesn't know about last night. He doesn't know how desperately I tried to get through to him. How steadfastly he denied me.

Ignoring me, Kendrick rises, gripping his side of the table. "*What do you want*, Cap?"

Before I can beg him to drop it—to leave well enough alone, to give me these last few minutes of time-out where Decker isn't on the outs with us, to give me a moment to pretend my heart isn't so broken and battered—Kendrick turns to me.

"Fine. He's forcing my hand. There's a way out of this. There's a way *through* it." He stands taller. "Cap and I had a conversation this morning. He knows there's a way to edge out his father once and for all. What I don't know"—he sets his sights on his friend again—"is whether he's brave enough to do it."

"You figured something out?" Locke sits up straighter and laces his fingers on the tabletop.

Kylian is silent as he watches the exchange.

"I had an idea, yeah. But it's Decker's choice. It comes down to what he wants to do."

Decker scoffs. It's a loud, indignant huff of outrage. "It's not that simple," he growls. He's gripping the table so tightly his knuckles are white.

"That's okay." I release Locke's hand and make my way to Decker. Gently, so as not to spook him, I rest my palm on his forearm, then glide my fingertips down to his wrist.

With a pained exhale, he allows me to peel his hand off the table. That's when I take my shot. I slip into the space between his body and the wooden surface. He doesn't budge, so it's a tight squeeze.

"I don't need simple," I promise, tipping my head up and brushing the hair from his forehead. "I want you, too, Cap. Whatever it is, I'm in."

"Josephine," he growls in warning. "No," I snap.

I'd stomp my foot if I had enough room to move. But as it stands, I'm trapped in his hold, even if he refuses to touch me. Refuses to look me in the eye.

"I want you. You want us. Don't you dare dangle the possibility of a solution in front of my face, then start up on your martyr shit again. I swear to God, Decker, whatever it is, I'm in. Whatever it takes, let's do it."

Onyx eyes find mine. His expression is pained, forlorn, but under the surface, there's a spark of hope, too.

"We have to get married. You and me, Josephine. You'd have to marry me."

Chapter 59

Josephine

My body jolts as if it's been struck by a shock of electricity. My bum slams against the table as a ringing sounds in my ears.

No, not a ringing.

A cackling.

Uncontrollable, maniacal laughter.

It takes a few seconds to realize the sounds are coming from *me*.

Delirious, possibly losing control of my sanity, I swipe the tears from my eyes and suck in a deep breath, willing my heart rate to level out. "I'm not marrying you." The statement comes out on a hiccup that sends me into another fit of laughter. "We aren't even *together* anymore because of you."

Lightheaded and oxygen deprived, I inhale, let it out, and do it again, equally amused and exasperated.

All that hope for this?

Sighing, I shove away from Decker and march back to my seat.

Except as I sit in my chair and collect myself, I realize the room is quiet.

Too quiet.

When I look up, all eyes are on me.

"Wait." I look from Kendrick to Locke to Kylian. "Did you all know about this? Is this some sort of prank?"

I've pulled plenty on Cap over the last few months. Maybe this is his way of retaliating. Although this one is unnecessarily cruel, given the circumstances. Sugary cereal and rubber ducks are no match for the prospect of not so wedded bliss.

Anxiety creeps up my spine when no one dares to respond.

"Somebody answer me." My lungs seize, once again stealing my oxygen. If they were in on this, if this is some sort of joke...

Kendrick speaks up, finally. "Not a prank, Mama. But it would work." He sighs, scrubbing his hand down his face as he looks from me to Decker.

I spin in my seat to analyze Decker's reaction.

"This isn't a joke? You really think I would *marry* you?"

He grumbles under his breath. His head is bowed low between his shoulders, and he's back to gripping the table.

"We're not even together, Decker. Just last night you refused—"

"Last night?" Kylian sits up straighter. "What happened last night?"

I dismiss him with a wave of my hand. I'm not interested in embarrassing Decker or myself by detailing our late-night run-ins.

Changing tack, I assert, "I don't trust you."

"You don't trust him?" Kendrick challenges.

I whip my head around to glare, my anger spiking again. "To care for this family? Sure. But with my heart?"

With my focus trained on Decker again, I shake my head. "No." I survey him, the defeat painted along every inch of him. After a few breaths, I go on. "Besides, even if I did trust him, even if any of this made sense, Decker isn't the only person I love. *Loved*," I quickly correct.

Even if I was willing to legally commit to him, my heart doesn't belong to just one person. I want a life with *all* of them. A future that's uniquely ours.

"It's a good idea."

Kylian's words are a punch to the gut.

"Wh—what?" I stammer out, gasping for breath. He can't be serious. Except Kylian doesn't joke.

"It's a good idea." He shrugs. "That may have been the worst proposal I've ever heard," he lobs a disappointed scowl at Decker, "but it's a solid plan. One Thomas likely hasn't considered."

"You don't mean—"

"I think you should do it."

Just like that. Cut and dry. Black and white. It's such a Kylian response, and yet my insides crumple into a heap at the prospect. A whimper escapes me as I work to school my expression, to keep my face from revealing the horror currently pummeling me.

I'm out of my depth here, blindsided, and very clearly unprepared for the other guys' reactions. Never in a million years—

"Jo. Come here," Kylian beckons, recognizing my mounting panic for what it is.

I race to him and nearly trip over my own feet trying to climb into his lap.

He pulls my hips closer so I'm straddling him, our bodies flush. His hands quickly find the hem of my hoodie and slip beneath it to smooth up the bare skin of my back.

I bury my face in his shoulder, wishing I could climb inside him and soak up the comfort he brings me. He rubs up and down my spine, assuring me that I'm okay in quiet whispers until the panic ebbs and my breathing evens out.

Eventually, his hands travel lower, grazing along my hips and cupping my ass.

"What are you thinking about?"

"Us," I admit without hesitation, my lips brushing his neck.

Kylian. Locke. Kendrick. The men who love me, but more importantly, the men who have stood beside me. Decker loves me, too, I know it, but he's proven time and again that love isn't enough. He's shown me that he's willing to give up things that aren't his to sacrifice.

"Baby." Kylian squeezes me. "Do you really think marrying Decker could change what we have?"

He grasps my upper arms and pulls me back so I'm forced to look at him.

When I do, the expression on his face is carnal and full of lust. "You think just because he'd be your husband, I wouldn't still be your daddy?"

My heart thuds against my breastbone. I whimper, craving the submission and safety that only Kylian can give me.

He senses my longing, just like he always does. Gripping my hair, he pulls, tipping my head back. "I told you, Jo. I'm never letting you go. Encouraging you to marry Decker doesn't mean I'm giving up. In fact, it's the opposite. It's me holding on tighter."

Shakily, I give him a subtle nod. I can't move more than that with the way he's gripping me. I don't like what they're suggesting, but I trust Kylian with everything I am. He would never, ever persuade me to do something that wasn't in my best interest.

Pulling me closer, he brings his lips to my ear. "But it's still your choice, Jo. *Always* your choice."

There it is. The closing argument—the freedom to be the one in control—that assures my rioting heart that this really could be okay.

"Why?" I ask him, continuing to ignore everyone else in the room. "Why Decker?"

For the first time since I crawled into his lap, Kylian looks past me to the other guys. "Ask him. My guess is, even if he lost everything—sponsorships, endorsement deals, other revenue streams—there's an inheritance to be claimed, and it would default to you."

"Exactly," Kendrick confirms behind me.

I turn, sitting with my legs draped over Kylian's lap so I can see K.

"Cap's mom left him more than five million dollars. It wasn't much of a consideration before, given his expected career trajectory."

"I've never heard anything about this. Was it a secret?" Locke asks, his voice quiet, reticent.

Decker lifts his head and grimaces. "Not intentionally. My mom set up a trust. She kept it from my dad. Neither of us knew about it until after she died. I get access to the money when I turn twenty-five or—"

"When you get married," Kylian pieces together. He nods once, satisfied. "This will work."

"How do you know?" I demand.

Kylian studies my face, calm, patient. Two things I am not right now.

"If Decker gets married, the money will be unlocked. If Decker marries *you*, it guarantees we all get to stay together."

I nod, because that makes sense, though trepidation still has me in a chokehold.

"It's more than enough money to move forward, start making a life. We can buy the mansion, or another house if you want. Thomas would have no say in any of it. Decker would be free. We'd be financially stable. We wouldn't be dependent on a career or a contract that wasn't in our best interest. It's simple, but it's effective. It will work."

The logic tracks.

But I never intended to marry for logic, despite being in love with the most methodical, logical man I've ever met.

I peek over my shoulder at Kendrick. Then at Locke.

"If I legally marry Decker…"

I let the idea float between us. Waiting, desperate, for one of them to object.

"It has to be him."

The pain in Locke's eyes cuts deep. I'm momentarily vindicated, then devastated.

"Why?" I demand, climbing out of Kylian's lap. As I cross the room, the heat of four sets of eyes sears me. They track me from every angle until I'm standing in front of my sweet, sensitive Emo Boy.

I lower myself into his lap and tip my head back onto his shoulder so I can speak directly into his ear.

"Your words say do it, but your eyes tell a different story," I say, my accusation a tender one. "I won't even consider this if you're not completely on board."

Big hands grip my waist, and inches from my face, his ink-covered Adam's apple bobs as he swallows thickly.

"I'm on board," he tells me with a gentle squeeze.

Shit on a crumbly cracker.

That was not the answer I expected from him.

"Why?"

He still hasn't answered the question. How can he so willingly encourage me to pursue a plan that legally binds me to another person? A person who hurt me.

"I want you so fucking bad," he groans, tracing one hand up my torso and past my neck so he can cup the side of my face. Angling it, he kisses me, but it's over far too soon. "But I want them, too. I want all of us, together. Safe. Happy. Secure."

I search his face for any hint of a lie but come up empty-handed.

"My arthritis isn't getting any better, Hot Girl. In the future, if I need disability benefits, it would be significantly easier to get approved without a spouse."

"Seriously?"

"Seriously." This from Kendrick. "It's almost impossible to be chronically ill in this country and get the support needed as a married person. I won't marry because of it. Neither should he."

With a deep inhale, I let the reality of the words sink into my bones. The reasoning makes sense; the reality still hurts. We've never talked about any of this before. To be forced to discuss it under extreme pressure doesn't feel fair to anyone around this table.

"Do you want kids?"

Kylian's words strike my already fragile heart. What kind of question is that? Snapping my head up, I stare at him, waiting for the punchline of the joke. Or maybe to wake up and discover this entire conversation has been a nightmare.

"Answer me, Jo. Do you want kids?"

It's too much. Too Fast. Too Far. Too Soon.

"I—I don't—" I grapple for words to string together to make him understand.

I don't want to do this.

I don't want to have this conversation.

Not with him. Not with any of them.

"Yes or no. Don't overthink it."

"Yes?" I guess. That's exactly what it is: a guess. I haven't spent a lot of time considering my future. It was so bleak for so long. Then, over the last few months, I've been focused on myself. On now. On starting fresh. On doing well in my gen ed classes. On picking a major. I thought all I had to worry about this week was registering for classes. Family planning was not on my bingo card.

"I do not. So it's settled."

"So that's it?" I snap, jumping to my feet. "You and I have no future because you're forcing me to decide in an instant whether I want kids someday?"

Kylian rises, too. Much slower, methodically. He approaches with measured steps, and when he's close, he pulls me closer. He grips both my wrists with one hand, while the other finds my chin.

He bows low, his mouth close enough to kiss. He doesn't follow through. Instead, he brushes his lips past mine as he whispers, "I can't wait to fuck the sass right out of this mouth later."

He kisses me hard then, a vow and a promise. I shiver on contact. He pulls away too soon, leaving me breathless and wanting.

"In the state of North Carolina, if a married woman becomes pregnant, the paternity of the child defaults to the husband both biologically and legally." He recites the law from memory.

I don't bother questioning him. For as ridiculous as it sounds, I'm sure it's correct.

"You want kids," he states. "Among the group, I'm sure there is another person who would like to procreate. I do not want to have children."

My stomach drops at the thought. His declaration was not only surefire, but it comes with many implications.

"Correction." He clears his throat. "I will tolerate and maybe even like your offspring. I like all of you, so statistically, that is likely. I will also participate in the agreed-upon parenting system when and if the time comes, but I do not want to contribute DNA and make children."

"I don't either," K declares.

I swivel, resting one hand on the table for balance, and take him in. His expression is pensive—low brows, firm jaw—but sure.

"Lupus is genetic. I want babies, but I always assumed I'd adopt."

How the hell did we go from the promise of strip poker to a full-blown family planning discussion? As my mind whirls, I cast my gaze to the ceiling and blow out a long, steady breath.

"Locke? What's your stance on kids?" Decker asks.

He glares at Decker—always on my side—then turns to me, the lines on his face smoothing out. "We've already talked about this. Joey knows where I stand."

I offer him a soft nod, confirming. Although when we talked about our future, I thought we were talking about the actual future. Sometime in the very distant future.

The room goes quiet once again as my ego battles with my heart.

I haven't had a chance to process any of this, to let the ideas simmer or to give myself grace to navigate what comes next.

But there's an urgency to the energy tonight.

Maybe it's because the clock is ticking down on our time-out.

Or maybe it's because this *is* the right call, landing in my lap at exactly the right time. Maybe the universe is nudging me so hard I'd be stupid not to listen.

I bend at the waist, gently drop a kiss to Nicky's cheek, murmur "I love you," and walk toward my fate.

Circling the table, I home in on Decker.

His eyes are dark, guarded, as he watches me approach.

"If we do this," I proclaim. "If I say yes to you, I'm actually saying yes to them."

He nods his acceptance. I refuse to make this easy for him, though.

"I'll marry you. I'll be your wife." I tamp down the unease rising inside me. "But in name only. Is that really what you want, Cap?"

He watches me, unblinking. Then he glances at each of the guys. "I want to make this right. I played it wrong for too long. If this is how I can fix it, for all of us, then yes, this is what I want."

"I'm not giving them up." I raise a brow to emphasize my point. "I'm not changing a single thing to cater to you. I'm not even sure I'll ever grow to trust you or let you in."

He swallows and exhales, stoic as ever. "I understand."

"You'll have no agency over me. I don't even want to hear your opinion unless I ask for it. Your influence ended the morning you broke up with me. Getting married doesn't change that. Is that clear?"

He glares but nods his ascent.

"Tomorrow," Kylian suggests. "You should do it tomorrow."

The words are like a sucker punch. Rearing back, I gape at him, suddenly panicked by just how final this is about to be.

"Why tomorrow?" I ask when I can breathe again.

"No cameras. No press. We'll catch them unaware. You can do it here."

Kendrick sits back and crosses his arms. "It's not a bad idea. I don't see any other way we can pull this off without tipping off the media. They'll find out soon enough, but it will be on our terms. I assume there's more to the plan, Cap?"

Decker nods once. "I'm breaking ties with my dad. Purposely in breach of contract with most of my NIL deals. I'm getting out, but it's going to be messy. There will be consequences, but I'll face them."

"*We'll* face them," Kendrick clarifies.

"Tomorrow, huh?" Locke runs his hand through his hair.

"Is everyone okay with that?" Decker asks.

The guys grumble their consent, the mood in the room noticeably sour.

"Josephine?"

Arms crossed, I prop a hip against the table. Waves of warning crash over me, even though there's no danger here. The instinct to oppose the situation is purely self-preservation. If I do this, *when* I do this, I have to protect my heart. So I press my lips into a flat line, doing my best to look unaffected at the prospect of marrying Decker Crusade. "I honestly don't care."

"Josephine," he mutters. This time my name is a scolding. He links his massive arms across his broad chest, mirroring my stance.

And just like that, we're locked in a face-off once again.

"What?" The unease inside me is quickly turning to agitation.

Decker wasn't even supposed to be around this weekend. Tonight was turning out to be chill, enjoyable, with the possibility of turning molten. Weren't we supposed to play strip poker? What happened to the damn time-out?

"Have you decided my opinion suddenly matters? Just like that, you've determined my words and actions have the power to change something you've already decided for me?"

"Easy," Kendrick chides.

His placating tone only raises my hackles more.

"No. I'll go through with this, but nothing about it will be *easy*." I'm not even mad at K, and yet I can't help but scowl in his direction. I'm out of my depth. Out of control. Panicking at the prospect of marrying—*marrying?*—Decker tomorrow. This can't be happening.

"Cap's made it clear where he draws the line with me. That doesn't mean I have to settle, though. Even if he is going to be my *husband*." The last word leaves my mouth like a bitter curse.

Never one to back down when challenged, Decker straightens to full height, rolling his shoulders back.

Gone is the remorseful, pitiful man who was stammering through his supper twenty minutes ago.

Before me stands the arrogant, egotistical asshole quarterback who broke my heart, then stomped on the pieces.

Holding his head high, he scans the room. "Guys. Can you give us a few minutes? I'd like to speak to my wife. Alone."

No one moves a muscle.

I also refuse to back down from his challenge, so I look from Kylian to Kendrick to Locke. "Go," I tell them. "I'll be fine," I promise when I note the concern in Locke's expression.

Planting one hand on my hip, I turn back to Decker. "Clearly, my future husband isn't going to settle until he gets his way. Once I deal with him, I'll meet you in the Den."

Chapter 60

Decker

I practically drag her into my bedroom. Our journey to this end of the cabin is punctuated by her huffs and exasperated sighs.

When we get inside, I close and lock the door.

By the time I turn around, she's perched on my bed, arms still tucked under her breasts in a way that rearranges my insides.

"What?" she pushes.

"Let me have it." Arms raised in surrender, I stalk toward her. I stop a few feet away, giving her space. Letting her choose how she wants to proceed.

"Let you have what, exactly?" she challenges. "I just agreed to marry you, Decker. What more could you possibly want from me?"

I laugh—a humorless chuckle. "What more could I *want* from you?" I grind my jaw so hard it aches.

She hits me with that haughty stare, her blue eyes sparkling like fractals of ice.

"I want it all, Siren." Fisting my hands at my sides, I risk taking one step closer. "Your anger. Your hate. I won't marry you with all this resentment and animosity hanging between us. Get it out of your system right now so we can start this right."

It's her turn to laugh.

She pushes off the bed, squaring up until we're toe to toe. "You think getting it off my chest will miraculously repair what's been irrevocably broken?"

I raise one brow, but I hold back a retort. I told her to let it out, so I'll keep my mouth shut and take it.

"You think we can just have a conversation and that'll reverse the hell you put me through? All the pain you caused?"

Shrugging, I push harder. "I don't know," I admit. "But it's worth a try. Give it to me, Siren."

"There's nothing left to give!" she screams, her hands fisting her hair in frustration.

"Come on," I goad, jerking my neck to one side, then the other, reveling in the shot of pain each crack sends through me. "You can do better than that."

My argument is nothing but a farce, but I play it cool. My insides twist every time I provoke her. Because all I want to do is hold her. Because she's dimmed so markedly over the last few weeks, and it's my fucking fault.

Her fire doesn't burn as hot.

The passion between us has been reduced to a flicker.

But it's not out yet.

And now that we're alone, I intend to reignite it and set us ablaze.

"I thought I was the coward here. I didn't think you'd give up so easily, Josephine."

That does it.

The ice blue of her irises ignites, and fury takes over.

"You think *I'm* a coward?"

There she fucking is.

"You think I'm the one giving up? You think I'll make this easy on you?"

I bite back a grin as she charges toward me. *My Siren*.

"Do you know how hard I worked to break through to you the first time? It took so much out of me to crack your shell. All that effort... all that *love*," she chokes out the last word. "When I'd finally tunneled my way in, you threw it all away. You threw *us* away."

She stands up straighter, glaring at me with so much force my instinct is to cower despite our size difference.

"I honestly believed you were worth it. Once we were finally together, I thought nothing could keep us apart. I never imagined you'd shatter us and just move on like I'm nothing to you."

I hold back all the words I want to say. Swallow down the apology on the tip of my tongue. It's all useless now. I've weaponized my words against her too many times. I've made promises I couldn't keep, and I've lied to her face to protect her. All I have left are actions.

Thankfully, because of the arrangement we came up with tonight, I'll have a lifetime to make it up to her and prove myself worthy.

Her shoulders shake with a dismissive huff. "You know what's funny about all of this? I'm not sad. I was at first, but now I'm just mad."

Good. I want her mad. I want to feel that fire.

"And why's that?" I ask, inching incrementally closer.

"Because I see right through you, Decker Crusade. I see through your bullshit armor and this martyr act you love to default to. You've been pushing me away to protect me, but I'm still so fucking mad at you."

She grits her teeth, her arms still locked tightly in front of her. Her leg twitches, as if she's holding back from stomping her foot.

"So punish me," I offer.

Her pupils blow wide—from surprise or desire, I'm not sure.

"What?"

"Punish me. Make me pay for putting you in this position, for all the pain I caused. I know there's nothing I can say to make this up to you. So punish me. Use me however you see fit."

Her face screws up. "What is wrong with you?"

"You're about to be my wife," I remind her.

Fire flashes in her eyes when I murmur those last two words.

"In name only," she sasses.

"Punish me," I repeat. "Let me have you tonight. Then you can go on denying me for the rest of our lives."

My proposition lingers between us, desire thrumming in the room.

She has me pegged. I am a coward. I'm weak. But if she's going to spend the rest of forever spiting me, then I'll take the scraps she's willing to give.

I'll do anything to be closer to her in this moment.

I'll give anything to chase the high only she brings, to taste her and savor her one more time. To make her come undone just for me. Even just this once. To prove to myself that the night I claimed her wasn't a fever dream. To remind myself that she was fucking made for me.

"Punish me or go back to your boyfriends, Josephine. We don't have all night."

Except we do.

But just as I suspected, my flippant remark sets her off.

She charges forward, claws at the back of my head, and growls. "You are infuriating."

She slams her mouth to mine as the energy notches up in the room.

Dipping down, I palm her ass and sweep her off her feet.

She clings to me with fervor and desperation as I march to the bed. Fuck, I can't help but revel in the moment. It's impossible not to get caught up in her desire.

When she nips at my lip, I remember it's not desire. At least not right now. It's anger. It's deeply seated frustration. It's loathing fueled by every fucked-up thing I've put her through, culminating in tonight's life-changing decision.

A decision that seals our fates, crushes her future, and unlocks my wildest dreams.

Tomorrow, she'll be my wife.

Tonight, right now, when it's just the two of us, possibly for the last time—she swears she won't give up the boys, and she means it with every fiber of her being—I'll fuck her like she's the most precious thing in my life.

Because she is. She was. And now, she always will be.

Her mouth fuses to mine again as she unleashes savage kisses. I groan, savoring each and every fucking one, letting the heat of her loathing coat my insides and lick up my spine like uncontrollable flames.

She bites up and down my neck and claws at my back with such ferocity I swear she's trying to break skin.

"Enough." With a growl, I throw her onto the bed. Then I make quick work of losing my clothes.

"Strip and spread, Mrs. Crusade."

Fury flares in her light blue eyes. "I never said I would take your last name," she contends.

I shuck off my boxer briefs and stand tall, completely naked before her. Gripping my cock, I give it a few pumps.

She's furious at me, but still, she licks her lips and tracks the movement of my hand as I palm my length and squeeze the tip.

"Oh yes you did." I step closer and grab the hem of her shirt when she makes no moves to remove it herself. "You said you would be my wife—*in name only.*"

Her leggings come off next. I rip them down her legs, removing her panties and her socks in the process.

"Fuck," I murmur, watching her breasts rise and fall with her labored breathing.

"Fine. Call me whatever you want. You know who I really belong to."

Her words are cool and flippant, in complete juxtaposition to the way her nipples harden under my gaze.

I crawl onto the bed, and her legs fall open, welcoming me right where I want to be. Right where she refuses to admit she wants me.

I nudge the tip of my cock at her opening and pull back to admire the sight of her arousal coating the tip. The way her hips tilt up, seeking more, makes my heart hammer so hard in my chest I worry it'll pound its way right out.

She wants me.

I want her.

And right now, on the night before our wedding, with no one else present and nothing left to keep us apart, I'll do the one thing I rarely allow myself to do.

I'm going to take what I want.

"Let me see what's mine, wife."

The hatred in her eyes is enough to light this whole cabin on fire. Yet her legs fall open wider. Then her back arches off the mattress and her fingertips graze her nipples.

Gripping my cock at its base, I glide it through her folds again, rubbing the tip over her clit.

"Your sass tells me one thing, Siren. But look how wet you are for me."

"Fuck," she murmurs just loud enough for me to hear.

So I do it again. And again and again and again. The crown of my dick tingles from the repetitive, blunt prods against her clit.

The prettiest pink blush blooms across her chest and up her neck, then transforms the color of her cheeks. And fuck if her sex isn't blushing for me, too. Glistening and dark, so fucking ready for me. It might be the hottest sight I've ever seen.

I skim my thumbs over her wet, warm pussy lips, spreading them open and staring at her perfect pink hole. "Look how needy and desperate you are for me. So responsive to your husband's cock."

Her eyes shoot open at that word. *Husband*.

Since I've got her attention, I take the opportunity to slide all the way home while she's watching me.

There's little resistance thanks to her wetness, but the grasp of her walls around me is even more exquisite than I remembered.

"Fucking perfect fit. You take me so well, Siren. Do you feel how much your body wants this? Get ready to experience just how good your husband can give it to you."

I thrust deep, setting a relentless pace, and crane up to kiss her again.

She turns her head, denying me.

"Josephine," I growl in scolding.

Keeping her head turned, she smirks. The look is just visible in profile. Then she scrapes her nails up my bare back, sending lightning bolts of need through me.

I pull out all the way, ready to plunge back in and fuck the sass right out of her.

Only, the moment I pull out, she scrambles back. Flipping over, she rises to hands and knees and gives me a cheeky smile over her shoulder.

"Fuck me from behind, Decker. Make me come and put us both out of our misery already."

I slam into her cunt, and she cries out, shifting back to match the pace as my hips piston forward. As soon as she finds her rhythm, I make my move.

Catching her by the hips, I pull her back against my chest, still buried deep, and find her clit. With two fingers, I rub hurried, uneven circles around the nub, then give it a sharp slap.

"Fuck. Decker. *Yes*." The first quivers of her pussy ripple over me.

I freeze and pull my hand away, then bring my lips to her ear. "Two can play this game, Siren."

I pull out, spin her around, and pin her to the mattress before she even realizes what's happening.

With my arms hooked around her shoulders and my body looming over hers, I slide back home and take her how I want her.

"You'll look at me when I make you come, wife." I punctuate the command with a thrust.

"You'll look at me." Thrust. "You'll scream my name." Thrust. "You'll give me what's mine." Thrust. "And you'll come on my cock, Josephine Crusade. *Now*."

She detonates on command, milking my length, hooking her legs behind my low back and screaming my name.

"Thatta girl," I praise, fucking her hard and fast until the arousal coiled tight inside me explodes and I come in rapid spurts.

I hold myself inside her as tightly as she can take it. Desperate to fill her up. Desperate to never let go. Because I know the moment the fluttering of her pussy stops, she'll shove me off and run to the bathroom.

So when she stills, smooths her hands up my back until they meet at my nape and pulls my forehead down to rest on her own, I'm staggered.

Tenderness blossoms between us as she clings to me.

Each inhalation quivers as she tries to catch her breath.

Her gaze is solely set on me, searching and forlorn, so full of all the pain I've caused her.

Her light blue eyes are wide and filled with unshed tears. Below me, she trembles, so I cuddle closer and hold her as tightly as I dare.

"Decker." My name on her lips is vulnerable and soft as she stares directly into my soul.

There's so much I want to say. So many words and actions I yearn to take back. So much pain between us, all dealt by my hand.

I don't apologize. I don't bother with words of reassurance.

They're meaningless. Useless.

I've lost the right to comfort her that way.

Only actions will prove my worthiness now.

I hope to God that, one day, I can show her that I'll always do right by her. Never again will I cut her out, force her hand, or make a decision without her input. Then maybe she'll know just how fucking sorry I am.

And just how much I love her.

"I know, baby," I relent, closing my eyes and grinding my forehead into hers as my own tears form behind my eyelids. I kiss the tip of her nose, her lips, and each tear as it falls. "I've got you now. I swear. I've got you forever, Josephine."

Chapter 61

Josephine

I cracked.

I splintered wide open in his arms, exposing all the pain, the sorrow, and the depth of my heartache to the man responsible for causing it.

I'm anxious and desperate to flee after such a vulnerable display. So when my limbs stop tingling and my pussy is done convulsing—which takes an embarrassingly long time, because damn, my future husband just fucked me senseless—I rise out of bed and dress quickly.

It's late. Dark. His room is warm, his bed annoyingly comfortable.

Just like all the beds at home.

My stomach sinks at that word. *Home.* I've had to correct that line of thinking far too many times over the last few weeks.

Now? The mansion is going to be my home again.

It's enough to give a girl whiplash.

With each second that ticks by, an urgency grows inside me. I'm eager to get out of this room, to get away from him. To find my boys, to give myself time to think, and to come to terms with what the hell I agreed to do.

I have no doubt Decker will take the prospect of marriage as seriously as he takes protecting the people he claims to care about by asserting control over their lives.

Even if this is a rushed, pragmatic means to an end, the man has used the phrase "my wife" no less than a dozen times in the last hour.

Stretching my arms overhead, I yawn, going for casual and unaffected.

"Shower?" he asks behind me. The sheets rustle as he hauls himself up to sitting.

"No. I'm headed down to the Den. Thanks for the fuck, hubby."

His growl rumbles through the room. "Josephine, I swear to God…"

I don't bother turning around. I have no interest in engaging in yet another battle. For tonight, at least, I'm done. At the moment, I'm desperate to get downstairs and crawl into Kylian's arms so I can soak in the comfort he so easily offers.

Tonight has been far too emotionally exhausting and mentally taxing. Not that I'll let Decker know just how much I'm reeling.

"See you tomorrow," I call over my shoulder. "I'd say something cute like 'I'll be the one in white!' but since I had no idea I'd be marrying a man I'm not even dating, I didn't pack anything appropriate to wear on my trip to the altar."

A wicked rush washes over me at the prospect of showing up dressed in the other guys' clothes. It would serve him right.

"I'll make sure you have a dress," Decker calls as I stride into the hall.

I can't help but roll my eyes. Then, once I'm out of his sight, I quicken my pace, wiping away fresh tears as I retreat to the Den.

Chapter 62

Josephine

"It's time." Ever our timekeeper, Kylian rises to his feet, pockets his phone, and offers me his hand.

I side-eye Locke, then look at Kendrick, who's sitting in the chair across the way.

"You're sure?" Hunter asks for the seventeenth time.

Bless my bestie.

She surprised me by waltzing in beside Decker a few hours ago. We holed up in the bedroom the girls had been sleeping in, and I filled her in between gasps and squeals. We may have also shared a bottle of champagne while going on an online shopping spree courtesy of Decker's credit card.

Hunter agreed that legally, Decker's plan should work. Despite only being in her first semester of prelaw, she knows her shit, and I trust her judgment.

As promised, Decker brought a dress for me: layers of gauzy red tulle that are impossibly soft and slightly shimmery. It falls just above the knee and fits tight through the bodice.

A traditional wedding dress, it is not.

Regardless, I love it. Just slipping it on instantly made me feel good. Beautiful. A little less anxious.

According to Hunter, Decker picked it out with minimal input from her. Naturally, that means I won't be gushing about how gorgeous it is in his presence.

I bat Kylian's hand away and pull myself up. "I'm sure. Let's get this over with."

The entire state is more or less shut down, but Kylian was able to apply for our marriage license online. With a few keystrokes and a confirmation that my social security number was input correctly, he declared us good to go.

Surrounded by my guys, I walk toward the double doors that lead out to the deck.

Decker is already standing outside with the minister.

She's an older woman, around Mrs. Lansbury's age. She smiles kindly at all of us, clearly unaware of who the guys are or what our dynamic entails. I'm sure that was intentional.

We've agreed to no photos of the ceremony. We can't risk news leaking before we're ready to make our announcement.

Still, I rest my head on Hunter's shoulder and smile when she pulls me in close and holds up her phone to snap a picture.

"I know this probably isn't what you dreamed about when you were little," she starts, taking in the guys as they line up along the railing of the deck that overlooks the snowcapped mountains. "But it's gorgeous out here."

My nose itches, signaling that I'm in danger of tearing up. She's not wrong. But it doesn't change the reality that I'd rather be committing myself to any of the other three men standing in front of me right now, and we all know it.

"Ready when you are," the minister announces.

Just like that, we all fall into place.

I stand toe to toe with Decker, like I've done so many times before. His onyx eyes bore into me: searching, longing, yearning for some semblance of a connection.

I give him nothing.

I can't.

I'm too raw, too hurt, too banged up from the breakup, to muster up anything more than civility.

Even that takes effort, as proven when it's time to say our vows.

He's a good man. I loved him. I still love him. In his own twisted way, Decker loves me, too. Nevertheless, I've been burned too many times by his particular brand of love to approach this marriage with anything but skepticism and wariness.

When the minister turns it over to me, I pull out my phone and read the promises I feverishly typed out during lunch.

"I, Josephine Meyer, take you, Decker Crusade, to be my lawfully wedded husband. I'll be loyal for as long as deemed necessary."

Hunter snorts behind me.

Then, looking past Decker, I swallow down the emotion clogging my throat and continue. "And I will love this family with all that I am, for as long as I live."

Kendrick is the first to mouth, "I love you," quickly followed by Locke. Kylian watches me with a predatory, protective glint in his eye, like he's about to pull a stunt and put a stop to all of this.

My attention flits back to Decker. He's wearing an expression I'm all too familiar with. It's equal parts amused and exasperated. It's his *Josephine* face. I bite my tongue to stop myself from reminding him that this was his idea.

"I, Decker Crusade, take you, Josephine Meyer, to be my lawfully wedded wife. My wife," he repeats, his tone sharp. Then his expression softens. "I'll try harder. I'll be better. I'll hold you in the dark and honor you in every way. I'll do whatever it takes to make this the life of your dreams. I'll love you forever and shelter you through every storm."

Hunter whistles low as I wobble in the heels Decker brought for the occasion.

His vows were perfect.

Everything I could have ever hoped to hear.

Even so, it's too late. The damage has been done.

I blink back tears as the minister declares us husband and wife.

I let him kiss me, and I fight like hell to keep my emotions in check as I silently pray that this idea works, and that my heart will survive the whiplash of being loved by Decker Crusade.

Chapter 63

Josephine

Sweet scents of lavender and honey waft off the water as I soak. Little jets along the bottom of the tub keep the bubbles thick and foamy and also keep the temperature piping hot.

My skin is starting to wrinkle, but I don't care. This is the most relaxed I've been in weeks.

For the first time since we arrived, I'm truly alone. Kendrick filled the tub in the bathroom attached to the Den and insisted I relax. He and my other guys are around here somewhere.

Decker promised he'd have Hunter home before dark. Since Greedy's place is on the opposite side of the mountain, that means they had to leave more than two hours ago.

Sighing, I skim both hands over the bubbles, collecting them into a massive pile in the middle. We didn't even have a bathtub growing up. It's wild to think that soon, I'll own the very one I'm soaking in now.

I've already decided I want Decker to buy this place.

Kylian has a space he feels comfortable in here. It's one of Nicky's favorite places in the world. After just a few days here, I totally get the appeal.

Visions of holidays spent at the cabin wash over me.

I want to make so many memories here, with my boys.

A soft knock at the door pulls me from my reverie.

"Okay in there, Mama? You know Kylian's worried about your safety in two feet of water."

I snort. "I'm fine," I call back. "Almost done."

"Take your time. We'll be ready and waiting."

Ready? And *waiting*?

My curiosity piqued, I pull the plug to drain the tub and run clean water to rinse off.

I get out and wrap myself in a robe Kendrick left in the towel warmer and practically melt as the plush cloth encircles my body.

My hair is still pinned up in loose curls from earlier. My makeup is still mostly intact, too. I love getting dolled up. Even if it's for less than thrilling reasons.

When I open the door to the bedroom, I stop dead in my tracks.

The room is filled with candlelight—battery operated candlelight by the looks of it. Dozens of flickering candles in all sizes cover every surface, emitting a warm glow.

White flowers are strewn about, creating a path from where I stand to the bed; the delicate, asymmetrical petals are as fragrant as they are unique.

But it's the sight of what's waiting for me on the bed that truly takes my breath away.

My boys. All three of them. Shirtless. Pantsless. Staring at me with intense hunger that radiates through me, from the top of my spine to the tips of my toes.

"What is all this?"

"It's your wedding night, Hot Girl." Locke's grin is as playful as ever. "And we're about to make the most of it."

"Get over here, Mama. You kept us waiting long enough."

I make my way over, still stunned that they planned such an elaborate setup as I take in the room. With each step, my excitement and anticipation grow.

"Drop the robe. Climb onto the bed."

Holding Kylian's gaze, I quickly untie the robe and let it fall off my body.

I'm naked, my skin still damp and warm from the bath.

"Like this?" I tease.

"Are you on the bed like I told you?"

Fuck. Yes. Daddy wants to play.

Obediently, I climb onto the mattress, immediately straddling Kylian's lap. The boys gravitate closer: Nicky to the side, and Kendrick at my back.

"Better, Daddy?" I question, grinding my bare pussy in his lap.

"Good girl." Cupping my face in his hands, he drops a tender kiss to my lips. "We all want in tonight, baby. We want to share you, and we're going to make you feel so good."

My core warms and my tummy flips at the prospect. I want them all, too. And more importantly, I want memories of my time here to consist of so much more than my rushed wedding to Decker.

"Share me," I practically beg. I kiss Kylian back, but then break away and seek out Locke.

His mouth replaces his friend's seamlessly. His tongue sweeps into my mouth with so much passion, slickness is already gathering between my thighs.

With Locke's lips still on mine, Kylian pinches my nipples. Quickly, he moves on to alternating between rubbing them and licking them.

Kendrick teases me from behind. He toys with my clit, then dips two fingers into my cunt.

"You're already dripping for us, Mama." His breath is hot on my neck. "You can't wait to have your boys filling you up." Kissing my nape, he snakes his hand between my legs again. "I need to feel this pussy come for me before anything else, Jojo. Because after I make you come, I'm taking this ass."

Flames ignite, licking up my insides as he sweeps one finger through my arousal and breaches my puckered hole. With his other hand, he circles my clit, then fucks me with two thick fingers, hitting the exact spot that sends pleasure sparking through my body.

"There it is, Mama. You feel me?"

Do I ever.

I arch back, resting my head on Kendrick's shoulder as Kylian tugs on my nipples and kisses my stomach. Eventually, he works his way lower, teasing my clit and rubbing in fast, tight circles while Kendrick penetrates my pussy and my ass.

The first orgasm hits hard and fast. It's a full-body release that's so intensely satisfying it hurts. My body convulses and aches, pleasure singing through my limbs as the guys relentlessly savor every inch of skin they can reach.

Kendrick crooks his fingers along my G-spot, extending the pleasure and leading me straight into a second wave.

"K," I whimper, needy and helpless, because he knows damn well what he's doing.

He grins into my neck, suckling on my flesh without stopping his ministrations on my inner walls. I spasm around him, then clench down tight when he swirls his finger in my ass.

"Keep her occupied," he tells the others.

He withdraws from my pussy, and I miss him instantly. But then a second digit pushes into my ass, and I moan.

"Shh," Kylian soothes, kissing me everywhere as Kendrick stretches my hole.

"Relax for me, Mama. You gotta breathe. You gotta let me in."

I take a breath and let it out, following his instructions, but my body is coiled too tight with anticipation.

"Hot Girl."

I turn to where Nicky's standing naked beside the bed.

"Bet you can't deep throat me far enough to kiss my piercing."

Kylian scoffs against my breast, the huff of air blowing against my damp skin and sending tingles coursing through me.

Before he can explain the mechanics or physical impossibility of getting all ten-plus inches of Locke in my mouth, I tip my chin.

"Let me try."

Gripping himself at the base, Nicky steps up and guides his cock to my mouth, rubbing the drop of precum along my bottom lip. "I love painting you in cum," he grunts.

With my eyes locked on his, I lick the salty offering from my lips, then tilt closer and press my lips to his tip. "More please."

Nicky pushes his enormous cock between my lips just as Kendrick works a third finger into my ass.

I'm stretched to the brink, unable to focus on one specific sensation. Kylian's words cut through my racing thoughts and center me once again.

"Good girl, Jo. Such a good fucking girl. How does it feel to be stretched open by one of your boys while the other feeds you his cock?"

I flush from the praise. From the heat. From the fullness.

All too soon, Kendrick retreats, leaving me so empty I ache.

Popping off Nicky's dick, I peer over my shoulder. "K. Come back."

I'm wholly unprepared for the raging desire burning in his eyes when he focuses on me. He's coating his dick in lube, spreading the glistening liquid from root to tip.

"This is it, Mama. I'm gonna take your last virgin hole and fill you up like you've never been filled."

"Do it," I plead, clenching when his cock presses against me.

"Nuh-uh," he scolds. "You've gotta relax. Breathe for me. Trust me, Mama. Your body's ready. Your heart's mine. Give up that control you love to fight Decker for, and I'll take care of you. We all will. We'll make you feel so fucking good. You just gotta let me in."

I blow out a breath and nod.

"Fuck," I whimper, resting my head on Kylian's shoulder as Kendrick breaches me.

"I've got you," Kylian assures me. "Breathe. Relax. Let K in, baby. You're doing so good for him. Such a good girl." He smooths his arms up and down my stomach, teasing my clit or tweaking my nipples with each pass.

Kendrick grunts as he pushes in so fucking slowly. I feel every inch he works into my ass. I love every second of the stretch and the pleasure as he claims me in a way I've never been claimed. Arousal gushes from my pussy, puddling on the sheets below.

"Fuck, Hot Girl. Look at that mess you're making."

Kylian drags two fingers through my folds and pops them into his mouth. "She loves getting fucked in the ass."

He sweeps his hand along my cunt again and plays with my clit as Kendrick slides in another inch, then another.

Behind me, K releases a guttural moan that vibrates through me. "I'm in."

My ass grips his hard length as I adjust to the fullest sensation I've ever experienced.

"Taste how much she loves this." Kylian's voice is a rasp as he lifts those same two fingers to Nicky.

Locke cants forward and eye fucks me. Without preamble, he wraps his lips around his best friend's fingers and siphons my cum off his hand. The sucking and groaning are obscene. His lascivious expression through the whole encounter pulls all the air from my lungs.

I clench again, and Kendrick hisses between his teeth. "Stop fucking around, you two. I need to move."

The slight jostling as he shifts sends a bolt of lightning through me. "Please," I beg. "I need him to move."

I've never needed anything more in my life.

"We both want in." Kylian nods to Nicky. "We're going to take turns, but tell us if it's too much."

I nod absentmindedly. My brain is so fogged with desire I can't grasp a coherent thought. All I can do is feel.

Kylian seeks my entrance, lining himself up like he's done so many times before. This time, though, is wholly unique. I don't know where he's going to go. I don't know how he thinks he'll fit. Not when I'm this full—

"Jo."

My eyes flit to his. To the man I trust implicitly. My safe place. My harbor in the storm.

He pushes in, never taking his eyes off me.

"You are here," he tells me.

"This is now," I murmur.

Pleasure surges to my core as the most delicious warmth pools in my belly.

They're both in. Sharing me. Filling me to the brink, promising uncharted pleasure. I slam my mouth into Kylian's, panting. "Fuck me, Daddy."

Following orders, he finds a rhythm, and once he sets his pace, Kendrick moves, too.

"Fucking hell. I can feel your cock every time she spasms around us," Kendrick grunts.

"She's perfect. So fucking perfect for us."

One pushes. One pulls. I'm alight with heat and pleasure as the fullness overwhelms my senses.

When I'm on the precipice, so blissed out I can't tell which way is up, Kylian pulls out and moves away.

Disappointment hits me like a sucker punch, but the pain instantly dissipates when Locke appears before me.

"Nicky's bigger than me." Kylian strokes himself, his attention fixed between my thighs. "You're going to have to breathe through this one, baby."

I'm ready. I want him so much I ache.

Locke slides into my cunt, and the stretch is so overwhelming I gasp.

Fuck. I'm not ready.

My ass is so full and my body is lit up with pleasure. With Locke buried to the hilt, with his pubic piercing hitting my clit with sniper-level accuracy as he thrusts up and joins us together, I almost black out.

"Fuck," I whimper, seeking out Kylian's mouth.

He kisses me greedily, one hand weaving through my hair and angling my head back so he can feed me his tongue. "Breathe out, baby."

I do.

Only to feel a sharp stretch, followed by the sudden urge to pee.

I gasp and tense up. "Oh shit—"

On instinct, I duck my chin, searching for the source of the sensation. Instantly, I find it. Along with Nicky's cock, Kylian's hand is between my thighs.

I jerk my head up and blink at him.

"Such a good girl." The smirk he gives me is one of pure arrogance. "You let us in. We're all inside you now, baby. Do you feel that?" He presses his finger against my G-spot for emphasis. "We've claimed you completely. You belong to us. And we're *never* letting you go."

He presses against my G-spot again, and I cry out.

Clear fluid gushes from my cunt, soaking Kylian's hand and Nicky's cock and even Kendrick's thighs.

"Holy shit," Kendrick grunts against the back of my neck. "Hottest fucking thing I've ever experienced, Mama. Do it again."

Focusing on the mounting pleasure Nicky's delivering to my clit with his piercing, I close my eyes and revel in the ecstasy. Kendrick uses one finger to massage the stretched skin of my taint: the only barrier between his cock, Nicky's cock, and Kylian's hand. My ass is gaping, stretched to accommodate all of Kendrick. Kylian brushes against my inner walls again, and the same urgent, unstoppable sensations overpower all my senses.

One more caress against my G-spot, and I'm squirting again.

"Soak us, baby. Don't stop. Keep going."

Kendrick ruts in and out, fucking my ass as I drench the bed. When he stills, one hand splayed wide on my belly, pressing himself as deep as he can get, I know he's coming, too.

Locke fucks me through Kendrick's orgasm, prolonging the pleasure for all of us until he also topples over the edge. With a curse, he pulls out of my pussy and grasps his dick, aiming for the literal puddle below me as jets of his cum combine with my release.

Kylian pulls his finger out of my pussy, and he and Nicky switch places. This time when Kylian pushes in, it's an easier fit, because Kendrick's dick is softening inside me.

K lowers onto his haunches, his cock still buried deep in my ass as he pulls me into his lap and spreads me open for Daddy.

The new angle gives Kylian better access to my clit. He makes quick work of stimulating the bundle of nerves as he thrusts into my pussy, praising me each time he's buried to the hilt.

"So perfect. So tight. Such a good fucking girl, giving us everything."

Panting, his hair drenched and his forehead slick with sweat, Nicky brings his face to mine. "Kiss me."

Our mouths meet, and our tongues dance. The connection is electric. I don't know how I'll go on after this. Nothing could ever feel this good, this raw, this right.

They're everywhere. They're part of me. My beginning and my end; my joy and my pleasure.

Working together, the boys bring me to the brink.

Biting down on my bottom lip to keep from screaming, I open my eyes as waves of bliss shudder through me.

"Fuck, I need to come again," I gasp against Locke's mouth.

He grips my chin and kisses me deeper, caressing his tongue against mine as he rolls my nipples between his fingers.

Kendrick's gazing at me with the most tender, loving expression. He kisses my forehead.

Kylian pulls me forward, wrapping me in his arms. He fucks me through a blackout orgasm, only letting himself come when he knows I'm good and truly done.

Done, I am. Done doesn't even begin to cover it.

Lifting my head, I kiss Locke again, sweetly this time. "I love you."

Turning to Kylian, I kiss him next, moaning when he quickly takes control and fucks his tongue into my mouth. I pull back and suck in a deep breath, steadying myself. "I love you."

Finally, he pulls out, shamelessly fingering my cunt and gathering up his own cum from inside me. With a feral grin, he smears it into the puddle of mixed release beneath us.

Kendrick smirks, kisses my neck, and works himself out of my ass slowly.

His release slips out of my body, joining the mix. It's an excessive amount of fluid. I giggle as I take in the visible evidence of our pleasure.

Who knew a cum puddle would be one of the highlights of my wedding night?

Kylian offers me a hand, but K shoulders in front of him.

"I've got her." He catches me under the knees and whisks me off the bed. "You need to pee, then I think you need another bath, dirty girl."

"Are you joining me this time?"

He snickers, then looks at the others.

"I'm pretty sure we're all joining you, Mama. I told you: you belong to us. That means we also belong to you. Never apart, ever again."

Tucking myself into the crook of his neck, I catch sight of Kylian and Nicky, who are indeed hot on our heels, their attention focused solely on me.

"I love you," I whisper into Kendrick's chest, cuddling closer, savoring the care, the fun, the sense of security, and the abundance of love I feel for each of them.

Chapter 64

Josephine

A yawn surprises me as I waltz into the kitchen. I lean into it, stretching my arms over my head, but startle when I open my eyes and find Decker cradling a mug at the kitchen table.

He's the first one up—my guys are still down in the Den—and a surge of smug satisfaction hits me as I take him in.

His hair is mussed, his face is drawn, and his eyes are rimmed red, like he hasn't slept at all.

Who knew marrying him would give me more ammunition when it came to riling him up?

Neither of us says a word as I prepare my coffee. I consider grabbing a blanket and heading out to the deck, but when I feel Decker's attention boring into me, I risk a glance at him. He's sitting at the table, watching me, wearing the saddest, most forlorn expression.

Taking pity on him, I sit in the chair across from him.

Clearing his throat, he sits up straighter and dons the stoic mask he wears so well. "How was your wedding night?"

I purse my lips and school my expression. How the hell does he expect me to answer that? Surely, he doesn't really want to hear the details.

My body aches in the best possible way as I squirm in my seat. "It was fine, thanks."

Decker glares over the steam rising out of his mug.

Wrong answer, I guess, but what does he want me to say? There's no response that could make this moment less awkward.

He clears his throat again. It's a nervous tic, I'm realizing, and one I've never noticed before. Probably because he's rarely nervous.

"I'd like to take you somewhere today."

My heart sinks. Here we fucking go.

I cock one eyebrow but say nothing.

"We don't have time for a honeymoon... but I thought we could spend the day together. Just the two of us."

Yeah. No. This isn't happening.

"We're married in name only, Decker. I'm with them," I remind him, bringing my coffee to my lips.

He grits his teeth and grips his mug until his knuckles pale. "I'm well aware of that."

I bet he is. The Den may be soundproofed, but I also may have noticed the door was left cracked open last night, and I didn't bother to say anything.

"This isn't how this works. You can't just tell me where to go or whisk me away like I belong to you."

"The guys know about my plan."

I frown. "They do?"

I take a sip of my coffee, savoring the warmth all the way down as I swallow.

"It's your choice, Josephine. Would you like to spend the day with me?"

His words surprise me—the very un-Decker-like offer and the acknowledgment that I have a choice.

"Where would we go?" I hedge, fully expecting him to withhold information.

Instead, he simply offers, "The beach."

I perk up just a fraction. "Really?"

A day at the beach—the sound of the waves, the warmth of the sun—sounds absolutely lovely. I'd prefer to go with all my guys, but I highly doubt that's part of Decker's plan.

Sitting a little straighter, Decker makes his case.

"I want to take you to the same place we went before. I have a buddy out that way who confirmed the roads are passable. According to him, that stretch of beach was untouched."

"And if I say no?" I ask, my heart rate picking up its pace, readying for another battle.

He examines me, his jaw ticking all the while, likely formulating his next haughty scolding.

Once again, I'm knocked back by his response. "I'll spend the day packing and closing up the house. Then we can head back to the isle first thing tomorrow."

I roll my lips, fighting back a smile, ignoring the little flicker of warmth in my belly. "Okay," I concede.

He squints, like he's searching for a lie. Or maybe he's expecting me to pull the rug out from under him. "Okay?"

His surprise is further proof that he still doesn't get it. I'm not the combative, obstinate thorn in his side he thinks I am. All I want is a choice.

"Okay," I repeat, standing up and smiling. "Let's go to the beach."

Chapter 65
Josephine

It's better than I remembered. Soft, lush sand. The brilliant warmth from the sun.

Sure, it's significantly colder than the last time we were here, but the temperature doesn't take away from the beauty of the place or the contentment that washes over me like the waves lapping along the shore.

Decker carries all our things, which is ridiculous, because I have arms, too. He also packed like our whole crew is here rather than just the two of us.

The car ride was surprisingly painless. It turns out we have similar taste in music, something I didn't know until today.

Decker didn't make any of the expected remarks when I queued up my favorite playlist, which Hunter has jokingly named my Sad Ohio Girl Songs. I can't help it if I have taste, while her preferences sound like a remix of the *Barbie* soundtrack.

I watch wordlessly as Decker works to set up our spot, shifting from hip to hip, sinking a little deeper into the sand with each movement. Awkwardness sinks in as I observe him quietly, but I'm determined to be noncombative today, so I don't dare offer to help.

I don't mind princess treatment from the other guys, but letting Decker do it all makes me anxious. The urge to help claws at me, yet the idea of helping stresses me out. It feels as though there's no solution for us. Either option will inevitably be the wrong move. With Decker, I'm always waiting for the other shoe to drop.

To distract myself from my spiraling thoughts, I turn and take in the ocean scene. I take a deep breath so I can taste the salt air on my tongue. A shiver runs through me, but it has little to do with the crisp temperature.

"Want to walk the beach?" he asks from behind me, his voice full of gravel and hesitation.

Peering over my shoulder, I inspect his setup.

"Sure," I agree.

See? I can do noncombative.

Clearing his throat and patting his pockets, probably to confirm he's got his wallet and phone, he takes a step closer. "Which way?"

I open my mouth to make a cutting remark about being shocked that he's actually going to let me choose, but I snap it closed just as fast. Clearly, I'm not the only one putting in the effort today.

"This way."

We meander along the water's edge, neither of us in a rush or with a destination in mind. The sound of the waves crashing onto the shore creates a melodic, meditative rhythm.

Decker's hand brushes mine every few steps. He doesn't course correct or shift away from the contact, but neither do I.

We pass two kids trying in earnest to fly a kite. Probably siblings, based on the way they bicker as the little girl tries to rewrap the string on the handle.

"Heads up!"

Lightning fast, Decker is on me, a hand pressed to my lower back and his body looming over mine, blocking me from the unknown threat. Heat crawls up my neck and paints my cheeks as memories of all the delicious ways he touched and pleased me two nights ago riot in my mind.

When we're not immediately approached, I peek over his shoulder and take in the scene.

A man's jogging toward us, shaking his head. "Sorry about that," he yells once he's in range.

Decker smooths his hand from my back to my hip and squeezes before releasing me. Warmth pools in my belly. His touch is intoxicating, even when we're fully clothed on a public beach.

He bends and snatches up the football that soared toward us a moment ago.

He tosses the ball—underhand; nothing like how he usually throws a football, which I assume is intentional—to the man, who thanks him, then heads over to a little boy.

We don't immediately continue our journey. Instead, still standing close to one another, we watch as the man grips the boy's shoulder and bends low to talk into his ear. He helps his son square his hips and then lines up the stitches in his hand.

The boy hesitates, barely holding the ball in the grasp of his small hand. He can't be more than seven or eight years old.

We can't hear the exchange because of the distance and the pounding of the waves behind us, but it's clear what he's seeking—what he needs.

The man squeezes his son's shoulder, whispers once more, nods, and steps back a few feet.

After another breath, the boy launches the ball into the air. It arches over the sand in a wobbly spiral. As it tumbles through the air, the dad claps and hollers so loudly his enthusiasm reaches us.

The little boy's joy is palpable as his dad scoops him up, hugs him close, and spins in a circle. It's a sweet moment. One I wish I could capture on camera.

When I peek up at Decker, he's got a massive grin plastered on his face.

I bump my hip into his to get his attention.

"Is that what it was like for you?" I nod toward the duo, who are running side by side to retrieve the ball.

"That? No." Decker grimaces, shaking his head.

"What do you mean *no*?" I frown up at him. "Your dad's a professional quarterback. You're telling me he didn't teach you how to throw a football?"

His hand once again finds the small of my back—why is that so sexy?—and he's quiet while he watches the boy launch the ball into another decent throw.

Finally, he pulls in a long breath. "Thomas is not a patient man. Or a good teacher. And honestly? I'm not a great student. Coach likes to say I have to learn my lessons the hardest way possible."

I snort. *If that isn't the understatement of the year...*

"What?" he demands, his expression going from hard to sheepish when I give him a pointed look.

"You? Not being receptive to training and coaching? That just might be the most accurate assessment I've ever heard."

Decker grumbles, running his hand through his hair over and over again. "You think that's funny, huh?"

I answer with silence and a knowing smirk.

"You'll love this, then," he murmurs, scanning the horizon. "I was the second-string quarterback on our U-12 Little Dukes team until middle school."

"Who was first?" I demand, because I have a sneaking suspicion I already know.

"Greedy," he admits.

I bite my tongue hard.

"I had the better arm. The quicker reads. But I couldn't nail the timing."

"That's what a lot of people don't understand about football. There's a rhythm to the game. A deep-seated trust between the players. It took being sacked a couple hundred times for me to trust my offensive line and step up into the pocket so plays could develop.

"Thomas hated that it took so long for things like that to click. He'd explain it a million different ways. Make me watch film for hours. Hired mindset coaches and throwing coaches and half a dozen other kinds of instructors and guides. He recognized my potential, but he wasn't willing to meet me where I was or do the work to help me learn in a way that worked for me."

"So you learn best by failing," I tease, thinking I'll get under his skin with the jab.

"Yeah." His knuckles brush against my fingertips. "Sometimes I think that's the only way I ever learn."

It takes a moment for the confession to really sink in. For me to catch on to the admission that he even has shortcomings. He's more self-aware than I thought. It irritates me in a way, but it's also really telling.

His hand hovers near mine, hesitant, close enough that I can feel his body heat. This time when he touches me, it's not just a brush. He circles my wrist while keeping his attention locked on my face, silently searching, as if to ask if the contact is okay.

When I don't pull away, he interlocks our fingers, slow but sure.

We walk hand in hand for a few minutes, quiet and lost in thought. Eventually, he turns to me, cups my face, and leans in close enough to kiss me.

Hovering until we're sharing breath, he confesses, "I'll rarely get it right on the first try, Siren. But I promise I'll keep trying until I do."

His earnestness makes me squirm.

Because I believe him.

And yet, my sense of self-preservation can't allow me to hope that he'll follow through. I've been burned too many times by Decker's words to take them at face value.

Sidestepping him, I squeeze his hand and hold on a bit tighter as we continue walking along the beach.

I appreciate that he's willing to do the work. I just hope like hell it doesn't always have to be this hard.

Chapter 66

Decker

I drive the umbrella into the sand with more force than I mean to.

I'm pent up and agitated, horny and frustrated.

I didn't think it would be this difficult to spend the day alone with her.

My wife.

Nothing is wrong, per se. But when her phone pings with a text from one of the guys, or when I catch her looking out at the ocean, lost in thought and wearing an expression that's far too peaceful to be associated with me, it scratches at the already raw wounds on my heart.

I've never employed more restraint than I did last night when I heard them.

The four of them.

Together.

On our wedding night.

Though it took all my self-control, I wouldn't allow myself to be baited. To go where I'm not welcome. To intrude on the genuine intimacy they share.

It felt like a mockery of our marriage to listen to her scream for them as I sat upstairs, alone with my bourbon. But I stayed the course and refused to engage.

I've gotten it wrong with Josephine so many times. It took a ridiculous number of failures to get here, but now, I'm irrevocably determined to get this right.

My words are useless. The way I wielded them in the past ensured that. All I have left are my actions—the consideration I give, the care I provide, and now, the privacy I can erect as she sunbathes on a blanket in her unbuttoned flannel shirt and shorts.

"What did that umbrella do to you?" she teases, her hand raised to her forehead to shield the sun from her eyes.

I take her in and will my dick to stand down.

She's so fucking pretty.

Toned legs and wide hips, her stomach curvy and soft as she lies flat on her back. Her breasts are perfect mounds, nipples clearly visible through the thin fabric of the crop top.

What I wouldn't give to slide my tongue—or my cock—along the curves of her breasts.

Swallowing back the desire threatening to take control of me, I inspect our setup, then finally join her on the blanket we spread out for lunch.

"Just wanted to give us some privacy."

"You built an entire umbrella barricade," she counters with a grin.

Yeah. I did.

Four umbrellas strategically circle us, none positioned in a way that block out the sun, but all of them creating enough coverage that we have the illusion of isolation.

"We've only seen a dozen other people here today," she reminds me, poking a finger into the side of my stomach.

I lurch back and bat at her hand.

She gasps. "Are you ticklish?"

Her eyes dance with mischief, and she's scrambling to sit up before I can reply.

She comes at me, arms outstretched, and when she makes contact with my T-shirt, I hiss in response to the featherlight touches. When she digs in and tries to tickle me in earnest, I snatch her wrists.

"Don't start something you can't finish, Siren."

She tugs against my hold halfheartedly. We both know it's useless. I've got her trapped.

"Believe me, Cap. I never have a problem finishing," she goads, hovering in my personal space until I release my hold on her.

This woman.

My wife.

We hover close, neither one of us pulling back from the other as we share breath. Eventually, she blinks, and the spell is broken.

"Aren't you cold?" I ask as she retreats and settles on her back again. I don't know why I bother asking. It can't be more than seventy degrees, and her nipples are very clearly on display.

Thank god for the umbrella barricade. Sharing her with the boys is enough. I refuse to let anyone else gawk at her perfect, perky tits.

"Feeling the sun on my skin is worth it," she replies, smiling at the sky with her eyes closed.

She holds one hand up to shade her face and cracks one eye open to focus on me.

"Lay with me?"

My heart stutters at the request. First from excitement. And then from fear. If this is a trick and she pushes me away? I told her to punish me. Use me. Make me pay. Fuck. Now it's time to man up and take anything she dishes out.

Nothing but sincerity emanates from her as I drop to the blanket beside her and lower onto my back.

I keep a healthy distance between us, trying in earnest to give her the space she insists she needs.

Rolling to face me, she props her head in her hand. "What are you thinking about?"

"How we're not out of the woods yet," I confess.

Getting married was just step one. There are a dozen calls to make, piles of paperwork to complete, and notices to send. Kylian is working hard today to get logistics lined up for the bulk of our plans. I can't help but be agitated, though, by the to-do list nagging at the back of my mind.

Sighing, she props up onto her elbow. "We can go. If you have things to take care of, or you don't have time…"

Fuck. I didn't mean it like that.

"No," I counter harshly. "There's nowhere else I want to be today, Siren. There's no one else I want to spend the day with."

It's true.

I'm just not great at compartmentalizing or managing the sense of overwhelm that washes over me every time I think about the consequences of what I intend to do.

"I want to be here with you," I confess. "More than I want anything in the world."

Her face softens, a small smile teasing at the corner of her lips as she wiggles closer and rests her head on my bicep.

The weight of her—her very presence—is the most gratifying sensation, a soothing balm to my frayed, anxious nerves.

She sighs. "This was a good idea. I'm really glad we get this day together." Fingertips brush the hair off my forehead. "We'll get through what happens next. We'll get through it together. Now is not forever. I promise it won't always be this hard."

"You can't promise something like that," I argue, my vulnerability on full display.

"Yes I can."

Swallowing past the trepidation clogging my throat, I wrap my arms around her and hold her closer. "How do you know it won't always be this hard?"

Shame washes over me. She shouldn't be the one doing the comforting. She's the one who compromised, sacrificed, gave up the option to marry any of the guys by settling for me.

"Because we'll be together. And because I won't leave you."

I close my eyes and nod. Swallowing past the frustration, I choke out, "I'm sorry I pushed you away, Siren. I'm sorry I broke us and went back on my word. If I could take it all back—"

Fingertips rest against my lips, silencing me. But she doesn't pull out of my hold. In fact, she cuddles closer, as if she knows exactly what I need in this moment.

She's perfect. Perfect for me.

I was a goddamn fool, thinking I could trudge through this life without her.

"I know you're sorry. I can't just say I forgive you, though, because I want to fully mean it when I do. You'll earn my forgiveness, Decker. I have faith you will. But you need to be patient with me. Respect that I'm still hurting. Give me time."

I hurt her so badly. My already decimated heart cracks a little more each time I remember.

"I know," I repeat.

"We'll get there."

Those three words feel more hopeful than any vows we've exchanged or promises we've made.

"I loved you," she reminds me. "I think…" She trails off, rubbing the stubble along my jawline as she considers her words. "I think I can love you again. Don't give up on me, Cap. Don't give up on us."

"I won't," I vow. "Never again."

Texts: The Fab Five

Kylian: Press conference is scheduled, media has been invited, and details have been leaked to Misty and Thomas. All systems go.

Locke: I'm telling you, bro. If stats doesn't work out, you've got a budding career in PR

Kylian: There isn't a single reason I can fathom that statistics won't "work out" for me. Probability is equal to zero.

Cap: What about the website?

Kylian: Done.

Josephine: What website?

Josephine: I'm sitting on the deck, you guys. I can see you with your phones in hand. Someone better answer me…

Kylian: I've created a simple static website and placed it behind a private firewall. It features in-

> criminating pictures of Misty Ann Paynter, several of which were manipulated using Photoshop. We don't intend to release the website, but she will be made aware of its existence and will be allowed to view the compromising pictures in full detail.

Jo: So we're blackmailing her?

Cap: We needed an extra layer of protection.

Locke: Sounds like it

> Kylian: Yes.

Kendrick: Only with your consent, Mama

Josephine: Cool

Cap: Cool?

Locke: Did you really just say that, Hot Girl?

Kylian: What does that mean?

Josephine: *eye roll emoji* It's a good idea. Misty is slippery to the core, so I'm glad we have an extra layer of protection against her. I don't love the idea of using doctored photos to blackmail her, but I do love the idea of her going away and leaving us alone.

Cap: She won't be a problem in the future, Siren. I'll make sure of it.

Kendrick: I doubt we'll even see the likes of her or Thomas ever again

Josephine: Cool

Locke: Cool *kissy face*

Kendrick: Cool *winky face*

Kylian: Affirmative.

Locke: Ahhhh come on man!

Kendrick: You spelled "cool" wrong, Daddy Genius

Cap: Leave him alone. He's still got work to do.

Josephine: Cap's right. Kylian has more work to do for tomorrow, and he's about to be distracted for at least thirty minutes…

Locke: *eyes emoji*

Cap: Josephine…

Kendrick: Where you at?

Kylian: That wasn't an invitation. More of an FYI. See you all at dinner. If I'm still hungry enough to join you, that is.

Locke: Damn

Kendrick: I keep telling y'all he's got jokes now

Chapter 67

Josephine

I'm racking my brain and pulling out all the stops, trying to lighten the mood.

Decker's nervous. We all are.

It doesn't help that I'm testing their resolve by insisting I navigate the lake.

It's been three days since we came home from the mountains. Three days since I moved back into the mansion.

It's been three days, but it feels like a lifetime.

Major decisions have been made. Strategic moves are officially in place.

Today is the last step. When it's done, we can finally move forward.

Life is restarting slowly in Lake Chapel. The guys haven't had to report for practice yet, and Lake Chapel University resumed virtually so they can stagger the start of in-person classes.

Easing back in like this has allowed us to prepare. To quietly work out the legal and financial pieces of the puzzle and to plan out today's press conference.

"Anchors away!" I call out from the helm.

Locke laughs, but he's the only one.

"Prepare to be boarded!" I holler, giving the throttle a bit more juice as we cruise across the smooth surface of the lake, headed for the marina.

"You know none of that makes sense," my husband grumbles.

He's got major Big Decker Energy rolling off him today, and it's hot as hell. He's dressed to perfection in a dark suit and red tie. His legs are splayed wide, and he's got an arm resting casually on the back of the bench seat, but the frantic jitter of his knee gives away his anxiety. So does the restless vitality rolling off him in waves.

"Excuse me." I furrow my brow and pop my hip, wagging one finger his way. "Are you the captain of this ship?"

"It's a pontoon," Kylian corrects. As if I don't already know that.

"Aye aye, matey. Don't make me throw you overboard or force you to walk the plank!"

Locke laughs again, and even Kendrick cracks a smile. Decker continues to scowl.

"Wait," Kylian says, perking up. "Is 'the plank' a euphemism for sex, or—"

"What the hell? Why is no one wearing life vests? Put them on," Decker barks, sitting up straighter and reaching for his own.

The hairs on the back of my neck stand at attention. We rarely wear them on the pontoon. I scan our surroundings, searching for what he's seen to make him panic.

"We're fine," he assures me as he joins me at the helm. He wraps his arms around my waist and buries his face in the crook of my neck. Then he wordlessly straps me into a safety vest.

For a long moment, he stays like that, breathing me in. I don't tease him or pull away, either. My heart aches for this stoic, heartbroken man.

"I'm sorry," he mumbles against my skin. "I'm just anxious about how this is all about to go down,"

Nodding, I look at the guys and mouth, "He's okay."

Then, hoping to lighten the moment, I shout, "You heard my first mate, you scalawags. Put on yer life vests or prepare to walk the nonsexual plank!"

Decker's breathing has evened out when he lifts his head and regards his friends.

"Hopefully the life vests deter our captain here from getting any dirty ideas."

I elbow him in the stomach, but my heart floats in my chest, because he's at least calm enough to make a wisecrack.

"Har har. Joke's on you, Cap. The skipper and my cabin boy got me off before we set sail."

Kendrick guffaws, nudging Locke. "You're the cabin boy."

"Yeah. Okay, Skipper," Locke replies coolly. "Apparently cabin boys get to come twice, so I'm not mad about it."

Decker grumbles as he sits again, resting his elbows on his knees and letting his head hang.

Kendrick makes his way over to me as we approach the marina, silently offering to take over and dock. He kisses me quickly as we trade places, then nods toward Decker.

I squeeze his arm in acknowledgment. "I've got him."

As soon as I sit beside him, he wraps his arm around me. It's awkward as hell because the life vests he insisted on makes it impossible for us to get close.

He scans the shoreline, then looks down his nose at me and reaches for the buckles. I purse my lips and use every ounce of restraint I possess to hold back the smart comment I want to make as he unclips us both and helps me shrug out of the safety device.

Once there's nothing between us but a few layers of fabric, he envelops me in his hold again and exhales.

"I want to give you something," he whispers once we're docked, "but I'm nervous."

The trepidation in his tone is so foreign it sends a wave of anxiety through me. Pulling back, I survey his face, searching for understanding.

"Meet you at the car," Kendrick murmurs. He kisses my head and squeezes Decker's shoulder, then he ushers Locke and Kylian off the boat.

Like he's purposely trying to give us a minute.

Decker shifts, holding me in his lap with one arm as he reaches into his pocket.

He pulls out a little black box, and all I can do is stare, mouth agape and pulse taking off at a fast clip.

"I want you to have whatever ring you want," he starts, popping open the lid with the flick of his thumb, "but for now—for today—I was hoping you'd wear this."

Nestled between the velvet pillows is a platinum ring encasing a brilliant dark stone.

"It's a gray diamond," Decker explains, plucking it from the case. "It was my mom's. Not her engagement or wedding ring. Just a ring she bought for herself. It's not as expensive or rare as a standard diamond, but she loved it. She wore it all the time."

"It's perfect," I whisper, suddenly trembling in his arms.

"I'll get you a bigger diamond. One you can pick out yourself... or something the guys help pick out. Whatever you want. But for now—"

"Decker." I cup his face and press a kiss to his lips.

"It's perfect," I repeat. "It's beautiful. And I love that it was your mom's." I stare at the stunning, significant piece, feeling completely unworthy of such a generous gift. "Are you sure you want me to have it?"

"You're my wife, Josephine," he says, grasping my left hand. "I want you to have everything." Then, softer, he bows low until our foreheads touch. "Will you do me the honor of wearing my ring?"

I grin at the formality of the request while fighting back a squeal, because he's finally, effortlessly, giving me a choice.

"Yes," I affirm, letting him slide the ring onto my finger.

The moment the cool metal notches into place, a sense of ease washes over me.

He's trying. He's trying so damn hard.

His earnestness and perseverance stitch a few pieces of my heart back together. It's still frayed, but it's healing. His devotion, *their* devotion, and the power he's finally willing to share are mending what he broke bit by bit.

Decker cradles my fingers for a moment, admiring the ring, then kisses my knuckles. With a small smile, he stands and helps me to my feet.

"This is it," he mutters as we smooth out our clothes.

Reaching out with my left hand, ring and all, I intertwine our fingers. Decker's eyes widen in surprise. Then relief, followed by contentment, wash over his expression.

I know it then. Right now, right here, beginning today, I want to start fresh with him.

Not because of the jewelry or the abundance of confessions he's made over the last several days. But because of the earnestness with which he offered me the ring. He didn't make a demand or try to tell me what to do, even though I clearly should be wearing a wedding ring for the press conference. It's the way he offered to buy another or turn over the selection to the guys. The way he asked me if I wanted to wear it and seemed fully prepared to respect my decision if I said no.

Options. Choices. It's all I've ever wanted—and I finally recognize and appreciate just how hard it is for him to give up that control.

We're not perfect. We're quite possibly two of the most mismatched people ever paired together. We're too similar—too stubborn and too hotheaded.

We're not going to see eye to eye often.

But watching him adjust—knowing how hard he's working to change—is enough.

"Ready?" he asks, guiding me forward with a gentle touch without letting go of my hand.

This is it. This is what it was all for.

I give him a warm smile and nod. I'm ready, and I've got him.

Then I let him help me off the boat and lead me to the car.

Chapter 68

Decker

I glance over my shoulder. Again.

I thought they were already back here, but maybe we got our signals crossed. I'm pulling up our group chat, ready to shoot off a text, when I hear them.

Nicky's boisterous laughter.

Kendrick's smooth reply.

Kylian's matter-of-fact retort.

Then Josephine.

Her voice carries above them all, enthusiastic and melodic, sassy and self-assured.

I love her.

I love them.

This is what it's all for.

They file into the tight space, Locke and Kendrick both conveniently avoiding my gaze.

As they get closer, I note a few displaced tendrils of Josephine's hair and the way she's tugging at the neckline of her dress, as if she's putting it back in place.

Kylian's smirk is all the confirmation I need.

I don't have time to scold them for sneaking in a quickie. Even if I did, I can't blame them. Stress levels are at an all-time high for all of us. Hell, I wish I could blow off some steam with our girl right about now, too.

Josephine steps up and winds her arm through mine.

"Ready?" she asks as she peers up at me, all doe-eyed and sweet like she wasn't just getting tag-teamed by my brothers in the bathroom down the hall.

Shaking my head, I lock my jaw tight and tamp down my jealousy. I'm trying so damn hard to communicate with her, to be vulnerable and express myself when I can, instead of bottling it up and stewing in my own frustrations.

"I was worried you weren't coming," I confess.

"Cap," she scolds softly. "I would never abandon you. I keep my promises."

Her words smack into me like an insult, even if they weren't meant to be. I'll forever regret what I put her through, but I'm trying not to live in the past. I'm ready to live in the now.

Turning my head, I crack my neck and blow out a breath, but it doesn't relieve the tension radiating through every fiber of my being. It's so acute my muscles bunch and revolt against this damn suit in a way I worry will split a seam.

Josephine pulls her arm away.

Before I can reach for her, pull her back in, tell her I need the comfort of her touch, she's turning toward the others.

"Hey, guys. Can you give us a minute?"

The boys murmur their agreement and file out, leaving us in the wings of the stage with nothing but the hum of the unseen crowd beyond the curtains.

She turns back to me and walks right into my space, loops her arms around my neck, and pushes up on tiptoes.

I snatch her waist and pull her closer, so damn grateful for the way she always knows just what I need. "A minute, huh?"

"Mm-hmm." She nods, smiling. She's so close I can practically taste the fruity notes of her lip gloss. "One minute, Cap."

She rests her forehead on mine and lets me hold her. Her fingertips find the hair at my nape, then she's pulling me so close our bodies are flush together. A perfect fit.

I hug her fiercely, holding on with everything I am, pouring out everything I hope to be.

I nuzzle into her neck, and she lets me. She scratches up and down my spine through my suit jacket, the caresses hypnotic and comforting.

Somehow, despite the reality of where we are and what's about to happen, she makes me forget it all.

It's just us.

In this moment.

Stealing away a minute that I dream transforms into a lifetime.

The warmth of her mouth against my ear sends goose bumps dancing along my neck. "Can I kiss you?"

Like it's even a fucking question.

I press my lips to hers and swallow her groan, greedily making love to her mouth as we race against the countdown clock.

I kiss her fiercely. Then I kiss her sweetly. I kiss her, knowing that my actions convey so much more than my words ever could.

The sound of a throat clearing breaks the spell.

Megan, my new PR rep, stands several feet away, headset on and clipboard in hand. "Mr. Crusade? They're ready for you."

I hold up one finger and dismiss her with a nod.

Josephine pops up on her toes and kisses me again, just a peck this time. "You're sure about this?" she questions for the millionth time.

I run my thumbs along her cheekbones, then cradle the back of her head, taking a mental picture of her in this moment.

"I've never been more sure of anything in my life."

"You don't have to do this, Decker. There are other ways."

"I know."

"The guys... they'll understand. If we have to figure out another plan—"

I grip the side of her head and brush my nose against hers to cut her off.

"No. I've made my choice. It's the choice I should have made from the start. I choose them. I choose *you*."

She beams at me, and it's all the resolve I need.

"You'll be here waiting?" I ask, as nervous as I am eager about what's about to go down.

"Right here," she promises.

"And after?"

"By your side. As your wife. No one's getting to you without going through me first." She cocks an eyebrow and plasters her version of a mean mug to her face, going for tough. Her attempt is weak at best.

I fight back a smirk and kiss her once more. Then I force myself to let go and take the stage.

Chapter 69

Josephine

I curl my toes in my heels, compelling myself to stay put when what I really want to do is chase Decker onto the stage.

I watch him walk away, leaving me in the wings.

The farther he gets, the tighter my chest feels. Though unlike every time he's walked away from me in the past, this time, I have no doubt he's doing it for us.

The fallout won't be pretty. Kylian confirmed that Thomas Crusade and Misty are both in the audience, although he didn't mention it to Decker. He assumed they would show up, but we've all been off the grid since the storm.

Little does anyone out there know that a new storm is on the horizon.

One that has the potential to destroy so much, and yet breathe new life into our future.

Subtle heat warms my back as a set of arms wraps around me from behind. It only takes a heartbeat to know it's Kendrick.

I lean into him, seeking support, craving his strength.

"He's got this," he murmurs. With a hum, he presses a kiss to the skin just below my ear.

I nod, trying to convince myself as much.

He's got this.

He wants this.

We're worthy of what he's about to do.

Nicky sidles up on my left side and takes my hand. He squeezes once, and I soak in all the comfort and care he provides.

On the other side, Kylian appears. He scans the wings, examines Decker where he stands behind the podium, and finally focuses on me. With Kylian, I am safe.

We stand together, united.

Waiting.

Hoping.

Dwelling in the last few moments before our lives change forever.

The press conference starts, and the room we can't see goes eerily quiet.

Decker greets the crowd and introduces himself, then gets right to it.

He admits to doping.

For years.

Using illegal substances—peptide hormones and metabolic modulators, mostly—to enhance his performance on the field.

He lists the website Kylian created that links to all the relevant evidence.

He mentions Dr. Kline, but insists he's not at fault, because he always used pseudonyms when scheduling appointments.

They're easy to track, because he was cocky enough to use the names of his friends.

Kendrick Crusade.

Nicholas Crusade.

Treatment protocols and records are all on file. He's been doping for years, but recently, worried the risks of implicating his friends were too great, so he decided to come clean now, before going pro.

He mostly reads from his prepared statement, but he's sure to look up often, to focus on the crowd—where I assume dozens of cameras are recording—as he apologizes to his team and his coaches.

"I will not be declaring for the draft as originally planned. I accept full responsibility for my actions, and I want to make it clear that I was not influenced or coerced to seek out these treatments. I will face the consequences from all entities involved—from the NCAA to the academic and athletic departments at Lake Chapel University."

He clears his throat and glances down at the podium.

The room is utterly silent as they wait for him to continue.

"I understand that I have disappointed many people, and that my announcement inspires more questions than answers. I've been advised by my legal team to not take questions today, but rather direct you all to the offices of Hensley and Horr."

The murmurs are hushed at first, but with each passing second, they grow louder. Raising both hands, Decker silences them.

He looks over to the wings again, and I nod once. I'm ready. We've got this.

The boys release me, and I step forward.

Decker holds his head high, his profile stoic and so goddamn handsome, his jaw ticking in the way it does when he's unstoppably determined.

"I respectfully ask for privacy during this time. Both for me..."

He holds out his hand.

"And for my wife."

Chapter 70

Josephine

I step onto the stage but keep my focus fixed on Decker.

He's the homing beacon, the eye at the center of this storm.

I'm not even halfway to him when the first camera flashes. In my periphery, it looks like lightning. I don't let myself panic. I won't. All I can do is move forward.

His eyes hold mine as I carefully walk across the stage toward his outstretched arm.

Each step I take is a promise.

Each second that passes is an assurance that this is really happening, that he really wants this, that he really wants *me*.

The slightest smile tugs at the corner of his mouth.

That single micro expression steals my breath, and another piece of my heart clicks back into place.

Walking toward Decker like this feels so much bigger than the trek I made to him at our wedding; it's so much more significant than anything I've ever done.

I see the vision he's cast for us. The sacrifice he's willing to endure, and the humbling, life-changing choices he's making.

His actions today communicate what's in his heart more than words ever could. His sacrifice won't be in vain, because with this announcement, Decker has finally proven how far he's willing to bend for this family.

By the time I reach him, my heart is beating triple time and tears are threatening to spill from my eyes.

He takes my hand, but protectively wraps one arm around me, too, pulling me into his side. He bows his head low, his words quiet, just for me. "I've got you, Siren. And now you've finally got me, too."

When he straightens, we look ahead, posing for photos as the media shouts questions at the stage.

Flashes light up the room in rapid fire, but with Decker by my side, they don't induce panic. They don't feel debilitating or threatening. For the first time ever, they feel like freedom.

Chapter 71

Decker

By the time I usher my wife off stage, my father and Misty are waiting in the wings.

We anticipated this.

Yet it's still unnerving to walk out of one upset and step right into another.

Sidled up close to my dad, Misty is pounding on her phone. Thomas has his pressed to his ear with one hand, and he's pulling at his hair with the other.

"Whatever you're doing is unnecessary," Kylian offers. Despite the tension so thick it's threatening to choke us all, his tone is dispassionate. It's exactly what I'd expect from him in a moment like this.

With his phone still pressed to his ear, my dad whirls around and points a finger at him. "I knew you had to have something to do with this, you freak."

"Whoa." Kendrick steps up so close my dad's eyes go just a little wide, and he takes a step back.

Josephine drops my hand and shuffles to one side so she's standing between Kylian and Locke. They move in, flanking her, with Kendrick blocking up front. She's safe.

"It's done, Dad," I tell him. "There's nothing you can do to change this. It's done."

He stabs at the End button on his phone's screen and turns to glare at me.

"You're married? Legally bound to that woman?"

Of-fucking-course.

Why am I not surprised that this is the issue he has the biggest problem with?

"You didn't even show me your prenup," he accuses. "According to our lawyers, they don't even have it on file yet."

"Those are *your* lawyers, Dad. And there is no prenup."

Misty makes a startled, choking sound, and my dad surges forward, getting right up in my face.

His hot breath wafts over me with each exhale. "What do you mean there is no prenup? When she leaves you, if she turns out to be a two-timing bitch like your mother—"

"Watch it," I snarl with enough vitriol to cause him to shift back on instinct. "That's my wife you're talking about."

"God dammit, Decker!" he shouts, the vein in his forehead bulging. "Have I taught you nothing? You let this whore pussy whip you into marriage? You don't realize what you've done."

He's wrong. I know exactly what I've done.

"If Josephine leaves me, she'll get half. Maybe more. Her best friend's going to be a lawyer. I bet the two of them could take me for a fucking ride." I look to my wife—see her trying to bite back a grin, just like I knew she would be—and wink.

Bracing myself, I prepare to shoulder my dad's outrage over what I say next.

"There's no prenup, and I don't want anything to do with you or her." I regard Misty. "Ever again. I've hired my own lawyers. I have new PR representation. I won't be entering the draft, but I still intend to make something of myself."

My father's eyes practically bug out of his head as he processes my declaration.

"You're nothing without me," he hisses. "You can't do this alone."

"I won't be alone," I quip. "I'll have my family by my side."

I knew the dig would cut deep. What I didn't anticipate is the way he whirls and storms toward Josephine with just as much fury as he was projecting onto me.

K sees it coming, thank fuck, and grabs him by the shoulders.

I'm on him a second later, nothing but a ball of rage. Was he physically going after her? If Kendrick hadn't stopped him, it sure as shit looked like he was going to put his hands on her.

He fights against our hold, hands fisted and face a mottled red, reduced to verbally assaulting her since there's not a chance we'll let him get even one more inch closer to our girl.

"You spiteful, evil bitch. I should have had them do more than chase you. I should have had them take out the whole damn boat. I should have ended you like I ended her."

Kendrick's wide eyes catch mine, the horror I feel mirrored in his expression.

"What did you just say?" I choke out, suddenly going numb.

"It sounded an awful like he admitted to murder," Kylian quips. He's ridiculously aloof, given the situation.

"Yeah." Kendrick nods. He's still playing the part of a shield, blocking my father's path to Josephine. "It sure did."

"It was you?" I accuse. "The boat incidents... *both* boat incidents?"

My father doesn't even bother acknowledging me as he fights against our hold. I dart a glance at Misty, who looks like she's going to be sick. Like this is news to her. Or maybe because she knew all along, and now she's worried about being caught.

"Do you have a hold of him?" Josephine asks, breaking me out of the mental spiral.

I close my eyes and focus on breathing. Tension coils in my gut as she takes a tentative step around K. I knew she was going to do this. I knew because, begrudgingly, I agreed to this plan.

And yet, now that I've had to physically restrain him so he couldn't go after her, all I want to do is whisk her back to the mansion and get her away from this scene.

"Cap," Kendrick murmurs.

He and I share the same concerns. We hate the idea of her even being in his presence, let alone giving him more opportunities to go after her.

But she insisted she wanted to do it this way, and we all reluctantly agreed.

I'm done making decisions for her. Not anymore. Not ever again.

Locking eyes with Kendrick, I tighten my grip, and he does the same, securing the older man in place.

"You're good," I tell our girl, bracing for what comes next.

Chapter 72

Josephine

Kylian warned me not to get my hopes up. That I might not get to do this. That it could be too dangerous, or we might not have time.

Now that the moment has come, I'm practically giddy with excitement.

I owe it to my husband to put his awful excuse of a money-hungry sperm donor in his place once and for all, and that's exactly what I intend to do.

Once the guys confirm they have Thomas secure in their grasp, I step forward, and I don't halt until we're standing toe to toe. Locke is standing so close behind me I can feel his body heat radiating off him. Just like they all promised, though, I'm the one who gets to deliver the final blow.

Peeking over my shoulder, I confirm that Misty is watching, face ashen and jaw slack, then I turn back to Thomas and smirk.

"This almost went down differently," I tell him calmly. "Decker had another announcement prepared for today, but I talked him out of sharing it."

"I bet you did a whole lot of *talking* to convince him," Thomas spits out.

I stifle a laugh. He thinks that's an insult.

"I don't know... my husband's pretty stubborn," I hedge. "He went as far as to draft it out before ultimately deciding to go a different direction."

"Hey, Kylian?"

"Yeah, baby?"

Misty's and Thomas's heads swivel comically to Kylian, then quickly back to Decker, searching for his reaction.

Plot twist. The joke's on them if they think Decker has any issue with the boys calling me by nicknames in his presence. It wasn't part of the plan to clue in his dad to our relationship today, but it feels like icing on the cake to confuse him while having the last word.

I bite back another laugh, but I can't hide the grin blossoming on my face.

Kendrick snorts at my apparent glee, chuckling low.

"Mama, you have no chill."

I hum at the callout, giddy at the way Thomas's eyes practically bug out of his head when he hears K's pet name for me.

Turning back to Kylian, I tip my chin. "Do you still have Cap's original speech saved?"

He's already pulling out his phone. "Yes."

"Could you send it to his former PR rep so she can see it?"

With a scoff, Misty whips out her phone and scrolls.

It only takes a few seconds for what she's reading to register. She sucks in a sharp breath and darts a glance at Decker before continuing on.

While she works her way through it, I turn back to Thomas. With my hands planted on my hips, I push down the wisps of trepidation fluttering through me and stand tall. I lift my chin and survey the man who has treated Decker so poorly his entire life, who's done things so vile I cannot comprehend them.

"In the original version of today's announcement, Decker planned to inform the press that he'd been doping for years *at the advice of his father*. At the *insistence* of his father."

Thomas surges forward, but I don't flinch. I trust the boys won't let him touch me. "You little—"

"Careful, Thomas," Locke calls out. "You're being recorded."

"Oh. Did we forget to mention that? We're all miked." I reveal, my hand skimming over the small, clear microphone Kylian affixed to my bra when we arrived. We almost didn't make it to the stage in time because we were messing with the high-tech audio recording devices.

Decker doesn't know about this part of the plan, but Kylian thought it best to collect any evidence we could get against Thomas in case things didn't go as smoothly as we hoped.

I scan Decker's face, searching for any sign that he feels betrayed by our decision.

His eyes are filled with nothing but warmth and affection when they settle on me.

I don't let myself get too lost in his stare. I still have a final threat to disclose.

Turning back to Thomas, I get as close as I dare. "Every comment. Every threat you just made, every potential admission you shared," I whisper. "We're ready and willing to release it all."

"Including that not-so-subtle slip-up about the boat incident and mom's accident," Decker growls.

Turning to Kendrick, I tilt my head and purse my lips. "What sort of evidence is required to reopen a case like that, K?"

"Honestly? His admission might be enough. I'd have to ask my Pops to be sure—"

"Okay. *Okay*," Thomas relents. He lifts a shoulder and tries to pull out of the boys' hold, but when they don't release him, he hangs his head and lets out a pained sound.

Though from the looks of things, he understands what we're demanding of him, I need to make myself very, very clear.

"Go away, Thomas. Go far away. Forever."

He slumps, but Kendrick and Decker don't release him. They won't, I'm sure, until we know we're in the clear.

"Oh, and Misty?" I ask.

Vitriol leaches from her as she eyes me.

"Kylian has one more email you may want to see."

Her phone pings, and she's quick to open it. Her eyes grow wider as she scans the screenshots of the blackmail website.

"The site isn't actually live," Kylian assures her. "Nor will you be able to find it online. It'll remain offline, unseen by the world, as long as you disappear."

"Don't contact us. Don't look at her," he growls. "And don't even utter the name Decker Crusade for the rest of your life. Unless you want people to see this. Unless you want to go to court and spend years defending yourself against the charges these pictures would require."

Misty raises her hand to her mouth as if she's going to be sick, then stashes her phone, bows her head, and scurries away.

Kendrick and Decker guide Thomas to the same door.

Locke and Kylian wrap their arms around me, each by my side.

"It's done," I whisper in awe.

"It's done," Kylian vows, kissing the top of my head as Locke blows out a long sigh of relief at my other side.

Chapter 73

Decker

Kendrick cuts across the lake faster than normal, chasing the light of the setting sun on the water as we make our way home.

I've received dozens of calls since my press conference: from the school, from my coach, from the NCAA rep at LCU, and from multiple partners severing contracts.

We knew that would happen.

It still stings.

Megan set up a control room for us in the executive suite of a nearby hotel, where we spent a few hours fielding questions and updating the lawyers. Kendrick signed with her, too, and Megan is confident she can navigate his image in the coming months and ensure he's still a top pick for the draft.

It helps that I just blew up my own life in a very public way. Kendrick's unsubstantiated charges seem trivial compared to the shitshow of drama I just created. It's the perfect distraction.

Leaving the team to continue handling the fallout was hard, but Megan insisted we go home and take some time to breathe.

And breathe we can. Everything else is handled. We worked around the clock over the last few days to ensure everything is done.

My lawyers submitted our marriage license to my mom's estate first thing Monday morning.

The money is ours. My dad is gone. There's still a lot of heartache around my mom's death to unpack, but as we cruise across the lake, I push that all out of my mind. In this moment, I can't help but feel like we finally made it. We're free.

"Hi, husband," Josephine purrs as she switches seats with Kylian and scoots closer. "How are you holding up?"

For a second, I really consider her question. I just blew up my life. Destroyed my career. Cut ties with my dad. Yet... "I'm good. *Really* good." I sling an arm over her shoulders, which she takes as an invitation to straddle my lap.

This girl.

My wife.

Once again, she's not wearing a life jacket. Fear flutters inside me when I'm hit with an image of the speed boat grounded on the isle and all the people I love pouring out of it.

I turn to Kendrick, ready to tell him to slow down, but before I can, he's backing off the throttle on his own. His chin tip confirms we're on the same wavelength.

Resting her forehead against mine, she rakes her nails over my scalp. I'm hit with a wave of tingles that only relaxes me more.

"What you said to your dad... about a prenup... I didn't even think of that. Is it too late? Is a postnuptial agreement a thing? I'm happy to sign one."

"Siren." I trace up the hollow of her throat with two fingers and gently lift her chin so she's forced to look at me.

Fuck. She's gorgeous. The sincerity in her eyes as she surveys me in return makes my still tender heart ache. She's mine. She's ours. And most importantly, she's letting me hold her now. She's willing to let me put in the work to stitch together the relationship she deserves.

"I didn't ask for one, because if you want out, then I want you to have that option. You'll get the house. Half the money. Anything you want." I clear my throat and lean into the vulnerability I'm learning to embrace. "I won't fight you. As long as you promise to stick with them and take care of them"—I jut my chin at the guys—"I won't fight you over anything."

She lets out a quiet sob, her chest heaving, and tears well in her eyes, but she blinks them back, never looking away from me.

"Thank you, Decker," she whispers, hugging my neck and resting her head on my shoulder.

I exhale and hug her back, keeping my cool, though the familiar ache of rejection sours my mood.

A defeated sigh escapes me anyway as I smooth a hand up her back. "We may have to wait for the dust to settle. Can you give me a year? Or at least until all the paperwork is official and you're on all the accounts."

She sits up, ramrod straight. "*What*?"

"I'm not trying to be difficult," I insist, keeping my hold on her gentle, praying like hell she believes me. "I just think we'll need to stay married long enough to make it believable before you get out."

"Decker," she moans, grabbing me by the shoulders and shaking. "I don't want out. I want to stay married to you."

Hope springs inside me like a geyser, soaking all the sorrowful thoughts infiltrating my mind.

"You do?"

"Yes. I do." Her voice is as tender as her expression. "I think we're in this too deep to turn back now, Cap. It happened too fast, but I'm here. This is now. I'm in. And I'm staying."

And then, softly, she adds, "I just wanted the power to make that choice for myself."

She kisses me, and I hold her tighter, the reality of her words sinking in. Her lips move against mine, transforming into the kind of kiss that begs to lead to more.

"Siren," I scold when she rocks her hips back and forth, teasing in my lap.

"We're *married* now, Decker. That *has* to earn me some sort of boat sex perks."

"You're infuriating," I murmur against her lips.

"You love it."

"Yeah. I do." I clear my throat, then share my truth. "I love you, Josephine. You make me a better person. You make us all better, just by being you."

"I love you, too, Decker Crusade." Peppering me with kisses, she continues to roll her hips in my lap.

"And just so you know, I'm pretty sure I gushed a little every time you said 'my wife' on that stage tonight. I'm so wet for you right now," she whimpers.

"Is that so?" I grin against her mouth and kiss her again, seriously considering bending my own rules about boat sex.

But when I glance up, I realize we're almost home.

I remind myself that we're in no rush.

That there are no more cameras.

That we don't need to sneak around or carve out private moments wherever we can.

We're almost home. And we're finally free.

Chapter 74

Josephine

> Mrs. Crusade: Hey, Cap?

> Cap: Yes, wife?

> Mrs. Crusade: Can you come up to my room, please?

He knocks and pushes open the door, then mutters "oh shit" and quickly closes it a second later.

"Decker," I laugh, peeling off Locke and scurrying after him.

I'm wearing my new bra and panties set. It's deep purple and compliments of the online shopping spree Hunter and I indulged in the day I became Mrs. Decker Crusade. Although calling it underwear is a bit of a stretch, considering the panties are crotchless and the push-up is completely sheer.

Kylian started this. He claimed to not understand the concept of crotchless panties, which I'm now realizing may have just been a ruse to get me to show them off.

There's nothing I won't do on that man's command.

"Hey. Come back!" I call after my husband, who's already halfway down the hall.

He turns, his cheeks pink. "I'm sorry. I didn't mean to walk in on you."

"Decker," I scold, planting one hand on my hip. "I asked you to come up here, remember? I want you to join us."

He freezes, and I swear his breath hitches, too.

"Join you?"

I exhale, ignoring the ache in my clit as I walk toward him. I move slowly so as not to spook him with my eagerness. Because I'm eager. I want this. I want all of them, together. What better way to celebrate our newfound freedom?

I try to even out my breathing. I've been driven to the brink by the boys over the last hour, only to be denied a real release. They promised me all the orgasms I could handle if I convinced Decker to join us.

As if I actually needed the motivation.

"You made your choice, Cap." I circle my arms around his waist and smirk at the way his eyes flit to my ample cleavage as I press my chest into his torso.

"You made your choice. So come be with us. Completely."

He says nothing, clearly warring with himself. I don't give him time to overthink it.

Turning on my heel, I grab his hand, then I march back to my bedroom.

I don't bother closing the door or enticing him further. He doesn't need to be coddled. If and when he's ready, he'll join us.

I've learned that trial by fire is the quickest way to teach Decker. So I jump right to it and reignite the flames.

"In or out, Cap," Kylian commands.

Decker is still lingering at the door, scrubbing a hand down his face, then cracking his neck from side to side. When he rights himself, his eyes are blazing.

"Yeah. Okay. I'm in."

Squealing, I skip back to the door and take both of his hands.

Pushing up on tiptoes, I ghost my mouth over his and plant a soft kiss on his lips. "You don't have to do anything you're not comfortable with.

Just do what feels right and don't overthink it. I want you, Decker. I want you here with us, completely in the fold."

He nods, and the briefest hint of relief flashes in his expression. I'm learning he doesn't do well when he feels like he's trapped or backed into a corner. He's more willing to loosen the reins and give up his beloved control when he knows he can snatch it back at any time.

Clearing his throat, he spins me around and hooks one arm over my chest.

All the guys are watching me. Meaning all eyes are on Decker, too.

"So, how does it work?" he asks, flexing his hand open and closed against my throat.

I crane back, seeking more of his touch. Wanting to feel him. Needing him to go all in.

"Sometimes we go for zone coverage," Kendrick starts. He's sitting on the edge of the bed, legs spread wide. "Then other times we play man-to-man."

"Man-to-woman," Kylian corrects.

Locke scoffs, rubbing his hands together as he approaches us.

"We take turns. We share. Sometimes we watch. Just do what feels good." He gives me a more than thorough once-over, his lip caught between his teeth. "Believe me, our girl can handle it. And she always makes us feel good."

The low flames still burning inside me grow gradually hotter. I have to grip Decker's forearm with both hands to keep myself upright.

"What are the rules?" I fight back a snort. "There are no rules, Cap."

But Kylian speaks at the same time.

And his answer is much more thorough.

"She comes first. Literally. Always. Nicky doesn't take her ass; he's physically too large. I'm the boss most of the time, unless K wants to be the boss, but only if Jo requests that specific dynamic."

He stands confidently before us, ticking off each supposed "rule" like it's straight from a checklist.

"Nicky doesn't take orders from me, but he *does* take orders from her. After sex, she has to pee. Even if one of us has to carry her to the bathroom. Peeing is nonnegotiable."

The room is silent. I glance to Kendrick and Locke to confirm they're also watching Kylian in awe.

"What?" he questions when he catches us staring. He scrunches up his forehead until his glasses slip down his nose. "Do you want me to keep going?"

Kendrick chuckles, rubbing his jaw. "That was intense, Daddy Genius. Even for you."

Catching on, Kylian looks around the room. "Wait. You all don't think there are actual rules to any of this?"

I roll my lips to keep from laughing.

"Or is this one of those neurotypical things where you don't acknowledge the guidelines, expectations, and structure of a social situation?"

This time, I really can't help but laugh. He's probably right. And it's sweet he wants to get Decker caught up to speed.

Only, I'm tired of rules. Tired of holding back. I'm so tired of *not* being together. I need to get lost in them all.

Kissing Decker's forearm, I wiggle out of his grasp and stride to Kylian.

Tipping my chin, I catch my bottom lip between my teeth. "Daddy," I whisper. "Come play."

That does it. Heat flares in his piercing blue eyes, and the switch is flipped.

Kylian lets me guide him to the bed and quickly climbs on top. He kisses me hard on the lips, then moves on to my neck.

"Daddy? Really?" Decker questions.

I'm too distracted by the way Kylian laps at the sheer fabric covering my nipple to explain.

Thankfully, K steps up. "Go with it, Cap. She loves it. Watch how good she looks submitting to him."

"I've never seen my wife submit to anyone," Decker huffs, closer to the bed now.

K chuckles. "You're in for a treat, brother."

Kylian bites my breasts through the sheer fabric and sucks my nipples into firm peaks. I press my tits together, making it easier for him to go back and forth and ravish me. Each nip sends a jolt of pleasure to my clit.

"Fuck, yes," I mewl. "Harder, Daddy."

He does what I ask, biting and sucking until I squirm.

"I need more," I whimper.

Kylian sits back on his heels, then pulls me down so I'm perfectly centered in the bed.

"Show me where you want me, baby."

I spread my legs, revealing everything through my crotchless panties.

Locke grins, gripping Decker by the shoulders as they take another step closer to the bed.

"See how wet she gets for him?" Locke's voice is low and gravelly. "She'll make a fucking mess of these sheets by the time he's done."

"Fuck," Decker groans, jaw ticking. "That's hot." The words rumble out of him just as Kylian runs his nose through my center and licks me from my opening to my clit.

"Your wife's a smoke show, Cap." Kendrick wastes no time joining us on the bed. He lounges against the headboard and pulls me up and back into his arms.

He hitches each of my legs over his, spreading me wider and putting me on full display.

Kylian lays flat on his front, teasing my opening with his tongue.

Kendrick's big hands find my breasts, massaging and kneading my sensitive nipples.

"Fuck. Yes," I moan as I grip the sheets.

I close my eyes, leaning back into K, and soak in each sensation.

A new sensation hits me, right on my clit, pulling a gasp from me. Though it's not unfamiliar, it is unlike anything I've experienced when we're all together.

I open my eyes, eager to discover the cause, and moan at the sight. Nicky is leaning over the bed, licking at my little bundle of nerves from above while Kylian continues to fuck me with his tongue.

"Oh fuck," Kendrick murmurs in my ear. "You're already tensing in my lap, Mama. They're going to fucking destroy you."

The boys work in harmony, licking and flicking, fucking and nipping. They take turns ravishing my hole and my clit, but never focusing on one pleasure point for too long.

When I swear I'm going to scream if someone doesn't let me fucking come, I feel it.

One thick, blunt finger, gathering up my arousal and massaging around my puckered hole, then pushing into my ass.

"Fuck!" I buck in Kendrick's arms as a burst of pleasure surges through me. He works a second finger inside and presses into my A-spot just as a clitoral orgasm tears through me, and I fucking detonate.

Waves of pleasure roll through my pelvis, the sensations warm and deep. My pussy pulses, needy, desperate, as it unravels from the double orgasm.

I'm a mess of curses as they work me through it. Writhing. Melting. Transforming right before their eyes.

When my body finally settles and my breathing evens slightly, I look up to find four reverent, heated gazes fixed on me.

"I've never seen anything so beautiful," Nicky murmurs, his lips—covered in my essence—on mine.

Kylian pops up next, smirking as he wipes my release from his face.

Kendrick just pulls me closer, arranging me so I'm sitting in his lap as he works his cock over with lube.

Kissing my shoulder, he whispers, "Help him out, Mama. Tell us where you want us."

"Everywhere," I reply without hesitation.

Then, looking to my husband, I make my request crystal clear.

"Decker, I want you in my cunt."

His gaze is heated, determined. He's got that Big Decker Energy going that I absolutely love.

"Come here," I demand of him as Locke makes space and Kylian sits up.

I'm still in Kendrick's lap when my husband drives into my pussy and thrusts all the way home.

"Fuck. *Decker*," I groan. "You feel so fucking good." I wrap my arms around his neck, clinging to him, as he begins to move.

"Look at me," he demands, the words gritty but sure.

When we lock eyes, I know it. I feel it in my soul.

He's in. He's all the fucking way in.

Finally.

"You said you wanted us to share you, Siren. Put your boys where you want them."

Fucking finally.

I grin, kiss him hard, and lean forward.

"Lay back and let me ride you so K can fuck my ass. Go all the way to the end of the bed."

Once we're in position, I look to Kylian and Nicky. "Can I suck you both at the same time?"

"Fuck yeah," Locke replies.

Kylian scowls, then opens his mouth in what I assume is an attempt to use words like *circumference* and *elasticity*, but I cut him off before he can speak.

"Just let me try, Daddy."

He snaps his mouth shut and assumes the position beside his friend.

"I love you," I murmur against Decker's lips as I sink down on his cock. "I'm so happy I could cry." It's the truth. This, all of us, together? I didn't think I'd ever get to experience it.

"Here it comes, Mama. Breathe."

I do as he says, melting into Decker and draping my limbs around him, bearing down as Kendrick pushes in.

"Fuck. *Ahh*, fuck," Decker grits out.

"Feels good, huh, Cap?"

Kendrick's words are all smooth swagger.

Wiggling my hips, I blow out another slow breath and give my body a moment to adjust to them both. To my boys. My men. To the people I love. To the family we've founded together.

Kendrick starts slow, guiding Decker as they work to find a rhythm.

All those years playing on the football field together make them synchronous as they fuck me between them.

As one ebbs, the other flows. I gush and undulate around them both, arousal trickling out of me as they bring me to the brink of pleasure.

I want to come from them all, though—with them all—because of them all.

I peer up at Kylian, and as if he can read my mind, he pulls Nicky forward so they're standing at the end of the bed.

"Open," Kylian demands, offering his cock. I wait until Nicky is beside him and their fat heads are fisted side by side. Then I open my mouth as wide as I can.

I can't move much or take them deep, but they both fit.

They all fit.

We all fit together, perfectly, messily, and so damn beautifully.

"Fuck her mouth," Kylian tells Locke, as Kendrick and Decker pick up their pace.

"Holy shit, Hot Girl," Locke groans, petting my hair as my eyes water. "You look so fucking pretty stuffed full of cocks."

It's impossible to see with the way they fill me, but I beam at his praise. My heart lifts and my eyes prick with real tears.

Every movement sends pleasure through me. Every thrust inspires a fresh thrill of sensation. But it's the rare moments when they all breach my holes and fill me at once that send me into a tailspin.

I clench and moan, unable to warn them as my orgasm builds higher and higher, but they know. They always know.

"Goddamn, you're a sight to behold. Just like that, Mama. You make us all feel so good," Kendrick grunts, his hands digging into my cheeks as he spreads my ass wider.

"You were made for us, Hot Girl."

"You make me better," Decker murmurs, gripping my hips and rutting up into me from below. "You make all of us better."

Every admission works its way into my heart, pushes me closer to the edge, but it's Kylian's command that finally sends me spiraling.

"Come, Jo. Squeeze and spasm and gush all over our cocks. We've got you, baby. We've got you."

The tension is so tight my muscles seize. I'm nothing but sparks, dancing nerves and quivering sensation. I liquefy between them as I cry out, my release rocking through me so completely and thoroughly it leaves no room for doubt.

And as my men come, one at a time, filling me up with their cum, claiming me and marking me as theirs forever, I can't fight back the tears of joy.

I am here.

This is now.

And in this moment, there's no place else I'd rather be.

Chapter 75

Josephine

I wake to the unmistakable pattering of rain on the windows.

Kendrick's arms tighten around my waist, though based on his deep, even inhalations, he's still asleep.

I blink open my eyes to find Kylian peering at me through his glasses, the light from his phone reflected in the lenses.

"Storm's still about twenty minutes away," he whispers. He caresses my cheek with his free hand but turns his attention back to his device. "Do you want to head upstairs now?"

I suck in a deep breath and close my eyes, considering. I take inventory of my physical state and my stress level and determine that I don't sense one iota of panic. Nothing but satisfaction, safety, and love course through every cell of my sleepy, sated body.

I am here. This is now.

"No," I whisper. "I want to go outside."

We wake the others, quickly assuring them that nothing's wrong. They're slow to rise, but more alert once they notice just how eager I am to get out onto the deck.

The grumbles start as I head for the sliding door off the kitchen, because, on the other side, it's pouring rain. I grin over my shoulder, silently assuring them that I'm okay, that I'm better than okay, in fact, and slip outside.

"What are we doing out here, Hot Girl?" Nicky hollers as the wind whips around us. It's a cold wind, a sure sign that fall is giving way to winter. It's a reminder that, just like the seasons, life is inevitably about to change again.

I cling to his massive frame, shivering when he wraps me up in a bear hug.

"We're embracing the storm." Pulling back, I take his hand and spin under his arm.

Kendrick catches my hips, pulling my back to his front.

"You want to dance in the rain with me?" he asks, nipping at my earlobe as he sways to a rhythm only we can hear.

"I want to dance with you always, K."

With my arms overhead, I circle his neck. He leans down and kisses me, skimming his hands up and down my sides as I grind back into him.

"I feel you, Mama. I feel you and I see you. You've never looked more beautiful."

My stomach dips, just like every time he makes those kinds of declarations. I'm so distracted by Kendrick's moves that I don't notice Nicky's covert attack until he swoops in and scoops me up in his arms.

"My turn!" he declares, shaking his head back and forth so water droplets fly off his hair and soak my face.

I laugh, relishing the pure joy emanating from him. His pain is under control, and despite the heaviness of yesterday's events, there's a deep contentment in his eyes.

He lifts me off my feet and spins me a few times before hoisting me onto the railing of the deck.

"It's slick out here, Locke. Put my wife down."

Nicky buries his face in my chest and snickers at the scolding, but he obeys without argument, turning me around to hug me from behind as he leans against the rail.

"We're about to be subjected to a lifetime of 'my wife' this and 'my wife' that, aren't we?"

Decker catches my eye and cocks one brow. If I have any say in the matter? We most definitely are. He knows what those two words do to me.

I duck out of Locke's embrace and approach Kylian. He's got one hand in the pocket of his sweatpants as he watches the radar on his phone.

"Dance with me, Kylian," I urge.

He doesn't look up. "I don't dance."

I expected as much.

So I pluck the device from his hand, stash it in his pocket, and wrap my arms around his torso in a tight embrace.

"Then just hold me in your arms and promise to never let me go."

"Never, baby," he vows as he bends to kiss me. "I'm never letting you go."

I sway back and forth slowly, savoring the sense of security Kylian imbues in me as rain pelts our heads. He follows my lead, moving to the rhythm I set.

Tipping my head back, I grin. "Look at us. We're doing it."

His brows pull together as he processes my words, then, with a nod, he kisses me again. "I guess we are."

I'm facing the lake when it happens.

A bolt of illumination that splits the sky. The first official strike of the impending storm.

Without uttering a word, Kylian hugs me tighter and turns so I'm facing the house.

"You're safe," he murmurs, running both hands up and down my back.

My heart aches, knitting itself back together just a little more. I can't help but tear up.

Not from panic or overwhelm or the memories that lightning usually inspires.

But because of him. Because of *them*.

"I know," I whisper against his lips. "I'm always safe with you."

He holds me as thunder rumbles in the distance, until my T-shirt is soaked through and I'm shivering from the cold.

"Can I cut in?"

It was only a matter of time.

Kylian guides me into Decker's arms. Decker, naturally, holds out one hand while resting the other on the small of my back, assuming a formal stance like we're in the middle of a ballroom, not out on the deck in the pouring rain. I roll my eyes and throw my arms around his waist instead, breaking his perfect posture.

"You're the most precious thing in my life, Josephine." He rests his cheek on the crown of my head. "The most crucial piece of the puzzle. The most important part of this family. It's an honor and a privilege to get to spend a lifetime loving you."

I tip my head back and press my chin to his chest.

"Promise me we'll dance in the rain?"

"Always, Siren. Through every storm."

Josephine

4 Years Later

Nicky hums to himself as he works, transferring notes from his volunteers into the program report he's compiling on the screen.

He smiles so much these days. His pain is under control, and he's so damn happy all the time.

As if he can sense me, he glances up.

"What?" He flashes me his signature grin.

It's like watching Kendrick run the ball down the field or observing Kylian while he calculates a complex stats problem. My Emo Boy has found his passion and sense of purpose. He's thriving, and it makes me so damn proud.

I shake my head. "Nothing. I just love seeing you in your element."

"In my element, huh?" He sets his pen down and snaps his laptop closed, eyeing me hungrily.

"'In my element' isn't one of my top five favorite places to be, Hot Girl. You know where is?" His hazel eyes darken as he lifts one brow.

"Oh no," I hedge. "Don't even look at me like that right now, Nicholas Lockewood. I have so much more work to do." Tearing my focus from him, I frown at the hospital form I've been working on all afternoon.

"Study break?" he tries.

I shake my head, adamant about staying on task.

"How about a snack break?" he teases, running his tongue over his teeth and tilting his head back toward the kitchen. To the pantry.

I know that look in his eye. I know exactly what he wants for a snack. But I really do have so much work to get done.

"I can't," I bemoan. "I have to get this paperwork submitted by tonight." Blowing out a frustrated breath, I bite the inside of my cheek to stave off tears.

I've always been an angry crier. Though I can't blame anger this time. I'm just so damn frustrated.

I worked my ass off to graduate with honors in three years. After undergrad, I decided to pursue a master's degree, and Nicky joined me.

We're both enrolled in Lake Chapel University's nonprofit incubator program. We'll graduate with master's degrees in nonprofit administration next year, and when we do, we'll each have developed startup nonprofit organizations we have to create through the program.

Nicky's organization is thriving. The Pick-Up Pals program provides safe transportation, tutoring, after-school activities, snacks and dinner, and more to the kids it serves. The organization is expanding by leaps and bounds, and already, other communities across the state are interested in adopting the concept.

It's a delicate balance, though. Nicky is so thoughtful about how he wants to operate the after-school programs and what sort of training volunteers must receive to be a Pick-Up Pal. He insists that either he or Ash has to interview and train every candidate. He rejects more applicants than he takes on, and only half of those make it through the thirty hours of required training and safety certifications.

He's a papa bear when it comes to protecting and advocating for the kids in his program. I'm so freaking proud of him, and I love seeing him work toward something he's passionate about.

I, on the other hand, am flailing through this program on my best days. The focus of my nonprofit is to bring spa and beauty services into hospitals, offering bedside treatments for child and adolescent patients and their families.

For almost a year, I've been working on it, and I haven't even been able to offer a single service yet.

I can't help but think this is how Decker feels more often than not: learning lessons the hardest way before he gets it right.

Early on, I discovered that my services can't be called "treatments," because that confuses the hospital staff and the patients' families.

Then I had to submit all my products and implement cleaning processes to the OSHA coordinator at the hospital, only to have to change a host of supplies and procedures to be compliant with their requirements.

If that wasn't enough, each hospital will have its own requirements and submission process, so there's no way to scale the organization effectively.

Cutting through all the red tape to get things going has been a huge obstacle.

But I refuse to give up.

"You look sad." Nicky nudges my foot under the table.

I bite back tears. I hate the idea of admitting defeat.

"It's a lot harder than I expected it to be. I can't help but think that I'm getting it wrong. Maybe this isn't the right path for me."

He rises from his seat and takes his time circling the table. When he's at my side, he squats and collects my hands in his.

"Or maybe," he hedges, "it's time that you finally ask for help."

I huff out a breath. We've been over this so many times. "I don't want to use my last name to get my foot in the door or to bypass the standard processes." The Crusade name still carries a lot of weight in this town—hell, in the state—but I refuse to rely on my husband's reputation to make my organization a success.

"Forget Decker," he says.

"Hey!" my husband calls out from the kitchen. He's on dinner duty tonight. "I heard that!"

"Stop eavesdropping, Cap," Nicky hollers back. Grinning, he turns his focus back to me. "Who else do you know who might be connected to a hospital?"

I huff. I have to figure this out on my own. There's no one else who can—

Oh. That's not true.

Squeezing Nicky's hands gently, I sit a little straighter. "I didn't even think of him."

"I'm sure he'd be more than willing to help."

He's right. Greedy would help me in a heartbeat. He's a med student these days, but his father is Chief of Staff at Lake Chapel General.

Why have I not considered this before?

Nicky pecks me on the lips, then kisses the tip of my nose. "I love that you're so independent, Hot Girl, but you don't have to prove anything to anyone or do things on your own anymore. Remember that, okay?"

"Thanks, Nicky," I murmur, melting into his hold.

He snakes his arms around my waist and lifts me off the chair.

Before I can protest, remind him that I have mountains of work to get done, he hoists me higher, cups my ass, and kisses me senseless while carrying me out of the room.

"You need a break," he hums against my mouth, marching right past my husband. "And an orgasm. What do you say, Hot Girl? Want to drive Decker crazy? Let's go at it in the pantry while he's stuck at the stove stirring risotto."

I snort at the very idea but can't stop the grin that splits my face. With my arms tight around his neck, I kiss him back with fervor as we make our way into one of his favorite places in the whole world.

Josephine

One Year Later

"They're back!"

Kendrick sits up quickly and reaches for me, but I'm too fast for the three-time Pro Bowl starting running back for the Carolina Cougars.

"Go easy on them," he hedges as I scamper to the door. Behind me, he stays where he is, perched on the edge of the couch, legs spread wide.

Training camp started this week, so he's sore as hell and extra grumpy from two-a-days. I promised him a massage and a whole afternoon in bed, but not until the guys got back from their meeting.

I'm bouncing on my toes as they ascend the stairs toward the house. Kylian's already lost his tie, and Decker's tugging at his with each step.

"They don't look happy," I fret, worrying my lip.

"They're not the most happy-go-lucky guys to begin with, Mama."

I shoot Kendrick a pointed look over my shoulder. "That's fair."

By the time they reach the house, I'm tearing open the sliding glass door. I can't wait any longer.

I barrel into Kylian's arms a moment later. He catches me with a *hmph* as Decker supports his back and guides us forward.

"How'd it go?" I demand, looking from one man to the other.

Decker's onyx gaze gives nothing away. If anything, he looks dejected.

Kylian's piercing baby blues are as cool and calm as ever, but I still can't get a read on him.

"It went well."

That's it?

"Meaning?" I press, pushing up on tiptoes and cupping his cheeks.

I want details. I need to know if this is it: their big break.

Kylian and Decker have been working on a real-time next-gen stats program for years. Originally, Kylian developed the software on his own and used it when he interned with the Crusaders, but he was the sole programmer, and from its inception, he's retained the exclusive rights to the technology.

Over the last few years, he's been scaling it for the pros, outsourcing additional development and hiring contractors to maintain the servers. It's taken some time, but he's finally elevated the program to a place he deems acceptable to pitch to professional clubs around the league.

Decker understands the program, but he has the knack for getting a foot in the door. Between the Crusade name and his natural charisma, he's secured meetings with several teams. No one has officially signed with them yet, but Decker knows the head coach and offensive coordinator in Atlanta well. If they really have a shot at this, then Atlanta is likely where it'll begin.

The software is unmatched. The presentation has been polished to perfection. Hell, I've sat through it so many times over the last few weeks I could probably repeat it verbatim.

They were so prepared. So ready. They've poured so much into this.

God, I hope it worked.

"It's good news," Kylian explains evenly. "But let Decker tell you."

He spins us, kisses me quickly, then releases me into the arms of my husband.

"So?" I demand of Decker. My patience is wearing thin.

He wraps me in a hug and guides me into the house. "It was good. Really good. We signed the deal." His words are even and reserved. I'm smiling so hard my cheeks hurt, and yet he's acting as if this isn't the big break they were hoping for.

"That's amazing, Cap." My heart squeezes with pride for my boys. "We have to celebrate!"

Shaking his head, he blows out a breath. "There's more."

Instantly, my elation turns to swirling anxiety. I cling tighter and pull in a deep breath before it overtakes me.

"After the meeting, the head coach pulled me aside." He licks his lips and regards me carefully. "He offered me a job. A coaching job."

My breath catches and my eyebrows shoot into my hairline.

"No shit," Kendrick murmurs, rising to his feet. "Quarterback room?" he guesses, clapping Decker on the back.

Decker shakes his head, looking from K to me.

"Assistant coach to the offensive coordinator."

"Oh, hell yeah." Kendrick grasps Decker by the shoulders and pulls him into a real hug this time. "That's a big boy job, Cap. They must really want you, brother."

Decker's smile is meek, his trepidation apparent.

"Well?" I ask. "Did you accept?"

Onyx eyes catch mine, then double in size. "Of course not." His response is pure defensiveness. "I would never make a decision like that without consulting you all first."

I bite back a grin and wrap my arms around his neck. He wouldn't. In fact, he can barely choose a dinner menu without checking in. These days, the idea of making a unilateral decision without talking it through first sends him spiraling. I love him all the more for it.

"You should do it." It's a whisper, not so much to cut out the others, but because I want to convey my sincerity. So he knows that in my heart of hearts, I want this for him.

Decker is good at everything. He can network, sell software, and open so many doors for himself and for their stats program, but at his core, he belongs on the football field.

He swallows thickly, his Adam's apple bobbing. "Atlanta's nearly four hours away."

I bite my tongue to keep myself from reminding him that I once drove four hours one way just to take him to an out-of-state hospital.

"You could commute. Come home on a regular basis. We could get a condo there so I could come stay sometimes. As long as we had a schedule, we could make it work." Then, again, with conviction and loud enough for everyone to hear, I repeat, "I think you should do it."

"I think he should do it, too," Kendrick agrees.

"Really?"

Decker looks to each of us, searching for any hesitation or hint of a lie.

"Really," I promise, pushing up on tiptoes and pressing my lips into his. "Plus, I'm tired of calling you Cap. Coach has a nice ring to it, don'tcha think?"

"Assistant Coach," Kylian corrects from where he's sitting on the couch, scrolling on his phone.

"What do you say, Coach?" I tease, nipping at my husband's bottom lip.

"Say it again," he practically growls.

"Oh, you like that, do you? I've never been with a coach before," I whisper.

"Josephine," he scolds.

I'm not playing. I want him, and I want this for him. Spinning out of his arms, I stride out of the living room, knowing damn well at least one of my guys will follow.

"I'm going to get the massage oil warmed up for my star running back. Just let me know if I should heat up enough for my favorite CEO and my professional football coach husband, too."

Josephine

Three Years Later

"Go! Go! *Go!*"

I scream at the top of my lungs, wrapping Emilia in a side hug as we cheer on Kendrick's team from our suite.

The chains are officially in the red zone, thanks to K's nine-yard gain.

I hold my breath and abuse my bottom lip with my teeth while I wait for the next play.

"Sit. Down," Kylian hisses in my ear, the words jolting me back to reality.

I sigh but obey. I know better than to argue with him. I just get so wrapped up in watching Kendrick play.

"Did you just get in trouble, Hot Girl?" With a grin, Nicky kneads the spot on my low back that's been bothering me.

"Technically you got me in trouble, Emo Boy. Your enormous genes helped create this massive baby."

I'm thirty-four weeks pregnant today and am on modified pelvic rest. Our baby is a boy, and Nicky is his biological dad.

I'm supposed to stay off my feet as much as possible due to the size of this baby. My hips burn by the end of each day, and my cervix is already thinning. Avoiding injury and staying pregnant are the key objectives for the next several weeks.

That's what I get for procreating with a massive, meaty hunk of man.

I lean into Nicky's frame and savor the feel of being in his arms.

I would never admit it out loud, but I'm grateful our first baby is his. All my guys will be amazing dads, but Nicky just has a way about him. He's so good with kids, and he's fully committed to being the kind of parent neither one of us had.

It's poetic. Healing the inner child through parenthood. Together, he and I are breaking the cycle of generational trauma. I can't wait to see him thrive as a father, or, as he's decided he wants to be called, Papa Bear.

Getting the guys on board with my presence here today was on par with how intense I expect labor to be, but since the Cougars were playing at home, against Decker's team at that, I wore them down—strategically and individually.

Kylian stands in the corner of the suite, wearing a concerned, intense scowl. He hasn't taken his eyes off me. I doubt I'll be allowed on my feet again for the rest of the day.

Jade and Emilia are here with friends, and their dad is with us today, too.

I swear Ken Taylor is almost as excited to be a grandpa as his son is to become a dad.

Just the thought of next season, when we're all together again, and I've got our son in my lap wearing his number 24 Taylor jersey, makes me weepy. I can't even wrap my head around the joy this baby will bring to this family.

I'm so lost in the visions forming in my mind that I miss the snap.

"*Yes*!" Emilia screams as she jumps up and down with Jade. "*Go, go, go!*" the girls shout.

Dammit. I can't see a damn thing sitting down. I peer over at Kylian, then at Locke. They're both distracted by the game, so I slowly rise to my feet again. Just in time to see number 24 dive into the end zone for the touchdown.

Heart leaping in my chest, I let out a little squeal.

I'm lowering myself back to my seat when a booming voice echoes through the room. "Why isn't she sitting?"

Kylian snaps up straight and homes in on me as my bum hovers a few inches off the seat.

"*Jo*," he exclaims, exasperated.

Shit on a crumbly cracker.

I plop unceremoniously back into my chair, then quirk one brow over my shoulder as my husband strides into the suite.

He looks good in his crisp black polo and headset. Damn good.

Pregnancy makes me hungry all the time. It also makes me horny.

"Hi, Coach," I singsong.

Decker scowls in reply. He rounds the seats, and when he's before me, he crouches low. "You know you're not supposed to be on your feet. You promised you would *behave*, Siren."

He places his palms on my upper thighs, smoothing over the scratchy fabric of my maternity jeans. I wish I could throw these suckers in the lake most days, but I do appreciate the way the stretchy waistband panel accommodates all the stadium snacks I've indulged in this afternoon.

"You're a buzzkill," I accuse.

"I am your partner, and I love you," he counters. Then, softer he adds, "I just want what's best for you and the baby, Siren. You know that."

"Kendrick scored a touchdown," I reason.

"Believe me," Decker chortles. "I know."

I fight back a grin. Decker's team is probably going to lose to the South Carolina Cougars today, and we both know it. It won't be the first time Kendrick's team has come out on top. In fact, the Cougars have beat Atlanta four years in a row now, much to Decker's chagrin.

"What if you stand behind me? I could lean against you. That way, I wouldn't be bearing all my own weight."

"Josephine..."

"Decker," I mock.

"I only have a few minutes." Relenting, he rises to his feet and hauls me up to standing.

Once I'm steady, I wrap my arms around his shoulders the best I can and give him a quick kiss. "I don't need a few minutes, Coach. All I need is one."

A smile tugs at the corner of his mouth. "One minute, huh?"

We situate ourselves so Decker is holding me from behind and supporting my weight. Special teams are on the field now as his team prepares to take possession. How he was able to sneak up here, I have no idea.

Caressing his fingers, I crane back to look him in the eye. "Do you miss it?"

"Every damn day," he replies with a sigh.

I ghost my fingers over the backs of his hands, silently honoring his loss and appreciating the vulnerability he shows me without hesitation. Decker loves football. He was made for this game. Although he finds joy in coaching, I know his heart still yearns to be on the field.

"Do you regret it?"

He sacrificed so much. For me. For our family. I love our life, and he does too. His life now, though, doesn't look anything like the dreams he once held.

"Not even for one second," he says, his tone strong, confident. "It was never going to be just football. I realize that now. My name... my dad's legacy... I never would have been in a position to just play the game. There would always be strings attached."

I sigh, acknowledging the truth behind his wisdom.

"Besides... this?" He brushes our joined hands over my belly. "This life is so much fuller and richer than anything I let myself dream of before you. All of this is so fucking worth it."

I melt into his confession, but quickly stiffen when he goes rigid behind me.

"Holy shit," he murmurs. "Hell *yes*!"

We watch with bated breath as one of his receivers flies down the field... farther... faster... and runs into the end zone for a ninety-five-yard touchdown on the kickoff return.

Decker spins me around, kisses me quickly, flips the mic of his headset down, and guides me back to my seat.

"Watch her," he hollers to Kylian as he gives me one more peck. "I love you, Siren," he declares, "but I've gotta go. We're not out of this game yet!"

I grin at the sight of him sprinting from the room.

My smile widens even more as I play back his words in my mind: *so fucking worth it.*

Josephine

Four Years Later

Leaning into Kendrick's side, I scan the status board again.

Patient 0623 is in pre-op

Patient 0622 is in surgery

I close my eyes and run through the facts: These are routine procedures. We're at one of the best children's hospitals in the country. Although they may not understand our dynamic, the surgeon and operating team are very much aware of the four foreboding men in the waiting room, chomping at the bit for an update on their little girls.

"You're okay, Mama." K presses his lips to the crown of my head and wraps an arm around my shoulders. "They're going to be fine. Better than fine. Jade got tubes when she was three, and her ear infections practically disappeared overnight."

"They're only twenty-three months old," I argue.

"You think either of our baby girls knows how old they are when they channel their mama's sass or their dad's stubbornness?"

I smile, and the pressure eases in my chest a fraction, because he's right.

"They're fighters. They'll pull through this and be so much healthier for it. I promise."

"I'm making two pictures for my two sisters," Archer announces, scribbling in one of the coloring books we brought to keep him occupied. He spent the first several minutes of our time out here cycling from one parent to the next, asking us each to hold him or snuggle him. He's such a love muffin, but he rarely has the undivided attention of all of us like this. He didn't know what to do with himself without the girls in the mix.

"Those look great, buddy," Nicky praises. "Your sisters are going to love them."

I check the status board again and find it unchanged. I flit my eyes back to Archie. His dark brown hair and rosy cherub cheeks make him look just like his papa. I smile as I watch him color and snack on the Goldish crackers we brought for him. He may only be four, but his appetite is unmatched. As long as he's fed, he's the happiest little boy.

Resigned to the fact that my babies are all okay, I bury my face in the crook of Kendrick's arm and inhale, savoring the smell of vanilla, musk, care, and home. "I thought the whole point of procreating with the great Decker Crusade was for his superior genes," I jibe.

Kendrick silently chuckles, his chest shaking beneath my cheek.

"Technically speaking, I have the superior genes." Kylian snaps his laptop closed and glances up at the status board. "Decker caught everything as a kid. He even got chicken pox in second grade, despite being vaccinated."

Cap glares from the row of plastic seats across from us, but he doesn't bother arguing. He works his jaw back and forth, his onyx eyes searching the status board every few seconds.

Kendrick kisses my head and nudges me, but I'm already rising to my feet.

With an encouraging smile, I plop myself right in the lap of my husband.

"I love you. Through every storm," I whisper, brushing his hair over his forehead.

He wraps his arms around me but says nothing. He's keyed up and just as anxious as I am.

"Lilah's almost done," Kylian announces, calling our attention back to the board.

Patient 0622 is in post-op

Patient 0623 is in surgery

I blow out a sigh of relief and crack my knuckles, itching to see my baby with my own eyes and ensure she's okay.

Decker captures my hand and brings my palm to his mouth. He places a kiss in the center, and murmurs, "Through every storm," his breath hot on my skin.

Soon, a nurse pops out and calls us back to recovery. Decker, Kylian, and I head back together. Nicky stays out in the waiting room with Archie, and Kendrick remains as well, waiting to be called back when Dylan is out of surgery.

Decker pulls back the curtain, and the moment our baby comes into view, tears spring to my eyes. She looks tiny in the hospital bed—her little body still and her light brown curls a halo on the pillow around her head.

As if she senses our presence, her eyes fly open as soon as we step into the room.

"Mommy!"

"Shh," I hush. She had ear tubes put in and her adenoids removed. She should *not* be screaming at her regular volume.

"Where Lanie? I want Lanie!"

"Shh," I soothe again.

Decker hurries to my side to assist, running a soothing hand over our sweet girl's head.

"Dylan's still getting her ear tubes, baby. She's almost done. She'll be with you soon."

"Lanie." Delilah sniffs, followed by a pathetic "*ow*."

"Try not to talk. We'll call the nurse and see if we can get you a popsicle."

"Wed," she requests pathetically, wiping at her sleepy eyes. "Boo for Lanie."

Decker cups her tiny cheek, palming half her face. He scowls as he inspects her, swiping at a bit of medical tape residue near her hairline.

"She's fine," Kylian assures him from the doorway. He's squinting at a device. "Totally routine, unremarkable procedure. The surgeon will be by to say the same thing soon."

It's no surprise he accessed the surgery report before the doctor's even done with our other child.

A nurse buzzes into the room, a popsicle already in hand. Thankfully, it's red. There's no reasoning with a toddler who sets her mind to something, especially when she shares DNA with Decker Crusade.

"She did wonderfully," the nurse informs us, checking Delilah's vitals and inputting the data into her chart.

"Can we hold her?" I ask.

"Of course. We already removed the IV and all the monitors. Just try not to jostle her head and neck too much."

Decker is lifting her to his chest before the nurse has finished her instructions. He lowers to the bed, looking so large and protective with our tiny daughter in his arms.

"Dada," she sighs, snuggling into his chest.

He holds her and soothes her, smoothing a hand over her hair and helping her rotate her popsicle so it doesn't drip.

I shift from hip to hip for a moment, in awe, as always, by the love my guys have for our children.

Kylian appears behind me, his mouth at my ear. "You did so well, baby. You're so strong, holding us all together. You're an amazing mother."

With a cleansing breath, I lean back, letting him hold me. When I release the air from my lungs, I release all the tension that has gathered over the last few hours with it. Because we made it past the worst of it.

"Where is she?" Kendrick demands from somewhere close by.

I stiffen as a bolt of adrenaline surges through my veins.

"She's fine," Kylian placates. "You know how he gets about his babies."

I will my racing heart to calm, but the anxiety I had just quelled is ramping up again.

"I think Dylan will want—"

"I'll go," he insists, guiding me toward Decker and Delilah.

We love to tease Kylian that Lanie is actually his biological child, given the connection between the two of them. Kylian loves all our babies, but what he and Dylan share is on another level.

"I'll text you pics, and as soon as Lilah falls asleep—in approximately ninety seconds from the look of things—you can join us."

Relief washes over me. It's a solid plan. I may be a good mother, but our family would be chaos without Kylian's calm, sensible leadership.

Decker is humming to our girl, and her eyes are already closing as she lets her half-eaten popsicle rest in her mouth. Decker removes it and hands it to a nurse, then wraps both arms protectively around our little girl.

"I love you," Kylian whispers in my ear. He approaches the bed, kisses Delilah on the head, and repeats the sentiment to her.

Kylian

Two Years Later

Tiny eyelashes catch in the stubble of my neck each time she blinks. A contented hum rumbles from my chest as I catalogue the sensation and make a mental note to remember this feeling forever.

"Okay, Daddy?" Dylan leans back and places her warm palm on my cheek, awaiting my response.

She calls me Daddy. All the kids do. Thankfully, I'm excellent at compartmentalizing.

The first time Archie called Decker "Daddy" instead of "Dada," I nearly went over the edge. Up until then, I had only ever felt that level of possession with Jo. But "Daddy" as a moniker is mine. In all forms.

"Okay?" Dylan repeats, her brow furrowed and her lips turned down in concern.

I nod, cupping her little head and guiding it back onto my chest. She snuggles closer, and a warmth I never knew I'd have the privilege of experiencing blossoms inside me.

Jo has trained all our children to check in with me like this, especially at the end of the night.

Kids in general are loud. Unpredictable. Overstimulating without meaning to be.

And yet, I rarely need to mask around my own kids. They accommodate me more than what's required of most parents, but there's a natural cadence and deeply rooted authenticity to the care and concern we show each other in this family.

Research shows that our kids will be more inclusive and empathetic than their peers because they're being raised by a parent on the spectrum. I take great pride in my contributions to raising good humans.

Dylan is nearly asleep when my phone vibrates in my pocket. I fish it out with one hand.

> **Jo:** You're spoiling her

> **Daddy:** You can't spoil a child. I read that in a parenting book. Babies don't keep.

> **Jo:** She's almost four

I don't bother arguing. Jo's weaponizing logic and reason, and for once, she's wielding it against *me*.

My phone vibrates again before I can reply.

> **Jo:** I'm getting tired. Why don't you come spoil me instead?

That'll do it.

I seamlessly transfer Dylan into her bed, then sneak out of the room to find my girl.

She's sprawled out on the bed, resting on her left side.

"Hi, baby," I murmur as I climb in and spoon her from behind.

The hint of a smile graces her face, and it only widens when I run one hand up her thigh and smooth it over her swollen belly.

She's pregnant again.

And this time, the baby is biologically mine.

All my opposition to procreating vanished the day Archer was born. I've never felt such an acute shift in my sense of self as I did then. That was the moment I realized my capacity to love can grow right alongside our family.

After that day, I started to consider what a biological child might look like, how they might act. Statistically they're guaranteed to have blue eyes. The moment I spoke my desire out loud, Jo was all in. So were the guys.

Kendrick and I had vasectomies years ago, confident we wanted to grow our family without contributing DNA. Though I was not fond of having a stranger slice into my testicles twice, I had the procedure reversed.

Jo made Decker and Nicky wear condoms while we were trying to conceive. Nicky was fine with it. His excitement for another baby trumped everything. Decker was not as patient, and very vocal about his displeasure. It only took two months for me to impregnate our girl, so we didn't have to listen to his complaining for long.

"Hi, Daddy," Jo murmurs. She catches my hand and lifts it to her lips, kissing the tips, then swirling her tongue around two of my fingers.

"Say it again," I grunt, my cock swelling at just the heady sound of her voice.

I love all versions of this woman, but now that her breasts are swollen and her stomach is expanding because she's pregnant with my child? I'm absolutely feral for her.

"Hi, Daddy," she repeats, sucking two of my fingers into her mouth.

She shifts like she's going to sit up, but she's six months pregnant, and the doctor wants her lying on her left side as much as possible.

"Stay down," I murmur, kissing along her body and smoothing my hands down her sides. I find the hem of her nightie and lift, exposing her glistening cunt.

"You're so wet," I praise. "Such a needy, horny thing when you're pregnant."

She groans when I tease one finger through her pussy lips.

When she moans, I bend low and pierce her with my tongue.

"Fuck, baby. You taste so sweet."

My girl's always insatiable, but pregnancy hormones are something else.

"Play with your nipples. I'm sucking those next."

I adjust her legs so they're pressed and bent at the knees. This way, I have unbarred access to her center. Then I dive between them and continue to assault her hole with my tongue. I alternate slow, languid licks with blunt, pointed thrusts, building her higher and higher.

"Daddy," she whimpers, flailing one arm in search of me, even though she can't reach me at this angle.

The first spasm takes hold, and I grin into her center, lapping and savoring every sweet drop she gives me.

A series of low moans informs me that she's nearly done. She's hypersensitive when she's pregnant, so I ease up earlier than usual.

A resounding "Oh!" fills the room.

My mind freefalls into a flurry of considerations and panic. "What's wrong?" I demand, sitting up and swiping her essence off my face.

Her hand is on her stomach—off to the side, above her hip.

"Are you in pain? Is it your back? Or your sciatic nerve?"

We're all well-versed in the side effects of pregnancy by now, no one more so than Jo. Growing a child with Nicky's DNA resulted in a nine-pound, twelve-ounce baby. If that wasn't enough, Jo birthed twins next. Though they were five pounds, two ounces each, the pregnancy and delivery wreaked havoc on her body.

I search her face, but when all I find is a serene smile tugging at the corner of her lips, I let out a breath of relief.

"I'm okay. Better than okay. But someone else wants to say hi to Daddy, too."

She reaches for my hand, and I'm quick to offer it, then she guides my palm to the side of her stomach and presses until the skin compresses slightly.

After two seconds, a jolt pushes back.

"Is that—"

"It's the first time I've felt him," she confirms, her eyes welling with tears as she searches my face. "Say hi to your son, Kylian."

My throat clogs with so much emotion I can't speak.

But then our baby kicks again, and the reality of the life we created propels me into action.

Bending low, I kiss the spot he kicked. "Hey, buddy," I whisper to my wife's stomach.

Another kick.

A sigh from Jo.

It slams into me then—the realization that I've never, not once in my life, felt the spectrum of emotions I'm feeling right now, in this moment.

It's stupefying to think a life we created is growing and flourishing inside Jo's body. Everything in existence can be broken down into logic, reason, or facts, and yet pregnancy never ceases to amaze me. I understand the biology, of course, but the shift that has to occur to spark new life into existence is nothing short of cataclysmic. I can't help but marvel at the magic a baby brings to the world.

Just like I can't help but marvel at the woman I get to call mine. The woman who has fought like hell to help me see more than just black and white so I can live life to the fullest in technicolor.

Up Next

Hunter

A hand lands on my shoulder, startling me so badly I fly three feet into the air.

Whipping my head around, I note the hands and forearm veins I swear I still see in my dreams.

Maybe not in my dreams, exactly. More like in that hazy transition between sleep and awake, where anything is possible and what I feel isn't so wrong.

I always see him in those moments. Always.

I lift a hand to my chest, willing my heart to settle.

It's beating erratically because he scared me. That's the only reason. Shrugging off his touch, I sit straighter and affect a glare.

"What do you want, Greedy?"

His face falls in response to my question. Good.

Before he can open his mouth to answer, I double down.

"Why are you here? You can't just let yourself into my room."

"I knocked a dozen times, Tem," he huffs, glaring right back at me.

"Don't call me that," I hiss for what might be the thousandth time since I returned to North Carolina.

Moving back in with my stepdad and stepbrother six months ago was not my first choice.

Or my second. Or third...

But after traveling the world for several years, running from the memories of the very place I've resettled, it was the only feasible option.

Greedy bites down on the inside of his cheek, making the muscle in his neck spasm like it always does when he's agitated.

I interlace my fingers in my lap to stop myself from smoothing a hand along his jawline and reminding him to unclench.

It's not my place. It's not my job. He's nothing to me nowadays.

He *has* to be nothing.

"We need to talk."

When he stops there, I rise to my feet and plant my hands on my hips. I go for nonchalant, even if there's nothing nonchalant about the towering heap of baggage and leftover damage between us.

"We don't have anything to talk about." I will my voice to hold steady, even as a tremble crawls up my chest.

He shoots me another glare, but this one lacks any heat. I wish he would hate me. I'd love nothing more than to make him loathe the day I reappeared in Lake Chapel.

Nothing I've tried so far has worked. Greedy never looks at me like he hates me. Like what I did to him is unforgivable.

If he only knew.

When he regards me, there's no hate. Only sadness.

Sometimes I wonder if he knows just how sad I am on the inside, too.

"It's about Levi. He's home. Well, not home. He's at Lake Chapel General. He's heading in for surgery in a few hours, and he's asking about you—asking if the two of us will visit once he's in recovery."

My heart stutters in my chest as Greedy's words sink in.

Flashes of hazy summer nights and skinny-dipping in the lake dance in my vision. Greedy brought us together, his best friend and his girl. Memories of blue eyes and country boy charm infiltrate my thoughts. Snippets of days when I called him Duke, and he loved to call me Daisy.

For that one magical summer, the three of us were inseparable.

It's been a long time since I've allowed myself to think about the other boy I broke when I fled to Europe unannounced.

Levi.

So Wrong
Boys of South Chapel Book One
Coming 2024

Afterword

It's been the highlight of my career to share Joey and her boys with you. Thank you from the bottom of my heart for going on this journey with me!

If you loved this story, please consider leaving a review on Amazon or Goodreads to show your support. I would also highly recommend signing up for my email newsletter. I'll be sharing extended excerpts and lots of updates about the Boys of Lake Chapel in the coming months. My email subscribers will also be amongst the first to learn all the details about Hunter's upcoming series, Boys of South Chapel.

Acknowledgments

Too Far is the longest book I've ever published, and I can say with certainty it was also the hardest project I've ever completed. From the feels to the spice, I was obsessed with getting things just right for Joey and her boys, but more so, getting things just right for my readers. I'd like to thank the following people for lifting me up and sometimes dragging me to the finish line of this series:

Mr. Abby—who would have guessed at the beginning of this year that you would get to "retire" and become a stay-at-home-dad because of Lake Chapel? Thanks for always believing in me like WHOA, and for lifting me up like no one else can.

To my three baby girls—your claps and hugs and encouragement are all the writing fuel I need. Well, that, and coffee. I love showing you what's possible through this career. Maybe just stop telling people your mom writes "smut" though, mmkay?

Beth—For jizzing up my words, keeping track of what my fictional men smell like, and laughing at my Abbyisms—you are so deeply valued and appreciated! It's hard to believe we're two years into this journey together... there's so much more to come!

Mel—For helping me make sense of my thoughts and leaning in to this new why choose era with me. And for handling all my schedule change requests with understanding and grace, even when I'm making things harder for literally everyone.

Megan—For sliding into my DMs to ask if I needed help... letting me say NO! And then letting me say "Wait! Come back!" about a week later. I appreciate all your support and encouragement. Decker's lucky to have you on his PR Team.

Alina, Ashley, Jen, Jessi, Kelly, and Krystal—For beta reading this book and providing such helpful, poignant feedback. There was still a lot to untangle and wrap up when I sent you the beta version, but we all powered through. The Boys of Lake Chapel series is better because of each of you!

To the readers, reviewers, and influencers who embraced Joey and her boys and have welcomed me into the why choose and sports romance subgenres. You've been instrumental in blowing up this series and and making Stats Daddy a household name.

To my Personal ARC + Promo team members, many of whom have been with me for years at this point. Thank you for embracing every story I dream up, and for loving my characters so well. I love you more than Kendrick loves winning board games. #YourCrownsCrookedCap

By Abby Millsaps

presented in order of publication

When You're Home
While You're There
When You're Home for the Holidays
When You're Gone
Rowdy Boy
Mr. Brightside
Fourth Wheel
Full Out Fiend
Hampton Holiday Collective

Too Safe: Boys of Lake Chapel Book One
Too Fast: Boys of Lake Chapel Book Two
Too Far: Boys of Lake Chapel Book Three

About The Author

Abby Millsaps is an author and storyteller who loves to write unapologetically angsty romance. Her characters are relatable, lovable, and occasionally confused about the distinction between right and wrong. Her books are set in picturesque settings that feel like home.

Abby started writing romance in 7th grade. Then in 8th grade, she failed to qualify for the Power of the Pen State Championships because "all her submissions contained the same theme: young people falling in love." #LookAtHerNow

Abby met her husband at a house party the summer before her freshman year of college. He had a secret pizza stashed in the trunk of his car that he was saving for a midnight snack— how was she supposed to resist? When Abby isn't writing, she's reading, traveling, and raising three daughters.

Connect with Abby

Website: www.authorabbymillsaps.com
Instagram: @abbymillsaps
TikTok: @authorabbymillsaps
Email: authorabbymillsaps@gmail.com
Newsletter: https://geni.us/AuthorAbbyNewsletter
Facebook Reader Group: Abby's Full Out Fiends

www.ingramcontent.com/pod-product-compliance
Lightning Source LLC
LaVergne TN
LVHW030312070526
838199LV00069B/6460